Praise for the Echoes of the Fall series

'It's addictively brilliant! The protagonist is vivid and sympathetic – and I love both the story and the world Adrian has created. It's meticulously thought out and utterly believable'

John Gwynne

'A classically brilliant fantasy writer, a pusher of boundaries, a great storyteller'   Paul Cornell

'This is a satisfying read, a story you can really lose yourself in'
SFX

'Equally deft in the realms of science fiction and fantasy adventure, Adrian Tchaikovsky knows how to take you to a place, no matter the setting . . . Maniye Many Tracks is a fascinating character; layered, strong, torn, constantly developing and hugely empathetic'   *SciFiNow*

'Brilliantly conceived and executed . . . . Readers will be captivated'
Publishers Weekly

'A clever, compelling page-turner'   *Sci-Fi and Fantasy*

'Tchaikovsky has woven a richly textured world, brimm difference and complexity'   S

The Hyena and the Hawk

Adrian Tchaikovsky was born in Woodhall Spa, Lincolnshire, before heading off to Reading to study psychology and zoology. For reasons unclear even to himself, he subsequently ended up in law. He has worked as a legal executive in both Reading and Leeds, where he now lives. Married, he is a keen live role-player and occasional amateur actor. He has also trained in stage fighting, and keeps no exotic or dangerous pets of any kind – possibly excepting his son. He's the author of the critically acclaimed Shadows of the Apt series and the Echoes of the Fall series, as well as *Guns of the Dawn* and *Children of Time* – which won the 30th Anniversary Arthur C. Clarke Award for Best Science Fiction Novel.

www.shadowsoftheapt.com

By Adrian Tchaikovsky

Shadows of the Apt
Empire in Black and Gold
Dragonfly Falling
Blood of the Mantis
Salute the Dark
The Scarab Path
The Sea Watch
Heirs of the Blade
The Air War
War Master's Gate
Seal of the Worm

Echoes of the Fall
The Tiger and the Wolf
The Bear and the Serpent
The Hyena and the Hawk

Other novels
Guns of the Dawn
Children of Time

ADRIAN
TCHAIKOVSKY

The Hyena and the Hawk

Echoes of the Fall:
Book Three

PAN BOOKS

First published 2018 by Macmillan

This paperback edition published 2018 by Pan Books
an imprint of Pan Macmillan
The Smithson, 6 Briset Street, London EC1M 5NR
EU representative: Macmillan Publishers Ireland Ltd, 1st Floor,
The Liffey Trust Centre, 117-126 Sheriff Street, Upper
Dublin 1, D01 YC43
Associated companies throughout the world
www.panmacmillan.com

ISBN 978-1-5098-3029-9

Copyright © Adrian Czajkowski 2018

The right of Adrian Czajkowski to be identified as the
author of this work has been asserted by him in accordance
with the Copyright, Designs and Patents Act 1988.

All rights reserved. No part of this publication may be reproduced,
stored in a retrieval system, or transmitted, in any form, or by any means
(electronic, mechanical, photocopying, recording or otherwise)
without the prior written permission of the publisher.

Pan Macmillan does not have any control over, or any responsibility for,
any author or third-party websites referred to in or on this book.

3 5 7 9 8 6 4 2

A CIP catalogue record for this book is available from the British Library.

Map artwork by Michael Czajkowski

Typeset by Palimpsest Book Production Limited, Falkirk, Stirlingshire
Printed and bound by CPI Group (UK) Ltd, Croydon, CR0 4YY

This book is sold subject to the condition that it shall not, by way of
trade or otherwise, be lent, hired out, or otherwise circulated without
the publisher's prior consent in any form of binding or cover other than
that in which it is published and without a similar condition including
this condition being imposed on the subsequent purchaser.

Visit **www.panmacmillan.com** to read more about all our books
and to buy them. You will also find features, author interviews and
news of any author events, and you can sign up for e-newsletters
so that you're always first to hear about our new releases.

For Darren Dale, greatly missed

Where the
Fords Meet

Salt Islands

Chumatla

Dragon
Isles

okawan

Whale
Seat

Prologue

This is how they tell the story:

That at the dawn of time the people of the world lived in the first lands and knew peace.

That amongst the people there were those who formed alliances with monstrous creatures and became the Plague People, who set out to devour all the earth and sky.

That the true people who were left were forced to flee, and that the three brothers, Owl, Bat and Serpent, called down a great fire to guard their flight, creating the ocean which forever protects against the Plague People, and serves as a dark reminder of them.

And the true people multiplied in this new land and took many gods, each tribe taking its soul and its shape from the god it followed. In the north the Tiger and the Wolf were constantly at each other's throat while the Bear slept and the Eyrie hovered overhead. In the south, the Serpent founded a great kingdom only to lose it to the Pale Shadow People, who we know to be the Plague People's exiled cousins, who suborned their servants and cast them out. So the Serpent came to the River Tsotec and brought civilization to the tribes there, and created the Sun River Nation. And in the middle the Plains tribes devoured one another, save for the Horse who sought trade and travel instead of tooth and claw.

And then, one day, today, the Plague People found them. They came with their wings and their hands of fire, and their rods that speak instant, invisible death; they came with their iron boat and

1

their flying ship. Most of all they came with their terror, which robs the true people of their minds and their ability to change shape, and makes them only animals.

Who will lead the true people against their ancient enemy? Maniye Many Tracks, daughter of Wolf and Tiger and Champion of the North, who discovered the Plague camp in the Plains where the Horse once dwelled; Loud Thunder of the Bear, who fought them on the northern coast and drove them into the sea; Asman of the Sun River Nation, consort of the Kasra and Champion of the River, who has only now seen his country unified; Hesprec Essen Skese, priest of the Serpent, who has seen human lifespans come and go, and is forced to seek allies in the worst of places, amongst the Pale Shadow; Venat, raider of the Dragon and Asman's one-time slave; Shyri, daughter of the Hyena with her own apocalyptic prophecies; Kailovela of the Hawk, who has kept hearth with one of the Plague People, the 'little monster' that the Eyriemen captured long before the invasion. Warriors, champions, priests and tribes from the cold north to the parched south muster against the threat of the Plague People.

This is how they told the story yesterday, today. Tomorrow is another matter, for the Plague People are the death of all stories.

1

The grand farewell had already happened before the palace at Atahlan. The Kasra Tecumet, robed and masked, had stepped down from the Daybreak Throne into the view of a thousand of her people, acknowledging their cries and benedictions with outstretched arms. Her message to them had been spoken by her chief priestess, Esumit of the Serpent, bland and reassuring. The news of what had happened out on the eastern Plains would not have reached many ears. The people of Atahlan had listened to the second-hand words of their leader with all confidence.

That would change soon enough, the newly named Asman knew.

Now he was at the docks and a war-barge was ready for him, a full complement of soldiers at his sole disposal. It was not the great army that the Sun River Nation could field, which was still being levied from every village along the river. Asman would lead the expeditionary force, to assess whether the world was just cracked, or broken in two.

He had on his new armour, segmented leather sewn with stone plates, edged in gilt. His *maccan* blade was freshly set with new obsidian teeth. He cut a splendid figure, if he said so himself: Champion of the River and Kasrani of the Nation. He was the man who had brought the Iron Wolves from the far north; had earned the favour of strange gods and travelled with the

Messengers of the Serpent. Even before becoming Tecumet's mate he had become someone they told stories of.

Probably people envied him, although the journey had not been a simple or easy one. He had earned a period of rest, quiet reflection, and a chance to enjoy his new station in life. Fate, it turned out, had decided he was not to have it.

'Would it be presumptuous to feel all this was aimed at me?' he asked his companion.

Venat of the Dragon stared at him blankly for a moment and then rolled his eyes. '*Of course.* The oldest enemy of *all* the people of the world is here because it heard *you* might be happy. That is how the world works.'

'It would lend a certain meaning to all that ridiculous business we went through,' Asman observed wryly. 'Thank you for coming back to me, by the way.'

The old pirate scowled. 'I thought it was to be rewarded, not for all this.' Venat had just arrived with news of Asman's father's untimely demise, a matter which was also not general public knowledge; nor, for complex reasons, a source of particular grief, especially as Asman had given the order. It was the act of a villain of myth to have one's own father assassinated, he well knew. His only defence was that those myth-makers had not known his father.

'Is not my company reward enough?' he declared, stepping onto the deck of the barge. The soldiers there clashed their spears against their shields, acknowledging their commander.

Venat shambled after, turning the bile of his expression on all and sundry. 'If you were a boil I'd stick a needle in you,' he grumbled as he followed Asman below decks. Even on a war-barge the quarters were cramped, and surely nobody had made allowances for a surly Dragon pirate when they were allocating rooms. Asman had already resigned himself to sleeping in Venat's armpit on the voyage upriver, and was about to say as much when the man stopped dead before the cabin door. Without thinking, Asman Stepped into his Champion's shape, that lean

4

sickle-clawed lizard that ran on two legs. He knew Venat, and in that instant the pirate had been a man about to do battle with a great enemy. A moment later, the Dragon shrugged and stretched theatrically.

'I'll be on deck,' he said. 'Never could abide these little boxes you live in.'

Asman, bewildered, pushed open the door to his cabin and found in that small space the sole and supreme ruler of the Sun River Nation in all her glory. Not the robe, not the mask, which were all her subjects and petitioners saw, but the woman beneath them.

He knelt immediately, and she put a hand to his head, fingers cool against the stubble where he had shaved the sides. He let himself look up at her face – a breach of propriety really, but who was here to complain? Still very much the girl he had grown up around, slight and dark and beautiful. He had loved her a long time, and if his love was divided, did that make the portion he reserved for her any less true?

Tecumet hooked a knuckle under his chin and raised him up. 'I wanted to say goodbye. Properly, not all the ceremony.'

'How did you even get on board?'

The Serpent priestess, Esumit, had arranged it of course. Probably the woman was delighted that Asman would be out from underfoot so soon, given that he and she had very much been on opposite sides of what had nearly been a civil war along the river. A little subterfuge for her Kasra was obviously a small price to pay.

He held Tecumet for a while, listening to the sounds of the ship's crew and the soldiers, and thinking of Venat somewhere on the boat. He had thought there would be some great reckoning between the Dragon and Tecumet, and only now did he realize he had been dreading it. And yet the man had just sloped off without a word, and taken with him all those missed chances for making Asman feel uncomfortable. *A wedding present, perhaps.*

5

He knew that Tecumet had her own role to play in planning for war. Emissaries were already on their way north to those of the Plains tribes who would speak to Atahlan – few enough, but perhaps with the new enemy that number would grow. This was the great doom, after all, that every halfway visionary priest had caught some fragment of. Surely even the legendarily divided Plainsfolk would set old grievances aside in the face of it.

Thinking on that, Asman had a sudden sense of being at the fulcrum of destiny, not a pleasant feeling at all. *This* was why the river had been torn in two after the old Kasra's death, after all. The Serpent had been desperate to have the *right* backside sitting on the Daybreak Throne, as Venat would put it. Tecumet and her brother had been the standards that different cliques of priests had flocked to, until their urgent need to second-guess fate had almost destroyed everything. Only the wide-wandering Messenger, Hesprec Essen Skese, had set things right, talked Tecuman down and raised Tecumet up. And just in time.

Tecumet would bring half an army. Tecuman was already sailing to raise the other half from the Estuary. But they would march where Asman directed. He was their vanguard.

'What's wrong?' Tecumet whispered. 'You're cold suddenly.'

'I am trying to think of what the Plague People will be like. I can't imagine them.' He had only the babbled words of Maniye's Crow, who had been half mad all on his own, no ancient monsters necessary. 'How can they be so terrible? He said there weren't even that many of them.'

'Maniye sent him,' Tecumet noted.

'And I trust her judgement,' he agreed. 'But . . . in my mind they are giants or monsters. How can they be so terrible and look just like men?'

'Perhaps we'll be lucky, and they'll not seem so terrible when faced with the warbands of the Plains and the armies of the Daybreak Throne,' she whispered. 'Perhaps they've grown less, or we've grown more, since the time of the old stories. Maybe this is no more than an echo, a ripple, after all.'

6

Asman wanted nothing more than to agree with her, but the words stuck in his throat and instead he held her close. She had been his friend for a long time, his enemy for a brief span of days. Only parting from her did he realize how she was rooted deep in him. But then he often found the closest attachment with people who had tried to kill him at one time or another.

There was a scuff outside the door, and then Venat was growling out, 'He's preparing. You just go play with your thumbs on deck till he's ready,' and Asman knew that the barge was ready to cast off, and that the Dragon was still being unnaturally considerate.

Tecumet held him a moment longer and then released him.

Soon after, he was on deck, waiting until he knew Tecumet had been safely smuggled away. Many of the soldiers and crew would know someone had visited him, but he hoped not a one guessed at the Kasra herself.

He stood at the prow as they let the current draw them out into the Tsotec's heart, Venat slouching at his shoulder. They would sail as far as the village of Umethret and then disembark on the north bank, marching for where Maniye had been. Nobody knew how swiftly the Plague People were advancing into the Plains, or if they even were. A similar lack of knowledge shrouded just about everything else. Asman and his warriors were going to be scouts as much as soldiers.

That far into his thoughts, Venat's pointed silence was like any other man shouting in his ear. 'What?'

The pirate snorted, then slumped forwards to lean on the rail beside him. He did everything as though he wanted to expend the minimum possible effort, right up to the moment he cut someone open. It was a Dragon thing, or possibly just a Venat thing.

'All those prophecies,' Venat told him. 'Your snaky priests flapping like fish on the beach.'

'You think it's nothing? They say Where the Fords Meet is taken, all of it.'

7

'I think most of the Plains tribes wanted to burn that place down. Horse Society, always acting like they know more than everyone else.'

Asman shook his head. 'You're wrong because you're right.'

'What kind of sense is that?'

'They would have taken the Horse if they could, raided them, stolen away the young and strong, set fire to the homes, emptied the storehouses?'

'In a heartbeat.'

'And yet none of them did. We saw that place. The Horse knew how to keep what was theirs. Walls and bows and good order. And now it's all gone.'

'If it's true.'

'I think the Dragon is scared to admit there's something worse in the world than him.' Asman was trying for levity but failing to find it.

'The Dragon isn't scared of *anything*.' And while the words might have been a bluff from anyone else, Venat said them with conviction.

'You'll go to them, won't you? Go back again?'

But the pirate wouldn't commit himself. He had been back once, since freeing himself of the River yoke. He hadn't stayed long. Something had changed in him – added or taken away until he couldn't quite see eye to eye with the rest of his kin; a man caught between two worlds.

Not shoulders the fate of the world should rest on. But whose were? Asman had no illusions about his own failures and frailties. Or should the world put its faith in Maniye Many Tracks of the Crown of the World, who didn't even know to what people she belonged? What about Shyri of the Laughing Men, whose people were no doubt sharpening their knives even now at the news of disaster, but only to feast after the fighting was done. Or Hesprec Essen Skese of the Serpent, who had travelled further than anyone alive, and was now on one more journey to a place nobody should ever have to go.

8

Asman stared at the river that was the life's blood of all his people and wondered how doomed the world must be, that such as they were its best hope.

* * *

Therumit's body was old, but she set a punishing pace, and after several days of travel Hesprec began to wonder if the old woman's withered frame was gnarled hardwood instead of flesh. They had borrowed mounts from the Horse Society to make the best time they could, and even so Hesprec was bruised from knee to waist after three days while Therumit just kept her narrow gaze on the horizon and pushed their beasts as far as she could every day.

And how had she coaxed the Horse into giving up the animals, without any handler to see them safe? It was unheard of, and yet here they were, their beasts laden with water and supplies as they left the southern bank of the Tsotec far behind and crossed the dry lands.

They were much like the Plains, these reaches, but sandier, and the grass was patchy. Here and there great pillars of earth stabbed at the sky like fingers, the castles of blind white ants that Hesprec harvested when they stopped at dusk, bursting their bodies between her teeth and spitting out the hard nuggets of their heads.

The Serpent had placed its mark on these lands. The journey that Therumit and Hesprec were making had been forbidden, long ago. But forbiddance was a word the Serpent considered more lightly amongst their own than they did when dealing it to others. They never buried anything so very deeply that they could not remember where it was to dig it up.

The priests of the Serpent had no leaders, but there were those amongst them who were oldest, those who were wisest. They had a complex and precisely measured tangle of respect that connected them to each other – and after all there were not so very many of them, not any more. In the eyes of their peers,

Therumit and Hesprec were both eccentric. Hesprec had always felt a need to travel and learn, far more than the others. Few had travelled so far from the safety of the River, fewer still had returned alive. The Serpent was not well liked, out where the world grew cold.

And Therumit had withdrawn from her people, these last few lifetimes. She had made herself a hermit of the Estuary, husbanding her secrets and growing slowly apart from her kin. Now Hesprec knew why: she had never lost her yearning for the Oldest Kingdom, first bastion of civilization when the Serpent had been young and strong.

Not even Therumit was old enough to remember, but the legends never went away, whispered from snake to snake in the dark places where they met. Once they had been greater than now they were. Once they had ruled a mighty city when all others had been savages living in caves and mud hovels. Once there had been a golden time, and then it had been taken away from them. And Therumit was not the only child of the Serpent who paused in the unceasing labour to shape the people of the Sun River Nation along the Tsotec to think *If only we could have back what we have lost.*

These dry lands they travelled through were not uninhabited, though the denizens were sparse and shy. Hesprec only caught sight of them a handful of times. Men with great curved shields of hide, watching the two riders impassively; tall women with feathered head-dresses and spears, who became long-legged running birds and fled when the Serpents glanced their way. Just as well they were so skittish; their beaks had seemed like hatchet blades to Hesprec.

None of these people had much contact with the Sun River Nation. It was not that they had nothing to offer, but that the Nation turned its back on them, and on anything to the south. Save for watchtowers and patrols, the River looked mostly to the River, and that was the way the Serpent had shaped it. For across the dry lands – close enough that sometimes raiding parties of

Jaguar had crept to the very banks of the Tsotec and been repulsed – were the forested valleys of the Oldest Kingdom.

Lost to us forever, Hesprec recited the old mantra. She had lived many lives, youth to old age to shed her skin and find youth once again; she had journeyed to many strange places. This was a path she had never taken, though.

The Serpent had been dethroned by a people they called the Pale Shadow, who had come from across the sea in the old days. They had been fair and broken, begging to serve the Serpent. They had been empty, but the Serpent had been wise and mighty and terribly, terribly complacent, and assumed that teaching would fill that void. And the Pale Shadow People had carefully, slowly, taken everything the Serpent had built and stolen it away with lies and promises and the outer beauty that hid their poisoned hearts. They had claimed the palaces and the loyalty of the Jaguar who had helped the Serpent build their city. And at last, those of the Serpent who yet lived had fled north to scratch out a new home with the squabbling tribes of the Tsotec, driven across the dry places from their own home. And though no snake now living had ever seen those palaces, that city, still they remembered.

And then an emissary had come from the Pale Shadow to Therumit. Hesprec had met with her: a pale, beautiful and hollow creature, unnatural as the sun at night. She had come to beg the Serpent to return, so she said. She had come to pledge their aid against a common enemy. By then, Hesprec had known the Plague People were finally bringing their hunger across the sea, and though the Pale Shadow were some offshoot of the Plague, they did not relish the thought of their devouring kin finding them. Or so they said.

Hesprec had not wanted to accept their barbed invitation. But now word had come that the Plague People sat at Where the Fords Meet in the Plains, and had destroyed or driven out the Horse from their own home. And so it seemed that there were

11

no unthinkable allies, no forbidden paths. The great threat from the oldest tales was *here* and *now* and very real.

Therumit believed they could take back their Oldest Kingdom. Hesprec herself just hoped that the Pale Shadow could be used, somehow, and that the Serpent had grown wise enough to grasp that weapon by the hilt and not the blade.

One morning, Hesprec woke to find herself alone at the fire. Therumit and her mount were gone, the tracks leading off south. They were close enough that Therumit's yearning had hailed her from their fire to go look upon the land of the old stories.

Heartsick for a home she never knew. But Hesprec understood. It touched all the Serpent's children. For all their teaching and their travelling, all they had built along the Tsotec and in the Stone Kingdoms, still they knew it was all second-best. The Oldest Kingdom dwelled only in the imagination; nothing real would ever compare to it.

She packed up the camp and scattered the ashes of the fire, knowing that there were hidden locals watching her, as their progress had been watched throughout these dry lands: the Curling Folk, the Tall Walkers, the People of the Hooked Claw. They kept their distance, hiding in the dust of this place so that even a Serpent would have a hard time rooting them out.

Hesprec loaded her horse and followed the hoofprints Therumit had left in the dirt, making no great speed and content to let her companion choose the moment of their meeting. *If we do. If the Pale Shadow hasn't closed about her like a trap.*

The natives showed themselves to her mid-morning. She saw two of them standing by a growth of cactus, just within arrow-shot had she held a bow. They had dust-coloured skin and lean bodies with curved spines, draped in shapeless ponchos. When she met their gaze, their long-nailed hands described some ritual gesture. A warding or a reverence? She couldn't know. Moments later they had Stepped and were scurrying away, armoured things with banded backs and claws tearing up the dry earth.

They must have been waiting to see if she was really going to that forbidden place, she decided later, for soon after that she found Therumit again. The old Serpent sat astride her own horse as it cropped at the dry grass. Her lined face was without expression.

Hesprec – no horsewoman – fought the reins a little and then let her mount amble to the side of its fellow. Beyond Therumit, she saw, the land fell away sharply. She had tried, all this way, to kill any germ of anticipation, but now the feeling leapt from her belly up into her throat. *For beyond the dry lands are the valleys and the forests where . . .*

'You've looked, of course,' she observed to Therumit. For a moment she could not tell whether the woman's stillness was triumph or despair.

Then the older priestess jerked her head towards the decline. Hesprec's mount followed when Therumit kicked hers into motion, and in mere heartbeats they were looking out over another world.

A skein of rivers had worn a great basin out of the earth, which stretched as far as they could see. The sun struck silver from their waters, or deep bronze from the greatest channel that came close to rivalling the mighty Tsotec itself.

A forest carpeted the basin, but Hesprec could see the patterns cut into it, where ancient husbandry had trained the trees into orchards, the ground into fields, so that all good things would grow in overlapping profusion without ever ceasing to be the forest. Here were the examplars of all the agriculture of the Sun River Nation, stolen from this lost place and taught to the people of the River and the Estuary.

And, rising from the trees, a single city of gold-warm stone; not a great concentration of life and architecture like Atahlan, but spread between the trees in mounds and temples and enclosures, each one placed precisely to please the eye, not to crowd its neighbours, to hold its own special beauty.

Hesprec glanced at Therumit and saw the glint of tears in the woman's eyes, the tight-clenched jaw that locked in the feeling of *Home, Home*. The older priestess looked back and asked, 'Do you not feel it?'

'I do not,' Hesprec said hoarsely. Yes, it was the Oldest Kingdom, but there was a reason the Serpent did not go here which had nothing to do with distance. The dry lands were not so impassable a barrier, after all. Raiders from the Jaguar came to the river, yes, and sometimes raiders from the Crocodile went to the forest, but they never returned. Hesprec looked out across the trees and the ancient, eroded buildings and saw only that the Pale Shadow had lain on this place a long time. But the Old Kingdom was where the Serpent had been wounded almost to death. It was where their old servants had been stolen from them, and if they took their new followers there, what else might they lose? Or perhaps it was simply that they would have to show any reconquering Riverman army just how they had fallen from grace, and nevermore be looked on with respect again.

At first it had seemed like mist to her eyes, but it did not move like mist, nor did it burn away in the sun. White sheets and strands shrouded the trees and blunted the edges of the buildings, so that the city and its surroundings were made into a maze of webs and tissue-thin walls. And within all of this there was precious little sign of life. Perhaps they saw some trace of people working the fields; perhaps bright birds soared over the canopy. But within the city itself, nothing. It was still as a tomb.

And Therumit smiled and seemed to see none of this, and then she was guiding her horse to find a path down the slope, and Hesprec's mount was following on.

2

She could not move. Moving let the pain in, and then she would have to give it the run over her body, leaping from point to point about her limbs and back. The same happened when she choked on the sweet, smoky air and the coughing set her every nerve on fire with agony.

Maniye hung beneath a foreign roof in a foreign land: too hot, wrong-smelling, all unfamiliar sounds from beyond the sloped wooden walls. There were hooks in her flesh, pulling her skin taut. She had been given plenty of time to see the lines set in the ceiling, the exacting measurements to match her small frame. She had expected a collar about her throat to lock in her souls, but that was part of the torment, to have that escape hung before her, just as she was hung. To Step would be to fail.

She had been hanging for a day, a whole day. Sometimes the door of the hut opened, and then a clay bowl of water would be pressed to her lips, just enough to keep her alive. Except even that little water was acrid with some drug that gnawed at the point where her mind met her body. She faded in and out, snapping back to her body every time she twitched or coughed, and the hooks about her flesh bit with their fiery teeth.

She had asked for this.

The world was ending, or it might be. There had been a doom stalking the visions of the wise from all lands, these ten years gone. The oldest stories told of it: how Maniye's distant ancestors

15

had fled their ancestral homes, pursued by the insatiable hunger of the Plague People. But those stories told of how Owl and Bat and Serpent had held the enemy off until the sea came to stand between Our People and the Plague. The old tellers of the old tales had never thought that one day the sea might not be enough.

And so, after Maniye had seen the soulless creatures in human form, after she had felt the dreadful fear they emitted that drove true people mad and imprisoned them in their animal shapes, she had gone to her father, Wolf's errant priest, and asked for his god's final blessing.

The hooks that pulled at her skin were iron, forged in a fire of wolf-wood in the Crown of the World, and carried ever after by Kalameshli because he had always hoped this day would come.

No doubt he had seen it as his moment of triumph over his rebellious daughter, but they had both run a long trail since those days. She was not the bitter girl she had once been, nor he the angry tyrant.

In the dark of the hut she drifted again, the pain of the hooks receding from long familiarity. Her mind took the sensation and made it into the prick of teeth, as though the Wolf were carrying her in his mouth across the shadowed hills of the Godsland. And had she not walked there, to tame her souls and become the Champion of the Crown of the World? Had she not walked between Bear and Wolf and Tiger in the north, and stood between the jaws of Old Crocodile in the south? If any mortal could know the gods, who better than Maniye Many Tracks?

In the next moment the hubris of her thoughts struck fear through her. Just as she was physically helpless, so her mind was being laid open by the pain and the incense and the faintness of hunger. She had fasted two days before Kalameshli had lifted her up here, her stomach shrivelling like dried fruit. Now food seemed just a memory, one more tie to the world that was fraying to nothing and leaving her attached by no more than a dozen metal hooks. And if her skin tore, if the hooks ripped free, she felt she would fly away and never come again to the world she knew. And that would not be so very bad.

Behind closed lids she saw a great vast expanse of moon-coloured grassland, while overhead the stars swarmed and darted angrily. She knew those lights, now. Surely they were the myriad lanterns of the Plague People, that great hungry host still trapped in a land they must have stripped clean. How long had they starved there, husk-like and hollow, before finding their way to these lands? *Our lands.* Maniye had felt their hunger – the insatiable yearning of the soulless for those who had what they lacked.

In her mind's eye, she sped across that vast grassland. Was she running or flying, or being carried? Was the Wolf truly bringing her home?

She jolted back to her body again, the bitter water at her lips once more, but her eyes no longer saw the inside of the hut. She felt them open, and yet she saw only the Godsland of the Plains. There were great shadows out there that made her tremble to see them. A maned cat stalked across her path, not deigning to acknowledge her existence; a high-shouldered shape heckled at her as she was rushed away, saying, *I am within you as much as the Wolf that bears you, do not forget! You are my Champion too!*

And there were others, further out – great lost forms that had no people to give them a human voice any more. She saw the solemn, endless tread of the Aurochs, its flanks vast enough to blot out the sky. She saw the great armoured shape of the Horn-Bearer mourning its vanished people, voiceless in the world of men. The Plains were littered with the ruins of dead gods and their lost children.

And then the silver grass was behind her and she was ascending into higher grounds, a land of hills and lakes and mountains that had been her home, while a home was still something she claimed or sought.

Her sudden access of speed brought her to the peak of a high

17

hill where stones had once been raised by men, then torn down by time. She rested there, feeling her body sway, looking out across the night-lit landscape of the gods.

When she turned, the Wolf was there as she knew he would be. His hackles were high enough to eclipse the restless stars, his mouth could swallow the sun. He was winter and night, privation and an empty belly, long journeys in harsh weather and the last test that everyone fails. But he was her Wolf, and she was his.

She put a hand out to him, touching the fangs of his lower jaw that could have served her as swords. Her relationship with the god of her father had been troubled and difficult, but that was how the Wolf liked it. He liked you to run so he would have something to chase. And sometimes, if you ran well enough, he would only savage you a little when he brought you down. He had savaged her at times: through Akrit Stone River who had thought he was her father; and through Kalameshli Takes Iron who truly was; in the pursuit of Broken Axe, who had been her friend.

She waited to be given the secret: would the Wolf breathe iron into her or drive it into her body with his teeth? And yet the great beast did nothing – did not even look at her, but stared instead across the rocky landscape. There were other hills there, and Maniye knew they would host other gods – the wolf-like beasts closest, then further to those other lords of tooth and claw that had come together to make her their Champion.

Slowly, Maniye turned. She could not keep herself from turning to see what the Wolf found so fascinating.

She saw the moonlit landscape, cut across with the shadows of rocks and trees. With her poor human eyes, too many heartbeats passed before she saw the other shadows moving there.

Coyote was skulking from tree to tree, creeping with his tail between his legs. The Wild Dog of the Plains was there too, with his high, round ears and his spotted coat turned to night and silver by the moon. He trotted after Coyote, pausing to glance behind him. Maniye could read the way he stood and saw anxiety in every line of him.

Then her breath caught, for here came Tiger like fire and smoke, only ever glimpsed but she was his daughter too and she knew him. Here he stalked in full view of the Wolf his enemy, and yet neither had any thought of fighting the other. At his heels he cast a dozen shadows that were other cats, of the north, of other lands, of long gone times. Then he too was sliding away after the others. And there were more.

Bear shambled, grumbling to himself. She heard the shrill cackle of Hyena receding, the grunt of Boar and the cough of Badger.

'What is it?' she asked the Wolf at her back and he growled, low and terrifying – all the more so because she heard the unease there. The god of winter and endings had found something beyond the furthest end of his world.

And she looked east – she knew it was east for all there was no sun – and she saw fire bright and burning on the hillsides as though, behind her back, those stars had begun to fall to earth. She saw flames destroy whatever they touched, the very stuff of the Godslands burned through, and the fire-edged holes spreading and spreading. And within them: nothing. A nothing that knew neither gods nor souls nor people. And though the fires were bright and devoured all they touched, Maniye knew that they were cold, and that the nothing they brought was colder.

And then Wolf turned away from her and began to run, and she was trapped on her human feet, stumbling in his wake. She called for him to come back for her, to help her, but that had never been Wolf's way. Wolf demanded that you run or you fall and die.

And she had run so very far to escape him; she had not realized at the time that she was running *to* him at the same time.

But I ran then and I can run now.

She took to her heels and, though she was just a human girl, she found her stride swiftly and danced across the hills of the

Godsland, emptied of their masters. Behind her, she felt the ground shudder and twist in horror at what was to come. Freezing embers flecked the air about her.

The Wolf was far ahead already and she put on a new burst of speed, seeking to catch him and knowing she never would. There was a reddish tint to the dark air. Above her, the stars were beginning to fall, each bringing another spreading ring of oblivion to the world. So she ran as only one born to the Wolf and then cast away from him can run. She gulped down breath like a fish in water, fought past her raw lungs and burning muscles, lowered her head and ran. She was Maniye Many Tracks, Champion of all the beasts that tore at flesh. She could outrun the end of the world if she had to.

And yet the world *was* ending all about her. There were spreading stains of nothing ahead, now, so that she had to weave her way through them, and there was a cold at her heels that had teeth and wanted to unmake her. She could sense it: not a mind but a driving need to transform the world into somewhere that Maniye Many Tracks would have no place in, where all she was, and all she knew, was dust and bones.

She ran faster, but the devouring cold was gathering all the world to itself, dragging the hills and forests out from under her like a cloth. Her poor human legs were not equal to the task of escaping it. The gods had left her behind to die.

She looked back and the Nothing was at her shoulder, looming all the way up to the sky. It teetered high above her, Nothing piled on Nothing, with teeth of icy fire.

It fell. In a shock of panic she clawed within herself, desperate for more speed, fighting against the bonds that trapped her in this inadequate shape. *Where are you, my souls, my kin?* she cried out, and something broke inside her.

Moments later she was slamming into the walls of the hut, bellowing and roaring, battering at the flimsy wood with her claws until it seemed it must give way.

She came hurtling out into the open, the door flung wide

20

before she broke it. The smoke-clogged air within gave way to the dust without, that Plains twilight when the heat that had beaten down was snatched away within a few breaths of the sun dipping past the horizon. The sky to the west was blood-tinged.

Around her, the Wild Dog people – the Black Eye tribe who were her hosts – were leaping up, spears and hatchets in hand. She smelled their fear but also their awe, because she was their Champion too. Only out in the open, her head beginning to clear, did she know for certain she had Stepped, and she had left the Godsland.

But the hooks . . .

She rounded on Kalameshli as he approached her, the old man with his hands out. Her jaws were full of words she could not say: she was angry with him for tormenting her one last time; she was ashamed at herself for failing the Wolf's trial. For a moment she just snarled and scored the earth with her claws because that was easier than taking on another shape and having to explain how she felt.

And there was a part of her that had always wanted to strike at Takes Iron, for all he was not quite the mean old man of her memories.

But she was not the angry child of those days, either. If she was the Champion, she must act like it. She Stepped, ready to receive whatever reproach he deemed fit.

The moment she did, the fire of the hooks was spread across her back and limbs like a net. They were still caught in her, and for a moment she panicked, wanting to tear them free, until she forced herself to be still.

The look on Kalameshli's face was not the long-familiar disappointment she had expected. Instead there was a simple happiness there: a priest whose god has been propitiated; a father whose daughter has done well.

She had taken the hooks into herself, *inhered* them, when she Stepped. She had freed herself from the ropes. She had brought back the secret of iron from the Godsland.

She remembered seeing the bare back of Akrit Stone River, shortly before she fled his shadow forever. The twin lines of puckered scars that had adorned him were hers now, just as they were the badge of every Wolf hunter who had entered into that final mystery.

Kalameshli found her an axe with a grey blade and she Stepped with it, feeling the slight tug of its unnatural metal before it became part of her, bound into her teeth and claws. He had a metal coat, too, that had belonged to one of her warband who had died on the river. It was too large for her, but Kalameshli was wise in the ways of iron. He would shorten it and unravel it until just enough was left to be strapped about her skinny human frame. That would become the strength of her hide, to turn away blade and arrow. She would be a true Iron Wolf.

Whether it would turn away the unknowable weapons of the Plague People, she could not say.

The Black Eye village was a strange piece of work: the buildings were up on low mounds and shaped like the longhouses she had grown up in, but with roofs of grass. The Wild Dogs had been Wolves once, and kept hold of some of their ancestral ways. Right now, of course, it was the heart of a great camp of Plainsfolk – men, women and children from a half-dozen villages to the east who had fled ahead of the Plague People. Maniye had always heard of how the Plains-dwellers loved nothing more than to kill each other, but here they were, Lions, Horse and Boar all within a spear's reach of each other and yet not drawing blood. Whether or not their fractious reputation was deserved, it was not hard to recognize the common enemy when that enemy went on human feet and lacked a soul.

That night, she sat in the Wild Dogs' largest hut, wrapped loosely in a blanket so it would not aggravate the little puckered wounds the hooks had left. The Plains-dwellers had made her an honoured guest, but she had little to say. She knew nothing of the

22

Plague People save what she had seen, and there were plenty of others who could tell similar stories.

A starveling-thin little coyote sat with her head in Maniye's lap, listening to the counsel of the Wild Dogs but not understanding the words. This had been one of her warband once, just a Coyote girl who never had the common sense of a stone. Then she had run ahead too close to the Plague People and the unnatural terror of them had taken the irrepressible girl and locked her away. And Maniye wanted to say, *But Sathewe feared nothing*, but in the end even she had feared the Plague People. Then Maniye thought of the foam-lathered horses running wild and mad about the Plains, and wondered which of them were truly born as beasts, and which had once walked on two legs as men and women in Where the Fords Meet. One, in particular, she thought of: Alladai, who had been kind to her when she had been in need, and dear to her later, when she was strong.

The chief of the Wild Dogs was a weathered old man, tough as leather without being as flexible. He was having a hard time believing what he had heard – without his own eyes as witnesses it all seemed like a trick to him. His fiercest hunter, a lean man named Grass Shadow, argued with him back and forth – not caution, but wanting to bring a warband to the Fords. Grass Shadow wanted to fight, and some of the others wanted to fight. The chief wanted nothing to do with it – or rather he wanted life to go on as it had until he was old enough to walk out of his human life and leave it all behind.

And there were others invited to sit at the fire within the chief's hut and give more counsel to be ignored. A scar-faced Boar woman was there, whose refugee people were camped outside the Wild Dogs' village. She joined her voice to Grass Shadow's, saying something must be done. At the same time, a lean Lion woman just shook her head and drank from a jug of Riverman beer. She was Reshappa, and her people *had* fought, she said, and the Plague had broken them. Their Champion had been pierced over and over by invisible arrows that filled the air like bees. Their people had fled – and those who had not fled quick enough had lost themselves to the Fear. She said the word as though it was a name, a living thing separate from the soulless Plague People themselves.

The great chiefs and warriors of the Lion – their men – had been too proud to come to the Black Eyes' fire, but Reshappa had slunk in of her own volition. She had no counsel to give, it seemed, but had come only to tear down the words of everyone else.

And there was Shyri, the Laughing Girl. She had travelled a long, long way – from her people in the western Plains up to the Crown of the World, and halfway across *that* before making her way down the Sand Pearl to Where the Fords Meet and the Tsotec estuary. Her people were the Hyena, who took the woes of others less than seriously. None of the other Plainsfolk liked them much, which Shyri repaid twice over. Maniye looked to Shyri for wisdom, or else to laugh. Neither was forthcoming, and indeed the woman's usual derision was so absent that Maniye shuffled her seat closer until she could lean into the Laughing Girl's shoulder and whisper, 'Why so silent?'

Shyri gave her haunted look. 'Just thinking of the stories my people tell, that these fools don't want to hear.'

'So tell me.'

'Oh, *you* don't want them either,' Shyri promised her.

'Tell me anyway.'

'My people are the bone-crackers, those who dance on graves,' Shyri whispered, voice shaking ever so slightly. 'We don't contest the Lion's kill, or throw ourselves onto the tusks of the Boar. We know they'll have our paw on their neck sooner or later. We tell stories of those people who knew their moment of greatness and then fell. Where are the Aurochs now? Where are the Horn-Bearers, raisers of walls? Worse than we have gnawed their bones, and nobody tells their tales.' Her whisper gave her words the cadence of a ritual. 'The end of the world will come, and find only the Laughing Men atop a mound of broken bones.'

24

'And you think this is that time?'

'It was never supposed to *be* a time,' Shyri hissed. 'It was just a story we told each other because the Lions were strong or the Boar were many. But now . . .'

'Will your people fight?' Maniye asked her.

'Everyone fights when there's no other choice. Will they fight with these fools? Why should they?' For a moment the firelight made her look desperately unhappy.

They argued back and forth, Grass Shadow, Reshappa, the Boar woman and the Dog chief, and in the end Maniye dozed fitfully, huddled in her blanket and woken every time she slumped too far and the hook-wounds bit. In her dreams she was still hanging from the iron, and beneath her was some vast and terrible abyss – but not bottomless, for there was something swarming up out of it and she hung on the hooks and could not get away . . .

She woke suddenly – finding herself alone at the ashes of the fire, the light of morning streaming in through the chinks in the thatch. Kalameshli Takes Iron had touched her shoulder, and for a moment she couldn't remember whether she was still scared of him, or angry at him, or what.

He led her outside, and she found her warband waiting for her, a circle of them and all of them geared for war, fierce painted faces, armour and blades. Spear Catcher, with his scar-torn face; his mate Amelak who had become the band's uncomplaining mother; mad-eyed Feeds on Dreams, the Crow. And all the rest, the misfits and the outcasts who had given themselves over to her because being a Champion's follower gave them back some measure of pride. Even Shyri, who was none of Maniye's, yet was given place and honour by the rest.

And now Kalameshli was taking his place at their head. His face was painted with the jagged maze of a Wolf priest standing before his god, and his robe sewn with bones rattled about his spare frame. He held for her an iron shirt that he must have been all night tailoring to her, removing links and resealing them with the tools that were as much a part of his calling as sacrifice and devotion.

She donned the iron, feeling its weight, less than the bronze scales she had worn before. Kalameshli had done his work well, and it lay across her shoulders evenly, ready to become a part of her the moment she Stepped. She had a great sense of the Godsland at her back – she who had walked there more than once. Iron was Wolf magic, after all.

'Are you ready, Champion?' he asked her.

Out there to the east, the Plague People were spreading their strange poison, unmaking those who could not flee and spinning their white walls to make the world theirs. How could anybody be ready for that?

3

They descended into the forested valley along paths narrow enough that the horses had to be led. Therumit seemed locked in her own thoughts, but Hesprec, the traveller of old, kept her eyes wide. What she could see of the cultivation looked slipshod. Whole swathes of forest that had once been carefully cultured by human hands had grown wild and untended. As she descended, so most of the buildings were hidden from her, but those she could see looked vacant, unlit, no sign of movement, and the vines reclaiming them.

'They have not been good stewards of what we left with them,' she remarked drily.

Therumit glanced back, and there was a blankness in her face that made Hesprec wonder whether they were even seeing the same sights.

Since being driven from this place, the Serpent had dwindled. A few hundred lived along the River, of whom perhaps a third performed active priestly duties. Children were yet born to them, but not often – most were very old indeed, and the urge to create new life and bring fresh souls to human form had waned in them. Hesprec had sired a daughter and borne a son in her time, but that was long ago, other bodies, other lives. The gift of shed skin, which let those born to the Serpent's coils live on and on, brought a strange, slow perspective on events. *No wonder, when we had to make a sudden decision, we panicked.* All that time spent

27

building a civilization on the banks of the Tsotec, and then one day the most ancient and terrible enemy was at their doorstep with no warning.

Except there was plenty of warning, but we would not believe it. I had to go all the way to the Crown of the World, and I was almost too late returning. She had left a skin in the cold earth of the north – the old man who had been Maniye's fellow fugitive – and become this young girl who felt so ill equipped to meet the storm.

And Therumit was a generation older, at least. But surely not so old . . . ?

'You were not here, before.' A statement, not a question. She would not believe Therumit was *that* old.

'No . . .' The old face turned towards her again, and Hesprec saw it then. Not of that lost generation who fled the usurping Pale Shadow, but perhaps the generation that came after. What tales would the infant Therumit have been raised on, save *We will have it back*, and *How golden were our halls*? And then time had swept back and forth across the Tsotec, and the River Lords had been woven from individual clans into a great Kasranate. The Serpent had gone amongst all the priests of the River and become a part of their creeds and teachings, not the ruling divinity, but the god that underlies all. There had been lessons in agriculture and architecture, mathematics, writing and government, and most of the Serpents had lost that dream, sloughing it away with one shift of skin or another. And most of Therumit's generation were dead, for the knife or the fever or just the weariness of too many lives still claimed the Serpent's long-lived children.

And through the centuries, one face after another, old to young to old to young, Therumit had guided the Estuary peoples and never lost her childhood dreams.

I am less than confident we are doing the right thing. But the revelation was too late. Here they were. The path was too narrow

28

even for her to turn her horse around, and she had a feeling Therumit might not let her go so freely.

Onward then, but still, not blindly. 'Therumit, do you not feel the servants in these halls are remiss in their duties?' She pointed at the heights of a tower emerging from the trees and the swathing sheets of white. 'I see a statue there that's nothing but two feet and broken shins, and the tower-top's not much better. And that tiered palace beyond it has gone back to the jungle. The roots pry between its stones. Do you not think this says something about the hospitality we shall receive?'

'Perhaps it says this place is ready for us to return,' was Therumit's dry response. 'The Pale Shadow were mighty once, to drive us out. Perhaps they have weakened to the point where mere force will win back our legacy for us.'

'I trust you've brought a force of invisible soldiers then,' Hesprec commented. 'It might tax just the two of us.'

'If soldiers are needed then the River will provide,' Therumit told her. 'But for now we have an invitation, or did you forget?'

Not something I am ever likely to, Hesprec knew. One of the Pale Shadow had come into the Estuary. A pale, hollow woman naming herself Galethea, she had been colluding with Therumit and some others of the Serpent there, with promises that the Oldest Kingdom was theirs for the taking. The Pale Shadow sought the Serpent's teaching, she had said. Hesprec believed not a word of it and, if that had been all, she would not be here about this foolishness. But of course there had been more, for Galethea had spoken about the Plague People. The Pale Shadow were less than overjoyed to find their distant relatives on these shores. They spoke of common enemies – and enemies that they understood as even the Serpent never could.

Another lie, probably. But the news from the Plains had been dire enough to spur Hesprec on. *And I should admit it to myself: one more journey; one more place so few have ever seen. I always knew wanderlust would get me killed.*

And now they were down, in amongst the trees, following a

29

stone-clad track that was humped and broken by the hungry roots, furred by moss. Around them, the deeps of the forest were shrouded, webs stretching in a maze of solid mist until look far enough in any direction and all you saw was white: the Pale Shadow.

There were animals – Hesprec heard the birdcalls quiet as they neared, start up again behind them once they had passed. She heard frogs creaking in the silted-up irrigation channels and there would be jaguars and capybara and peccaries winding their ways between the trees. None of these were seen though, knowing the presence of man enough to flee it. What she did see were the spiders.

They were small, for the most part. Tiny eight-legged motelets drifted on the faintest breeze, trailing silk. Thumbnail-sized skitterers crept on every leaf and branch. Hairy hand-sized monsters bumbled across their path, their ambling turned to a sudden flailing rush as the hooves came close. And none of this was what concerned Hesprec, who was only thinking, *None of these spun those great webs I see, not alone, not all together, not in a hundred years of weaving.*

And at last, after hunting the branches and canopy, she spied one, and tapped Therumit's bony shoulder to draw her attention. The creature squatted in the crook of a tree, its bulbous body as great as Hesprec's own, its short legs drawn in and kept so still she might have missed it – as she had perhaps missed many of its kin already. A Kasra of spiders, architect of the enshrouding sheets and nets that hung all about them.

Therumit just grunted, unsurprised.

Do they have souls, I wonder? But the question was not one Hesprec would voice to her companion. There were sacrileges even the most irreverent priest should not consider.

Then Therumit stopped, swiftly enough that Hesprec's mount jostled hers. The old woman took out a gnarled cane from the sling on her saddle, holding it like a switch for striking.

Hesprec let herself down to the earth, spiders or not, because she was not the rider Therumit was. In case of trouble she would trust to her fangs and her coils.

There was movement about them – the sense of large creatures moving quietly. For a moment Hesprec was still thinking of spiders, but long experience told her this was a more familiar threat. She knew the scent of a big cat, the soft pad of its feet. The People of the Jaguar had raised this city along with the Serpent, in the distant past. Serpent had been wise and Jaguar had been strong. Strong, but ultimately dissatisfied and easily suborned, as history had borne out.

'I don't think they've come to welcome us home,' she murmured.

Therumit said nothing, but her visage was terrible. It would be a brave warrior who would face that gnarled countenance, all the bottled scorn and bitterness of a dozen lifetimes. Still bravery was a crop raised from numbers, and Hesprec reckoned there were a dozen men and beasts out there, at least.

Then one made himself known: a tall, broad-shouldered man with skin as dark as the Serpents or the Rivermen, but features distinct from either. Others were slipping out from between the trees on all sides. The Jaguar were heavy-jawed, heavy-browed; they wore their hair in long plaited tails. Some of them had spotted pelts slung over their shoulders; others wore quilted tunics. A few had faded rags and swatches of silk given pride of place about their bodies that said to Hesprec *favours* or *cast-offs*. They had stone-beaked clubs and jagged spears.

In between the men were the cats, shoulders high as Hesprec's ribs, eyes narrow with green fire, their coats leaping out from the shadows when they moved, fading into nothing when they were still.

Therumit faced them down with a masterful arrogance. 'You will not raise a hand against the Serpent.'

To Hesprec's surprise, that sent a shiver of wariness through them. There would be some strange old stories told at the hearths of these hunters about the old times. Did they have

31

doom-filled prophecies of Serpent's vengeful return? Did they all bear the mark of their forebears' ancient treachery?

Therumit guided her horse forward one more step, stick upraised. Hesprec knew full well how fierce her fellow priestess could look, no matter what face she wore. The warriors before her backed off, anger vying with fear naked on their faces.

She almost saw the movement in time to cry a warning, but by the time her mouth was open, the jaguar was already in the air. The big cat landed claws out on the haunches of Therumit's mount and the beast reared up, screaming. She fell back from the saddle, landing in a looping nest of coils, rearing up higher than a man to menace them with her fangs. Hesprec Stepped alongside her, choosing a more slender shape that might go unseen for vital moments, dropping into the thick greenery that was sprouting between the stones of the path.

The attacking jaguar was still mauling the horse, but the others had made a move for Therumit. More than half had lost their nerve almost instantly, leaving only a handful with the courage to brave her. Hesprec lashed her body forwards, striking five feet out and then recoiling herself, seeing one Jaguar warrior drop with his leg gashed, the venom already starting to shake him. That sent another tumbling back, swiping at the undergrowth around him as though there were serpents everywhere. The remaining two met Therumit's full wrath.

Her coils surged and coursed within one another like wheels, impossible to know where she was going until she was already there. One of the Jaguar was lost within them instantly, looped about the chest and arms and throat, legs kicking frantically. The final attacker swept his club at her body, the beak slanting away from her scales. Therumit reared higher, almost to the branches above, then struck down at him like a hammer, driving her fangs into his eyes.

Momentarily, Hesprec thought they would flee, but there was a sound from deeper in the overgrown city – a braying horn sounding some uncomfortable, jarring note. It did not give the warriors courage, but it gave them desperation, and abruptly they were thronging in, getting in one another's way, spear-shafts rattling against each other as they tried to pin the Serpents down. Therumit Stepped again, from great constrictor down to ribbon-thin viper that squirmed between their legs like an eel. They lashed at her – carved up the earth and bloodied their own shins – but she was out from their knot and already lunging back to send a jawfull of poison into an errant foot. Hesprec took that moment to Step larger, erupting from the undergrowth as a great black snake rising as high as their heads, spreading a hood that flashed fierce eyes at them and sending them tumbling back. They were terrified, yet they were not fleeing, and all this show would only work for so long. Neither she nor Therumit had limitless venom and the numbers would tell. They must either flee into the unknown jungle or fight and fall.

A club cast its shadow over her and she shrank and darted away. Feet were trampling everywhere, threatening to crush her even if their owners did not realize it. She darted for the nearest leg and wound up it, climbing the man in rapid zig-zags as she would have done a tree. He cried out and tried to grasp her slender body but she slipped out from his fingers and threatened his face with her fangs. Then one of the others lashed at her and struck his fellow full in the head. She heard the skull crack like an egg from the force of it and dropped to earth with the dying body, already twisting to see where the next blow would come from.

But in that moment they were fleeing, gibbering and calling to one another in some bizarre speech from which she could make out one word in three.

We scared them off! But the thought died even as she tasted it. They had been crammed full of fear of serpents and still tried to fight. Some other force had mastered them in the end. She watched them plunge between the trees and her heart almost stopped when a great grey shape lunged from the shadows to bowl three of them over, seizing one in its fangs and bearing him away. A shape with many legs, larger than a horse. The spiders she had seen in the canopy were mere hatchlings compared to it.

She Stepped back to her human shape, feeling new bruises. Beside her, Therumit had done the same, levering herself to her feet and drawing her dignity about herself like a mantle.

Their hosts had arrived.

At first they seemed too bright to look at: radiant with silver and gold as though they had stolen the secrets of the sun and moon, striding through the forest like gods. Perhaps that was what the Jaguar saw, but Hesprec had lived enough lifetimes to see through such trivial matters. They were not truly lustrous, but it was the thought they placed in the eyes of those who looked upon them. *And if you were not looking for it, you'd not see the emptiness within them. Maybe that's how they fooled our ancestors.* Which was less shaming? That their ancestors had lacked the wisdom to pierce this glamour, or that they had been blinded by their own pride.

Hesprec saw a dozen of them: eight women, four men. All were very fair, unnaturally pale. Had that inner absence not been apparent to her, no doubt she would have found them beautiful. They wore robes of shimmering gossamer that were likewise beautiful until she considered what must have spun them. Some had armour of hide that was ornamented with gold. Most wore bands of precious metal at their wrists and ankles and necks, enough that they could not have Stepped – although of course they had no shape to Step into, without a soul to gift it to them. *So are they children, then? Children who never grow up?* She felt it was a dangerous comparison.

There were spiders amongst them – some that crawled on their bodies or amidst their clothes, toying with the silks as though adjusting their fit. Others with iridescent bodies crouched on their breasts like jewels. Larger beasts ran beside them, grey and hairy and long-legged. If Hesprec had only glanced, and not truly seen, she might have thought they were accompanied by nothing more than hounds.

34

Therumit glanced for her horse, seeing it mauled and dead. Hesprec's beast had remained nearby, more spooked by its surroundings than the bloodshed.

'When last we met,' she said, 'a companion of mine introduced you to our customs of host and guest.' She faced the glare of their glamour with barely a narrowing of her eyes. 'Now see how we are met, who were invited.'

She expected them to retort with some piece of arrogance, but instead one of their women stepped forward, and she recognized none other than Galethea, their ambassador from the Estuary.

'We are not all of one mind, one heart here,' she said. 'Please, come with us to the palace of our house. You will be safe there.'

Hesprec doubted that very much, not sure whether division within the Pale Shadow was something to fear or exploit. She glanced at Therumit in time to see the old priestess nod curtly. Without a word she snagged the reins of the surviving horse and hoisted herself into the saddle. She held a hand out to Hesprec, who Stepped into a little serpent and climbed up it, finding a roost about Therumit's shoulders. Let the other woman do the talking; she would watch.

And watch she did, as the party of the Pale Shadow passed through the forest, noting how the buildings grew less ruined – how there were signs of occupation: cloth at the doorways, lights in the windows. She saw men and women of the Jaguar who were plainly the servants or slaves of the Pale Shadow – they knelt when the shining entourage passed by, and averted their faces from any sight of the Serpent.

And yet so few, Hesprec thought. She was reminded of the Shining Halls of the Tiger, a great power laid low by their losses in the war against the Wolf. *So what war came here?* But she sensed some more final hand was laid on this place than mere brawling. There was a gauntness to their hosts' faces, a brittle precision to their motions. Had they been real humans she might have thought that a plague was stalking here, eating away at them

35

even as they ate away at themselves. She had the sense of arriving at the ending of something nobody should witness.

But then that's true of all the world right now, and if it were not for that I would never be walking in these shadows, and nor would any sane human.

The little band of northerners had attracted a lot of interest from the Plainsfolk. Grass Shadow's people showed them off like a trophy: *See who our guests are!* Lion and Boar warriors turned up in bands of four or five to stare and measure themselves against the foreigners. Many wanted to touch the Wolf-iron. Sometimes they tried to barter for it: tools, livestock or the gold and bronze jewellery the Plains people were so adept at crafting. Amelak appointed herself chief diplomat to these people, pointing out tactfully that the Plainsfolk could not Step with the metal: strong as it was, it was useless to them.

Others came for purposes of their own. Errant children from some fire or other would chase the little coyote Sathewe through the camp. It hurt Maniye, but the little animal her friend had become seemed to enjoy the attention – *just as she would when she had a human face* – so she let it be. She was more concerned with the lean Leopard man, Tensho, who had taken to standing at the edge of her camp, staring directly at her. It was a challenge, Maniye knew. She asked Shyri about the Leopard, and the Laughing Girl had little good to say. They were an ill-omened people, living in the shadows and good only at stalking and killing. Most of the Leopard stories they told on the Plains were about murder and treachery, unwanted guests, missing children.

Maniye wondered what stories the Leopard told. At last,

because she couldn't ignore the man, she hailed him to the war-band's fire, ready to make a fight of it should matters go that way.

Tensho reminded Maniye a little of the Tiger, in the face and the coppery skin. The Tiger had come north from the Plains long ago, kin to the Lion and the Leopard, they said. One generation ago, two maybe, and there had been a loose-knit alliance of Cat tribes that had held a swathe of the Plains and half the Crown of the World. Then the Wolf had broken the Tiger, and some similar fate had fractured the unity of the Lion, but what of the Leopard? They were not numerous, not empire-builders. So . . .

'So what do you want?' Maniye asked flatly.

Tensho arched his eyebrows. He sat very still at the fire, like a branch drawn back that could be released at any time. There were neat parallel scars on his cheeks and shoulders and his shaved scalp gleamed. 'You are the Champion, they say.' His voice was low, enough that Maniye had to resist the urge to lean in to listen.

'If you've come to see the Champion, you've seen her,' Maniye pointed out.

'You ask your guest to leave so soon?' That raised eyebrow again.

'You come to my camp uninvited. Tell me your purpose and I will share our food with you or I will ask you to go. Until then you've not become a guest of mine.'

Tensho stared at her for a long time and Maniye matched him, glower for glower. She could tell just how dangerous the man was – swift and strong and eminently confident in his ability to kill. On the other hand, Maniye *was* the Champion, and the Champion's soul within her would not let her back down. So she just locked gazes with the man and waited to see which way the branch would spring.

And at last Tensho's gaze dipped. 'These fools will not listen to the Leopard,' he said sullenly, a cock of his head taking in perhaps the whole Plains.

Maniye just shrugged, as if to say the doings of Plainsfolk were hardly her concern.

'Since when does the Leopard care?' Shyri's voice cut in. Maniye grimaced inwardly, but she would have to trust her friend knew what she was doing.

Tensho spat, eloquently showing just how much the Leopard would normally care. Then he shook his head. 'One came to my fire, seeking words with the war chiefs of the Plains here.'

'Why did they not come to the Black Eyes' fire?' Maniye asked him.

'For the same reason I do not. They are not welcome. The Wild Dog and the rest have made themselves mad telling spirit stories about them over their fires each night, until even to see a Leopard has them scrabbling to deflect our curses and our magic.' He sounded more amused than annoyed at this. 'But as the Leopard are to these fools, so the one who came to my fire is to the Leopard. So I intercede for them, and ask you to intercede for me.'

'Who asks a Leopard to be their speaker?' Shyri demanded incredulously. 'Why you?'

A new emotion rippled on Tensho's face briefly. 'It was payment of a debt.'

Maniye opened her mouth to ask, but something in his expression suggested the debt had been a complex, perhaps shameful thing. Certainly nothing that could have been paid off with meat or hides.

'So who is this friend of yours?' Maniye asked him. 'I can't just go to the Black Eyes and say "Someone wants to sit at your fire."'

Tensho told her, and she didn't understand who the man meant, or the reason for Shyri's sudden intake of breath in her ear.

Then the old stories came back to her and she remembered the Owl priest, Grey Herald, talking through How We Escaped the Plague People.

39

'Yes,' she said immediately. 'Bring them to our fire. I will take them to the Black Eyes, to the Lions, to all of them.'

A commotion struck up from just beyond the circle of her warband and she leapt up, ready for anything. Even that was enough for Tensho to slip away, for when Maniye looked back he was already gone.

She Stepped to wolf feet to run. The world resolved itself into a texture of sounds and scents her human senses had not guessed at. Instantly she knew who was at the centre of the ruckus, and normally she would have turned away, exasperated. This time there was a new odour clinging to him that was not just the reek of his own mischief.

Most of her warband were Wolves, hunters and warriors and renegades seeking a banner and a cause. One had been a Coyote before the Plague People lessened her. One was a Crow. He called himself Feeds on Rags but his true name was Feeds on Dreams. The name was a curse on him for destroying the lives of others with his ill-thought schemes and rash actions. She should have turned him away, no doubt, but he was useful and there was no malice in him, any more than there was fore-thought. The Coyote, Sathewe, had been his closest confidante. He had sworn some sort of vengeance against the Plague People after their power touched her. *Whatever vengeance a Crow can enact.*

Now he had swooped down and Stepped, hopping from foot to foot, waving a bronze mace in one hand and crying out that he had slain the enemy. There was something at his feet that smelled sharp and wrong to her wolf nose. *But he couldn't have flown with one of their bodies . . .*

As she arrived, Feeds was already arguing with Spear Catcher. 'It is one of them!' the Crow insisted, brandishing his cudgel. 'I have taken the battle to the Plague People! I have slain one!'

'They look like men!' Spear Catcher insisted. 'That's no man.'

'It is one of them, Stepped to their beasts,' Feeds insisted furiously.

40

'They have no souls! How can they Step?' the Wolf warrior demanded. Then Maniye took on the shape of the Champion and bellowed in all their ears because it was the quickest way to remind them whose warband they were a part of.

In the echo of that, she took her human shape again and asked, 'What is it? What have you killed, idiot bird?'

He cringed a little from the insult, but she still held him responsible for what had happened to Sathewe, as did he when he remembered. 'Here!' he cried, though, kicking at the thing by his feet.

She saw an insect there, save that it was the size of three of her hands together. Feeds must have been labouring in the air to carry such a thing. It was clearly dead, its shell cracked open and the curled body smeared with yellowish ichor. A beetle, and not the largest she had seen in the company of the Plague People.

'It is not one of them,' she said quietly.

'I *told* you—' Spear Catcher started, but she held up a hand to quiet him.

'It is *of* them,' she stated. 'It is a thing of theirs. Unless the Plains breeds these creatures?'

The Plainsfolk who had been drawn by the noise were quick to deny it. She drew a deep breath, thinking, *Why must I always do the thinking? Where is Hesprec when I need her?* 'Where did you find this thing?' she asked the Crow. 'How far did you fly?'

'There and back between dawn and noon, yes,' Feeds on Dreams confirmed proudly.

Maniye said nothing, listening to the realization leap from head to head. Once people had begun to run off, to fetch their elders and betters, she asked over the murmuring, 'Was it alone?'

'There were others. Human-looking others,' Feeds confirmed, and then skittered back at her expression. 'Why are you angry? Was it I who put them there?'

'You didn't think to start with that?' she yelled at him, once more regretting ever bringing him. *The Plague People are already close. How far can a crow fly in half a morning?* Feeds was swift

41

when he wanted to be, but nobody had guessed the enemy were already gnawing at the edge of their cloak. She saw Grass Shadow pushing his way through the gathering crowd, demanding to know what was going on, and dragged Feeds close to her.

'You remember everything, now. Remember, and tell it in the right order at the right time.'

There had been more than five, less than ten of them, Feeds wasn't sure exactly. He hadn't wanted to look at them much, nor attract their attention. Listening to his meandering account, his corrections and reversals, Maniye tried to imagine him there – off on a mission of his own making, seeking a revenge he couldn't possibly exact. The Plague People had been pale and armoured, he recalled abruptly, breaking into his own recollection. They were dressed in the colours of sun and darkness.

Many of the Plainsfolk didn't want to believe it. How could the enemy have come so close, so swiftly? Others – those who had already lost their lands and villages – broke in: they fly. No, not like birds. Not riding their beasts. They just *fly*. And the undercurrent of fear that came with the revelation: *they are the Plague People. They can do anything.*

Then the arguments started up again – the same as last night but whetted to a razor's edge by the urgency. Some of the refugees were already packing what they had salvaged and preparing to head west, as though the Plague People would someday lose interest and cease to pursue them and consume the world. Others were taking up spears, axes and knives, donning armour of linen, hide and bronze. A band of ten Plague People was not so many.

Grass Shadow was the loudest voice of the war faction. His own chief was trying to speak for caution, but the old man had no arguments.

'So what is your plan?' one of the Boar demanded. 'Kill these scouts of theirs, and what? What, when the rest come?'

'Kill these scouts and the rest won't know where to come!' Grass Shadow insisted.

'If they can be killed,' another of the Black Eyes said, one of their hearth keepers. 'They have no souls to part from their bodies.'

'Then we'll destroy their bodies, burn them until nothing's left but ash and teeth,' Grass Shadow swore.

'And when they fly off, do you think the terror of Grass Shadow will keep them from coming back with ten times the numbers?' the Boar pressed. 'Or will you fly after them, dirt dog?' This last some Plains insult Maniye wasn't familiar with, which made Grass Shadow bristle.

'My arrows will fly swifter than they can,' he spat. 'And when we have killed each one of them you can be sure we will remember who feared too much to stand beside us.'

Maniye felt a great urge to be elsewhere and started shuffling to the edge of the circle. This was not her land. Anything she said would be wrong. Then she saw a shadow at the edge of vision, and turned to see Tensho standing at the firelight's furthest reach, dappled with the moving shadows of others. He nodded at her, just once, but his message came through clear.

So I will have to speak after all. She tried to gauge how the argument was going. Reshappa and some of the Lion were fierce for fighting, giving Grass Shadow more voices for him than against, but not by many. And of course many were not speaking at all, and most were more likely thinking about packing up their tents than taking up spears.

'I will speak!' Maniye called, but they were none of them listening to a skinny little Wolf girl. The Champion shifted impatiently within her. She did not want to abuse its shape, but it was plainly not used to being ignored.

She Stepped, readying herself to bellow at them and take the consequences, but the sheer size of the wolf-cat-bear-kin creature she became sent a wave of shocked quiet through them until everyone was looking at her. She felt a growl of challenge from a pair of big men, scar-chested and broad-shouldered, who must be Lion Champions. The other people here had none, and in some sense that made her *their* Champion. She was of no single people.

She walked to the fire, and they all made way for her. She could smell their hope and fear, and was only grateful that it was not *she* who would be their war leader. Stepping, her human feet were left surrounded by the great space she had occupied a moment before.

'What would you say?' Grass Shadow asked, plainly wanting her to support him.

'Not me,' she told them. 'One comes who would speak with you. A voice you'll want to hear.' There were complex nets of etiquette about inviting a guest to someone else's fire, and she did not know the Plains way of it. Thankfully Grass Shadow simply said, 'Then let them come forward,' and that dealt with that.

The figure who stalked in, through the broad channel Maniye had cut in the crowd, was tall and emaciated, wrapped in a loose white robe. Maniye could not decide whether it was male or female – or perhaps time had erased that distinction. Its face was high-browed, hollow-cheeked, its skin the yellow-brown of old bone. There was something of the Plains in it, but only a little, and nothing at all of any other people Maniye had ever seen. Tensho the Leopard skulked in its wake.

For a long time nobody there seemed to know who the visitor was, save that there was some uncomfortable power in every line of that lean frame. Then the whispers started up, and Maniye heard the name being passed back and forth, in awe and horror and incredulity. *The Bat have woken at last. The Bat Society is with us.* The Bat, the Owl and the Serpent were the three brothers who held off the Plague People before, so said the oldest tales. And while the Serpent had gone to build a kingdom and guide the River, and the Owl had become just one more tribe of the

Eyrie, the Bat had vanished themselves away, seen only in the dreams and darkest rituals of the Plainsfolk.

The gaunt creature nodded, accepting as its due the whispering and protective gestures, the wary retreat from where it stood.

'We were brought back,' it told them in a low, dry voice, a woman's voice. 'If not to fight the Plague People then why? I will go with you. You will not hear my battle cry but it will strike fear into the enemy. We will drive them and their world away from here.' The Bat's voice was flat and impatient. *We were brought back*, she had said, and Maniye guessed she wanted nothing more than to return to wherever she had been conjured from.

'And if we fight and fail, what then?' one of the Boar challenged from the safety of the crowd. 'What, when we have drawn their anger?'

'Do not fear their anger,' the Bat said, but not to reassure. 'Do not fear their hate or rage. Fear *them* and what they are, for they are soulless and hungry. Do you think it will be better for you, if they are calm when they come to eat you and your ways and your gods? When you are no more than rooting pigs or voiceless dogs, will you feel relieved that they did not do that to you in *anger*? Know this truth: they do not *care* about you. They do not even *believe* in you. You are the shadows in their world. They come to set the fires that will unmake you.' She spoke with a dreadful patient conviction. 'So flee if you will, like the shadows flee the fire. One day the fire will be everywhere, and the shadows will have nowhere to go. Or fight. I intend to fight.'

'And I!' Grass Shadow cried, and Reshappa of the Lion was echoing him a moment later, and dozens of other voices besides. There were still those who would leave, Maniye knew, though they would not be arguing it here. The Bat's intervention had brought round the majority at the fire, at least for now.

And then Grass Shadow was looking for her, pushing through the crowd to clap a hand to her shoulder. 'Champion!' he said. 'Will you fight? Will you stand with us?'

Some small part of her wanted to claim that it was not her

fight, but in truth she knew that this was everyone's fight, and the mood about the fire had caught her up just as it had caught so many.

'I will bring my warband!' she shouted, as loud as she could. The Plague People had come too far without being shown that the world they were invading had teeth.

5

Hesprec remembered a Kasra's son from a hundred years ago, the most beautiful man she had ever set eyes on. He had been his mother's pride and joy, but he had not lived to be Kasra. A fever had taken him that all the lore of the Serpent had not been able to draw from his body. Hesprec had sat by his bedside at the end and watched the heat of his disease consume him, bright in his eyes and gleaming just beneath the surface of his skin. He had never stopped being beautiful, not even when the fever had hollowed him out.

That was what the Pale Shadow People reminded her of. They were beautiful – as statues could be beautiful when executed by a master. Their beauty hid a gnawing disease though. It was not their soullessness, or not just that, nor was it the legendary hunger of the Plague People. There was a sickness abroad in the Oldest Kingdom.

Galethea had led them through the overgrown streets of that ancient place, and every sight had only shown the Serpents that the world of their ancient enemies was collapsing in upon itself. The stories they had inherited had told of a city of gold, every wall a library of carven knowledge, every word set with gems. Hesprec had been more than prepared to find all that no more than hyperbole, and certainly the gold and the jewels were, unsurprisingly, absent. The carvings had been there, though, and she ground her teeth to think what knowledge had been lost.

Everywhere she looked, the stone had crumbled or been worn smooth until what had been written there was lost to the eye. Vines and roots crept up from the ground and creepers fell from the boughs, all with the intent of smothering the stonework and thrusting into every crack to prise it all apart. In other places she saw a deliberate effacement: statues beheaded or their stone faces ground flat *(so the eyes of the Serpent can no longer see here?)*. Elsewhere, the Pale Shadow had evidently tried to emulate their predecessors. Whole walls had been re-faced with new carvings in an alien fashion. She saw marks that were not writing, but aped it, set into orderly rows of meaningless repetition. She saw elaborate geometrical carvings, lines, circles and angles, interlocking and radiating, leading the eye in a spiralling inward dance. And yet many of these had been vandalized too, hacked at and struck from the stone.

'Those who attacked us?' she prompted Galethea.

'Unhoused,' came the reply, after some shared looks between their pale guides.

'Meaning more than lacking a roof over their heads.' Hesprec's sidelong glance took in a dozen palaces that must have been abandoned for five generations, the jungle swallowing them stone by stone.

'Renegades,' Therumit said.

'Are all the Jaguar renegade?'

'No.' Galethea's answer came swiftly. 'Those of our house serve us loyally. Those of other houses are happy with their lot. But some are of fallen houses, and others . . .'

'Are less happy to serve,' Hesprec finished for her.

'Ungrateful,' one of the other Pale Shadow women said.

They were approaching a walled compound where the greenery had at least been held back. White webs spanned the wall-tops and hung about the place like veils, a skittering motion wherever Hesprec looked. She wanted to make some comment to Therumit, about how neither of them would sleep well here. A little humour to puncture the tension had always been her way,

48

old or young. Therumit's face was so serious though. The words went unsaid. *She must see the same sights I do.* But if so, Therumit obviously gave them very different weight. Her face still had that hunger for lost times in it, and in that she was almost akin to the Pale Shadow.

Entering the compound of the silk-ragged palace, Hesprec almost thought she could reconstruct the entire history of the Oldest Kingdom from the moment the Serpent had been driven from it. *They came as our guests, the stories said, and then they suborned our servants and betrayed our trust. They put themselves in our stead and drove us to new homes on the River. And we were never many, and those who survived the exodus were fewer still, and had so little hope of reclaiming their home that they made a new one along the River.* Though some thread of that hope had survived, sufficient to bring Therumit here, and Hesprec in her shadow.

Then they rose and grew mighty. Most of the buildings around her must have post-dated the Serpent exodus. She looked up at the older carvings that sheathed the great tiered walls of the palaces and temples within the compound. She could not read the jagged almost-characters there, nor interpret the interlacing lines of their art. Where the Pale Shadow's carvers had represented their masters, though, they were shown huge and grand and radiant. Women mostly, those early rulers: some cut in the old style of the Jaguar and the Serpent, stylized in stolen attitudes of benevolence and benediction. Others were cut to be startlingly naturalistic, and Hesprec could read the natures and vices of the originals in those stone masks. She looked on those long-dead queens and kings of the Pale Shadow and knew them to be cruel, proud and arbitrary, and that they must have seen such as virtues to so glorify them in their art.

But those were old, those exacting carved portraits. They had been cherished, but she saw the cracks and the wear of centuries on them. Their lips and eyes had been painted and repainted, and she could read the longer and longer intervals in which anyone had cared to take up the brush, for they were flaked and the colours faded. The silk hangings that graced the walls, which were shot through with gold and silver, were washed out, the images hard to descry. What she did see hinted at a history stretching back to the times before the Pale Shadow came to trouble the Serpent. There were great armies shown there, seen from a lordly distance so that the fighting knots of men might as well have been ants. There were unfamiliar ships pitching upon great waves, and terrifying beasts made of hooks and blades and too many legs which made the ubiquitous spiders seem tame and harmless in comparison. And yet she could see, too, that many of these tapestries were but copies of the past, copies of copies perhaps. Whoever had woven the image of that ship had never *seen* the ship itself. She could find the most ragged and light-bleached of the hangings and plot their descendants, generation to generation, each more stylized than the last until the image of ship and wave had become a mere abstract swirl of lines and colours.

Whatever the Pale Shadow had been, it was that no longer. And perhaps there had always been a core of rot, a lack of inspiration. Where the Pale Shadow had ordered their servants to raise palaces to their greater glory, the style was that of the halls the Serpents had left behind. The Jaguar masons had simply carried on their traditions, and the Pale Shadow had brought nothing new to their craft.

There was spider imagery more often than Hesprec was happy with, and she could not help noting that it was generally newer than the rest. Columns had chains of the creatures forming ascending helices up to the web-dusty ceilings. The brighter tapestries showed tessellated arachnids, mazes of interlocking legs, or else individual monsters rendered in a thousand attitudes of waiting and hunting, threat and display. The new art overlaid the old and its constant repetition of theme spoke of a strange desperation. Yes, the Patient Ones of the River revered Old Crocodile, but they did not practise such a mindless echoing of his image.

With that thought, Hesprec wondered if she had found the secret after all. She itched for a moment alone to take counsel with Therumit, but most likely their hosts would have ears everywhere. *Ears and eyes and legs, far too many legs.*

And then Galethea was breaking out into a grander chamber, and the two Serpents were abruptly standing before some three score of the Pale Shadow, and twice that many Jaguar. *And did they lead us through all those little halls so they had time to assemble this host?*

There was a throne at the far end of the chamber, and for a moment Hesprec thought that, too, was cut in the shape of a spider, its limbs arching upwards around its occupant like a cage. Then she blinked and saw it for a half-open flower, leaves and petals carved from a single piece of white stone. The workmanship was fine and old and she wondered whether this was something left over from her own ancestors' craft, still used by the usurpers so long after.

A woman sat in the throne, haughty and pale as any of the old stone images they had passed. She might have been three decades old or six, her skin so pale as to be near translucent. She wore silks dyed blue and red, ornamented with gold and precious stones, fantastically elaborate in the interweaving of layers and colours. A high collar stretched behind her, spined and spread like a fish's fin. Clusters of gems dotted her robe, and Hesprec saw they had been fixed to the shells of tethered insects that wandered on mindless, circular paths, so that the eye was constantly being drawn to their glittering burdens.

Such finery! And yet Hesprec had a keen eye. She saw where that fabulous garment had been darned, where a previous owner had trailed the hem too long on the ground. All around was the height of the Pale Shadow finery, gathered to overawe their visitors, and she could see the holes and the stains, the missing stones, the unravelling threads. Some instinct prompted her to glance up and she had to fight back a shudder. The lofty ceiling was a dusty mass of ragged webs: just as the city was time-worn cast-off upon cast-off, so the spiders had recreated the same story with their own art, knotted with the corpses of desiccated flies.

And it is the same with their faces. With such a host of the Pale Shadow to examine she could pick out the common sickness afflicting them. Even that matriarch on the throne was gripped by the same fever, and many were worse. The hunger – the *need* – in their eyes as they stared at the two Serpents was palpable. It seemed to reach out towards them, then flinch away, fearful of what it might find. For her part, Therumit could match the Pale Shadow pride for pride, and she made her simple white robes seem more than the equal of all those jewels and faded colours.

'You are made welcome to the House of the August Hand,' the matriarch declared, the words comprehensible though given a stronger twist of accent than Galethea's. There was such masterly arrogance in her voice that Hesprec wondered whether the speaker saw all the signs of decay, internal and external, or whether to her it was all gleaming and new. The Pale Shadow queen waved her slender hand, and dust motes glittered in the wan light like tiny jewels. 'Long has it been since the Serpent was our guest.'

Hesprec waited for Therumit to make some caustic rejoinder, for the queen made it sound as though the Serpent had simply been poor friends, to leave the visit so long. *Centuries, it has been centuries and yet she speaks as though we had just been away a year, and all been close as kin before then.*

'Yes, long,' Therumit said dismissively. 'Let us not talk of past *hospitality*.' She waved her hand dismissively, and that, apparently, was that. No raking up of the old grievances, no accusations of the betrayed against the betrayer. 'Much water has flowed since then. Much has flowed, even, since your emissaries came to me in the Estuary.' And now she was waiting for the queen's response, and Hesprec recalled that the early overtures of the Pale Shadow had not been well received. Galethea was not the first ambassador, but she was the first to return alive. 'So long we have been away, and you did not think to *invite* us back,' and *here* was what Hesprec had expected, that hard tone she well remembered from a dozen arguments with the woman. 'But now you desire us to come and see your wonders.'

Hesprec tensed, ready for Therumit's angry tone to go down badly. There were plenty of weapons there: spears and clubs in the hands of the Jaguar guards, and some of the apparently lower-status Pale Shadows had knives and longer blades of bronze that were like little swords.

She saw the pride and offence build behind the face of the queen, but before it broke the surface it was consumed by something greater, which rose beneath it like a sea monster and gulped it back down.

Despair. She was shocked to see it there so nakedly, stretched across the chasm of the woman's hollow nature. It was the most human expression she had seen on any of their faces. Hesprec saw the need writhing there beneath that near-translucent skin, and yet the words that came from the Pale Shadow's lips were mundane. 'And what do you think of our wonders?'

She gestured, and in that moment Hesprec could have been persuaded that all about them was bright and opulent. But then the moment passed and it was dust and time-faded silk.

'Long have I lived, and wished to look upon these sights,' Therumit said. Hesprec heard the edge in her voice, though perhaps their hosts would not. 'Long have my people told tales of these halls.'

The queen had been leaning forward as she spoke, and Hesprec realized abruptly that Therumit's accent must be as strong, to her, as hers was to the Serpent. 'And it is past time you returned to them, in peace,' the woman said, after a moment's pause. 'Ask what you will of my servants. Nothing shall be denied you.' And still that need beat beneath the words, but the queen was too proud to ask what it was her people wanted – no, she was too proud to *beg*, though Hesprec saw the begging in her and wondered at it.

★

53

Later, a woman of the Jaguar led them to a chamber that was taller than it was wide, the walls positively swathed in ragged tapestries where the efforts of a thousand battling warriors were slowly being eaten away by the work of the worm. There was food – some manner of stew too highly spiced for Hesprec's liking, containing unguessable meats. And there was the company of Therumit.

She caught the older woman's eye. They had a lot to talk about and would have to do so without words. No doubt the Pale Shadow were listening.

She gathered up dust in the hem of her robe and dumped it out on the cracked stone of the floor, flattening it until she had smoothed out a regular surface. She and Therumit both took up slender sticks, and set to writing. One would scratch her swift characters in the dust, then the other would erase and write her reply, so swiftly that, even had someone been looking over their shoulders, they might not have been able to catch any of it. *And I have seen none of our writing on their walls anyway.*

Hesprec started. *You have a plan.*

We have a plan. Therumit drew an oval box about the single character she had erased and replaced.

Hesprec wiped the words away. *Do we remember why we are here?*

Why else would a child of the Serpent come to the Oldest Kingdom?

I never thought I would.

You have always looked towards the wrong horizon. Therumit marked that column of characters with a sour look at her.

Hesprec's return expression was mild. *Well, we are here now. You have the ear of their queen. How will you use it?*

I will find my way about our city and see what they have left of it, Therumit picked out quickly. *I will learn all I can about our enemies and I will bring that knowledge back to the River.*

Are they our enemies now? Hesprec set the words down in the half-smudged remnants of Therumit's own.

How can you ask? Therumit marked out below that, and then angrily swept all the characters away and set out, *You learned the same histories I did.*

Some I learned from you, Hesprec followed. *We are guests here.*

When we return here it will not be as guests. Not now we have found them weak and foundering.

Hesprec swept that aside and then took time to gather and flatten the dust again, so that she could think. *And the Plague People?* she wrote, feeling her hand rebel against setting down that name.

Therumit stared at her. *We do not even know if they are the Plague People*, she wrote.

We do. Hesprec would not let her get away with that. *I did not go all over the world and nearly get sacrificed to the Wolf just to bring back empty stories. All the foresight in the world has been screaming at us about the doom to come, and now it is here. The Crow told us, and even the Pale Shadow told us.* She was cramming her characters in, smaller and smaller to make them fit.

Therumit hesitated, but then let her sleeve sweep all those words away, to be replaced with, *What are the Plains to us?*

It is not just the Plains, Hesprec wrote under that. *It is the Crown of the World and it is the River. And why should it not be here?*

Why should it? The Plague People will glut themselves long before their eyes turn here.

Hesprec looked into her fellow Serpent's eyes and saw the utter certainty that never visits the wholly sane. But Therumit was writing again. *We held them back before. When all the Serpent are gathered together in their own kingdom, the Plague People will not dare come near us.*

And the rest of the peoples? Hesprec scrawled through Therumit's writing.

The wise shall come to our gates, Therumit set down. *The foolish shall perish. And when all listen to us and do as we bid, we shall drive the Plague People from the world and into the sea again.* She scrubbed out her own writing hurriedly to make room for more. *Because the whole world will move with the coils of the Serpent. No more factions, no more little wars, no more tribe turned against tribe.*

Hesprec looked at her levelly. *What a grand plan,* she thought but did not write. She felt very cold inside, that Therumit could look on what was happening in the Plains and see it all as a means to an end. A glorious end, perhaps, but such terrible means. And yes, a Serpent's long life did lend itself to a certain lengthening of perspective, but either Therumit had far outstripped Hesprec's vision of the future, or she had fallen very short.

Hesprec swept the floor clear, but had no more words to write. Instead, she stood and brushed down her robe. 'I remain unconvinced,' she said – aloud so as to forestall further argument. 'I am going to ask some questions.'

'You believe the answers will be worthwhile?' Therumit growled.

'I want to know what they really want with us.' Hesprec turned to the doorway to leave, finding that Therumit behind her was an uncomfortable thing.

56

6

A pack of Laughing Men arrived just as the Black Eyes and their many guests were readying their spears. They were led by a craggy-faced woman calling herself Effey, wearing a cloak made of lion-hide with the manes as a luxurious mantle about her shoulders. She had a grin Shyri recognized as almost a religious obligation amongst her people.

These were not her tribe but they were her kin, some other band of the Hyena blown in on the bad tidings of what was happening to the east.

'So, little daughter.' Effey stretched lazily, watching the frenzied preparations. 'You are far from home.'

Shyri bristled at that. Effey might style herself Malikah of this little band, but she was no mother to Shyri. 'The Hyena goes where she wills, if the Lion doesn't chase her off. And the Lions around here have other problems.'

Effey had brought thirty warriors, which was a lot of armed Laughing Men to have in one place. It showed this was not some mere scouting expedition. She eyed Shyri, that grin still in place. 'We like it when the Lion has problems.'

'These are not just the Lion's. The Horse you see here – their home is gone. Those Boar there as well.'

Effey shrugged, the worries of the Horse and the Boar beneath her. 'And so all these brave warriors will draw knives

57

together and not kill each other.' She sounded disappointed, displeased even.

'You have brought many knives,' Shyri noted. She had a bleak feeling she knew where this conversation was going.

'You can never have too many knives.' Effey's grin widened. 'Word has come even to the ear of Hyena that a great dying time is on the wind.'

Shyri had been waiting for that, but knowing it was coming and mustering arguments against it were two different things. 'A great threat, yes.'

'Better a great dying,' Effey said firmly, taking in all the war-like preparation around them. 'The world goes badly for Hyena when the Lion is friends with the Dog.'

'Be friends with the Lion, then. Right now the Lion needs many friends,' Shyri tried.

'And Hyena has no friends, and needs none,' Effey pointed out. 'It's the act of a bad friend to gnaw on your friend's bones, little daughter. Who has been filling your head with these stories?' She regarded Shyri with easy contempt. 'You sound like a River priest.'

Shyri felt herself full of words – just like a River priest. She wanted to say that this was bigger than the Hyena and the Lion, bigger than the Plains and the River. She wanted to talk about how Hyena's dreams of a world of bones and Laughing Men was a grand dream but a poor reality. She wanted to say many things, and for most of them she didn't even have the words or any way of stringing them together. And then there was the other part of her which just wanted to agree with Effey's comforting world view, that the Laughing Men were on their own, waiting their turn when all the rest had been broken against the rocks of the world. She was *not* thinking like her mother's daughter any more. Too long spent trailing after that cursed River Lord boy because he was pretty and made her laugh. Too much seen in foreign places. So she said nothing, ashamed at where her thoughts were taking her.

58

Effey clapped a patronizing hand on Shyri's shoulder. 'Run with us, daughter. Let us stalk the Lion and see where he hunts. I am curious.'

Perhaps when she sees the Plague People she will know we must hunt as well. It was a faint hope, but Shyri clung to it.

So she walked at Effey's shoulder when the Malikah sloped between the camps, her people strung out behind her, some on two feet and some on four. The great gathering around the Black Eyes' village was breaking apart. Those who could not or would not fight were fleeing further west, in the hope that . . . what? That the blood of others would save them? That the Plague People would advance so far and no further? Shyri saw a terrible fear stamped on the faces of those who had already met with the enemy – some were shepherding children, some were old or young or crippled, plainly not able to take up a spear. Others could have been warriors, but the fear had stripped that from them. They knew only to run.

But there were still enough left with a warrior spirit in them. Grass Shadow had won his argument with his chief: there were close on a hundred of the Wild Dogs ready for battle, whooping and clashing spear and shield. The fugitive Lion had produced a fair number, too, led by a grey-bearded old man but with Reshappa clearly doing all the work of keeping them in line. Their two Champions prowled through their ranks, already Stepped – great barrel-bodied cats who could have walked shoulder to shoulder with Shyri, long fangs like curved knives jutting down below their chins. And there were many of the Boar, their faces and bristling hides painted in angry colours, and a score of the Horse with their famed bows that could shoot to the horizon.

Beyond these, Shyri saw the others. There was Maniye Many Tracks and her warband, a cluster of tan-skinned northerners in their iron coats. Shyri wanted to run over to them – they had made her one of their own, after all – but she felt Effey's stern eye on her. When she travelled with Asmander or Maniye, she had done what she wanted. Now she was back with her own, and she felt the pressure to walk in the Hyena's footsteps. For a moment she bucked rebelliously. *Not my tribe; not my mother.* But her own Malikah was enough like Effey that a surrogate authority still bound her.

Striding through it all was the Bat Society warrior. No grand speeches from that one – her mere presence was enough. Effey stopped and stared at the lean figure, and for the first time a little uncertainty crept into her.

'A *great* dying time,' she murmured, and Shyri hoped she was considering just how far that dying might go, and that being born to the Hyena did not make anyone immortal.

Grass Shadow was boosted up to shoulder height by a knot of his hunters, while another Dog blew a blaring note from an aurochs' horn. There were too many there, too much muttering and shuffling, for any great inspirational talking. Instead he just waved his spear in the air – a clutch of bright feathers and cloth below the head – and then he was down and his people had Stepped, surging forwards as a dappled pack for the rest to follow.

For a moment the rest were just milling and then the Horse were following, tossing their manes and stamping their hooves, the Boar at their heels. By then the Lion had motivated themselves to slink along after, and Maniye's band was a little river of grey at their side, with a crow circling overhead and calling out dire warnings. At their very edge Shyri caught a glimpse of Tensho the Leopard's spotted coat before the cat faded into the landscape, and she felt a stab of loss. *I should be one of them. That's my place.*

She even started forwards, horribly aware of Effey at her shoulder. But then the Hyena warband had Stepped too and was flowing after the others, an unwanted rearguard. *But they are going, at least.* Shyri fell in with them, loping along through the dust.

★ ★ ★

Feeds on Dreams landed smoothly, only Stepping once he was under cover of the long grass. 'They're at some huts,' he announced.

The great bulk of the combined warband was still some distance away, spread out across the plains with the Wild Dogs acting as runners between different groups. The leaders had gone forward to take a look at the enemy. Now Maniye, Grass Shadow, Reshappa and the Bat were crouched in the grass, awaiting Feeds' report. A pair of Shadow's people were crouched nearby, still Stepped, ready to play messenger when they were needed.

'Fifteen, I counted,' the Crow told them.

'That's more than you said,' Maniye noted.

He shrugged. 'Maybe some were away.'

'You're sure, fifteen?'

'Maybe twenty. Less than us. A lot less.'

'Whose huts?' she asked Grass Shadow.

'Uglies,' he said, and then swiftly corrected that to, 'Tooth Markers. Boar – we have plenty of them with us.'

'Not your friends, normally?'

Reshappa chuckled softly. 'Not his friends ever, till now. Everyone knows the Uglies and the Dirt Dogs hate each other.'

'Until now,' Grass Shadow echoed. 'What are they doing there, Eyrieman? Are they building the white walls?'

'Didn't see any.' Feeds shrugged. 'These Uglies, there's some bigger place of theirs, sunways?'

'This close by is just for their herdsmen to rest in,' Grass Shadow agreed. 'Their village is close, too.' He drew out some lines in the dirt, showing the relative positions of *here* and *there*. 'We should have some good hunters circling round to get between them.'

'The Lion will do it,' Reshappa said promptly.

Grass Shadow cocked an eye at that, but then just shrugged. 'Well then, that's the Lion's due. We'll have the Tooth Markers as

61

our left horn, the Horse and whoever wants to run with them as our right. Many Tracks, will you be the teeth with me?'

'Of course.' Straight down the centre while the horns curved in at either side and the Lions waited to catch the runners. Maniye remembered her previous encounter with the Plague People and felt her heart speeding. 'There will be fear,' she warned them. 'Not just fear of harm or death, but a fear that goes deeper. A *Fear.*'

'Then let's make them fear in return,' Grass Shadow said. 'What else can we do? Run and abandon all we have? The fire has already heard that one talked out. We fight.'

Maniye slunk back and found her warband again, the wolves lolling in the Plains heat, tongues out. She didn't need to brief them; they would follow her lead to where they needed to be. She just set Feeds to go ride the shimmering air above and watch for when people started to move.

The waiting was hard, but she knew the Lion would be moving slowly, sliding between the grass so as to leave barely a ripple while the Plague People performed their nameless rituals in the huts of the Tooth Markers.

And then Feeds dropped down on them, cawing news that didn't need human words, and they were moving. She saw the dust kicked up on either side as a great host of Boar and Horse and the rest rushed forwards, trampling the grass flat, blowing horns, squealing and thundering. A moment later, Grass Shadow's people were running too, all Stepped, and Maniye's warband needed no sign from her. With their iron worn beneath their skin they surged ahead like a single living thing, and Maniye just a wolf amongst wolves.

She saw the huts ahead, sooner than she had thought. There was movement there that had a human shape but no human soul. The Plague People were swarming out – more than twenty of them, and they had long rods she knew were weapons. Their attention was focused to Maniye's right, where the stampeding Horse made the largest targets. She saw a handful of them lift and point their rods and – snap! – a half-dozen Horse were tumbling, rearing and dying.

The Fear touched her, then. She felt it ripple through everyone around her.

But the Tooth Markers themselves were now curving in, the other horn, so that the Plague People had to divide their attention – Maniye saw them running from one side of the huts to the other. They were killing Boar, too, but fewer of them, the lower targets half-hidden in the grass. Then they looked for the centre of the charge, and Maniye felt a jolt through her as the attention of the Plague People at last rested on her.

Something like an insect whistled past her and one of Grass Shadow's people was abruptly dead, dropping to tangle the paws of the dog behind him. The Fear reached out like a living thing to touch them, making their souls recoil. For a moment, Maniye felt the whole grand assault tremble at it, as though they were running from the warm air of the Plains into some other medium fatal to everything they were.

Then a keening rang out across the sky – horizon to horizon, it almost seemed. A great vane-winged monster swooped across the roofs of the huts, making a sound heard only partly with the ears, more with the whole body. The sound was a stab of pain for Maniye and the others, but it seemed to turn their own fear back on the Plague People. Even as the swiftest of the Boar and the Horse were reaching them, Maniye saw the enemy's nerve suddenly break and they were fleeing.

Some were running, others took off into the sky, veering madly to avoid the battering wings of the great bat. The air about their shoulders shimmered with the ghostly flicker of their wings. Arrows were beginning to fall about them – warriors of the Horse taking human shape for a breath to release the string, then Stepping back to thunder forwards and trample whatever they could.

Maniye found a new lease of speed within her, rushing ahead. *They flee!* And they were taking their Fear with them. She saw one of the Plague People tumble from the sky, two arrows in him. Ahead, those trying to escape on foot were discovering the Lions.

She kept running, seeing that the enemy above could not just hold to the air like birds. Their flying was more like great arcing leaps, as though the metal of their armour weighed them down. They dropped behind the Lions and then ran with all the teeth of the Plains snapping at their heels.

Yet they were fast, still. She was close to the front of the charge now, the Horse a little ahead to her left, the Dogs and the Boar the same distance behind on her right. Every time she thought that a final burst of speed would catch the enemy, they would throw themselves madly into the sky again, soaring across the clear blue and then coming down far out of reach, forcing her to make up the distance all over again. She saw one of them veer above her, abruptly off-course, and then the huge-winged shadow of the Bat emissary swept the flailing man-like figure from the air, clawed feet and fanged jaws shelling it of its armour.

Ahead she could see a village that must be that of the Tooth Markers. Her heart stuttered when she saw the Plague People had taken the Boar's low huts and strung a white wall between most of them, leaving only one gap she could see. The surviving Plague People were rushing madly for it – but then the back half-dozen turned and levelled their rods again. She steeled herself, knowing nothing would save her if they chose for her to die. Instead, one of her warband was struck down from beside her, a young Wolf named Kolomiti who had never earned a hunter's name. She saw a Horse go down in a flurry of breaking limbs as well, and then the Plague People were making a final leap, their wings taking them well over their own walls.

Maniye started slowing, because she could see plenty of movement within those walls – far more than the scouting party they had set out to deal with. She had no way of turning aside the assault, though, and she was as much a part of it as anyone. Courage was what they needed, and if she fled where would that courage be?

Feeds wheeled past wildly, a feathered black blur in her sight before he was behind her. She had a moment to wonder if he was trying to tell her something. Then the killing started.

There were Plague People up on the hut roofs, or on platforms they had built against their white walls, and they were pointing their rods and striking down the warriors who came against them. Maniye saw their movements, calm and practised, as though that hollowness inside them had eaten up all the places where passion lived. She felt the great Fear hanging in the air, waiting to swoop on the attackers like a hawk the moment they faltered. And yet they did not falter. Those who fell were left in the dirt and the rest rushed on, hooves and claws digging up the earth, and their banner the great dust cloud their progress had kicked up. They had run a long way but Maniye thought they had not even slowed. They were fine warriors the Plains bred, all of them!

But the sleeting invisible death zipped and danced all around them like bees, and then the Horse – still the fastest – suddenly began falling and stumbling. Several who had been galloping at top speed crashed down into the grass and others began to slow. Some Stepped to their human shapes, bows in hand, and Maniye heard the cry go up that there were snares about the walls. She did not slow, but then she saw the pale lines the ground ahead of them was strewn with – more spider-leavings and silkworm trails from the Plague People's crawling beasts. The advance began to slow, the Horses falling away to her left, and still the killing rain scattered across them – picking away at them one by one.

Then Grass Shadow went bounding past her with his people flooding behind him like a tawny tide, and there were Lions and Boar mixed up amongst them. Maniye found that burst of speed she had been husbanding and caught him up, with the iron grey of her own warband shouldering for room. The Plague People kept killing them, but suddenly their attacks seemed like spitting into the storm instead of the storm itself. She saw movement within the white walls and it was quick and panicked. *There are not so many of them after all* . . . Feeds on Dreams whirled past her as though a plaything of the wind, his wings battering briefly at her face, but she shrugged him off.

There were Plague People clogging the gap that led to the Tooth Marker village. They pointed their rods together and a whole dozen Black Eyes just died, struck down together without warning. Maniye felt the Fear reach for the hearts of the attackers and she Stepped, from wolf to the great Champion, bellowing at the enemy, looking down on them. The Fear broke, unable to touch her Champion soul, and the sight of her gave the rest heart. A heartbeat later the two Lion Champions were either side of her, smaller than she but bigger than any normal lion. One was dead seconds after, the little metal deaths the Plague rods sent tearing up his flank and opening him up. But then they were all at the gateway.

It seemed to her, as she reached that line of Plague Men, that she was under a shadow, that the sun shone only dimly on her. It was the way of things, to call the dominion of a people or a chief its 'shadow', and now she thought, *Is it real, for the Plague People? Are we in their shadow now?*

Then she glanced up and saw what was crowding the sky above her.

She had seen it before at Where the Fords Meet, a great boat like a moon in daylight, striped with the Plague People's warning colours. Now it hung low above the Tooth Marker village, coasting forwards so that its shadow stained all the attackers below.

Then she was almost on the spears and swords of the Plague People and she had to give them her full attention. A line of them was trying to hold the gap and she slammed into them, feeling their blades bite at her and grate, iron on iron. Roaring, she swept a handful of them aside, their bodies tumbling over each other, light as though they really were hollow inside. One tried to challenge her, striking at her face with a flare of fire from its hand, but she just shook her massive head and snapped down on him, blood filling her mouth, her fangs ripping into unnatural flesh.

Grass Shadow Stepped beside her, his spear skittering from the Plague warriors' mail. On the other side, Spear Catcher struck down one of the enemy with his hatchet, splitting the creature's bare head.

The Plague People tried to hold, but the attackers had too much sheer momentum and Maniye was within their walls with the warriors of the Plains at her back.

Then there was thunder and the ground shook, enough of a shock that everyone stopped fighting for a moment. She had no idea what had happened but the air was full of burning and she heard cries and screams from behind her.

She slapped down the closest Plague Man warrior, trying to understand what had changed. There were still warriors fighting all around her, but the great surging charge she had expected was absent. Where were the rest? She looked round . . .

A great column of smoke was rising from out beyond the walls. There were bodies strewn all around the base of it, where the earth had been torn up. She did not understand what she was looking at until the thunder spoke again from the flying ship. She saw a flash of light and motion from it, and the ground erupted in the thick of the attacking warriors, tearing them apart, throwing mangled animal and human bodies up into the air. Her heart seemed to stop for a moment. She could not believe what she was seeing. She forgot to fight.

That was when the Fear came back.

That was all it took. The terror rolled out from the white walls like a tide, surging either side of Maniye to crash into the Plains warriors as they tried to get through the gates. She fell back, feeling its pincers pluck even at the edge of her soul. Wheeling about, swatting a couple of the Plague Men out of her way, she saw the entire attack disintegrating. Not the thunder of the flying ship, but the Fear itself was tearing the assault apart. She saw the warriors about to funnel through the gate: Boar, Wild Dog,

Horse, Lion. She saw their eyes roll, foam at their muzzles, and the great iron purpose of their attack rusted away in an instant so that they were fleeing in all directions. Fleeing on four feet, because Maniye knew what that Fear fed on. Even as they turned away they were boars, dogs, horses, lions. The human part of them had been locked away, unable to face the Fear. And still the Plague warriors killed them with their rods, striking them down and not caring if what they killed was a beast or a man in a beast's skin.

Her own warband were still close about her, as were Grass Shadow and a handful of his people, but they had no force to back them up, and the Plague People were all around. She Stepped for a moment, bracing against that storm of Fear, just long enough to cry for them to go, to get clear of this terrible place and these terrible people.

They fell back for the gates, and then past the gates, and still they were her people, Stepping to two feet and four as the need dictated. Some were killed by the swift death the Plague rods brought, but they held their minds because they held to her. Her Champion soul cast a broad shadow.

Still, they ran and there was no shame in it, but now the Plague People were coming after them, not content to let their enemy vanish away. *It was a trap*, she thought. *They baited us in and then they closed their jaws on us.* But another part of her was thinking that they had done nothing of the sort. They had been oblivious to their enemies, and this appalling counterattack was little more than a reflex.

There were Plague Men in the air above her, lancing down their lethal bolts, and more landing ahead, weapons raised. She saw something appear from the grass and launch itself at them – a swift spotted cat that bore one of them down and spoiled the aim of the rest. It was Tensho – but it was not Tensho, for when the bloodied muzzle lifted to yowl and snarl at the Plague Men there was no human thought behind it, just a maddened beast that they struck down. Then the warband was upon them.

More Plague Men were dropping down, but before they could strike they were sent reeling by the piercing shriek of the Bat emissary as it swooped low. Maniye put on an extra burst of speed, crashing into one of the Plague warriors and smashing his brittle bones beneath her feet. The air was raked by a swift scatter of death from their weapons. She saw the Bat falter in the air, one wing beating wildly, and then the creature wheeled from the sky to crash, broken and diminished, off into the grass.

A spear of pain ripped across Maniye's side and she fell.

The warband faltered, and she knew the great rolling tide of the Fear was heartbeats away from claiming them. She Stepped, although pain tore through her to do it, screaming at them to run. Grass Shadow and Spear Catcher were coming back for her, but the Wild Dog warrior was struck down even as he did so, and she yelled her orders again, desperate not to see more of her people die. Spear Catcher was human for a second, scarred face agonized, and then he was a wolf and running, just as they were all running, and Maniye forced herself around, reaching for her knife, as the Plague People came to earth all about her like a poison rain.

And off on a hill overlooking the carnage, Shyri tried to break away from the knot of Hyena warriors to go to her, for all she was too far off, for all she was too late, but the hand of Effey was on her shoulder, clenched painfully tight to remind her who and what she was. Shyri saw the Plague People take up Maniye – the sole living human figure there save for themselves – and haul her back towards their white walls, and tears ran down her face, but she could do nothing. She hated herself for it, and she hated Hyena and all the Laughing Men for it, even though she could have done nothing but share her friend's fate.

7

It took Hesprec some skulking in the shadows – serpent and girl-shape both – before she could find Galethea. In that time she saw something of how the compound worked – that the Pale Shadow had a complex hierarchy, the great and the lowly. Where did Galethea fit in all this?

Somewhere in the middle was her best guess. Important enough to send as an emissary, expendable enough to send where her predecessors had not returned. The woman was weaving silk in an overgrown garden, when Hesprec's sinuous form finally caught her scent amongst all the strange and exotic odours.

Did she collect it direct from the myriad spiders themselves, Hesprec wondered, or did she go about the palace unpicking cobwebs? She Stepped, standing on human feet at the threshold, waiting to be invited in. Galethea's eyes flicked up as her nimble fingers worked. Again Hesprec was struck by how pale she was. Amongst the Serpent, only the very old were such a pallid shade, those ready to split their dry old skins and move on.

'You would talk with me, Messenger?' the Pale Shadow woman asked, borrowing the River term of reverence.

'It's time for that.' Taking the words as an invitation, Hesprec walked in and sat cross-legged in front of her. 'Because there are terrible things happening, and the lands north of here will know my tread sooner rather than later.'

Galethea's fingers tangled the strands and stopped moving,

70

though her face retained a detached expression. 'When we met last, you told me your people took host and guest seriously. It is too soon for you to leave.'

Hesprec raised her eyebrows. 'How long then, for politeness? A month? A year? Ten years, or a hundred, before someone finds a way to tell me what you brought me here to learn?'

The Pale Shadow woman settled her hands in her lap and said nothing.

'You said, when we met in the Estuary, that you wanted what we had,' Hesprec recalled. 'You asked us to teach you. The teacher must know what lesson is required. Your queen will not speak of it.'

'Can the wise Messenger not guess?' Galethea asked bitterly.

'The wise Messenger wants to hear you say it.'

Those pale hands clenched into fists for a moment; in the next they had relaxed, letting the tension fall away like the tangled silk. 'You know we want souls.'

'That can be taught, can it?' Hesprec prodded.

'Can it not?' Galethea hissed, locking eyes with her at last. 'Do they not say the Serpent went to the River and taught the men there how to farm and heal, write and rule? Do you not bring the secrets of learning wherever you go?'

'The River men already had souls. They were born to the jaws of Old Crocodile long before we came to trouble them,' Hesprec pointed out.

'Stop,' Galethea said abruptly, cutting off whatever might have come next. 'Do not name it as impossible. We can learn. We will learn. We *must*.'

'You did not need souls to take our kingdom from us, so long ago,' Hesprec pointed out mildly. And she was teaching, in a way. Her favourite means of encouraging students was to set up arguments they could attack. 'So why must you? Do you envy the Jaguar who clean your fine robes and polish your jewels?'

'Yes!' Galethea snapped, surprising her. 'We envy them. Because they will live and we are dying. They are not the ones the world's dream is killing.'

71

Hesprec went very still, feeling herself on the edge of something. Yes, she had known they wanted souls – she had come here on that assumption, believing it some fashion or superstition amongst them. But some malaise was eating at the Pale Shadow, that much was true. 'So tell me,' she invited.

Galethea stared at her for a long time. 'You don't know,' she said at last.

Hesprec shrugged. 'There are many things I don't know. That is what questions are for. Tell me of this dream.'

The Pale Shadow woman took a deep breath. 'The land we came from, the people are different.'

'The Plague People made it different. They devoured everything that was not of them.'

Galethea shrugged. 'Or you were hollow, before you came here. That is how we tell it.' *That is how we need it to be*, was what Hesprec heard behind those words. 'Who knows if your ancestors could change their skins, before they came here? But the dream of this land is a *changing* dream, so you are changing people. The dream of the land we left behind is not the same. But that is *our* dream, still. We breathe this changing air, but we cannot *change* with it.'

'It has taken a long time to poison you, this air,' Hesprec remarked.

'We thought we *would* change. We were strong with our own dream when we came, but we lost it generation after generation. We came to love this land and its people – yes, we did!' She must have seen the doubt in Hesprec's eyes. 'We were proud when we came, and we fought your people, suborned them and drove them out – I know it. There are ways we tell that story, which excuse all we did and paint it in better colours, but I admit it to you. We wronged you. We abused your trust and we took from you all you had. We thought we could become you. Once you were gone, we became many and we became strong, but we never became you. We feuded against each other, we wove our intrigues and our dramas, but we were dying and we did not

72

know it. We have never become people fit for this place. We never grew souls.'

Hesprec thought of the obsessive spider imagery on all sides, seeing it for what it was. The Pale Shadow People were diminishing, and they laid the blame on the emptiness within. They were trying to entice some non-existent Spider to bless them with its patronage. She tried to decide if that was better or worse.

'So what are the Plague People then?' she asked. 'Will they not just die as well?'

'Do you believe that?' Now Galethea's smile was sharp. 'Will you wait for them to shrivel like slugs? I do not think they will. They have brought their own dream with them, Serpent. It is a dream where nobody changes skins. Animals are animals to them, and people are people, and the two are nothing alike. They bring this dream to your land and they do not even know they are dreaming it.'

In Hesprec's mind was the panicked jabbering of the Crow, Feeds on Dreams, speaking of a terrible Fear, of his friend who had been a girl of the Coyote, but now knew nothing of human speech or a human shape. She shivered, and Galethea marked it.

'But enlighten me,' she said. 'Surely this is what you want, this dream of theirs. You will not need souls in a land that does not dream of them.'

'There are some families who have said just that,' the Pale Shadow woman confirmed, 'but the rest of us have seen your dream now. If our kin the Plague People win, then perhaps we will not die, but we will never live either. And perhaps they will kill us anyway. When we came here, we were fleeing our kin. We are not them any more, but we are not you either. We are . . .' Her hands made a tearing motion, and abruptly her weaving was nothing but loose threads, blowing away across the garden. 'Speak to your gods. Beg them to open the way so that we may have souls, and be *true* people in your dream. You may live with us in your kingdom if you will. The greatest of us will share their thrones with you, if only you will transform us.'

73

'And the Plague People?' Hesprec asked.

'We will help you,' Galethea insisted.

'How will you? You fear them almost as much as we do.'

'I will go with you to face them, as my queen's emissary.'

'How will that help against their dream?' Even speaking of it, Hesprec felt sure things had gone terribly wrong in her absence. Abruptly she was desperate to be rid of this place. What good were these decaying creatures?

'I can stand before them, and their dream will not destroy *me*,' Galethea said fiercely. 'The very thing that is our curse can be our strength! And I can speak with them. It is hard to learn your language, but that other language comes easily to us, the speech of our past, of the old lands we left. It creeps into us by dreams. We speak it back to our mothers almost before they speak to us.'

That feeling of being at the edge of revelation was abruptly tight about Hesprec's chest again. *The world dream*, she thought. The Pale Shadow are of that other land's dream still. Can we bargain with the Plague People? Can we give them gifts to go away? Can we blunt their hunger somehow, if they can hear our words?

She let out a long breath. *I am too small for this whole world to balance on me.* But there was nobody else. 'Help us turn away the Plague People and I will speak to the Serpent on your behalf. I do not know if what you want can ever be made real, but we will grant you such wisdom as the Serpent has, to help you.'

There was a terrible hope in Galethea's eyes. *I am making deals with an old, old enemy*, Hesprec knew, but she felt the world burning around her. She must hope that these creatures, these bywords for treachery in all the old stories, had somehow grown honest in the years that had passed since.

'What about your friend, the other Serpent?' the Pale Shadow woman asked at last.

'I do not know what she will do,' Hesprec admitted. *Save be very angry that I've done this and not just done her bidding. I don't think letters in the dust will suffice for our next conversation.*

★ ★ ★

The town of Umethret sat on the north bank of the Tsotec, three-quarters of the way between Atahlan and the fortress of Tsokawan. It had been just another little village once, but three generations ago the Plains raiders had grown bold, and troops from the fortress could not march out swiftly enough for punitive retaliation. The Kasra had ordered Umethret fortified and garrisoned, and since then it had become the muster-point for troops levied along that stretch of the river. Asman had sent messengers ahead, and by the time his barge arrived at the town the first troops were already trickling in. Some were regular soldiers, well trained and equipped and come from their posts along the river. Most were levy, farmers' sons and daughters with spears or slings and a little practice under their belt. Asman chose to believe that all were proud to answer the Kasra's call.

They would keep coming over the next days, and he met with the clan head who governed Umethret and told her to keep bringing the recruits in, and to send men to all the villages to ensure nobody was having difficulty in finding their duty. Asman and his scouts were going to look at the enemy and make cautious contact with the Plainsfolk.

They took their leave soon after, travelling as swiftly as they could after so long on the cramped barge. At night, when the dry heat of day fled the world and left an icy chill in its wake, they made camp on a tall rock, setting a watch of crocodiles whose eyes were better than a human's after dark had fallen. Asman huddled close with Venat, grateful that the old pirate had stuck with him. Oh, he'd been rewarded for his service to the Sun River Nation – treasure had been sent to his tribe, the Black Teeth, and the fires his people had set along the river had been forgiven, his victims compensated by the Kasra. Still, profit had never been Venat's motive and Asman had half expected him to either slope off to the Dragon Islands or else start a new wave of raiding and piracy along the Tsotec. Instead, the man was still at his side, and could he hope that so meek a thing as companionship might motivate so brutal a man?

75

That night they spoke of many things, yet not the most important things. They talked about the first time they fought, when Asman and his father had tracked Venat's drunken band of pirates down to apprehend them. They spoke about the cold north, though never how Venat had been a slave then. Venat chewed over stories of his people, which were all the same and began, continued and ended in blood. Asman remembered Maniye Many Tracks and the Wolf hunter Broken Axe, whom he had admired, and who had died.

He did not speak of Tecumet the Kasra, his mate, nor did he speak of hopes for the future, and where his divided heart might find its rest. Venat knew that heart, after all, in all its sharp-edged pieces. His followers were optimistic about the war with the Plague People, but a darkness was heavy on Asman. He was no priest, to read omens and foretell dooms, but still he could look to the east and see a change to the quality of the sky. It was as though the stars, which he knew were the gods and heroes of the stories, were changing. And true, they were different gods and heroes to different tribes, but now it seemed they were just pale and distant lamps that meant nothing at all.

The next day they met the first refugees heading for the river. Not so many, but then the Plains people had learned not to associate the banks of the Tsotec with a friendly reception. The first group was perhaps a score of the Boar, none fit to fight. They were of the Tooth Marker tribe, they said, when the soldiers had risen up before them and brought their journey to a halt. Their village had been taken by the Plague People. Even with Riverland spears and stone-toothed *maccan* swords pointing at them, they were still more frightened of what they had left behind.

Asman found an old woman who was the closest thing they had to a leader, a solidly built grandmother who looked as though she could grind corn in her clenched fists. He sat with her and talked, while his followers grudgingly donated some of their rations. In other circumstances, Asman guessed, the old

76

woman would have been no friend to the River, but right now she was willing to share the burden of what she had seen, for all her words could barely stretch to describe it. Hollow men had come, yes. They had dropped from a clear sky, and the very sight of them had bred a terrible Fear. They had imprisoned the souls of those closest to them, and anyone else who had not run fast enough. Asman questioned her choice of words and she looked him fiercely in the eye.

'The Fear attacked their *souls*,' she said harshly. 'These hollow men, just the *being* of them is more than a soul can stand. And when we are men and women, our souls are here, in our mouths, so we can talk.' She stared at him as though he should know this, and he had no idea if it was her personal creed or some secret of the Boar. 'But they would suck the soul from our lips, if it stayed there, or burn it out with the fire of their being. Those who were caught by them, the souls fled deeper – they Stepped, and that was the end of them. Mute brothers and sisters, all who could not escape. No more going on two feet for them. No more singing or painting or telling the old stories.' She spat the words at him as though it was his fault. Only then did he realize she was fighting the tears back, for close kin lost when the Plague People came.

He gave her the name of the governor of Umethret, and words that would show the woman that the Boar came with his blessing. At that point he had no idea how many more fugitives he would meet.

But they kept coming: men, women and children of a half-dozen tribes, and all with similar stories. The luckiest had fled just on hearing the news from others, the worst-off were those who claimed they were all that survived of a whole people. But they told the tale of warriors gathering with the Black Eye tribe, who were to bring the fight back to the Plague People. Some were hopeful, speaking of a quick tomorrow when they could return to their homes. Those who had laid eyes on the Plague People did not waste time on optimism.

And then the refugees were behind Asman, and he was left with the knowledge that the trail of them fleeing south must be only a fraction of those who had fled west, to the Black Eye lands or beyond. Still, there was a muster of warriors, and he picked up the pace, driving his soldiers in the hope that they might play some part in the fight that was coming.

He expected Venat to be twice as keen to get his teeth bloody, but the old pirate was unusually subdued. His lantern-jawed face was closed and brooding. Asman asked him what ate at him, and he shook his head irritably.

'Even the Dragon tell the oldest stories, you know that?' Venat scowled. 'Just about the only stories where it's not us against the world, because it's the whole world against the Eaters – what we call 'em, in our tales. Eaters of Everything.'

'That's not just you,' Asman told him. 'I've heard that, in some versions.'

'Well we only have the one way we tell it,' Venat snapped. 'But if you know it, you ever thought about that? I never did, but I'm thinking now. Eaters of Everything.'

'They took all the food and lived on all the land and—' Asman began to recite, but Venat broke in.

'That's not "everything". That's just what we do, only bigger. You heard that old woman. You saw what they ate, of her people. And the Crow was saying similar, wasn't he? They're not come to eat our food and houses and *things*. They're come to eat *us*, what we are.' The thought obviously unsettled the old pirate more than Asman would have believed possible. He thought of the Dragon, who lived for their fearsome reputation. They did not build, and they did not write. What they were was *all* they were, moment to moment. If the Plague People came to the Dragon Isles there would be nothing left to show Venat's people had ever lived, save for a few huts and stone blades.

Then they met another wave of refugees fleeing a new fight in the Black Eyes' lands. Hearing that, Asman pushed his soldiers on even more, but in his heart he knew he would be too late.

Soon after that, it was just cold fires, abandoned tents. The turned earth showed how many had been here, and how recently, but they were gone now. Some had marched east but from that direction few had returned. Animal tracks Asman found in plenitude, but they were meandering and random, a panicked rout of beasts and not the ordered retreat of men.

Asman thought of what that might mean, given what he knew of the enemy and their weapons.

'We're going to get our blades wet now?' Venat asked him. He had his own greenstone *meret* out, that was sharp as a razor and harder than metal.

'That's not the plan,' Asman said. 'We'll go east, but keep your eyes open, and be ready to run the moment we see them.' He didn't like saying it, and was ready for Venat to chew him up for a coward, but the old pirate just nodded soberly. *Truly it must be the end of the world.*

The vultures led them to the first bodies, boiling about them like gigantic flies, lurching off their feast only reluctantly. There was a people of the Vulture out on the Plains, Asman thought, but if they were here they did not Step to welcome their southern guests. Or else they could not.

Most of the bodies they fed on were unrecognizable now. The scatter of weapons and effects showed they must have been Plainsmen, but the marks of their tribes and their deaths had been erased by the scavengers already. Asman looked at the sky, in case any of those circling wings belonged to something worse than vultures. Then he looked east. He saw a distant village out there and a road of vultures leading towards it. The walls shone bright, like the sun on water, yet cheerless.

'Trouble,' Venat snapped, and abruptly the Rivermen had their spears levelled, pulled together into a defensive circle. It was not the Plague People, though, but a particularly Plains style of trouble. Slinking through the trampled and bloody grass came a pack of spotted hyenas, grinning and snickering at the southerners.

79

Asman thought that was all they were, for a heartbeat, but then half of them Stepped into lean, copper-skinned women who heckled and jeered just as they had when they were beasts. All save one, and that one he knew.

Shyri almost didn't approach him. He saw her exchange some harsh words with the woman who must lead them, before slinking over to him like a whipped dog. He wanted to be pleased to see her, but for once she plainly didn't want his praise or his smile. Some terrible thing had stamped itself across her. He had never seen her ashamed before.

'Laughing Girl,' he greeted her. She just nodded, standing fidgety in front of him and not meeting his gaze.

'We heard of a battle, Plainsmen marching,' he prompted her.

'And this is your army to help, is it?' She spared a glance for his little band of followers. 'Go home, Longmouth.'

'What's happened here? You fought?'

The look she gave him was agonized. 'There was fighting. The Black Eyes, Tooth Markers, all of them, they tried to run down the Plague People. They're gone now. Dead or changed.'

'All of them?'

'One in four got to run.' At last she was looking at him.

'You're scouting?' He was giving her every opportunity to lie to him.

The muscles of her jaw twitched and she told him, 'The Laughing Men do not fight the battles of others. We wait until the day is done, and then we come to the field and take what is left. A mountain of bones, remember, Longmouth? The Hyena's brood will own the world one day, when the rest of you are carrion.' The words were spat out, infinitely bitter.

Asman looked at the pack of Hyena, no more fit to take on the Plague People than his own followers. 'Perhaps the Laughing Men have the right of it this time,' he said softly.

She glared at him, a look that said, *And this one time you won't criticize me?*

The lead Hyena called, 'Shyri, say your farewells.' Her expression showed she bore Rivermen no love.

Shyri cast a look back at her and then turned round and gabbled out, 'Asmander – Asman, Maniye was there. She was at the front of the charge.'

Asman felt his stomach drop. 'Dead?'

'Taken or dead. I'm sorry.'

'Shyri!' the Hyena woman snapped, her patience plainly ending. Shyri snarled and then Stepped, skulking back to her people without another glance at her former friends.

Asman watched her go, wishing he had some magic words that would make things right between them. His mind worked, thinking about Maniye dead or Maniye taken. Could he storm the walls of the Plague People, a Champion to help a Champion? Was that not the right thing to do?

And yet he knew that, if he had ever been the man to do it, he was not that man any more. He was the Kasrani of the Sun River Nation. He could not just throw himself onto the spike of his honour, simply because it was right.

'Well?' Venat asked him.

'We head for Tsokawan. Tecuman must know what has happened. We need to rally the Estuary.'

* * *

When Hesprec went to find the horse, Therumit was waiting for her. Perhaps the woman had followed her to Galethea and overheard what was said. Perhaps she was just a crawling knot of suspicion. Certainly, finding her fellow priest leaving without saying farewell would confirm a lot of that distrust.

Hesprec had not really thought she could just leave without this confrontation. All her stealth had felt like going through the motions. She might as well have gone to face up to the woman and have done with it.

'You're just stretching the animal's legs a little,' Therumit suggested, 'of course.'

Hesprec couldn't tell if she meant sarcasm or if she was genuinely giving her colleague a way out. Therumit hadn't been able to say anything pleasantly in living memory, and either way it didn't really matter.

'I'm riding for the Tsotec.' *And not alone, but let's have one betrayal at a time, shall we?*

'No.' As though the simple word from Therumit would lock the doors and close the borders.

'I'm going to try and turn back the Plague People. That's what Serpent did, in the first stories. That's what Serpent must do now.'

'And you speak for Serpent?'

'How else is his voice heard?' Hesprec shrugged. 'I've heard your plans, Therumit. You want our people to retreat here and abandon the world. Not a path I can follow. Not even for the Oldest Kingdom.' And then she stepped back, because Therumit was abruptly in front of her.

'This is our place. Don't you recognize it? Don't you know it, like a memory?' the oldest priest demanded of her. 'Not the dry lands out there. Not Crocodile's river or the rest of the world. *Here*. It can be ours again – they'll even throw the gates wide for us! The world's too wide to save, but this one place—'

Hesprec shook her head. 'You know what, I don't recognize it. Nor do you. You were born on the Tsotec, just as I was. I don't feel Serpent in the earth here. Not like he moves on the banks of the River, not even as he moved under the Crown of the World. Maybe we can bring him back some day, but right now I'm going to where he still *is*, not where he was a thousand years ago.'

'You'll die.'

'Or worse,' Hesprec agreed.

'It's not worth it, not for *them*.'

So there it is. '"Them" meaning the Riverfolk, or the Plains-folk? How about the Estuary people you've spent five lifetimes amongst? Or my dear Champion, Maniye and her people?'

'Their brief lives,' Therumit insisted, 'what are they, compared to us?'

Hesprec felt a great sadness settle on her small shoulders. 'They are souls that go on from life to life, just as ours do. What Serpent made of us was not an end in itself, but so we could help those who were doomed to forget, birth to birth. But I see you don't believe that.'

'The Serpent eats his tail,' Therumit said flatly. It was an old saying, and one she would never have voiced amongst their peers back on the River. It meant that the long lives of the Serpent priests had no purpose but their own longevity; that to teach, to build, to nurture and harvest, these things were meaningless.

'Then stay here and gorge yourself,' Hesprec told her friend. 'I'm going.'

She went to get the saddle and Therumit jumped her, old hands twisting at her flesh in an effort to bring her down. Hesprec slapped her off and then they were both snakes, writhing across one another, rearing up with fangs bared in threat.

Serpent did not fight Serpent, that was known. It was the oldest law of a people who knew each other intimately and had lived many lifetimes in each other's company. And yet she saw real intent in Therumit's gaping jaws, and a moment later they were darting at each other, scaled bodies whipping apart, then clenching together. They lashed and wrestled, the knot of their bodies slithering about the cracked stone of the floor as the horse snorted and stamped.

Abruptly Hesprec was larger, from a slim viper to a great serpent as thick as a man's thigh, Therumit springing off her as she grew. For a moment they were both Stepping into larger and larger shapes, each trying to put the other in her shadow, and then Hesprec was slight and slender again, tracing a swift and crooked path forwards, lunging to bite between the scales of her opponent. She had no venom in her fangs, and they slid away from those thick scales anyway. She hoped it would count, that Therumit would fall back, knowing it could have been the final strike of the fight.

A moment later, her enemy had her by the throat. Therumit

was a woman, her gnarled hand at Hesprec's neck, and then Hesprec was human too, unable to regain her serpent shape. Therumit shoved her until her back hit a wall, driving the breath from her. And then the older priest had Stepped again, her body collapsing into a towering coiled shape, her hand becoming jaws, the fangs piercing Hesprec's skin, ready to unleash a mouthful of poison that would kill in seconds.

For long heartbeats they were locked together, Hesprec waiting for the end, Therumit steeling herself to deliver it.

But she was Serpent, in the end. Those born within the Serpent's coils did not slay one another. They argued, yes; they held grudges that lasted mortal lifetimes. But they did not kill, for each one of them was an old, old friend.

Therumit let go, and abruptly was nothing but a withered old woman, at the end of yet another life, her wrinkled skin so loose she was almost ready to shed it for something younger. She collapsed back against a wall and sat down.

'You'll die,' she echoed her earlier words. 'Don't go. Or go and bring the others. We can make this place safe. We can make it ours. Please.'

Hesprec let out a long breath, feeling the blood flow down her neck and pool at her collarbones. 'I have a duty, Serpent's oldest duty. I will go, and I'll take one of the Pale Shadow with me. I will do what can be done, and if that's not enough then that'll be the end of me, along with all the rest of the world.'

'Except here,' Therumit insisted.

Hesprec shrugged. 'If all the stars go out north of here, but this place is somehow proof against the end of the world, then remember me and remember everything. But probably I'll be back, and with some of the others too, to look over the old place and meet the old neighbours. Probably it will all go perfectly.' She swung herself up into the saddle. 'You must understand, though, there's one little thing I have to do before that.'

8

Foolish, of course, to think she could just *go*. A woman great with child, who had lived her life amongst the Eyriemen, a captive bride of one warrior or another, and then *he* had come to her and told her she was free. Free to do what, precisely?

Kailovela stared down at the child in her arms – sleeping, for now – and thought the world had expected her to die, but here she was.

Loud Thunder had expected her to live, but then she had been given ample opportunity to know he didn't think ahead as much as he should, especially now he was Warbringer for the whole Crown of the World. *Fly*, he had said, and so she'd flown, while the Eyriemen stared after her with angry eyes, but dared not defy Thunder's word.

But he had given her a place to fly to, at least. It was his place, a cabin near a lake. His directions had just been adequate enough for her to find it. There was food stored in the cold depths of the cave the cabin was built around, and there was firewood cut and ready, just as he had promised.

Still, left solely to her own devices, she would have been looking death in the eye. The child had been very close, when she had Stepped from her bird shape onto the ground, and Thunder's cabin did not come with a midwife. But she had help. Help no others would have taken, but she was desperate.

The ground before the cabin had been cleared of trees a long time ago, and now she stared out at where the dense green of the pines took up again, that boundary beyond which lay all the threats in the world. Were there eyes out there, even now? What would they make of her, a Hawk woman living in a Bear's cave. She had cut her dark hair short, so it could not be used as a halter about her neck. Childbirth and shifting for herself had surely added a crease or two to her face, and yet it had never been that which had drawn others to her. There was something in her soul evident to all. Beasts would not attack her, nor even run from her. Men wanted to own her.

There was a Deer village some distance south – her unlikely helper had found that much. Kailovela had forced herself to Step again, to haul her aching bird body into the air, feeling the child too close, as though she would be wrenched back to her human shape in mid-air. At least she could fly – she had been given very little chance to try out her bird shape before Thunder had freed her – only a few brief months of rebellious freedom before her first mate had claimed and shackled her. The skill had come swiftly to her, and her wings remembered it, no matter how many chained years she had languished through.

She had flown to the Deer and begged their hospitality: a pregnant Eyriewoman from nowhere. Still, if there was one gift she had, it was that people welcomed her. It had been a poisoned gift for most of her life but this once it saved her. The chief and the tall warriors of the Deer strutted around her, but she threw herself on the mercy of their hearth-keepers, and the women took her in and kept the men away.

She had the child, in blood and pain: a boy, the son of a Hawk warrior who had been killed by the Champion Yellow Claw before he even knew his seed had found a hold.

She had left the Deer as soon as she was strong enough, and before the men could bring themselves to pierce the wall of propriety the women had put up about her. They gave her gifts – of course they did; everyone liked Kailovela. She had a pack of food and clothes and wraps for the baby.

86

The path to Loud Thunder's cabin had been a long one, on foot. She had stopped often. Again, had she been alone she would surely have died, or the child would have. But her help, the little monster, had stayed close. Kailovela tried to ask her why she did not go. The answers she got were fragmentary and unsatisfactory. She had to piece together her own narrative from them, and could not know if she was right.

But she was back here now, and the child was suckling well. She was eking out Loud Thunder's supplies. And she was waiting.

He had done the best he could by her, in sending her here. He had taken her out of the hands of those who would claim her and he had fought down his own urge to take her. She had seen that hook in him, grimly familiar. She had felt the same in her: perhaps this time things would be different. Loud Thunder was a kind man and a strong one. In his shadow she would not fear any others' hands.

She had her own struggle, to make herself see that she would still be in shadow. He had given her a choice, and she had chosen to be free, even if freedom and death came as one.

Looking down at her child, she weighed how she thought about gambling his life with her own. *No regrets*, she thought. *Forgive me, but I needed to be free.*

And still she was waiting. Many days had passed since her flight, since the birth. She had seen no humans aside from the Deer; when snow had fallen, none of the tracks the beasts left had suddenly become shod feet from one stride to the next. But one man knew exactly where she was; she knew Loud Thunder would come to visit soon enough. She hoped she was strong enough to survive it; she hoped he was. She had seen how hard it had been for him to simply free her and let her fly.

Now she stood before the heavy hide that closed up the warmth of the cabin, looking across Loud Thunder's clearing. Her child slept in her arms. She should put him down and draw water or cut wood. Even though she was not quite alone out here, she must still work to live. Something had caught her mind's notice, though. She could not quite tell what, but it held her out here in the chill morning air.

He's here, then. She had not set eyes on him; the world had given her no proof of Loud Thunder's return to his home, but somehow she knew. It was just one of those things about her. The gods had blessed her with gifts, the priests said. She felt so loaded with them she could barely stand.

But oracular visions would not cook a meal or make a fire, and so she went inside and set her son down, tucking him in as warm as she could. Then it was out with the hatchet she had found, to cut more of Thunder's logs into billets. Luckily, though the Eyrie did not like its women to fly or talk or think, it had no problem with them working. Most Eyriemen hunters viewed taking a mate as the end of their ever having to make a fire or a meal again, and in making her tend to them, her mates had inadvertently taught her to look after herself.

He was there when she straightened up from the work to wipe her brow. He walked softly for such a big man.

Loud Thunder: strongest of the Cave Dwellers who were the sons of the Bear, a great awkward shambling man uncomfortable with the space he took in the world. Except some of that had sloughed off him since he had taken the battle to the Plague People and driven them from their nest amongst the devastated Seal tribes. When he had returned from that fight, she had seen a new power in him. He had become the war leader that the Bear tribe's Mother had always seen in him.

There was enough left of that awkward, shy man in him, as he looked at her, to make her smile a little. His face lit up when he saw, then lost its expression when she flinched back as he approached. He halted, and she saw he was not alone. There was another Cave Dweller standing back by the trees: Lone Mountain, Thunder's cousin. Mountain was almost as huge as Thunder, wearing a greatcoat of hide studded with bronze knuckles, a nine-foot spear sloped on his shoulder. At his side, virtually under his elbow, was a slight figure she didn't know: a youth with short dark hair and something strange about him – her? An emptiness to the face that Kailovela thought she should recognize.

Thunder still stood there awkwardly, and she realized that he must be waiting for her to invite him in. He could just have strode into the cabin – it was his home, and she was surely his guest. But he waited, and wrung the edge of his sheepskin cloak a little in his hands, and did not speak to her.

Something gave inside her, and she said, 'It's your house. Come in if you will.' Not exactly gracious, but the business of host and guest was strange with the Bear and she wanted to just sidestep it. He nodded, though, and there was relief in every movement when he headed inside. The short-haired youth bolted after him but Lone Mountain remained outside.

'You'll want fresh meat, I reckon,' he rumbled, and Kailovela nodded cautiously.

'Saw some hare spoor back there. Might go and dig them out.'

'You do that,' Loud Thunder agreed. He grimaced apologetically at Kailovela. 'There will be others, probably. Soon, probably. If I were you I'd fly off or something.'

'I can't,' she told him curtly, and saw understanding make its belated way onto his face.

'Of course,' he muttered, and ducked inside.

She found him there, looking down at her sleeping son. When he asked after a name, she just shook her head. Eyrie children had no names until they had seen a handful of winters. Hawk was a cruel god.

Thunder went to the fire and built it up a little, becoming the master of the place again without ever thinking about it. The skinny youth sat back on his haunches – no, her haunches. She was a girl, a Seal tribe girl. Kailovela regarded her quizzically and Thunder grunted.

'Don't know what to call her either,' he admitted.

'Empty Skin,' the Seal girl said, her voice toneless.

'No,' Thunder said, obviously not the first airing of this argument.

'I am Empty Skin.' The Seal grinned horribly. Kailovela looked at her, and saw she was right. You could not give yourself a hunter's name, but nonetheless that was surely the name she must have. That part of her which made her human was gone.

'You were with the Plague People,' she said, hushed, a hand before her child's face so that the evil she named would not alight there.

Empty Skin nodded. 'They took us, when they had killed or changed our parents. They like children. But I stopped being a child when I was with them, and the Seal could not find me to give me a soul.'

Kailovela digested that. What was there to say, to such a calm confession of ruin? Best change the subject to those matters that threatened her. 'Loud Thunder, you have been kind to me,' she observed. *Will you take that kindness back?*

He grunted. Plainly he was not just here to see how his cabin was holding up, but she had spoken with him enough to know how the words got choked inside him. So she must prod them loose herself.

'I will take my child and leave. This is your house.'

'No, no,' he said, but then would not supply any alternative. At last it was Empty Skin who spoke for him. 'The Bear wants you to go south where the Plague People are.'

'What?' Kailovela snapped. It was the one thing she had not considered.

'It's not like that,' Thunder protested, but then he shrugged. 'So it's a little like that. We had some Horse come up the Sand Pearl on their boats, but not trading. They said their place down south is gone, that the Plague People ate it and put up their white walls about it. Sounds like those we didn't kill up here have gone down there to join their kin. I'd hoped it would be over when we drove them into the sea and the sky.'

'You thought that?'

90

'I hoped it.' He let out a long breath. 'But no, I didn't think it.'

'So why would you think of me?' She knew, even as she asked the question, but made sure nothing of the knowledge showed in her face. *Please let me be wrong.*

'When I saw you, you were keeper of the little hollow monster,' Loud Thunder said. 'It was calm, with you. I know you spoke with it, a little, or it spoke with you. And it was one of *them*, one of the Plague People. Just a little one.'

She held herself very still.

'We're off to fight them,' Thunder went on, staring into the fire. 'Us, the Wolf, the Tiger, your people, those two Coyote trouble-makers, Boar, Deer, even those Bat Society magicians. Axes, we've got. Spears, bows and wisdom from the priests. But I said to Mother, when tribes fight there is a time when the fighting gets slow, and neither side wants to go on. And then we talk, and there's peace.'

She glanced at Empty Skin, for surely the Seal girl had filled herself with revenge after the deaths of her parents and people. Skin's face was solemn and calm, though; an expression far too old for her.

'You could talk to them,' Thunder prompted. 'Even a little. I have heard them, the little chittery noises they make. To me it is no speech, but you . . .'

'This is why you came? Because you think there will be peace with the Plague People?' she asked sadly. 'And the Wolf think this? And the Tiger?'

'They are not Warbringer,' Thunder pointed out, and then Empty Skin twitched round to stare towards the cave-dark that dominated the far end of the cabin, the stone hollow Loud Thunder had built around.

'We're not alone,' the Seal girl said.

Thunder stood abruptly, his head brushing the beams. She saw his jaw work: who was it that had come before him to visit Kailovela? She watched the possessiveness and the embarrass-ment war in him.

91

'Don't,' she whispered.

'Who is there?' he rumbled, and he couldn't keep the threat out of his voice.

'Please . . .' But then her guest, her helper, stepped out into plain sight, perhaps cued by the sound of Thunder's anger. The best she could say was that it wasn't what the Bear had suspected. Instead his face froze – a little revulsion but mostly shock.

'It's still *here*?' he demanded.

'Where else would she go, after you drove her people away?' Kailovela asked him.

Standing in the cave mouth was a figure whose head was at a level with Kailovela's navel – meaning below Thunder's waist. Its shape was that of a woman, but pale and strangely featured. Her hair was hacked short like Kailovela's and she wore clothing of fleece and hide, just like a person. She was hollow as a pot where it mattered, though; not the physical flesh of her, but her soul. The lack of it shone out from within her, turned her pleasant features into a void, her body into a scar on the world. The little monster, as Kailovela thought of her. She had fallen from the sky one day, long before her kin came to slaughter the Seal tribes and take their children. The Eyriemen had bound her, and she had come into Kailovela's hands because all living things loved Kailovela, even the empty horrors that were the Plague People. Only she could live with it and be its handler. And when Thunder had freed her, he had freed her fellow prisoner as well to go take word to its people. Yet the little monster had not left her.

There was a bronze knife in the creature's hand, that looked about the size of one of Thunder's thumb-nails. The creature was ready to defend the only human she knew.

'She helps me,' Kailovela said. 'She finds food. She flies, and leads me to where I need to go. I would have died without her.' Her words felt flimsy before Thunder's wrath, but that last admission softened his look somewhat.

'It will serve,' Empty Skin said. Again, Kailovela looked for the vengeful anger that must be there and could not find it, as though the girl's emotions had gone to find her soul.

'What will you do, when you reach the Plague People?' she asked.

The Seal girl's hard, dark eyes flicked to her. 'I will try to talk, as you will. When there is a moment for such talk. I will try to find the human in them. You speak to this one. I was their prisoner for many days and heard the sounds they made. And they cannot take from me what I have already lost.' Her delivery was flat and dull, abrasive on the ear.

'And you want me to come too?'

'Yes,' Thunder told her. 'I want every voice we have that the Plague People might hear. We will fight them, because we will have to fight them. But I want there to come a time when even the Plague People send an emissary begging peace, and I want there to be you and the Girl,' he would not call her Empty Skin, 'so we can try and speak. But this one . . . will this one come too? Will it serve you?'

'I can only ask,' Kailovela said, thinking, *I can hardly even ask. How little the monster and I can talk, even now.* But that little was more than any other true human in the world. Perhaps that little might be the difference between survival and extinction. Because she did not share Thunder's assessment. If one side was brought to bay and forced to beg for peace, she did not think it would be the Plague People.

9

At Tsokawan, the Kasra's brother Tecuman received them with all ceremony. Asman and Venat stood before the throne, before the gaze of the serious young man in elaborate robes, as a priest spoke for him. Last time, Tecuman had been in the mask of a Kasra, and still in open conflict with his sister. Asman had half feared that he might come to find those ambitions rekindled – a new civil war just when the Nation needed unity the most. Whatever peace the priest Hesprec had kindled between the siblings, though, it held.

Matsur, the priest who was speaking for him, droned on with a long roll of announcements: how Tecuman welcomed Asman, both as his friend, as the Kasrani and as an emissary of the Kasra herself; how Tecuman had received the Kasra's word regarding the mustering of the Estuary; how he extended wishes for the health and reign of his sister, on and on. Asman shuffled, and he could see Tecuman fidgeting as well. This wealth of formality had its purpose, but he wanted to speak to his friend *now*. He was in Tecuman's court, though. He could hardly start giving orders.

And then the enthroned youth rapped his rod on the arm of his seat, and Matsur drew back to listen. The priest was obviously attempting to demur, but Tecuman was insistent. Even as the priest was stepping aside, the Lord of Tsokawan stood, drawing his robes about him. 'Matsur was about to say that there will of course be a feast in your honour,' he said, his own voice almost lost compared to the priest's grand declarations. 'But let them be long preparing it. You have words for my ears alone, I think?'

News of what had happened in the Plains would come to everyone's ears soon enough, but rumours of bloodshed north of the river were common. Heard from travellers on the road, they might find little purchase amongst the people of the Tsotec. Heard from the Kasrani, they would light fires of panic halfway back to Atahlan. Gratefully, Asman retired with Tecuman, Venat trailing mulishly after.

They found the youth shrugging out of his heavy robes, leaving them in the care of a half-dozen servants. He rolled his slender shoulders – his war with his sister had not made a great warrior of him; he was still the boy Asman remembered under all the finery.

They embraced fiercely. 'You're visiting sooner than I'd thought,' Tecuman told him. 'Surely my sister hasn't sent you to check up on me?'

'I'd rather bear her suspicions than the news I have,' Asman stated. 'Sit yourself. You'll need it.'

Tecuman did so, and had the servants bring grapes, mangoes and beer, and then leave the room to the three of them. 'Well then, you'd better tell me.'

And so Asman did, all of it: that the Plainsfolk had already fought a great battle against the Plague People, and had lost as decisively as they could. 'And don't just tell the old tales about the Plainsmen being all mouth and no stomach, when it comes to war,' Asman added. 'We know it's a River lie. They fought, with as much strength as they could muster in the time. I heard tale of the Bat Society there, and . . . Maniye's warband was in the teeth of it.'

Tecuman drew a deep breath. 'We've had Horse refugees trickling in since before Tecumet's message arrived. We knew this was no small fish, even then.' He tried a weak smile. 'It's *them*, Asa. They scared us with stories of the Plague People to keep us in line as children. Of course they're strong. Of course they're terrifying. But we have to fight them. Even if I hadn't heard what you said, even if I didn't know what they do, I'd know that. Everything you've said just makes me more determined.'

'How goes the muster?' Asman pressed him.

'Ah, well, the Estuary folk are slow to take up arms when you want them to, though swift enough all other times,' Tecuman said, with a rueful expression. 'We have had some come in, and the rest will follow. They're remembering where they put their spears and their courage, but they'll find both.'

It struck Asman how much Tecuman was talking like a man, not the youth he was. Not the rebellion against his sister but the mending of it had taught him how to grow up. Asman found himself grinning.

'You sent a man to the islands?' Venat broke in.

Tecuman eyed him warily. 'For the form of it. Unless I take a force over there to remind your people of their duties, I don't see the Dragon rushing to aid us. Or am I mistaken?'

Venat shrugged. 'Probably not. I'll go.' Seeing the expression on the youth's face, he grinned. 'You think I'll raise a thousand raiders to come pillage the River while you're all off fighting.'

'And would I be mad to have such a thought?'

'Teca—' started Asman, but Venat spoke over him.

'No. Can't say it won't happen, with or without me. You know how we are.' The Dragon smiled broadly the way they did: just a threat of teeth. 'But I'll go anyway. The chief of the Black Teeth, Gupmet, he knows me. I know him. If anyone can get Dragon knives into Plague bellies it's him. I'm not saying we'll do it for you, but we tell the stories too. And it'll eat everyone up over there, to hear there's a bigger bastard than us in the world. We'll have to do something about that.'

Asman couldn't tell if he was serious. Venat would do as he willed, and laugh when people complained.

But it wasn't his decision anyway, and Tecuman just stared into the man's hard grey eyes and then nodded. 'You'll have what you need. My writ, gold, greenstone even.' For the Dragon loved the hard-to-work stuff: almost as stubborn as they were, but it made blades that would break bronze.

'And you, Asa? I'll find you a fast boat to Atahlan if you need it?' Tecuman suggested bravely.

'My brother,' and it was strange, that his brother-in-spirit was his brother-by-marriage now, 'I will have a message for my wife the Kasra, to go with all haste, but I will stay and watch the Estuary muster, and I will march out with you.'

Tecuman's smile filled out into something genuinely warm. 'Terrible things, Teca.' The old childhood warcry the two of them shared with Tecumet.

'The most terrible,' Asman agreed.

'Someone mentioned a feast,' Venat grunted.

'You won't like it,' Asman told him. 'There'll be a dozen Estuary headmen as guests and they'll all hate you.'

'Sounds like my favourite kind of feast,' the Dragon told him. Asman felt the mood in the room lift; surely there was no threat to the world that the Sun River Nation could not defeat, now it was unified and whole. His mind kept slipping to think of Maniye, though. She had not just been a fellow Champion; she had been one of the strongest and most resourceful people he had ever met, and now the world was without her just when her strength was needed most.

He trailed after the other two, trying to keep a confident smile on his face but feeling hollow inside.

* * *

Maniye woke. Every part of her hurt, but most of all her side, where the pain had driven deep, the flesh there hot and pulsing. The slight movement of waking had set it all on fire and she clenched her teeth against it, but long-learned instincts meant she made no sound, nor motion. She did not know where she was.

So she listened, and heard movement and voices nearby.

Voices, but no speech, only *sounds*, harsh and broken, rising and falling in rhythms that sounded almost meaningful, and yet conveyed nothing. Beyond that, she could hear footsteps, the clink and scrape of metal, and there were other noises she had no name for. Something kept up a grumbling roar that never varied. Other things crackled, hissed and hummed, sounds that were not made by humans or animals or the weather, or any other source she could think of. At the same time, she was assailed by a battery of peculiar smells – sharp and offensive, like nothing alive or dead, save for a faint tinge of rot.

And while her ears and nose informed her of all this, some other sense was marking the pressure in the world around her. It was not a physical sensation, though it was so strong in her mind that she could almost fool herself into thinking it. Her surroundings did not consent to her being there. She could feel them prising away at her very being, rattling at the gates of her soul with claws and pincers. The Champion stood over her inside, warding her all the time she had lain here.

She remembered the battle and how it had ended, and knew they had taken her. The understanding came with a flurry of panic but she fought it down without moving a muscle. Whatever they had done with her, she was alive, and she guessed she had been away from the world for some time. She had few enough weapons but surprise was surely one of them.

She risked opening an eye. She saw white. Just a glare at first, but then it resolved itself into one of the Plague People's walls, two feet in front of her face. She followed it as far as she could without moving her head: there was a corner there, where the material was pulled out into shape. She guessed she was in a prison of some sort.

There was light beyond the wall, that eerie, steady light the Plague People used, which owed nothing to flames. The wall itself blurred her vision like mist, but she could see shapes past it. There were platforms there at waist height, each with a burden. Beyond them she saw more walls, cluttered and hung

98

with things that might have been food and herbs stored out of the reach of rats.

There was movement. She had to fight all her instincts in order to remain quite still. One of the Plague People was within the larger tent with her. It – he? – stood at one of the platforms, its back to her. She heard metal clatter, and then a high whining sound that sent a buzz of pain through her teeth just to hear it.

Her eyes were becoming more used to the haze of the enclosing walls. She could see a little of what was up on the platforms now, and wished that she couldn't. The Eyriemen and some of the Plainsfolk practised sky burials, so she'd heard. They pinned out corpses for the elements and the scavengers, especially for those who had died as humans and needed their soul freed from its prison. What the Plague People were about here looked like that, save that they were indoors. There were bodies on the tables, and some were whole and others were separated into parts. A lion skull stared bleakly at her from the nearest table. Beyond that was the part-flayed body of a wild dog. She caught her breath when she saw, spread out across one part of the outer wall, the huge wing of the Bat Society emissary, unfolded to its full tattered extent.

The Plague Man stopped what it was doing briefly, and she held very still. Some movement, some too-loud breath had alerted him, but then he continued his work, and she knew what that work must be. She did not want to see what cadaver he was desecrating.

She did not want to be in the place of death and perversity any longer, either. She risked shifting her head, keeping one eye on her busy jailer. The walls enclosed her entirely: no door, no window, no hatch or hole. She could be almost glad of that. Beyond those shrouds she saw only the carnage of the failed attack, Grass Shadow and the others being cut down, the terrible hammer of fear that had shattered them. That Terror was still all around her, tainting the air, weighing on her back, squeezing at her heart. Within her mind the Champion stood between her and

99

dissolution, but she felt it constantly, a dread that would not let up or let her forget about it.

She was not bound.

Keeping so still, she had not even thought about it, but there was no halter about her neck, nothing to stop her Stepping. All these walls, and the enemy had missed a trick that any young hunter would have known.

She felt the hurt within her and wondered how much harm she might do to herself. Was that the chain they sought to bind her with? The wound was still fresh and deep, seeming deeper now than when it was dealt, lancing at the heart of her. She felt feverish with it, and who knew what toxins would follow from a Plague warrior weapon? *Will I heal with this in me, or just sicken?* And the leaden thought followed after: *or will I die?*

The Plague Man set down some tool. The metal-on-metal sound sent chills through her. *And were they dead before this creature separated out their pieces? Or would I have heard the screaming had I woken a little earlier? And no need to ask what they're keeping me here for.*

It turned around, staring her right in the open eyes, and she could not keep still, but fled across the meagre confines of the gauze-walled cell, pressing away from him. The whole structure swayed with her motion, and she realized her prison was suspended within the greater tent, and that the Plague Man could get to her through any of the walls.

He approached, winding between the platforms with their grisly burdens. Something metal glinted in his hand. He was one of the south-dark Plague People, short and stocky, and wearing an apron smeared with ochres and yellows.

He was still looking straight into her eyes, and she felt the Terror prying there, trying to get into her skull and change her, diminish her into a mere wolf or tiger. The Champion gave her strength, though. And anger. She had forgotten how invigorating anger was until it coursed without warning through her body.

100

Let us die, then. She Stepped. In an eyeblink the cell was filled with the great furred shape of the Champion.

There was a second when the walls were taut around her, but holding, and she thought she would be trapped despite all her strength. Then she got her claws dug into the cell and unseamed it, just tore it to shreds around her and stumbled gracelessly onto the ground.

The Plague Man had fallen onto his back like a beetle, eyes so wide she could see the white all round them, mouth open and yelling. She smelled fear, yes, but it was subordinate to the sheer disbelief she could read in that face.

She lumbered forwards, snarling, shouldering platforms aside and spilling bones and tools and half-opened corpses. Her enemy scrabbled backwards on his elbows, shouting himself hoarse as she got closer and closer. And yet incredulity at what he was seeing shackled him. He did not just get up and run. He stared at her as if, any moment, she would simply not be there.

The wound stabbed at her, even as she stood over him. She felt it buried in her, that long line of hurt the Plague weapon had driven through her flesh. She stumbled, and what was meant for a disembowelling slash just cuffed the Plague Man, spinning him across the floor. She roared in her frustration, and then there were more of them spilling in from outside. She had a brief, tantalizing glimpse of the sun.

There were many of them, some with the killing rods and some just with swords or empty hands. Those empty hands spat flame, though – they seared across her, burning her hide and filling the tent with the reek of singed hair. She roared at them, driving them back with the sheer force of her rage. She was desperate to reach the outside. She wanted to die in the open air.

So she charged. It was a weak, staggering thing, but she was many times greater than any of them. She scattered them, bullied them out of the way. A sword drove into her shoulder and another gashed her about her jaw. More fire lit across her skin

101

and she got her teeth into one of them and flung him away with a savage jerk of her neck.

Then she was out, and the sun glared in her eyes, and she let loose a cry, the voice of the Champion in despair, a sound the world had not heard since the dawn of time.

The Plague People were everywhere. Some ran from her, some brandished weapons. The little camp she had seen was now twice, three times the size. Everywhere they had raised their web-walled tents and their scuttling beasts were still building, ceaselessly building. Everywhere their dread soaked into the soil until it must be poisoned for a hundred generations. They were making the world their own place with every foot they laid upon the earth.

She bellowed again and tried to see a way out of the maze, but the wound was already sapping at her, draining even the Champion's strength. She thundered forwards another three steps, the Plague warriors dancing back to keep out of her reach, and then, abruptly, it had all gone from her. She felt her grip on her souls slipping, and the next step she took was with a bare human foot. She reached for a knife, for a stone, for anything, but there was nothing, and the white walls were spinning around her, the sun revolving madly in the sky. Maniye dropped to her knees, seeing the Plague People all around her awaiting their moment.

'Come, then!' she screamed at them, hearing her own voice thin and scratchy from disuse. 'Finish me!' But they stared at her, somehow more aghast to see her there as a slight, broken girl than their man had been when she became the Champion.

And he was the last thing she saw before her wounds got the better of her and she lost the world again: the stocky dark man with his stained apron and his sharp little blade.

10

'It's always this way,' Loud Thunder grumbled. 'Always I have to go tell people things they don't want to hear.'

The scent of woodsmoke was on the air: not far off, a great host was encamped. The forest south-west of the lands of the Tiger had suffered a plague of axes: wood for tonight and wood to float south. Everyone in the Crown of the World knew there wasn't a single decent tree once you got onto the Plains.

Thunder had not rejoined his people yet, and Kailovela could see that he wasn't keen on it. Of all his qualities, perhaps she liked that the most: his awkwardness within his own skin; his unwillingness to become what they wanted him to be. He had said more than once that he'd go off and live in his cave, away from his people, if only the world wouldn't keep making demands of him.

And now he was bringing one of the enemy into the heart of his people. Just a little enemy, it was true, but he was sure they weren't going to like it. He had sent Lone Mountain ahead to bring word to his Mother, the forbidding woman who ruled all the Bear by sheer force of personality. And while Lone Mountain was away, he paced and fretted in a clearing.

At Kailovela's side, the little hollow woman also fidgeted and shifted from foot to foot. She had told it what was going on, but how much it had understood she wasn't sure. It knew some of her words, she could understand a few of the sounds it made.

Kailovela felt that they were both striving across a gap that actively did not want to be bridged.

She really did not know why the little monster stayed with her. It could fly, after all, and it had kinfolk somewhere south. Why hadn't it just scudded away like the weather, never to be seen again – or appeared at the head of some Plague army come to avenge those killed by Thunder's warband . . . And yet it had helped her through the tearing pain of the birth, and stayed with her when she was weak, and was still here now. When it looked on her son, the expression on the creature's face was indistinguishable from human tenderness, save that there was no soul behind it to give it true life.

And that made her think of Empty Skin, the soulless Seal girl. *Is that why she wants to talk to them, not fight them? Because they are like her?* It was a mean-minded thought, but the girl scared Kailovela. *She should be hurt and screaming from what she's been through. How can she stand there like a normal person?*

When Empty Skin met her gaze, the girl just smiled. But then everyone smiled when they saw Kailovela. Thunder paced ponderously back and forth, butting his fists together as he waited. 'It should be someone else's turn,' he complained to himself – though he was making sure the words could be heard by everyone else. 'Why make *me* do all the work again?'

'Are you fishing?' Kailovela asked, because she could only take so much self-pity. 'You want me to say, "Loud Thunder, it's because you're so strong? You're the great war leader of the Crown of the World"? Is that what this is for?'

He stopped, looking so wounded that she knew he would be angry – that was how men covered their hurts and humiliations. But then a sheepish grin broke over his face and he said, 'Well, if you want to say that, I'm not going to stop you.'

She laughed at him, a single bark before she bit down on it. But she couldn't strangle the smile altogether. Even the little monster seemed to understand the joke, despite knowing none of the words.

'You say what you will,' she told him, an apology that was not quite an apology. 'Your Mother scares me too.'

He had some rejoinder to that, but Lone Mountain was back before he could give it, announcing, 'Cousin, put on your serious face, our Mother is here.'

The Mother of the Bear filled the clearing. It was not just that she was huge – though all the Cave Dwellers, the Bear's children, were taller and more heavily built than other peoples. She was old, her hair shot with grey and white, but still a little black in there too. Her face was craggy and heavy-jawed, yet with a commanding beauty – the kind normally reserved for mountains. She was vast and bulky and moved with a deceptive slowness, leaning on a gnarled staff, but then you could never hurry a bear, and this bear least of all.

Standing before her, Kailovela felt Mother was a natural force more than a woman. Until the woman looked on Loud Thunder, at least, and a very human expression of exasperation came to her face.

'When you set out on your diversion, I was against it,' she said, as though continuing a conversation from last time they had met.

Thunder shuffled. 'Would I do a thing you were against? You were . . . unconvinced.' Even that much rebellion seemed to scare him. He was a chastised ten-year-old in the body of the Bear's strongest warrior.

'And can you convince me, yet? Why do I feel you have not even done the thing you said, but some other worse thing?' That imperious gaze swept the clearing, passing over Lone Mountain, who stood to one side with all his body saying, *This is none of my fault*. Mother's eyes rested briefly on Empty Skin, who met them quite without fear, and then found Kailovela.

'So here she is, the woman who talks the Plague language.'

Kailovela bowed her head. The sheer force of the woman's personality compelled her.

'Well?'

She looked up sharply. The Bear woman had taken a single step, and now made up Kailovela's whole world. 'Well?' she demanded again.

'I . . . have made myself understood to one of them, and she to me.' She was aware that the little monster was hiding behind her, crouched in her shadow to avoid the stone weight of Mother's gaze. Kailovela could only envy it.

The Bear rumbled, deep in her chest. 'My war leader believes there will come a moment when you will be useful.' She spared Loud Thunder a sidelong look. 'Or that is the excuse he has given for seeking you out.'

Kailovela hunched her shoulders, making herself smaller, looking away: all the tricks she had used to survive being the property of one warrior or another. 'I can't say what he thinks.'

'Like that, is it?' Mother looked sharply at Thunder and Lone Mountain. 'What are the two of you doing, just standing around? Go show your faces at the camp, remind people you still exist! Not you,' she added, stopping Empty Skin mid-stride. 'You stay. We'll talk sense, we three, where it won't addle the heads of the men.'

The baby woke then, and began to fuss. Kailovela knew his moods enough, now, and nestled the boy inside her robe, letting him find her nipple and feeling the dull ache as he latched on. Mother stared at the child as though he was just one more complication.

'Not Yellow Claw's get,' she murmured.

'Five Cuts, the man that Claw killed.' She wondered if she was supposed to feel sorrow about the death of her son's father. When she reached for it, though, there was nothing.

'Yellow Claw is still the Eyrie's Champion, and still causing trouble,' Mother told her sourly. 'You will have to face him, and Thunder will not always be there.'

Kailovela looked her in the face. 'Will you?'

'If you hide from everyone behind me, who will save you from me when I'm tired of you?' Mother countered, but her face softened slightly. 'If you come to help against the Plague, then my word will shelter you until we're done. After that, nothing. The Bear will return to its cave and sleep again.' Her eyes narrowed, and she stepped back abruptly. 'You brought *it* with you?'

'She has stayed with me. She won't go to its people.'

'Stand aside.'

There was no refusing that voice; it shoved her away as easily as if the huge woman had put out a hand to do it. Before Mother, the little monster seemed tinier still.

'Loud Thunder's idea was foolish from the start,' Mother said, staring at the creature. It looked up at her defiantly, but Kailovela could see the tension in every line of it: one threatening move and it would take to the air and flee.

'Why did you let him go then?'

'Hmm.' Mother's mouth twitched, not quite a smile. 'Can I stop him, when he's being a fool? Perhaps. But after he had gone, I brought the Wise together at my fire and told them of this foolish thing my son had set his heart on. I spoke with the Coyote and the Wolf and the Tiger. Many were angry, or else they laughed. But there were a few who had words worth hearing. One of the Moon Eaters said he had travelled further north even than the children of the Bear would go, to where all the land is ice. He said that there are shining people there, who live where there is no tree, no blade of grass, no beast or bird. He said they dance beneath the cold sun and are beautiful, yet as hollow as the Plague People. And there is an old woman of the Horse, one of those who fled Where the Fords Meet. She had travelled past the Tsotec once, and said there was a land of monsters living amongst a cat tribe, far, far away. All hollow, and yet they did not disturb the earth like these invaders. So Loud Thunder went to do a foolish thing, but while he was away that thing became less foolish. And now you have your own tame hollow child to speak for you. Does it have a name?'

It did, though Kailovela could never quite say it properly. She put a hand on the thing's narrow shoulder, seeing that so human face turn to her.

'Speak your name,' she prompted. 'Your *name*.'

She felt that brief connection with it, as she had felt with so many things before – which had brought wild beasts of all kinds to eat from her hand, and then men to contest ownership of her.

It spoke, a sound most like '*T'k*'.

Mother rolled her eyes at that, but the exercise had not been about learning what the creature called itself, so much as seeing whether it could be bidden by Kailovela.

'Well, it's here. We will bring it before the war host and perhaps they will kill it and hoist it on a spear.' Her lip curled a little, seeing Kailovela step closer to the creature. 'The Owl's priests had it leashed.'

'It doesn't need to be.' Kailovela tried to stare the huge woman down. 'It will stay with me.' She took a deep breath. '*She* will.'

Mother rumbled contemplatively again, deep in her throat, but said nothing, and so Kailovela went on, 'Will you really bring all the warriors of the Crown of the World south to the Plains?'

'The Crown of the World, the Highlands, the Eyrie. And we have some three score of the Horse Society with us, and a handful of Plainsmen who have fled north begging for help. The Horse, at least, are earning their keep. They have good minds for moving things from place to place. I have left feeding the host to them. You'll travel with me,' Mother told her shortly. 'I don't intend walking all the way to the Plains. Your monster can travel in your shadow, or someone'll put a knife in it no matter what the Wise decide. And now you'll present the thing to everyone.' She turned and bellowed off into the trees. 'Mountain! I know you're skulking out there. Round them all up!' Her voice seemed loud enough to echo from the far peaks.

Yellow Claw stood front and centre, at the gathering. All the chiefs, the great hunters and warriors, the priests and wise women and just people who had somehow made enough nuisance of themselves, they were all there. At first she thought it was the whole war host, but no – just its leaders. How large was the force, then, that Loud Thunder commanded? She could not guess. Behind the gathering the sky was smudgy with the smoke from all the fires.

In truth perhaps there were a hundred who had come at the summons, but to Kailovela it might as well have been thousands.

Loud Thunder stood to one side, arms folded and giving Yellow Claw filthy looks, which the Eyrie Champion ignored. Her former mate was still bruised from the time that Thunder had called him out and bested him, but he stood straight and proud and arrogant, as he always had. Mother was already stepping from the trees, holding her staff high to quiet them, and Kailovela began desperately looking for friendly faces.

There was Seven Mending, the Owl priestess who had first given the little monster into Kailovela's care. Her eyes were blind-looking, her face painted with the Owl's mark: grey with a white band across the eyes. There was power in that mark: a shiver of fear that came to all who looked on it. There would be no friendly welcome for Kailovela there; Seven Mending would still be smarting at the loss of her diminutive captive.

Mother was speaking to them, but Kailovela could barely understand the words. The massed regard of all those powerful men and women was buckling her knees and she knew she could not leave the shelter of the trees. She found more faces, stern and hostile all. There was Aritchaka, the priestess who led the Tiger warband. She had eaten souls in the name of her god. There were two dozen Wolves of different tribes who would be sniffing for the first hint of weakness. They stood beside the Tiger like comrades, united by a greater enemy, by shedding blood together.

When Kailovela stepped forward they would be united against her. Mother had finished speaking; the moment had arrived.

Just before her nerve broke entirely, Kailovela caught sight of two unassuming faces in the crowd. They were Coyote, the only two of that people present. She knew them; when the tribes had come together at Loud Thunder's invitation they had been guests at every fire, spreading rumours and telling tales. His name was Two Heads Talking and hers was Quiet When Loud. The Coyote woman was already growing large with the child inside her, and setting eyes on her brought much-needed calm. *Allies*. The least of the least, perhaps, but Coyote accomplished more in the shadows than the mighty could beneath the sun, as they said.

So she stepped forward, her son cradled in one arm, and the other hand on the little monster's shoulder.

Afterwards she was most surprised about Yellow Claw. He had been there, eyes boring into her with a cold, patient hatred: the man who had claimed her, finding her almost within arm's reach again. And yet he did not reach out. When she spoke, he did not speak over her. His mocking humour hung like a ghost over the meeting, and yet never quite reached his lips.

She told them Loud Thunder had brought her here. She used his own words, mostly, about speaking with the Plague People after they had been bested in battle. For the warriors of the Crown of the World had already routed the enemy once. They knew they could do so again, and she must assure them that her presence was not to diminish theirs. Then her words broke free of the little Thunder had said. She spoke of the old stories – the first flight to Our Land from The Place Where We Were, the pursuit of the Plague People who devoured whatever they touched. There was another land beyond the sea, she told them. Did her listeners think these Plague Men were the last of their kind? Their very numbers were at the core of the old tales, a locust swarm of them across the land.

So there must be words, when spears and axes had done their work. The Plague must be made to bind themselves by whatever gods they followed, never to come back. That was her role, and that was what her little monster, her *T'k*, would aid in.

Some doubted her. Aritchaka of the Tiger was openly scornful.

Hunters of the Wolf spat, and Yellow Claw just stared and stared as though willing her to burst into flames. Yet others murmured and nodded, the wise seeing wisdom, the strong seeing strength. And Mother stood close by, her great shadow behind everything that Kailovela said. But there was more than that. She felt the power in her, that unwanted gift, as it reached out to them. Usually she could move just a single mind to like her – often even when she did not want to. This one time, she felt the curse-magic expand to all of them, tilting them just a hair's breadth towards her. And in the end there were more who nodded than spat, and it was decided.

She only started shaking after. She sat on a stump amongst the trees and held her child, who had been miraculously quiet all through, oblivious to her tension. But then he was a solemn child, not serene but watchful.

She had been a fugitive when she bore him and perhaps he had come into the world with the knowledge that sometimes to go quietly was life. Certainly Yellow Claw would have dashed the boy's brains out, had she still been his. That was the Hawk's prerogative.

A step close by made her look up; it was Loud Thunder with his usual awkward approach.

'That was good,' he said, fumbling with his hands. 'Better you than me.'

'I live another day,' she agreed, and saw his face darken. 'It is not as it was with Yellow Claw. Did I ever thank you, for standing between us? Did I thank you for letting me out of your shadow, once you had taken me from his? I am thankful, Loud Thunder.'

'Less thankful for being dragged back into this nonsense.'

'Your nonsense, yes.' But she couldn't help smiling a little. 'But I am a warrior in your war host now. I will do my part when the time comes.' She looked at the little monster, who was sitting cross-legged beside her, eyeing the Bear suspiciously. 'We both will.'

He shambled over and sat down himself, keeping a careful

111

distance. Even seated on the ground, he towered. 'If we could just do your part, and save the rest, I'd be happy.'

'You do not want to fight? They call you Warbringer now, don't they?'

The pain that came to his face surprised her. 'Many died when we fought the Plague People. Died, or were lost. And we will have to do it again, and maybe many times, before they will let you talk to them. But I don't want it. Not our deaths, not even killing them. I just want it done the quickest way.'

'That is why you are war leader,' Kailovela told him, 'and not Yellow Claw.'

11

They had moved her from the tent of dead things. She awoke in another cage-within-a-cage, and with her wrists bound with metal, but still they had not collared her. Maniye felt her souls stir rebelliously, but at the same time she was weak, and there were Plague warriors staring at her.

She stared right back, feeling the Terror eroding away the Champion's bulwark, trying to get her mind to flee deep inside her, her body to become a beast's only. But she held out.

Their expressions, at least, were wary, but she had noticed that they had no great courage themselves – as befitted creatures that breathed fear, perhaps. They were miserly with their hollow little lives.

Some word must have been given out, because one of them came in that she recognized. It was the dark Plague Man, the one who had been so deft with his knives in the tent of corpses. Now his stained apron and his knives were not in evidence, and he had a fellow, a stout woman very similar to him, whose greying hair was drawn back severely from her round face. They both stared at her for a long time, but it was not a warrior's stare. Rather, they reminded her of hunters examining a trail made by a beast they did not know.

She shifted uncomfortably. Rather the hostile glower of the guards than this calm scrutiny.

They talked to each other, or at least made gabbly sounds she guessed was speech, and then they went, and that was that.

Maniye understood her duty then. She heard the Champion's voice in her heart: *Step, and kill as many as you can.* It would not be many, she knew. She was still weak, and their weapons were terrifying. She did not know why she was not already dead.

Or she did: it was written in the faces of the two who had come to stare at her. They were curious about her.

Why me? Why no other prisoners?

That night, she thought over it. They had fed her, in their way – some kind of stew with precious little meat in it, which sat leaden in her stomach and kept her up half the night with nausea. The answer came just before the moon went down: she had seen what had happened to their other captives, butchered and preserved in the tent of dead things. Only Maniye had lived, because she shared their shape. Only she had shown them a living human face.

And they're curious. Perhaps they think there is some secret in me that can defeat all the peoples? Perhaps they will cut me open soon, to try and find it.

She thought of her pack, abruptly, Spear Catcher and the rest. All dead now, perhaps, or had they scattered and fled with the Plains people, to fall in some desperate last stand another day? Or had they come for her, and fallen to the invisible lances of the Plague People or run mad with the Terror, and here she was, oblivious of their futile sacrifice? Soon enough, the thought of them became a part of that constant, sapping ache within her, pain and grief and guilt all tangled up together.

The Champion made its demands again, but she fought them down. It had its honour, but when she reached for her own she found it had been wounded and broken by the darts of the Plague warriors. Every thought of resistance stirred the deep, feverish ache of her wound as it tunnelled into the heart of her. She did not want to die in a final flurry of teeth and blades. *When I am a little stronger*, she told the Champion, and a few days later, when she might have been a little stronger, *When I am a little stronger still.*

And in between her confrontations with her soul she fell into a strange routine. She was fed, and they gave her a metal bowl to void her bowels in. She marvelled that metal – iron! – was so plentiful to them that it was used even for such menial things. There were guards who watched her through all these tasks, and they took shifts in turn but their faces seemed interchangeable. And each day the two curious Plague People came to study her. She could not work out what they were for. Plainly they were not hunters, nor did she ever see them at any other useful task, but they did not have the air of priests. The woman drew pictures sometimes. The man had the guards bring Maniye out of the cell and measured various parts of her. She felt the Champion roar, deep in the recesses of her skull, but it seemed to be further away now. Perhaps it would abandon her for the coward she was, and one day the Plague People would find just a wolf or a tiger staring dumbly at them through their gauzy walls.

Then they tried to speak to her.

They made their sounds, at first as fast as a woodpecker's drumming, then slowed down and given heavy emphasis, as though that made them any easier to comprehend. The Plague Man would hold up objects, some familiar, some mysterious, and repeat sounds to Maniye, who just stared sullenly back. The woman sketched out pictures of things. Most of these were baffling to Maniye, abstract lines and corners that meant nothing. One she recognized as a horse, though the perspective was strange, and tears welled in her eyes as she remembered Alladai, who she knew now she had loved, and who had been wiped from the world with most of his people. Once or twice, listening to their babble or staring dully at their scribbling, she felt herself on the brink of a great chasm of understanding, as though all their madness might suddenly fall into patterns of reason. She shied away from such revelation. It was a door through which her souls could not pass. She did not want to become the empty thing she would surely have to be, to make room for their meaning.

Day in, day out, they came. She felt them becoming frustrated. She felt no pressing need to respond to them.

One picture, though, she could not ignore. It was crude work, a poor likeness, but she saw the Champion there, as if a child had sketched it. The Plague Woman pointed at it, then at her, and made more of her babble.

'Yes,' Maniye told them. 'I have a *soul*. You cannot understand that, can you? I am of the true people. You are just our echo.'

The Plague Woman seemed to find this a triumph, and scribbled away on the thin bark she used to draw on. Maniye craned to see, despite herself, but it was just lines of scratchings, no picture of anything she could recognize.

A few days later, they brought in one of the children.

He was a Plains child, and she guessed he had probably been born to the Horse about seven years before. The thought made her imagination push towards how it had been, when the Plague came to Where the Fords Meet. The Terror would have rolled down upon the people of the Horse, driving their minds away. The marshes around their home would have been mad with panicking horses sinking haunch-deep in the muddy ground as they careened off the paths, screaming as their legs broke. The defensible stronghold of the Horse Society must have become a deathtrap, and into it the Plague warriors would descend, their rods spitting death like invisible hornets.

But the children would have no Horse shapes to be forced into. They were yet to gain their souls. Maniye had barely thought of it, save to assume they must all be dead.

The boy did not want to speak to her at first, but the dark Plague Man was at his shoulder, pushing him, making sounds. And the Horse boy shook his head and said '*Hkt! Hkt!*' That was how Maniye learned a word of Plague-speech despite herself. *No*, he was saying.

'Speak to me,' she said, as kindly as she could, but the boy was more and more agitated, caught between the soulless creatures that had claimed him and this reminder of his life before. Eventually, they took him out.

The boy would never get his soul, she knew. And what would that make him? When he was full grown, cut off from the gods and the cycle of birth and rebirth, what would he be? He would be a Plague Man, just another of the consuming host. Would he even remember that his parents had souls and were human?

When she was left alone again, save for the stony gaze of the guards, she could not keep from weeping. Helplessness, her injuries, the obliteration of the Horse, the end of everything she knew, it built and built within her until she was screaming, raging at the unseen sky. She Stepped then, howling her pain out, hissing at the world with wide cat-eyes and flattened ears, roaring into the faces of the warriors who had come running. She did not tear through the walls though. The fear was buried in her. She did not want more hurt, more weakness.

When she was done she was human again, standing there with her metal fetters at her feet, loosed the moment she Stepped. The two curious Plague People were back. They had watched her pain and anger, and made careful notes.

* * *

The armies of the Sun River Nation were slow to muster, but then the Nation had never needed all of them at once. Usually they were deployed against raiders – Plainsmen or the Dragon, and some small fraction would suffice, raised locally or an elite detachment sent downriver from Atahlan.

Tecumet was taking the Plague People seriously. She had sent her Kasrani Asman ahead with scouts, her brother was raising the many and diverse forces of the Estuary, and she had sent word to every village and clan chief, ordering them all to bring their spears. Here, on the north bank of the Tsotec some miles downriver from Atahlan, was the greatest gathering of Riverland soldiers that history would ever record.

117

She had four score scribes keeping track of the soldiers, the supplies, the gold and flint and leather, and a dozen priests overseeing them. It was a testament to the lessons of the Serpent over the generations that there was a corps of men and women who could count and calculate and set it all down in writing, so that of all those soldiers not one starved, not one was missing a helm or a blade.

And still there were matters that required her attention, or troubled the courts of the priests. There would always be clan rivalries, enmities passed down from parent to child from some mythical time when *they* offended *us*. Punishments for breaking discipline were severe, but human nature would find a way to express itself nonetheless. Add in the Plainsfolk and the problem doubled and then doubled again.

Most Riverlanders knew the Plainsmen as raiders. There had never been a great deal of love between the Nation and the many tribes of its northern neighbours. Now there were hundreds of Plainsfolk in Tecumet's camp, and her people were being asked to welcome them.

Some were simply messengers, because intelligence from the north was at a premium right now. She had received Asman's report at around the same time as the Plainsfolk themselves were telling her the same thing, that a force of their warriors had already been broken by the Plague People. Now the spears of the Plains were gathering west of that battlefield as they tried to prevent the Plague's spread. The number of their warriors was dwarfed by the numbers of their refugees, however, and while most of them sought sanctuary further west, plenty were descending on the river, desperate for aid. Many of Tecumet's advisers told her to turn them away, but the Serpent disagreed. Esumit Aras Talien and her fellows were making provision for any who fled the fighting to the north: finding them what shelter and food was to be had, though it strained their supplies to breaking point. Tecumet had followed the Serpent's guidance. If nothing else, aiding the children and the hearth-keepers of the

118

Plains warriors would make them more likely to fight under the direction of the River when the time came.

And yet there was friction. There were face-offs, fights, deaths even. The refugees were many, frightened and desperate. The Riverlanders were all too often hostile and grudging. And that was before taking into account the small number who had come just to cause trouble, it seemed. Some bands of Plainsfolk had no cares about the Plague People, but simply stole and raided and intimidated locals and refugees both. Tecumet had received plenty of reports about the Laughing Men in particular, who held all others' laws in scorn. She could only hope that they would add their spears to the rest when the fight came, but until then they were a constant thorn in her side.

Tecumet was strong for her people. She walked in their sight, with the formal robes of her position and her savage war mask. She stood in their sight while Esumit made rousing speeches in her name. And then she retreated into her own palatial tent and shucked off all the burdens of state, and collapsed, feeling the shadow of the Plague People looming high over her.

At least I have Tecuman still. The thought of facing this crisis without him was terrifying. *We came so close to killing each other.*

Lying there after dark, in the only solitude the world afforded her, she fought for sleep. The murmurous sound of a thousand people reached her: talking, snoring, crying. Beyond that, she seemed to hear the soul of the world itself moaning in fear and hurt as the Plague ate into it, an infected wound whose rot only spread. Sleep would not come for her, and she was left with tortured imaginings: the last Kasra of the Sun River Nation presiding over the death of the entire world.

Then someone moved at the entrance to her sleeping chamber and she froze, picturing Plague People assassins; picturing, despite herself, Plainsfolk raiders, because she had grown up on the same tales as her people after all.

But it was Esumit of the Serpent, her right hand. Tecumet sat up hurriedly, because the priestess would not disturb her without good cause.

'What is it?' *What has gone wrong now?*

'Kasra . . . Hesprec Essen Skese is in the camp.'

Abruptly Tecumet was wide awake.

Like so many petitioners before her, Hesprec met with Tecumet along with Esumit Aras Talien, currently the most influential of Atahlan's priesthood, and therefore of all the Serpent. Unlike so many others, Hesprec would not be asking Esumit to intervene with the Kasra. In fact, she might be doing the precise opposite. Therumit had not let her great rival Esumit in on her plan to travel to the Oldest Kingdom, nor even that the Pale Shadow had begun making overtures. Now it would all come out.

In the Kasra's tent, with the ruler stripped of masks and ceremony, Hesprec told them as much as she thought was wise. The ancient usurper and enemy had made contact with the Serpents of the Estuary. Therumit had begun a dialogue. The Plague People had been mentioned. She and Therumit had gone on a journey.

What she held back pertained to the Pale Shadow's deepest desires: to cross that divide that separated the soulless from the ensouled; to fill the hollowness within them. That was a matter for the Serpent alone. Enough that Tecumet knew she had more allies than she had guessed, although of a most doubtful nature.

Esumit's tightly controlled expression promised angry words in the near future, but before Tecumet she held her peace. If Hesprec had expected the Kasra to just swallow every bite without comment, though, she was to be disappointed. Most especially she wished to see the Pale Shadow ambassador.

Hesprec had walked Galethea through the press of the camp, and the experience had deeply disconcerted her. She had expected the woman to go hooded and veiled, to hide the emptiness within. Instead, the Pale Shadow woman had let the world see her face. There had been many stares – and more than a few

120

admiring. Of course, most of the Riverlanders had never laid eyes on the Plague People themselves. They had no basis for comparison, that was what Hesprec had told herself. But then there had been the Plainsfolk, come fleeing that enemy, and many must have stolen a glimpse before the Terror drove them away. And yet nobody was drawing the obvious conclusion. Galethea was exotic and unfamiliar, but they did not see past her face to the nightmare depths.

Looking at her charge, Hesprec had seen why. As some wealthy River youth might use cosmetics to disguise a disfigurement, so Galethea had painted over her hollow core somehow. Hesprec could see it, if she reminded herself that it was there, but there was a magic the Pale woman had layered about herself that bewildered and enticed the eye.

This is how they fooled us when they first came, she thought, and it was a salutary lesson, reminding her how little she could trust these creatures. *But let them help us now, and we can sit in judgement on them later if needs be.*

And now Galethea stood before the Kasra of the Sun River Nation, practically radiating glamour and charm. Esumit stared at her, slit-eyed as though trying to glare at the sun, while Tecumet herself kept her face without expression, as though the mask was still there.

She asked what help the Pale Shadow could bring, and Hesprec heard Galethea trot out the same answers: insight and understanding of their enemy. At what cost? The familiar story of a common enemy, wrongs lost in the mists of time. The words fell flat before Esumit, whose suspicious glower had only grown as each one was uttered.

'The timing of this is *convenient*,' the priestess remarked coldly. 'A perfect opportunity for the Plague People to place a spy amongst us.'

Hesprec found herself about to launch into a defence of her charge – *already they divide us against each other!* – but she was cut short when Galethea laughed.

121

It was no part of her act, that laugh. It came not from the mannered face of the beguiling diplomat, but from whatever passed for a heart within her. 'Do you see them spying on you?' she burst out. 'Do they send many to infiltrate your camp and learn your plans? Have you had any sense that they even *care* what you plan or what you think?'

Esumit had an answer, but she too was stalled, this time by a gesture from Tecumet.

'Speak,' ordered the Kasra.

'Great Lady,' Galethea addressed her, 'my people understand your people, because we have lived long amongst you and learned by rote your words and your expressions. And they must be learned, generation to generation; there remains a divide that separates us. That divide counts a thousand times for the Plague People, our distant kin. They have no concept of you, they may not even have noticed that you are at war with them. If they have, then probably they take it as you might take a pride of jaguars moving to hunt your herds, or an infestation of rats in your grain. They cannot imagine you, Great Lady. You are not real to them. It took us many generations before you were real to us.'

'And now?' Tecumet asked her.

'Now we are all real.' Galethea's voice sank to a hushed whisper, and Hesprec could not tell if she was play-acting or not. 'Or, if the Plague wins, none of us are, or ever were.'

Later, after the Pale Shadow emissary was found a tent where she could be watched, Hesprec commandeered one of her own. To Esumit, she pleaded exhaustion, which was not far from the truth. The ride from the Oldest Kingdom had been many days, the horses driven hard. Once they had found locals surrounding their fire – representatives of the strange tribes she had seen on her way south. They had never quite stated their intentions, but Hesprec had offered them wary hospitality, and they had fallen to swapping stories while Galethea looked on. Enough word of the Serpent had filtered down to them that any harm they had meant remained undone. Perhaps they would even send some spears north to the muster, for they had their tales of How We Came To This Land, just as everyone did.

But now she did not want to argue with her sister priest. Let the morning look to that. She needed to sit and take her thoughts out, one by one, and see which might have been veiled by the webs of the Pale Shadow.

Perhaps Therumit was also on her way – she could arrive tonight and tell a completely different story, and mire them all in arguing just when they needed to be most unified. And was that Galethea's true purpose, to sow doubt and disruption?

There came a time when ten lifetimes of wisdom ran out, and she just had to guess.

She was brought out of her meditations by the sound of something scratching about the edge of her tent. Hesprec Stepped, letting her tongue taste the air as she hunted out its scent. To her surprise, she knew it well enough: not a friend, but perhaps a friend's friend.

She returned to her human form to say, 'Come in, Laughing Girl.'

The hyena that slunk through the tent flaps stared at her balefully, long enough that Hesprec wondered if she had made a mistake. Then Shyri Stepped, and the Serpent priest saw that she had indeed returned to Hyena's shadow. Her face was painted with black and white, and she wore stiff linen armour studded with bronze. She looked like a full-grown warrior now, not Asman's sometime follower. Her capricious mockery had been harnessed to the more malevolent humour of her god.

Nonetheless, Hesprec raised a smile for her, from that diminishing stock she had left these days. 'I'm not supposed to be here,' Shyri said, so softly that she might have feared listeners within the tent itself.

'You are welcome nonetheless,' Hesprec said, and sadly, because there had been a time nobody could forbid this Laughing Girl anything.

'Effey, she'd be angry,' Shyri muttered, as though trying to talk herself into leaving.

'This is not Effey's domain, whoever she is,' Hesprec noted. 'I make you my guest, for as long as you stay. What is it, Shyri? What help does the Hyena seek from the Serpent?'

That was a mistake; the girl's eyes flashed angrily. 'Hyena needs nothing from any of you!' she spat. But something tugged at her and she went on, 'But there is someone else. Maniye.'

Hesprec went cold. 'Tell me.'

12

The River Lords – those like Asman, born within the jaws of Old Crocodile – were fierce soldiers, disciplined, well armed and well trained, but the Estuary tribes were many and diverse, each with their skills and cultures. The Estuary had a hundred strengths, if a wise commander could make use of them.

Tecuman wore heavy mail of crocodile hide studded with flint, and on his face was a scowling mask, an echo of the war-face that Tecumet was surely wearing even now. His servants had laid out a path of rushes for him, and he walked it between the many camps, looking at none of them but letting himself be seen. Beside Asman, the priest Matsur murmured the numbers each tribe had sent.

Such a host, Asman thought as they trod the camp's winding ways. *Not one nor the other could have called so many spears, but only Tecuman and Tecumet combined. The whole Estuary has heard their voices.*

There were the Hidden Men, crept out from their secluded groves. They went into battle in only their painted skins, which shifted and changed until they could hide right before your eyes. They nodded solemnly, eyes never still. Next was a camp of the Milk Tear, a cauldron roiling over their fire as they cooked up what might have been dinner or one of their deadly poisons. Beyond them, in loincloths and cloaks of sharkskin, were a band of Salt Eaters off the coast, their hair greased into jagged crests, whalebone clubs at their belts. They crouched over their own fire, smoking pipes of kelp and snorting white plumes from their nostrils. They hissed at Tecuman, which set Asman's teeth on edge even though they meant it as an accolade.

The Shellbacks and Foot Cutters were both Turtle tribes, and never great friends, but they were set up within sight of each other and yet no Foot Cutter youth had tried to steal from his enemy or cut the straps of their bulky armour. They clattered spear on shield to welcome their prince, each camp trying to outdo the others. Past them, a band of Rain Watchers watched with mild exasperation, midway through mending their coats of reeds, better known for their wisdom than their warlike natures. *But we will need wisdom.*

Warlike and peace-loving, cunning and forthright, many or few, here were the spears of the Estuary, accepting Tecuman as their leader, as he had accepted Tecumet as his. There was a flurry of wings above them – for a moment he looked up, expecting the black of Maniye's Crow. These were blue-grey and far broader, though – a heron large as a man descending at a prudent distance from Tecuman before Stepping to a long-limbed woman who knelt with her head bowed. The Wryneck people had been running messages between brother and sister, up and down the river, as well as other more dangerous tasks.

The Wryneck proffered a scroll, more word from Tecumet on how the muster down the Tsotec's back was going. When Asman stepped forward to take it, she lifted her head. 'There are scouts at the fortress,' she said. 'Weary from much flying, but they have grave news.'

Tecuman and Asman exchanged glances. The only scouts the prince had sent out had been heading north, to fly high over Where the Fords Meet and see what the Plague People had done with it. Herons did not fly swiftly but they could fly far when they needed to.

But they had left too recently to have gone to the fallen Horse stronghold and come back. Something was wrong.

*

126

Three of the Wryneck had gone out the day before. Only two were back, looking weary and shaken. They were an aloof and reclusive people by nature, their long-headed spears deadly when they were forced to fight. Their women were bolder than their men, and Asman remembered the scouts before they set off, like three tall sisters in reed armour tied with grey feathers.

Tecuman took the throne in his regalia, and Matsur bustled forward to greet them. The Wrynecks swapped glances before one stepped forward.

'We did not go to the fortress of the Plague People, mighty prince,' she said. 'For this, forgive us.'

'Yet you have found something worth bringing back, nonetheless,' Matsur said on Tecuman's behalf. 'Lay it before the throne of Tsokawan.'

'We followed the road north past Chumatla,' she explained, naming the laketown at the Estuary's edge that had grown fat on trade with the Horse. 'We had thought to fly swift that day, fly high the next. But we found the enemy before we were ready for them.' She shuddered. 'We found them on the road.'

Asman felt the Champion become very still within him. It had been restless since he reached Tsokawan, knowing that others were fighting a war denied to it. Now here was word of that war, already on their doorstep.

'We saw a warband of the Plague People travelling,' the Wryneck said. 'I counted ten hands of warriors, with monsters alongside them that bore their burdens and trailed their heels like dogs. We flew over their heads, and we felt the Fear of them touch us. Isiliqua did not stop flying,' she explained, meaning her comrade who had not returned. 'She let the Fear take her and did not know us.'

'But you escaped them,' Asman broke in, against custom. 'You dodged their darts and arrows, and fought off their Fear.'

The Wryneck speaker just looked at him, biting back what she wanted to say for shame, but her fellow lifted her head and said, 'They sent no darts. Even their Fear was not sent. It just *was*. We were strong in heart and it did not master us, but they took Isi-liqua from us without even knowing she was their enemy. And we saw them fly, just as the Plainsfolk said. If they had taken wing after us I think we would not be speaking these words, or have words left in us to speak.'

Tecuman had murmured a prompt to Matsur, who asked, 'How far were they?'

'In two days at most they will be in Chumatla,' the Wryneck reported. Everyone there knew that from Chumatla the Plague People would see the crown of Tsokawan.

* * *

Some lesser chief of the Dragon had tried to kill Gupmet while Venat was away. The lord of the Black Teeth, the most powerful man in the Dragon Isles, had survived it, not because he was stronger and faster, but because he had a hundred ears all over the islands. The challenger had not even reached the Whale Seat from which Gupmet ruled.

Venat had returned briefly to Shark Hilt, to the general dismay of Uzmet, whom he had left in charge in his absence. Renewing a life of petty tyranny was not his plan, though. He made a show of approving how Uzmet was running the place – not well but no worse than he himself would – and then had a woman go with a message to Gupmet. Time was short.

Last time he had met with Gupmet just like any powerful chief would – out in the open and both of them backed by war-riors. This time he waited a day and then set off for Whale Seat on his own, taking a canoe through the maze of islands, slipping past the notice of rival Dragon chieftains. It was the end of the world, after all. It was a time to break traditions.

Gupmet was not a typical chief of the Dragon – that was what Venat was relying on. All too often, the outsider view of his people was no more than truth: that the most brutal and the strongest ruled, and only until a younger and more vital challenger arose. Gupmet had not been young for many years but none had usurped him. He was clever and managed his underlings well, setting them against each other. He understood that there was more to a ruler than blood and greed.

Still, the look on his face when Venat strode into his hall was worth the journey. The best part of a hundred Dragon raiders, their women and their scrum of children in that long house, and all of them stopped and silent, staring. If he *had* come to just call Gupmet out, open his throat and take the Whale Seat as his own, perhaps none of them would have stood in his way.

The old instinct tugged at him, the one that said, *Who cares if you ruin tomorrow, just so you taste blood today?* But Venat was not that man, either. Not any more. Often he wished he still was, but travel and foreign friends had soured him to the Dragon's old song.

'Let's talk,' he said, and Gupmet nodded. Soon after that, the hall was cleared save for a dozen warriors who were obviously considered more loyal than most, and the woman who served as adviser. Venat remembered her from last time – a little younger than Gupmet, but still with plenty of life written on her face. Women had no place at a Dragon war council – or any formal position within their rough structures of power. Except of course every man of worth had women at his fire, and those women talked to each other, and talked in the ears of the men they lay with. And so they had their own chiefs and their own influence, hidden in the Dragon's shadow, and here was the hub of it, sitting at Gupmet's shoulder and murmuring to him.

'I'm here for a warband,' Venat said straight off.

'You *had* a warband,' Gupmet noted. 'Strange tales they told me, when they came back. Burning the houses of the River Lords, that's one thing. I'd expect no less. But they say you let yourself be taken by them too, and you had the man who enslaved you as a guest at your fire.'

'And these men who talk so much, they came back cut and empty-handed, no doubt?'

Gupmet smiled grudgingly. 'They came back with Crocodile

gold, and if they were paid it rather than took it from dead hands, gold is gold.' The woman bent to his ear again. 'They say you cut the head off a River Lord Champion. They tell a story at the fires about it – not the way it was, but the way they want it to be: that you killed the boy who made you a slave.'

'His name is Asman. He's a boy no longer.' Naming Asman before the Whale Seat was giving a warrior's honour to one of the soft River Lords, and one whom Venat should hold as his direst enemy. Except being Asman's slave had not been the worst thing in his life. Except he had killed the Champion, Izel, to save Asman's life.

Gupmet was watching him narrowly.

'The Dragon are called to muster,' Venat stated.

Gupmet made a flicking gesture in front of his face: a man waving away a fly that was of no great concern to him. 'For this you want a warband? And will it be that while the River Lords go to shake spears at this enemy of theirs, you will set fires in their villages and take their treasures?'

'Not this time. You have heard what is said of this war.'

'The Plague People.'

Venat's heart sank, for there was no belief in the chief's voice. 'No more than the truth.'

'Children's stories.'

'The Horse have been driven from Where the Fords Meet.'

Another fly-swat; what were the Horse to the Dragon?

'The warriors of the Plains have been broken. Everywhere the Plague Men go, they bring a fear that drives men's souls mad and robs them of their minds,' Venat pressed. 'I have seen where their shadow has passed.'

Gupmet sighed. 'None doubts you are still strong,' as though Venat's words were just smoke, already dispersing. 'You are not young, but you have plenty of blood in your teeth. But you are too in love with the River Lords. Or with one of them.'

The spike of anger Venat felt was no less fierce because the words were true. He held himself very still, seeing Gupmet's warriors tense and ready.

'But this is foolishness,' the chief went on. 'You and I know there is more in this world than strength, but this is too far. Ask the Estuary men who died fighting River Lord battles. The Dragon has a destiny. It is not to sit here tearing at ourselves and wasting our strength against Old Crocodile's back, but perhaps it is to wait until he shows his belly. And he is rolling over now.'

'And the Plague People?' Venat demanded.

But again there was the fly-swat. Gupmet did not believe in the Plague People, not as anything more than a cautionary tale dulled with over-use.

'I honour you, Venat. Go back to Shark Hilt and live well. Or lead your own warriors in our vanguard, while I muster the rest of the Black Teeth to lay open the throat of the Tsotec. But the time has come to break free of the River Lord yoke, now and perhaps forever.'

* * *

Shyri knew she was in trouble soon after she left Hesprec's tent. She thought she had slipped away from Effey's band subtly enough, but there were hands on her within a few heartbeats of leaving the Serpent behind. Two Hyenas had her by the elbows without warning, but the hand that went to grip the nape of her neck missed its mark. Instantly she had Stepped, bloodying some fingers until she was free of them, but by then the entire pack had turned up to surround her.

Effey swaggered to the fore, looking down on her. 'Now there you are,' she said with exaggerated surprise. 'It's time we were on the move, little daughter.'

'On the move where?'

Effey's gesture took in all the bustle of the camp around them. 'Thin pickings here. The Kasra has far too many knives keeping the peace. It's all a pack can do to keep their bellies full.' She

131

started off between the tents, and Shyri found herself at the woman's heels as always.

'But where, though?' She hated the whine in her voice, that little cringing tone that was an inferior talking to a superior.

'Plenty of bones just lying around to the north. Now we've seen what foolishness the River Lords are up to, it's time we went back to the Plains where we're supposed to be.'

The warriors of a score of Plains tribes were gathering to the north, because they must either unite or be destroyed piecemeal. Messengers passed back and forth between them and Tecumet, and Shyri could only think, *What if they're not enough, what if none of it's enough?* The previous defeat of the Plains forces had been so complete that perhaps nothing could stop the Plague People going wherever they wished.

And she did not think Effey meant to join that muster anyway.

'You're going back to where the Plague has been,' she divined.

Effey cackled. 'Plenty got left behind when the Boar and the rest ran away. Plenty more piggies to hunt down, too, that were once proud warriors that looked down on the Laughing Men.'

'But what about—'

Effey rounded on her suddenly. 'You haven't worked it out yet? None of them have, with their armies and their wars. This is no war for winning, little daughter, because the Plague People, they're not even fighting a war. They're just *being*, and that's enough to turn aside all the knives in the world. But we don't need to fight them. There aren't so many of them; they can't be everywhere. And they won't care when a little line of hecklers goes past their gates. They won't care when we go to the places the Lions abandoned and take what we want of their trophies and their food. We're beneath their notice, little daughter. The only thing that would change that is if we were stupid enough to bring a war to them.'

But they're destroying everything, Shyri thought, but that was no argument to sway Effey. Hers was the creed that most of the Laughing Men might mouth, but Effey truly believed. Here was the end of the world; it was the time of the Hyena. Hyena did not come to mend wounds, but to watch them fester and gnaw on the dead.

'I thank you for teaching me,' she said bitterly, and made to move on, but Effey gripped her shoulder painfully.

'I do not teach you; you will not learn,' the Malikah said. 'Even now you creep off to speak to your southern friends, as if their struggles were your business. You have chosen your place in the pack, Shyri. When we go into the lands of the Plague People, you will go first. You will make our fire, you will prepare our meat, and you will feel my hand, and the hand of any of my warriors, when anything is amiss.'

Shyri started back. 'But that's a man's work.' Always in a pack there would be one at the very bottom, to be bullied and pushed about at the whim of the rest, but it had never been *her*.

Effey glanced at the handful of men in her band. 'Oh, but they have been true children of the Hyena, as much as a man can. While you have taken your coat to the river and tried to wash the spots from it. But you are of the Hyena, and perhaps you will remember it after we have beaten you enough.'

133

13

In careful stages, the Plague People had trained her to perform for them. They did not cut or burn or twist her, or even threaten these things. A physical threat she could have met with physical defiance, and perhaps the Champion would have overcome the ache of her wound and the louring pressure of the Terror and she would have died at last, as a warrior should. Instead, though, they tormented her with bright light and close walls. They offered her more food. They brought the soulless children in to beg her. That last wore her down, eventually. It was not that they were punishing the children for her refusal – the boys and girls that came to her gossamer cell seemed well fed, starved only in the soul. But they hurt her. Just the thought of them burned at her, and the sight of them even more so, watching them die inside a little each day as the taint of the Plague People seeped into them. She saw them when they were unhappy and confused, wailing for lost parents and homes, then she saw them when they were quiet and obedient, and that was worse, because the price of such contentment was everything they had once been. And so at last she did what they wanted when they demanded it, just to spare her the sight of the misery of others.

They wanted her to Step. She thought at first it was because they were trying to trap her in an animal body, as they had all the others. Then they would kill her and take her body apart, for their art or their ritual or why ever it was that they did such things.

As they watched her, though, she watched them. Their words remained nonsense, but the way their faces moved was not such an alien language. A look came into their faces when she Stepped, and though they asked her each day to trot through her captive assembly of shapes, they did not seem happy with her. Their features twisted into strange concern, and then the two curious ones would gabble at each other, back and forth at such a pace that she had no chance of learning any of their words. Then perhaps they would bring out the thin sheets they made their drawings on and compare pictures. Craning forward, Maniye once caught a glimpse of bone sketches – the skeleton of a man made so lifelike she almost expected it to leap from the page, and next to it that of a dog or wolf, lines connecting different elements.

And after days of this, feeling her spirit wither a little each time at her capitulation, feeling the deep pain that festered within her grow, she understood. She understood that they did not understand.

They had no souls. They had no shapes to Step to. Their Plague magic let them fly without wings or kindle fire in the palms of their hands, but they could not understand how she did what she did, and it bothered them. They could not let it alone, like a scab they picked at. They beat her down with their bewilderment. Their incomprehension felt like weights being piled on her shoulders. The Champion gave her strength, but she felt it dying with the rest of her, starved of wholesome air.

Some nights she tried to escape her body and reach the gods. Whether the influence of the Plague People trapped her, or whether there were no gods left to reach in this part of the Plains, she never found them, not even the abandoned hunting grounds they had left behind.

One day, without really making a conscious decision to, she stopped eating.

135

The thought came to her almost like an unlooked-for gift. *I don't have to take this any more.* They gave her a bowl of stew, and some raw horse meat because she had eaten that greedily enough before, and never mind whether the beast it had been cut from had walked on two legs once, or been someone she knew. But now she stared dully at it all and found her hunger had been cut loose from her, to drift away into the numb distance. *I don't have to.* The Champion still wanted to explode out into the midst of the Plague People, to crunch their bones and taste their flesh. But there were so many of them, and their weapons drove so deep – the wound she had taken when the Plainsfolk fell was still inside her, inching towards her heart. And she feared that they would not kill her, no matter how she provoked them. They were interested in her now. They might have ways to prevent her dying, no matter what pain they caused her. In the pit of her stomach she was afraid.

But she did not have to eat. She could send her body the way of her soul, dwindling day by day. That way she could escape them.

Her stomach protested, but she felt as though a river was bearing the sense of hunger far from her. She could sit in her cage and stare dully at the blurred world beyond, and feel only satisfaction that she had found a way to escape. The wound burned inside her; it ate her but she would starve it. She and her hurt would fall into the darkness with hands about each other's throat.

When the two curious Plague People came in, they marked the uneaten food but were not concerned. They showed her pictures, and she Stepped from shape to shape after enough prompting. Each beast just lay there on the cell's silk-lined floor, though, staring at them. They did not understand or know anything was wrong.

And then they came the next day, and still the food had not been touched, and they began to realize something was amiss. The Plague Woman spoke to her, and perhaps her tones were

136

meant to be cajoling or even comforting, but were so alien that they imparted nothing. Maniye just stared at her with a wolf's dumb eyes, with a tiger's mute misery at being caged.

She did not return to her human shape that night, and was a tiger again for them in the morning. Her yellow eyes watched their reaction, their pacing about the outside of her prison as they tried to work out whether she had just gone the way of the others. She wondered if they would be relieved if she had become no more than a beast. Would they burn their sketches and their scribble and pretend she had never been human at all? Would that make things easier for them?

But they brought the children back, and she could not maintain the pretence before them. They knew that the girl was still within the tiger's skull, not just her soul but her mind. She watched them stare back at her, fellow prisoners but ones who had lost so much more than she.

After five days of lapping desultorily at water, taking no food, they let her out under the open sky again. The two Plague People who were so concerned with her seemed genuinely worried that she would come to harm. Their studies were not yet concluded and so she was a thing of value to them. Under the stern gaze of a score of warriors, killing rods at the ready, she paced slowly out into the bright sun of the Plains and felt its heat, and the breeze in her fur.

She could not help herself. She returned to the form of her birth and stood there on two legs, staring up at the cloudless expanse of the sky. It was not the dour colours of the Crown of the World, but it was the same sky nonetheless. She barely marked the ripple of horror that went through her captors as she changed shape, that act of the soul they would never understand if they studied and anatomized her for a hundred years.

She saw the children had been let out, too. They were sitting in rows before one of the larger tents, and another dark Plague Woman was standing before them. Maniye began to walk towards them, feeling their stares on her thin body – she was barely a couple of years older than the eldest. Were they in her sight just to torment her, or was there some other purpose . . . ?

In the Crown of the World, children learned from their parents or a priest, but Maniye had seen how the Sun River Nation brought many together to heed one teacher, to learn all the complex things that land had invented. And the Plague People went about things in a similar way, she saw; they were not interested in torturing her with these children. Instead, they were busy turning these unsouled bodies into more creatures like themselves. Plague People would hatch like flies from the minds of these youngsters.

Their looks, to her, were filled with guilt and shame. They would remember their parents and their grandparents, dead or fled, and their villages abandoned to the scavengers. The oldest, at least, understood that they were being made to betray everything they were, but what choice did they have?

Then one more step had taken her too close to the guards, and her eyes abruptly focused on the levelled rods that were practically in her face. The Plague warriors' expressions were taut with fear of her; that was what she remembered most, afterwards. Even in this little shape, with blunt teeth and no claws, she remained The Unknown to them, the thing they could not conceive of. She terrified them, her whole world terrified them, and she had seen what they did with the things they were scared of.

She drew a deep breath, locking eyes with the Plague Man who was so curious about her. She would take one more step. Their weapons would lance at her and pierce her fragile human flesh. She would die in this shape before all these stolen children. Perhaps it would remind them of how a true human was, in their last sight of one. Her ghost would be trapped in her flesh, but then she did not think her souls could fly free from this place anyway, even if she died in the body of a beast. How could they find their way from the silk-walled warrens of the Plague People all the way to the Crown of the World to be reborn?

138

She made to take that fatal step, seeing the warriors tense, about to strike her down. The eyes of the curious man widened, bright in his dark face. He shook his head slightly, trying to communicate with her, speaking his sounds.

She made to take that fatal step and the wound within her stabbed out, as though it collaborated with its makers. She remembered instantly that great pain, where every part of her hurt to move; she remembered waking to the weakness. She would step forward, but the wound was suddenly too great a burden. She could not move. She could not stand. They almost killed her when she dropped to her knees.

When the curious man and woman came for her, she Stepped into her wolf shape, which always came easiest to her. She wanted to threaten them, but the snarl she intended was more of a whimper and she shrank from their touch. Without being forced, without even being herded, she slunk back into the tent, back into her cell. Her limbs shook with fatigue and hunger and she lay with her muzzle on her forepaws and whined and could not stop. They waved food in front of her, virtually putting their hands between her teeth, but she ignored them. Inaction was the last form of protest left to her.

She had one more visitor, though, before they left her with her misery for the night. Just when she thought she had plumbed the depths of the Plague People, there was more. After the two curious ones had gone, bobbing with concern and yammering at each other, another man stepped in past the guards. The weird pale light the Plague People made shone on his face and sent a new kind of fear through Maniye. Now she understood.

He was not tall or strong-looking, a slender man in a simple robe. He was not of the same people as the pale guards, nor the dark scholars, nor the little people or any of the others. His skin was grey and his eyes were blank white as though he was blind, though he saw her well enough. She knew that face immediately: when the priests of the Owl painted themselves with ash and drew a line of chalk paste across their eyes, there was a terror to

139

that simple mask that no part of it could account for. Now she was looking on the original that the Owls had preserved. It was the face of the enemy their ancestors had fought in the beginning alongside Bat and Serpent, so that the people could flee the Plague and come to these new lands.

He looked on her, his pale gaze like ice, and she saw something behind it that was not incomprehension or fear, the two reactions she was used to getting from the Plague People. Instead, she saw knowledge. He knew what she was, and that she was his enemy. He understood in a way that the guards with their killing rods did not. He held all the learning that her prying keepers would never be able to dig from her, even if they cracked her bones to the very marrow. He knew what the Plague People destroyed, just by coming to these lands, and he was glad.

Nothing about him that met the eye should have recalled Kalameshli Takes Iron to her, but the old man loomed in her thoughts as she looked on the grey-faced Plague Man. The figure of her childhood with his switch and his strap who had known no other way but to beat the Wolf into her. There was something about the contemptuous arrogance of this creature that brought those unfond memories flooding back, and she knew that the Plague People might have no souls, and perhaps they had no gods, but they had a priest.

The day after was when everything changed. It started just as all the others had, with her lids clenched shut to keep out the glimmering of dawn that the tent walls could not block. She listened to the Plague People rising, exchanging their meaningless stutters. Somewhere one of them laughed and the sound was so universal, so human, that it startled her fully awake.

There was a child crying, behind it all. *One of ours.* But she did not know if that was true any more.

The two curious ones came in soon after and regarded the food she had not touched. Under the stern eyes of the guards they took it away and brought in more to replace it. The man crouched down and spoke at length, the tone of his voice entreating. They had grown complacent around her. She was a wolf still, and she could have ripped out both their throats before the guards raised their weapons. They were right to be complacent, though. When the thought of moving against them touched her, her wound set up such a savage bone-deep ache that she retched, the nothing in her belly struggling to get past her lips.

She waited for them to command her to Step again. She was feeling so hollowed out by hunger that she wasn't sure she even could. *I was going to die a human.* But that no longer seemed so important against the ravening hunger she was keeping at arm's length. *Let me die like this. Let them wear my pelt as a trophy. Why should I care?*

Her wolf senses were telling her something was different, though. She cracked open an eye and stared at them, understanding belatedly that there was a distance between the two, who had always seemed inseparable. The change dragged a few dregs of curiosity from her and she forced herself to shrug into her human shape, though she could not make herself stand.

The woman was speaking to her. Maniye didn't know why they bothered, but apparently this was something that needed to be said, if not understood. She talked at length, and her fellow grew angrier and angrier until he interrupted her. Then they were at it like dogs, not fighting but arguing, their chittering speech thrown back and forth like the rage of idiots. Maniye watched them, fascinated. The woman had made some decision and the man was ridiculing her – no, he was trying to dissuade her, or was he worried for her? She could not keep up with the expressions, and they were never quite the ones she was used to.

And she would never know: there was no stolen child here, who might have learned enough words of their speech to translate. In the end, the man stormed out with a forced laugh, a shot at mockery that fell flat, and the woman stayed on and stared and stared. If the grey priest had reminded her of the Takes Iron of childhood, so Maniye found herself thinking of the Testing, where she had proven herself a Wolf at the end of Kalameshli's lash. The Plague Woman was bracing herself for some great trial.

Will she kill me now? Maniye wondered. *Has she some plan to take my soul to fill that gap in her?* But there was no sense of danger, or no more than the whole camp was steeped in, with the Terror of the Plague People in every breath.

Then she too left, and Maniye was none the wiser for any of it.

She lay down on her side, trying not to think about hunger, and a voice whispered in her ear, 'Many Tracks,' so faint she could not tell whether it came from within her head or without it.

She froze. There was a guard at the door but his eyes were set outwards.

'Many Tracks.' Like the voice of a ghost.

She shifted, trying to make it no more than a tired body seeking comfort, not a suddenly alert body trying to look around. The words had been her hunter's name in true human language.

The suspended walls of the cell had a new shadow, tucked at the back, as far from the guard and the entrance to the tent as could be. Maniye stared and stared, because she could not believe what she was seeing. *She is in my mind. She is just what I wish to see.*

I cannot be seeing Hesprec Essen Skese in the midst of the enemy.

But she blinked, she squeezed her eyes shut until flashes of colour burst across them, then opened them wide as could be and still Hesprec was there, a little River Lord girl with rainbow scales painted across her face and winding cloth covering her head from the sky, just as the Serpents always did.

'How?' Maniye made the word a breath. At the door, the guard was half asleep in the muggy sun.

'I rode in the beak of a Heron, all the way from the banks of the Tsotec.' Hesprec had her lips to the stretched web of the cell, and Maniye her ear to the other face of it. The words passed through but the Serpent's soft breath did not, as though it was her thoughts alone that crossed the barrier. 'For a priest, not a dignified way to travel, but I had to find you.'

'Why?' Maniye could feel sobs welling up inside her, wrestling for control of her throat.

'Isn't this what we do, Many Tracks? Rescue each other?'

'You must go,' Maniye made herself say. 'This is a bad place.'

'The Serpent is indebted to the wisdom of the north,' Hesprec noted, with all of her old dryness. 'I will hide beneath your cell. I will be the smallest serpent in the world until there is a chance to cut you from this bag.'

'You have to go. I will die here. I have no strength left.'

'Is the food poison?'

'It is not hunger. I'm hurt, Hesprec. They hurt me, and it burns.' Even the thought of escape brought back the pain and she shrank from it. *Better to just lie here and just let go . . .*

'Show me.' Hesprec was all business. When Maniye tried to ignore her she just demanded again and again, until surely the guard was within a whisker of hearing. If only to shut her up, Maniye turned and pulled up the thin white shift she had been given. She did not look, herself. She did not want to see how it must be consuming her, purpling and then blackening the flesh, eating deep into her innards. In her mind, the wound was a great abscess, enough to put a hand into, shining with the corruption of the Plague People.

She flinched as Hesprec shifted, even though the girl could not have touched her through the cell's wall.

'It is a severe wound,' the Serpent admitted in her whisper-voice.

Maniye could only nod.

'It must gnaw at you.'

Nod.

'Escaping this place would put a great strain on it.'

The very thought made Maniye grit her teeth.

'Maniye, I have some Serpent magic for you, a great secret of my people,' Hesprec told her. 'You must stay very still, and in

143

your mind see the Serpent's jewelled back that runs even beneath this dead place. The Serpent has been your friend before; you know him well. Call to him now, in your mind.'

Unbidden, behind closed lids, that rainbow path appeared in Maniye's mind. The Serpent was not like the gods of her cold homeland, who tested all and punished those who failed. The Serpent brought gifts and guidance. She had walked his back before, when life had seemed impossibly hard.

'The Serpent is within your wound, Maniye,' Hesprec murmured. 'He knows poison of all kinds. He draws the hurt from your flesh and takes it to himself. He drinks it, every drop. Where his body passes through you, he brings purification and life, like a river. You understand?'

Despite herself Maniye nodded, lulled by the soft whisper.

'The wound is gone,' Hesprec told her. 'So sudden are the gifts of the Serpent.'

Maniye's eyes flicked open and she reached within herself for that hurt; ready at any moment to flinch from a resumption of the ache. Yet . . . nothing. For the first time in days she permitted herself to lay a hand where the dart had gone in. There was puckering there, and the flesh was a little tender, but no pus, no oozing corruption, no deep wound.

She sat up suddenly, and still there was no stab of pain. At the entrance, the guard stirred, then lapsed back into his slumber.

'The Serpent cannot do such things,' she stated. 'I know you, old Snake. If you could mend such wounds . . .'

'Such wounds I *can* mend, and such wounds alone,' Hesprec told her. 'The wounds that are left, when other wounds have come and gone, these the Serpent has power over. For the rest, I have a few remedies the Milk Tear taught me, but the wound in your flesh had healed itself already. Champions have a robust constitution, in my experience. But the weapons of the Plague People are laced with despair like a poison. Small wonder it made a home within your flesh. Small wonder it grew the wound within your mind until you felt its teeth about your heart. And now you must be ready to leave.'

Maniye stared at her, still feeling within her for the great abyss of that wound, and knowing without a shadow of a doubt that Hesprec was right. *Was it just the fear of pain, not pain itself?* She felt ashamed for her cowardice that had preserved her. *I should have let the Champion off its leash and torn them ragged.* She felt just the faintest echo of the wound, then, and knew it for all the hurts she had seen done, the failure of the Plainsfolk attack, her own capture, the constant leaden pressure of the fear. How much easier a story it had been to say, *I cannot act, I am too hurt*, than to know all the chains that bound her.

And yet there were more chains. 'They will not let me go,' Maniye told Hesprec.

'I do not propose asking their permission,' Hesprec replied mildly. 'I will find some way.' And only those last words admitted a little uncertainty. Hesprec had come for her, but for once she had no more plan than this.

'They will make you fear,' Maniye whispered. 'They will drive your soul into hiding until you are no more than a snake.'

'Remember the three brothers who fought the Plague People in the story? Who held them back, back then? Owl, Bat and Serpent had that honour. I feel my ancestor in me, Maniye. Serpent shields me as the Champion shields you. For now, eat,' the Serpent advised, and the hunger Maniye had been holding at bay for days took her by the throat and dragged her over to the meat they had left out for her. As a wolf she tore into it, startling the guard into falling from his seat. He came over and stalked about her cell, staring in at her with horrified fascination as she ripped and slobbered. He never saw the tiny serpent coiled beneath the strung floor of her prison.

Then, long into the night, screams erupted from the camp, and Maniye knew that, even if Hesprec had no plan, the Serpent had made a path for them anyway.

145

14

When the Plague People had taken Where the Fords Meet, if they had simply advanced, they could have swept the world before them. They could have poured across the Plains like a tide, swarmed on the banks of the Tsotec, darkened the skies with their insubstantial wings. But they had delayed, building their new home instead of destroying their enemies to the west and to the south.

Especially to the south, Orabin of the Milk Tear People told himself, because it helped to think of the Sun River Nation as a great hammer poised above the Plague People, ready to come down and smash them. It helped to fight his fear, which was jumping all through him as he hung in the water with only his bulbous toad eyes above it, waiting.

Then the Plaguefolk had gone west. Enough fugitives had come to Tsokawan who had witnessed that fight. The Plains warriors had been broken. First the Plague weapons had killed them, and then had come the Terror that stole minds. *Plenty lions on the Plains now. Plenty lions without thumbs trying to remember what they used to be.* Orabin felt his warty skin shiver at the thought.

But they had not come south, not even then. They had crouched and spun their webs about the place the Horse had once called home and they had brawled with the Plainsfolk, and all that while their real foe had only grown in strength. Surely they knew nothing of the world, to ignore the River Lords and their allies so.

Brave words. Orabin did not feel brave. The Milk Tear People did not count it amongst the virtues they valued. They had never brought a war to some other tribe's village. Their god, into whose wide mouth they were born, did not exhort them to rule or fight, but only to live and learn and prosper.

But they were terrors when wronged, were the Milk Tear. Plenty of stories all around the Estuary about those who stole from them or disrespected their Mata, the wise women who ruled them. Enough stories that the other Estuary people treated them with care and seldom crossed them. Sometimes a reputation for vengeance was better than actually having to be vengeful; it was certainly less exerting. The Milk Tear did not like having to work up a sweat.

But the Plaguefolk don't know those stories.

He blinked, eyes sliding half down into his broad skull then popping up above the waterline again, and he saw shadows in the north, past the edge of the water towards the dry horizon. Heart hammering, he tilted himself back and saw the great blue-grey wings of the Wryneck circling. The enemy were coming.

His nerve faltered, and for a moment he thought about just sinking down into the murky, comforting depths of the lake Chumatla was built on. He was just one young warrior after all. Who would notice if he did not fight? Who would know?

But there was a ready answer for that. Mata Heppa would know. Mata Isilwe would know. And Mata Embe would know most of all, for even the Toad came to her with respect and a downcast gaze. So Orabin would not follow his sinking heart and let himself hide in the mud of the bottom. He would fight.

He shifted in the water, the slightest paddling with his broad feet to keep him steady, and let himself focus further and further, past where his eyes were happy, until he could see the enemy properly.

Many of them were walking, and he tried to focus on them

147

because they seemed least fearful. Most were tall, strong-framed men, pale as fish bellies, wearing armour banded in black and yellow as though they were warning the world they were poisonous. Some were dark as Riverlanders, though no more familiar-looking for that. Some were slighter of build; a few seemed full grown but were small as children. None of that mattered. Orabin had heard the Plainsfolk talk about their souls, or the hole where their souls should be, but he had not believed them. When his eyes rested on the enemy, it seemed as though clouds covered the sun and the whole world darkened.

And they were many; more warriors than the Milk Tear had brought certainly. Perhaps more than the Milk Tear and the Salt Eaters together. Were there a full hundred of them?

From there, his gaze was drawn to the things that accompanied them. Again, the warnings of the Plainsfolk had not prepared him for the sight of insects large as men, loaded with burdens or trotting at the Plague warriors' heels like dogs. But for all their size they were still things that Orabin recognized and could understand. His Toad-soul even managed a stab of hunger, for if a water bug or a crayfish was good on the tongue, then here were walking meals that could feed a whole tribe. Their masters were by far the more unnatural.

Then the movement above caught his eye, because of course these Plague creatures could fly. The Wryneck had given over the sky and now human shapes darted there, lifting up from the mass of them to circle overhead, then drop back down, keeping watch. *Is it because they do not have the weight of a soul?* Orabin wondered. *That emptiness within them makes them light, perhaps?* And he scrabbled to continue the line of thought, because he could feel the Terror reaching for him.

They know we're here! But the Terror was not a spear in the hands of the Plague People, it was a cloak that swept all around them.

We will kill them, he told himself, trying to fortify himself against the fear creeping under his skin. *This is our land and we*

148

will drive them from it. But the traitor thought seeped in: *That is what the Plainsfolk said.*

By the command of Prince Tecuman, all those who lived in Chumatla had fled for the shadow of Tsokawan. Now the village was just a collection of vacant huts and floating walkways, built out across the surface of the lake. The Plague People paused at the water's edge, and a party of them set out around the lake's periphery, but that was a long, long way – when the River Lords had deepened the water here generations ago they had done a good job, making the biggest fish trap the world had ever seen. The majority of the Plague warriors were already crossing, stepping carefully onto the shifting walkways, their gossamer wings seen and then not seen as they caught their balance. Their rod weapons were pointed like arrows at the nearest huts.

Orabin fought his heart, which wanted to speed and speed. He fought his mind, which was screaming to him of how close these unnatural monsters were coming. He fought his legs, which wanted only to kick away into the safe depths.

Without warning they were at the first hut, dropping from the sky to shove their weapons through the doorway, finding no enemies. He could see their mood in the way they moved: tense, frustrated, curious in turns. And stupid, or at least blind to the most obvious of things, things any child of the River would know. *Watch the water.* But the Plague People watched the sky and the doorways of the huts, and now they had pushed far enough into abandoned Chumatla that their enemies were all around them. This sign of their fallibility gave Orabin the strength to stave off the Terror. For how long? Abruptly it did not matter, because the signal was rumbling through the water: the shuddering boom of a bull crocodile, more felt through the skin than heard. The Plague People did not react to it: to them it must be just one more alien sound in a world they had no place in.

Orabin found his courage and Stepped.

He had kicked out with his toad legs first, but he erupted from the water's surface as a man with a bow in his hands, string

149

already drawn back. All around him the first wave of Tsokawan's forces was leaping up, some springing onto the walkways or the platforms that surrounded the huts, others keeping to the water to loose their shafts.

Many simply missed – there was a lot of panic tugging at the hands that released the bowstrings. Orabin saw his shaft wing past the hollow man he had been aiming at but gash the face of another beyond him. Just a scratch, and the Plague Man slapped at the line of blood irritably, but then he was down, trembling and kicking as the venom took hold. The Milk Tear were no great warriors but they had never needed to be.

In that first moment he thought the entire battle would be done within heartbeats. Milk Tear archers were sending their darts into the ranks of the Plague warriors, and though most just broke against their armour or hung uselessly in cloth, those that pricked even a little could be fatal. Others in the water were rocking the walkways, trying to tumble the invaders into the water where the River Lords cruised, long jaws hungry. Some of Old Crocodile's children were in amongst the Plaguefolk, lashing at them with stone-toothed *maccan* swords. Above circled the Wryneck, Stepping for the heartbeat it took to loose an arrow and then catching themselves on their wings before they could fall.

Death to the Plague People! Orabin whooped and sent another shaft at them, almost expecting there to be no living enemy left by the time it landed.

But the Plague warriors' armour was strong metal. The teeth of the *maccan* shattered against it; arrows could not pierce it. Instead of topple into the waiting jaws of the crocodiles, most of their warriors had wings that could right them. After that initial flurry, Orabin saw that, no, they were not all dead; they were not even mostly dead. Perhaps a dozen had fallen in the ambush but the others had drawn together and weathered the assault, letting the fury and the shock of it vanish into the holes they had for hearts. Their faces had no fear in them, just a bloody-minded determination.

Then they turned the killing back on their attackers. They stabbed at the River Lord soldiers with blades of silver metal that made no distinction between hide and armour, flesh and bone, but clove through them all equally. Death sped from the rods they carried, so that the Heron warriors above were plucked from the sky, the great graceful birds turned in an instant into sodden masses of dead feathers as they struck the water. Their darts, too fast to see, skipped over the water and pierced the soft bodies of the Milk Tear People. Orabin saw his uncle die, his cousin, then his oldest friend, and none of them even saw their death before it touched them.

The attack faltered, surprise lost. The Plague warriors kept killing, and now the Terror came rolling out that had been driven back while the warriors of Tsokawan thought they were winning. Orabin felt it grip him and pry into his mind. *Flee!* it said, but it did not mean the mud at the bottom of the lake, or to run to the far reaches of the river, or even to go to some far-distant land. *There is no place you can go that will be safe from the Plague People,* that fear told him. *There is only one direction that will let you escape them. You must flee inside yourself, where they cannot find you.* He felt the need screaming in his ears. He was floundering through the water then, trying to get away and yet knowing the urge was right: there was no escaping this on human feet. But he did not Step. He did not Step because he knew that if he took his toad shape now, his mind would burrow deep into that amphibian flesh and never come back. All around him he saw his kin, faces twisted in horror, and some of them were abruptly just large toads kicking off into the water, and in their bulbous, staring eyes there was no human connection, no empathy, no shared bonds of family. He was losing them. They were losing the fight. They were losing everything. The fear took him in its jaws and gaped wide to devour him.

And then the others arrived.

*

151

Lekat was one of twelve; the Hidden People were never numerous nor much liked by the other Estuary tribes. Still, when Tsokawan called they had come to fight the great enemy of the old stories.

The Terror had frozen her even as she braced herself to strike at the enemy. She had thought that, unseen as she was, their power would likewise overlook her. It was a poisoning of the very air though.

She stood beside one of Chumatla's huts within three steps of the enemy, invisible to them. Naked, her skin painted with the intricate, eye-watering patterns that were the secrets of the Hidden Ones' priests, she blended perfectly with the wood and the cane. She kept one eye on the foe, another open for the signal.

The Milk Tear and the others were falling back, and a bitter despair rose in her throat as she saw them transform: human to beast, and not just Stepped but lost. Like so many others, she had not believed it. Everyone knew Plainsfolk were great liars. Except this, the most incredible of their tales, had been truth.

But then the drumming started – the Rain Watchers on the far bank sending the signal for the rest of the warriors to attack. *Madness!* Lekat thought, because this was a time for flight, not rushing into that hideous wall of fear. Brave men might charge in, but only beasts would exit that invisible barrier. Lekat could feel its claws in her, and only the knowledge that she was beyond their notice was keeping her from it.

But they came, the warriors of Tsokawan and the Estuary. The water was abruptly running with the ridged backs of crocodiles, the crested bodies of lizards and the hard shells of turtles. Toads leapt onto the walkways and became desperate, terrified men and women with bows and flint knives. Salt Eaters, dark men in sharkskin cloaks wielding clubs of whalebone, rushed forward with fear-widened eyes. And Lekat waited for that terror to consume them all, because it cared nothing for numbers and it already had its hooks in them.

But in the lead, rushing faster than any of the other warriors, was a shape out of deep time, a two-legged reptile rattling its quill-like scales in warning, keening at the enemy at a pitch that sawed into the brain. Running Lizard, they named it, Swift Reaver, Killing Claw. It was the Champion of the River Lords, and its shape was worn by Asman of the Bluegreen Reach.

Lekat felt the Terror reach for the man like a child for a flame, and he burned it. It could not touch the Champion's soul within him. The darts of their killing rods went wild and then he had leapt – as high as two men and half again as far – and driven his sickle claws into the heart of them, scattering them and shattering the fear so that his warriors could flood in after him.

There was a signal somewhere – one of her fellows flashing colours across one hand to tell her to go; she did not need the prompt. She was already running in, feeling the colours flow across her skin, hunting. The Plague warriors were beset on all sides – from the water, from the land. For a moment they held together, blades out and making bloody work of the River Lord vanguard, but Asman tore into them and abruptly they were fragmenting, bands of them taking to the skies and coming down elsewhere, trying to escape the scaled tide but finding jaws and spears everywhere they went.

Lekat watched, seeing more colour language from her fellows. *There*. One of the Plague People was rallying his fellows, some chief of theirs gathering his warriors to him. She ducked into the water and eeled her way past the rolling bodies of crocodile tearing off flesh from their prizes. Suicide at any other time, but for once the beasts were on her side.

The Plague warriors were trying to defend a hut. Beneath the water she saw Shellbacks already cutting at the ties that held the wood together. Chumatla would give the enemy no stronghold to regroup in, and Lekat would give them no leaders to obey. She slipped from the water with barely a ripple, feeling the air around her dance with the killing darts of the enemy. They did not see her, though. Her skin crept with the colours of the earth and the water, the wood and the moss. Their leader was bellowing out: yaps and hacking sounds that must be commands, and his followers aimed their rods and killed crocodiles and toads that thronged in the water, but they did not see Lekat.

She swayed as she moved, and she moved with them, each step closer made a part of their own pattern. Her knife was cupped in her hand, blade along the line of her arm so she could hide it.

She saw their leader point, mouth open for another order. One moment her arm was folded close to her, pulled tight; then she had lashed out to full extension, the movement swift with the ease of long practice. The point of her knife jutted out of his nose; the hilt she left sticking down from under his jaw. She caught his own metal blade as he dropped it and then she was gone, before the enemy even knew she had cut off their head.

Asman felt the instant when the Plague warriors broke. One moment he was leaping and darting amongst their gleaming blades, cut already and knowing that at any minute they might pin him down and make an end to him. Then they were flying, or trying to. Some obviously lacked wings or were too hurt to flee, and those died swiftly, dragged into the water by crocodiles and torn apart, run through with spears or hacked down by the heavy blades of *maccans*. Asman himself pulled back from the fighting, from warrior to leader as he Stepped. Some Plague warriors were trying to get away overhead – a few would doubtless make it, but there were a lot of arrows up there and the Wryneck were merciless. Others were trying to group together towards the north end of Chumatla, plainly hoping to force a path back to where they'd come from. For a second Asman thought his attack's final set of horns was not in place, but then the north edge of the lake was thronging with Plainsfolk and Horse archers, all the displaced and the broken who had fled to Tsokawan's shadow. He had not trusted them to be his front line, not beaten and grieving as they were, but now the Plague

154

People were in retreat they would make a fine chasing force to kill as many of the runners as they could. After all, there were few who could outpace one of the Horse.

The beasts their foes had brought with them, the lumbering insects, had not fought. He had dreamt up strategies for dealing with their hard shells and their shearing mouthparts, but the creatures had just milled or blundered into the water and drowned; another element of the Plague People legend that was not as fearsome as the stories had led him to believe. They were just mute animals in the end.

The band of enemy that had split off along the edge of the lake was done for by now, as well. The Foot Cutters had attacked them from the water, fighting viciously with hatchet and shield, while the few warriors the Rain Watchers could muster had come from the trees, backed by more River Lords. Asman could see the victors dancing at the water's edge now, the Plague People scattered or dead. The Terror, which was the enemy's greatest weapon, could be broken, or at least held back long enough to break the enemy, and who feared a foe that was running away?

He took a deep breath, seeing the last of the fighting coming to a close, the last arrow-struck body dropping from the air to fall amidst the thrashing tails and jaws. They had beaten the Plague People.

We have beaten these *Plague People.* This force was only a fraction of the creatures squatting at Where the Fords Meet and their other strongholds in the Plains, though he hoped it was a significant fraction. *And we outnumbered them many to one, and I do not know how many of us died to bring them down.*

But for now he must grin for his people, lead them in cheering. The enemy dead were one thing, but knowledge that the enemy *could* be driven back was surely the greater victory, a future shield against the Terror that might save hundreds of lives.

And Tecuman would be happy with him. And word would race upriver to his mate, Tecumet, and perhaps news of this would even go as far as the Dragon Isles where it would reach

155

other ears. Asman smiled fondly, and let his followers take it as joy in their triumph.

He set watchers to keep an eye out for more of the enemy and began organizing his army for the return march to Tsokawan.

The scouts were not long in reporting. Messengers had scarcely been dispatched upriver before Wryneck were descending on the fortress. Something was coming: something like a bulbous fortress suspended in the air. Its course, cutting across all wind and weather, was directly for Tsokawan itself.

15

At night, they could see the lights of the Plague People. Their unwavering white lamps, like a hundred little moons, sent a cold, pale light out across the surrounding Plainsland and made their white walls gleam.

Shyri had caught a moment's glimpse of the hollow creature Hesprec had brought back from the south at the River camp. She had heard the old Snake legends too, far more than most of her people. Easy enough, then, to see that Hesprec's creature was distant kin to those occupying the Tooth Marker village. Easy enough, looking at those web-strung walls, to know that 'Pale Shadow' did not refer to their pallid skin.

And yet here were the Hyena, trotting across the midnight grasslands with their shadows thrown long by that dead still light.

And Shyri was at the back, behind even the men. While Effey's word was on her, she was less than a slave. Any curse they had, it was for her. Any frustration became a cuff or a kick, a snap or a snarl directed at her. And if Effey herself had some spleen to vent, well . . .

But it was Hyena's way. There was always someone at the end of the boot when a kicking came around. Shyri had put that boot in, had bloodied her teeth on some wretched male often enough. She had never thought it would be her.

Beyond the Tooth Marker village was another Boar camp that the Plague People had not spread to yet, despite it being within sight of their beacons. It was a cluster of huts that probably the Boar herdsmen had used when grazing their cattle. Effey had the pack circle it, sniffing out any ambushes, but the Plague People seemed oddly complacent. Rivermen would have a sentry or two out here, at least, to deny their enemies haven. Effey remained suspicious. Eventually she Stepped, crouched in the long grass, and nodded to Shyri, who knew it was no more than her due.

She crept amongst the huts on soft feet, nosing about the open doors and ready to flee at a moment's notice. First impressions continued to hold, though: the Plague People's shadow had not fallen on this place.

For a moment Shyri found herself considering how that might be used against them. A force could muster here, under cover of the huts, and be at those glowing walls before an attack was even suspected. She pictured Asman leaping into their midst with his keening warcry, Venat's long dragon shape launching at them from the grass.

Then she stopped, and unthought all those thoughts, unsaw the inner images, because that was not the Hyena's way, and why was she doing these menial tasks if not because she had forgotten what she was?

She had a further sniff around because, despite the absence of the enemy, her nose was telling her all was not right. Perhaps it was just the cattle that had trampled about the place after their masters had gone, and still stomped between the huts like noisy white ghosts . . . but no, there was more in the air: blood and a touch of smoke.

She let her nose guide her: carrion always spoke loud to the Hyena. Past the edge of the huts there was a dead cow, and that was no unusual thing when the herdsman had been driven away. Probably a lion kill, or . . .

Close enough to see the mound of the body, she froze. Not a lion. Something like a grey knot the size of a man was clasped to the dead animal's body. It smelled like bitter ashes. For a long while her eyes, good as they were in the moonlight, could not make sense of it.

But then she knew. *Their beasts.* It was a spider larger than she was, escaped from its spinning duties. Or did the Plague People let them out to hunt, maybe? Were they nearby? Just like the cattle, there was no trace of a master, just this crouching grey monster.

Abruptly the pack were around her, Effey's patience having run out. Shyri felt their teeth nip at her flanks and legs, their heckling cries ringing in her ears. The thing on the dead cow shifted its many legs, and they fell silent.

Shyri was forgotten. Effey advanced a few paces, growling, her hackles up. The spider regarded them all glassily, enough eyes to go round. When she was close enough it lifted its front legs high, reaching over her, showing fangs like curved yellow daggers.

Shyri stepped, becoming human crouched low, her spear held close to the ground. With a few terse words Effey had two of the pack circling left, two right, surrounding the thing.

'Now you, runt,' she said out of the corner of her mouth, meaning Shyri.

Shyri looked at the creature's fangs and didn't much like the idea, but there were three of the pack at her back, and Effey right next to her. She took out her knife and then Stepped, touching her teeth together and feeling the metal of them meet.

The spider retreated crabwise a few paces. She wondered if it thought. Was it lost? Or was it glad to be free of its hollow masters? Or perhaps it just killed and ate and rutted and had no thoughts at all.

It didn't want to give up the carcass of the cow, that was certain. The monster shifted and shuffled, trying to keep them all within its broad view. Shyri moved every time its attention seemed to wander left or right. She felt she must be within the span of its limbs now, certainly within reach if it went for her.

Even as she had the thought, it charged her. She had a brief

159

sense of furious motion, all those legs flurrying, and she fell backwards, human again and knife before her. She felt something hard scrape against the bronze – one of the monster's fangs. The scream she heard was her own.

But then the rest of the pack had taken the opening she'd made and were snapping and stabbing at the thing from either side, and surely that was the end of it. Except the spider made a shrill hissing sound and abruptly the air was filled with panicked yelps and whines from hyenas, the shouts of women.

The spider, still very much alive, arched over her, trying to bring its fangs to bear, surely venomous as any Serpent priest. Shyri held it off with one hand, stabbing at its leathery hide with her knife until yellow ichor jetted from it, and still its legs clasped about her, trapping her in a living cage.

Something lanced from its hairy abdomen, driving into the earth between her legs, and she screamed again, thinking it had a stinger as well. It was Effey's barbed spearhead, though, having ploughed through the rest of the monster. When she yanked it free with a yell of effort, the innards of the monster came with it, and Shyri was drenched with its fluids, stained yellow and blue. She scrabbled out from beneath the stiff corpse and dropped to the ground, breathing heavily. *Let that be enough*, she begged Hyena. *I am prostrate before you. Let it be enough. I don't want to be the runt any more.*

But Effey didn't look as though she was in the mood for making friends. Half the pack had their waterskins out, dousing their faces, their swollen red eyes and gasping mouths. The spider had filled the air with a stinging shower of dust or hair from its back when they leapt at it. Only Shyri's position beneath its fangs had spared her.

'Effey, here,' one of the less affected warriors said, drawing her leader's attention to the dead cow. She had found something nestling between the beast's forelegs, a lumpy ball of white like a goitre.

For a moment they all stared at it blankly, but then it moved, just a little, as though many tiny things within it all shivered at once.

'Eggs,' breathed Shyri, and the pack fell back with revulsion.

'Make a fire,' Effey said. 'And keep watch.'

They lit the flames within one of the huts, and then it fell to Shyri to carry a torch to the beast's corpse and burn the egg sac. The huts stood between her and the Plague People, but she was still keenly aware of them: they could fly, after all. Who knew where their eyes were? But the eggs popped and sizzled fiercely, and no hollow man swooped down to punish her for it.

So how many of their beasts are loose? she wondered grimly. *How many eggs to hatch?* A spider that could bring down a cow could bring down most other prey, she'd guess. And what predators were there that would contest with such as that?

She Stepped and loped back to the huts, only to find that Effey had unearthed a little unexpected treasure.

Not all the Tooth Markers had fled when the Plague devoured their village. Certainly there were plenty of pigs running about that might once have had human names and faces, but these little piglets had kept their home *and* their shape, hiding out under the very gaze of the enemy.

There were four of them: an old man, a worn-looking woman, a boy of maybe twelve and a child of five, gender uncertain. They had been hiding in a store beneath one of the huts. Shyri guessed she had smelled a trace of them, but the dead cow and its monstrous rider had dragged away her attention. Now, the pack had them.

What might have happened had Effey's band all been well fed and content was anyone's guess. Perhaps they would have been lenient; perhaps things would have played out just the same. Half of them were still stinging from their fight with the spider, though. They would have had plenty of curses and kicks for Shyri, but fate had served them different prey.

When Shyri arrived, they had the Boar family out in the open, ripped clothes and bruises showing that the eviction had been none too gentle. The pack ringed them, some human and some hyenas, their voices rising together in mockery. The Boar were terrified, the adults trying to shield the children.

It was hardly a novel scene to Shyri. Her own tribe had treated captives just the same at times. Effey was different, though. For her, this cruelty was the breath of the Hyena. Shyri could see it in her face. Of course Shyri knew the stories about how Hyena was kept out of the counsels of the other gods, forced to the margins and slighted at every turn; about how Hyena would pick the bones of the others at the end of the world, the sole surviving deity of the sole surviving tribe. Everyone told those stories, but then they got down to building homes and raising crops, herding beasts and raiding the neighbours. And in a bad year, or if the Lion had raided you harder than you raided them, you told those stories and took refuge in the thought that one day it would all be carrion and bones for you, rather than the Lion's leavings. But they were just stories, where nobody asked what people would eat when the last of the carrion was gone.

Nobody lived their lives in joyous anticipation of the end of the world. Except now she had met Effey. Effey had heard of the Plague People and her thought had not been, *We must fight them.* It had been, *Now is our time.* Shyri watched her jab at the Boar with her spear, not to kill but to make them dance and beg. She was grinning hugely, Hyena seeing the joke of the world. Effey cared nothing for any future, not her own, not the world's. She cared only that these were the end times and they were hers to enjoy.

It was a strangely religious moment for Shyri, that here was someone who had swallowed down those stories night after night until she had become closer to the Hyena than any priest. She felt she should throw herself before Effey's feet and worship the woman. She should grovel with thanks at being allowed to be Effey's runt. She should kiss the foot that kicked her.

Except she realized then that gods are all very well in stories, or off in that far country where priests and dreamers went. Gods

162

standing before you stabbing at a five-year-old child with a spear were less palatable.

Surely the Plague People can hear this? For the whole pack were cackling and yammering, following Effey's gleeful lead, and the Boar woman was screaming at them, breaking down past her ability to bear. There was blood on all of them from a dozen shallow cuts.

Then the boy Stepped into the scrawniest boar Shyri had ever seen and tried to charge Effey. She tripped the animal effortlessly with her spear-half and gashed its leg with the tip so that the animal was abruptly human again, a child suddenly reminded he was not yet a man. As the boy howled, Effey's eyes narrowed.

'You have forgotten what you are, pigs,' she told them. 'And we have grown lazy eating dead meat. It's time for a hunt.'

The Boar woman cried out, and Effey adopted a pose of puzzlement. 'Would you not prefer a chance? If you run well enough, perhaps you will outpace this band of fat and idle hunters.'

The woman just shook her head, and Effey pretended not to understand her, speaking over her whenever she tried to plead and beg, goading and goading until suddenly she mimed revelation.

'Oh, it's *this*!' she exclaimed, as if seeing the five-year-old for the first time. 'Of course you can't run with *this* dragging behind you!' And she laughed, and Shyri saw the woman relax slightly. Something kicked inside her then: the knowledge of how this would look to any of her new friends. *Even to my own people surely? We were never like this.* But who knew what her own Malikah was up to, off in the west? *We tell ourselves we were wronged and it gives us the right to take our vengeance however we want, and on everyone.*

Effey stopped laughing and skewered the child on her spear. Moments later the only sound was the Boar woman's keening cry of grief and loss.

'Now.' All the laughter was gone from Effey. 'Run, piglets.

163

Give Hyena something to hunt. Or we will kill the other little piglet.'

There were words in Shyri's throat, words the Hyena would not have owned to. She wanted them to stop. But if she so much as spoke, they would hunt her along with the Boar. Effey was right about her. She was a poor daughter of Hyena.

The pack had their spears out, and were pushing the Boar stumbling beyond the huts, out into the open grasslands. The old man broke first, abruptly just a hairy back rushing off. The other two followed, the boy already falling behind his mother. In a heartbeat the pack were all Stepped and spreading out, and Shyri saw the plan immediately. They were not just hunting, they were herding. Ahead, spreading its deathly light across the grass, was the luminous domain of the Plague People. Effey was curious, perhaps, or she reckoned she would enjoy the spectacle. Or she had chosen to make an end to her captives in a way that would torment their souls instead of just their bodies.

Something twisted in Shyri that had been lodged there a long time. To her surprise it felt like Hyena speaking to her after all. Not *Save the innocents*, but *Take no more of this*.

* * *

When Maniye heard the screaming she thought it must be some victims of the Plague People, that they had learned how to take human prisoners without driving their minds away and making animals of them. In the next heartbeat she knew otherwise: the voice yelling itself hoarse and waking all the camp was familiar to her – more so now it broke into a high gabbling of alien language. It was one of the two curious Plague People: the male.

She was standing in her cell, trying to see past the entrance to the tent. The guard was craning out to see too. Past him there was a shadowy gathering and she heard dozens of their stuttering voices raised in shock and horror.

Good.

Then Hesprec uncoiled from beneath the cell and Stepped,

164

becoming a girl with a sharp flint blade in her hand. She dug it into the side of the cell and made hard work of cutting the silk, one eye always on the guard. Maniye watched her work and despaired. This was their chance, and it would surely last only a few breaths, but even flint's keen edge struggled against the Plague People's work. The blade was just not strong enough; it would take Hesprec forever to cut a hole large enough for Maniye to creep through.

But that was not her plan. Instead she tore a gash just a few fingers wide and then pushed the knife through so that it fell at Maniye's feet.

Their eyes met and Maniye understood. She took up the knife, and let the Champion rise up within her, bulking out into its great burly bear-dog body, its boundless strength held in hooked claws now sharp and hard as knapped stone.

Hesprec was already darting for the guard, like a woman running towards her own death. Maniye rose up on her hind legs and raked her foreclaws down the wall of her prison, throwing all her weight and power against the unnatural material, feeling it resist and resist and then suddenly part like the gossamer it resembled, unseaming from top to bottom and letting her spill out into the tent with a thud.

The guard whirled, already fumbling for his weapon, and Hesprec lunged for him. Maniye was lumbering forwards, seeing only a slight River girl with an empty hand thrust at the Plague warrior. Then Hesprec was a serpent, her hand the snake's gaping jaws latching onto the man's arm, fangs scraping at his armour. Her narrow body whipped about his throat, and then it was not so narrow, growing and growing as coils thicker than a man's leg wound round about the hollow man's body. Maniye saw the loop about his throat tighten, cutting off his cry of pain or warning. His eyes bulged and his face darkened, and she heard ribs shatter as Hesprec constricted with every breath he took.

Maniye Stepped to her wolf shape and padded silently to the entryway. There was still a great deal of fuss, and a half-dozen of the Plague warriors were trying to bring something out from one of the larger tents. Many others had gathered, and she saw a shudder pass through them as they laid eyes on it. Despite the precariousness of her position, she found an unlooked-for curiosity rising in her. *What can horrify the Plague People?*

'Come.' It was Hesprec whispering in her ear, and she knew they should just leave, as swiftly as possible. She slipped from the tent into the night, hoping that the noses and eyes of the enemy were no better in darkness than any human's.

Hesprec, now a ribbon-thin snake again, slithered past her and Stepped in the tent's shadow, eyes glinting. *And she's right, we have to go*, but a thorn jabbed Maniye even as she thought it. *I am leaving too much here.* There was plenty she wanted to be rid of, but some things belonged to her. Some things she had earned.

Without explanation she turned and slipped away into the camp, looking for that other tent, the house of dead things where she had first awoken. That was where the curious Plague People kept the human things they had found, and not just the corpses.

She paused at the threshold, scenting the bitter stink of whatever stopped the piecemeal bodies rotting. A stab of the old fear cut into her, as though her wound was back, but she shook herself from nose to tail and threw it off. Then she was inside, nosing through the reeking exhibits for that subtle scent that only the Wolf knew.

Her coat. She had been wearing it when they took her, but not when she woke. Swiftly she hunted across the nooks and platforms of the place, hoping and hoping. She had hung on the hooks for that coat. It was her inheritance, the one gift she would take from her true father.

The faintest scent of metal came to her amongst such a cacophony of other odours, but she felt it was her Wolf soul that truly let her find it. It had been discarded in a heap of broken arrows and bronze knives – the greatest secret of the Wolf just a commonplace trinket to the Plague People. Quickly she Stepped and shrugged her way into it, shivering at the cold metal. When she turned, Hesprec was at her back, wide-eyed and anxious to be gone.

She spared one thought for the children. They also represented something the Plague People had stolen from her own. Probably she could find them in the camp, but she could never have freed them. And perhaps some would already be too far gone, and not want to escape. It was a cold thought.

So, a Wolf once more, she darted from the camp, and stopped. The great gathering of the Plague People had begun to disperse, but the curious man and a handful of others were left there, standing before . . . something. The sight of it brought Maniye's gorge up, and she knew she was feeling a kindred revulsion to that of the Plague People themselves. It was a pooled thing, a malformed, lumpy thing that glistened wetly in the pale lamplight. Parts of it were shiny brown shell, and here and there joined legs jutted from it, crooked and useless. Other parts of it showed dark skin, and she saw a hand there, though two of its fingers had become a barbed claw. A bulbous compound eye glittered from the midst of the amorphous mass, but it was set in part of a human face.

The other Plague People were angry, disgusted, arguing fiercely with the curious man, but he – some different emotion had him in its jaws. He was jabbing a hand at the hideous mass and though he was plainly shaken and saddened, there was a weird exultation in him as well.

'Maniye,' hissed Hesprec, and she knew the Serpent was right. They had overstayed their welcome. Even as she took off, she heard a shout from across the camp and caught a fleeting glimpse of white eyes set in a grey face. Their priest had sniffed her out and was calling for pursuit.

A thin scaled body looped itself about her and Maniye ran with all the speed a wolf can muster, the presence of Hesprec reminding her of all the other times the two of them had run from danger's mouth just before the jaws closed on them.

167

16

Loud Thunder's problem was that he couldn't stand his own war host. Part of this was that his war host couldn't stand his war host either, but he had already chipped away at that problem until all those sharp edges between the Tiger and the Wolf, and between the Wolf and everybody else, had been smoothed away just enough. They would never be friends but they could be foes of the Plague People together.

Did that mean that they marched uncomplainingly south along the bank of the Sand Pearl? It did not. Tribe did not war against tribe, but individual most certainly had grievances against individual, and these grievances hunted up and down the river looking for a pair of ears to trouble. And if Loud Thunder was present, those ears would be his.

And his own people were worst of all. Of course they were! They couldn't even live with each other, let alone anyone else. Loud Thunder sympathized deeply, but when the Bear fought, even if it was no more than shoving, breakable things got broken. Things like the people of smaller tribes.

And so he went ahead with the vanguard as much as he could. Sometimes he was called to speak to Mother, which meant he had to wade back through the great migrating mass of the host to her sled. Mother rode in a sled; nobody else did. It was a privilege that not the proudest warrior or most august priest had argued. She was hauled in it by eight of the Bear, and everyone said what a grand honour that was, except for the expressions of whoever was doing the hauling which said something else entirely.

When he was called to Mother, he generally had to wait, ambling along beside her sled as others of the Wise got to talk to her first. Waiting, he could at least steal glances at Kailovela as she sat in Mother's shadow or walked along with her child in her arms. Her look for him was wary, but sometimes she smiled. The smiles hurt him, because a part of him always wanted to take them in its teeth and run with them, far further than they were meant to go. *She smiles at me; that means she's mine.* He could at least recognize the fallacy in that. But it was a smile, nonetheless.

He had been to Mother yesterday, answering her questions about the land ahead, and who had joined the war host. That was the other thing – they were still taking on new warriors. Another band of Tigers had come in yesterday, and a few Swift Back hunters, and another half-dozen Horse who'd fled Where the Fords Meet. And they always lost a few too – some sick or hurt, some just too far from home and losing their nerve. Loud Thunder knew that as war leader he should do something about this, but he did not have the heart to. Most of those with him had already fought the Plague People once, on the Seal coast. The memory of that battle made him shudder even now; plenty had not come back from it. Let the chiefs and priests keep their people on the path. He would not be shepherd to every hunter who found one more step south one step too many.

In the vanguard, he could almost pretend none of it was there. So long as he didn't look back, he didn't need to acknowledge the great tail of warriors he was dragging behind him, stretching back along the river. They Stepped to move swiftly, so he really was trying to herd wolves and boars, deer and tiger and bear. If he didn't look left he didn't have to acknowledge the fleet of rafts that the Horse had built to carry everyone's tents and tools and baggage. (Could Mother not have ridden on a raft? No, apparently that was not dignified enough.)

The vanguard changed constantly. Loud Thunder would go to one tribe or another and give them the honour, and then two score or so of warriors would run forwards with him, to become the point of the long twisting spear that they were bringing south to stick in the Plague People. Ahead of those two score, another score or so of the best scouts would already be moving through the countryside, keeping a wise eye out for any sign of the enemy.

Now some of the scouts were coming back with company: at first Thunder thought it was more Wolves, but when they Stepped they had the coppery tone of Plainslanders. There were a dozen of them, mostly men, with the look of people who had travelled far and slept little.

He listened to their story for just long enough to understand how bad things had become. The Plainsfolk had already fought the Plague People, who were apparently pushing deep into the Plains. Fought, and lost.

Only these *Plainsfolk*, he told himself. *There are plenty more to the west. We just need to join up with them somehow.* Part of his mind was running through what he'd say to the Eyriefolk – sending their Crow out in all directions to find the limits of the land the Plague had already touched. The rest was with his mouth, telling the Plainsfolk to come with him, because Mother would need to know.

They were resting one night out of two, a pace that was punishing but possible. When they got closer to the enemy, Thunder knew they'd have to slow to give people time to catch their breath. Every day spent travelling was another day for the foe to grow stronger. He saw in his mind's eye their web walls expanding outwards from Where the Fords Meet, creeping like a fungus across the world and bringing the devouring Terror that was the enemy's greatest weapon.

Of course, the news from the south was all through the camp by nightfall, and nobody was happy about it. The young and the brash cursed the Plains warriors for being weak, and Thunder had been ready for that. What surprised him was that *only* the young and the brash were saying it – and of them, mostly those who had not fought on the coast. The mood amongst the rest was grim. Everybody remembered how hard it was to fight the Plague, with their lethal weapons, their sea monster, their flying ship and their fear.

That night, the two Coyote, Two Heads Talking and his mate, Quiet When Loud, came to his fire. He was old enough to have grey in his beard, a ragged-looking wanderer who was also probably a priest – with the Coyote it was always hard to tell. She was younger, and rounder now, with a child swelling her belly. She rode with Mother a lot, or on the rafts, but she could Step and run with the best of them when she needed to.

'I know all the stories about what happens when Coyote comes to your hearth,' Thunder remarked, nonetheless beckoning them forward, making them his guests. 'I don't want to wake up and find out you stole all my teeth while I slept.'

'It wasn't stealing,' said Two Heads, who knew everyone's Coyote stories. 'Wolf agreed to it in the wager, he just didn't realize that was what the wager meant. And besides, he got them back eventually.'

Thunder managed a smile at that, but it was short lived. 'What bad news are you bringing?'

Quiet When Loud grimaced. 'The Wild Dog that you brought, their words are guests at everyone's fire.'

'That much I know.'

'The worst sort of guests,' she went on. 'Fear is all through the camp before we even see the enemy.'

'They'll get over it,' Thunder decided.

'They will,' Two Heads agreed. 'But when it's darkest, they'll look for something to burn.'

They told him what they had heard, the words flowing from camp to camp like poison, and his heart sank. One more problem he should have foreseen.

171

'Mother won't allow it.'

But the Coyote just looked at him, and he knew that Mother would expect him to deal with it before it came to trouble her.

The only thing that remained was to see who would broach it with him. The next day, as he ran ahead with a score of Razorbacks, a tiger came to pad alongside him. He knew her, and his heart sank: easy enough to argue down a warrior of the Wolf, less so Aritchaka, priestess and war leader of all the Tiger.

If she had just Stepped and started speaking, he could have remained a bear and pretended not to listen. She said nothing, though, just padded pointedly beside him, as impossible to ignore as a thorn in his foot, until he gave up and Stepped, human ears to hear her human words. She followed suit, becoming a lean woman in mail of bronze squares, a feather-crested helm on her head.

'Well then, let's have it,' he said gruffly.

'The Bear is a long way from here,' she remarked.

'The Bear is right here, as far as anyone needs to care about.' He struck himself in the chest to show where he meant. 'Not that the Bear is much use to anyone at the best of times.'

'The Tiger is closer, but still not close,' she went on. 'The Wolf too. We are leaving the places where they are strong.'

Thunder rumbled, deep in his chest.

'When we fought the Plague People, our gods were with us,' Aritchaka said. 'The Tiger brushed past me, in the fight. I felt his pelt against my hand. The storm that covered our attack was his breath. Or the Eyriemen would say it was the Hawk's wings casting their shadow over us, and probably the Wolf have some story too, and the others. But all our gods dwell in the Crown of the World, and we must find a way to bring them with us.'

'Good luck getting the Bear to go anywhere or do anything,' Thunder grumbled, but he knew what she meant. 'So what are you saying? What will bring the Tiger on our path?'

'A sacrifice. Proper meat laid before him.'

172

The sacrifices the Tiger made to their god were the stuff of campfire stories, and not the funny Coyote ones. They were called Shadow Eaters; they devoured the souls of their prisoners so that their god might feed, or so people said.

'Well then,' Thunder said heavily. 'You have something in mind for this proper meat?'

'The blood of our enemy will bring the Tiger from his temple to run with us,' Aritchaka said. 'The Wolf too, and the rest.'

Thunder sighed. It was not the worst outcome; it was even perversely attractive, in a way. He could see the logic. But Kailovela would not like it. It would be breaking faith with her. 'No.'

'Give us the hollow monster. Let us put the taste of its blood in the mouths of the gods. Why is this even a question that needs asking twice?'

Thunder almost said that the Tiger would have to look elsewhere for a sacrifice, but that would be inviting all the trouble in the world to his fire when some young Wolf went missing. Instead he just shrugged off the Tiger's demands and stomped off.

Icefoot came next. He was a Wolf priest from the Moon Eaters and had proven himself amongst the wisest of the wise. Loud Thunder's heart sank to see him.

'My warriors live further north than the rest of the Wolf,' Icefoot remarked. 'It's a long way you've brought them.'

'I know what you would say,' Thunder told him bluntly.

'Saves me asking.' Icefoot shrugged. 'I know the Tiger woman has been at you already.'

'And I thought if she said push, you'd pull,' Thunder pointed out. He felt genuinely aggrieved. The enmity between Tiger and Wolf was something he should have been able to count on.

'Not in this.' Another shrug. 'You'll do what you'll do. I know the Bear. But you can drag bodies where you want; minds are different. If you want to bring them too, you'll need something.'

But at least he ambled off of his own accord without any threats.

173

Towards evening Thunder sent the Boar scouting for somewhere to camp. Even he was beginning to feel it now: the *south*-ness of things. The air smelled wrong. The sky was too clear. He was too warm. The ground was hard in the wrong ways.

Then something stirred in the branches nearby, and he looked up to see a great white-winged owl Step to become Seven Mending the priestess, with her blind-looking gaze.

'You too, is it?' he muttered.

She cocked her head, obviously reconstructing everything the others had said to him. 'You took the creature from our hands, when you took Kailovela from Yellow Claw,' she pointed out. 'It was ours to keep, ours to kill.'

'Freed,' Loud Thunder stated. At her blank look, he expanded. 'When I freed her. The priestesses of the Owl live different lives to the women of the Hawk.'

She stared past him for a long time, pinning him with her attention even though her eyes never quite fixed on him. 'She won't be yours,' she said at last. 'Not without a leash about her neck. You're not the first man who's thought she would roost at his hearth of her own will. But until you cage her, she's no more yours than the sky is.'

Thunder felt the words strike home, but he bore the hurt without showing it. A moment later she was an Owl again, and flying away into the gathering gloom.

All the next day a new pair of wings was in the sky, far greater than Seven Mending could have spread. Thunder kept expecting Yellow Claw to stoop down and gloat, but the Champion of the Eyrie kept his distance, making sure Thunder knew he was there, his shadow criss-crossing the vanguard's path. Small wonder whose idea this sacrifice had been. *You can take her from me*, that shadow said, *but I can make you hurt her.*

* * *

Tecuman had no idea how to fight the thing. None of them did. The wise had no advice, nor even the Serpent, who knew all the

174

secrets under the earth. The floating ship of the Plague People was the antithesis of such lore, a great bloated thing like a false moon that hung in the sky against all nature. The old stories said nothing of it.

And so the warriors of the Estuary stood ready, watching it course leisurely towards Tsokawan, passing Chumatla, where the Plague Men had been routed. Those few survivors of that battle, who had skipped off into the air and evaded the spears and the poisoned darts, they had gone to this thing. They had told their fellows what had befallen them.

Let it put fear in their hearts, Asman thought, but if it had put fear in their hearts then why were they here? *How large is it, truly? How many can it hold?* For unless it was far further up than Asman could imagine, surely the vessel could not carry enough warriors to break the will of the Estuary people and let the Terror in.

There was no clue to the Plague People's intent in that steady approach. The more the warriors on the ground had to wait, with their enemy in full sight like that, the more their nerve started to go. Asman felt it himself. More sinister than fires on the horizon, more sinister than a marching warband was the slow nearing of that floating ship.

Tecuman had sent some of the Heron to fly close, but the Plague People killed some, and the Terror took others, leaving only two to report that they suffered no other thing to share the air with them. Even those whom the Terror had turned had been struck from the sky by the Plague warriors' weapons.

Would they stop beyond the great camp around Tsokawan so they could marshal their forces on the ground? They would not. The floating ship showed no signs of slowing until it was virtually above the spires of the fortress, turning slowly like a fish in deep water. Asman stood next to Tecuman on one of the balconies, staring up at its swollen silhouette against the bright sky. Either side, a score of soldiers waited with spears in case enemy soldiers began dropping on them.

'Could we take it from them, do you think?' the prince asked, his voice shaking slightly. 'If they brought it low enough, perhaps we could leap from the spires to board it. Then it would be ours, and follow our commands, like something from the stories. We could travel all the world as easily as going up and down the Tsotec.'

'It would carry you to places you'd not want to go,' Asman decided. A handful of Milk Tear had entered the chamber at their back, some delegation of their wise women. 'It is a creature of theirs, nothing of ours,' he cast over his shoulder as he went inside to meet them. 'The Salt Eaters say they have a metal-skinned beast of the sea too, that brought more of them to the coast to strike at Where the Fords Meet.'

'A beast, or a made thing?' Tecuman speculated, squinting up. 'It seems made, to me . . .' His voice trailed off.

'Teca?' Asman turned to see him staring upwards.

'Seeds,' the prince said distinctly, and then the world beyond the balcony erupted as though Tsokawan had been built on a volcano.

Fire came in through every window, a glare that blotted out the sun, and Asman was plucked at by a score of stone blades as the elaborate carvings of the doorway and balcony railings were blasted apart. He heard the screams of the soldiers, some cut short, some drawn out in horrible agony, and above it all one voice he knew.

Tecuman crouched on the slanting, cracked floor of the balcony, one half of him blistered red by fire, his robes blazing. Asman let out a roar of grief and rage and Stepped, the Champion's leap carrying him to the doorway, then his human hand reaching for his friend, trying to close about the scorched ruin that Tecuman held out to him. Even as he did so, the stone of the balcony gave, slumping and peeling away from the shattered wall. Asman lunged forwards, but his prince was already sliding away, one good eye finding his gaze as he fell. Asman could hear himself screaming, bellowing over the cries of the soldiers as they toppled away too, or clutched at the floor of the room, seared by the heat and carved by the stone.

And over it all, another thunderous retort, so that the whole of Tsokawan shook. *Seeds*, Tecuman had said. They fell from the ship above and grew death wherever they landed, cracking stone or belching fire. He could hear the assembled Estuary forces in their panic. If the Plague warriors were to come down now, then the Terror would tear through the whole army, hundreds lost in an eyeblink. Asman ran from the room, heading down, feeling the stones shift and shudder with each new blow, ordering every-one he saw to get out under the sky, for the stone would be no shelter.

He found Matsur and some of the other Serpent, and then some officers and courtiers, and then some of the Estuary chiefs found *him*, and everyone wanted to be told what to do. Asman's heart screamed *Tecuman would know*, but there was no Tecuman, and he could not even mourn his friend because he was needed. The Champion was a staff within him that kept him standing when he wanted to fall to the ground and howl his grief to the sky.

The seeds were still falling on Tsokawan, and as he watched a whole spire tore away, fire trailing from its windows like flags, collapsing down and then sloughing from the rest of the fortress, exposing the honeycomb of smashed floor and walls within. Some seeds had already fallen wide of the mark, beginning a blazing harvest of the close-packed Estuary forces, who were already fleeing into the trees.

So Asman cut out his own heart, or tried to. He gave clear, curt orders to any who would hear him. He had the chiefs scat-ter their people through the trees, to hide beneath the branches and make no grand targets for the death magic of the Plague People. He told them they must take their people up the river, by boat or on foot or Stepped. Tecumet was gathering the strength of Atahlan and the Tsotec's back. She would need them

177

all, and perhaps she would have a plan that could survive the fire and the broken stone.

And tell her that her brother is dead, but he could not say it. That task was for him alone.

They begged him to come, each one of them wanting a Champion at their side, but he told them he would be the last; he would stay until all ears had heard him. It sounded very brave but he just did not want to leave Tecuman behind.

The Boar were fleeing now. Their shadows slid sidelong, human and pig-shaped holes cut in moonlight, but as Shyri caught up, she saw them breed other shadows, thrown by another pale radiance. The Boar tried to break away from it, but always a set of cackling jaws lunged out of the dark at them, forcing them back on the path to oblivion. The mother had the worst of it, always slowest, always with the pack chewing at her heels, tearing at her robe.

Then the old man stopped running. He couldn't have been far from passing out of his human skin altogether, leaving age and infirmity behind to run with his mute brothers and forget he'd ever stood on two legs. He had been trying to keep pace with the woman, and his bristling hide bore a dozen nicks and grazes where the pack's teeth had chivvied him along. The woman stumbled and fell, then staggered back to her feet. One of the Hyena ran in front of her, trying to trip her again, and she wailed in rage and frustration. It brought the old man round, and though he had been a bag of bones as a man, he was burly and savage as a boar.

His tusks tore into the Hyena, ripping into her ribs until white bone showed through the red. The warrior Stepped briefly, screaming in pain and driving a bronze blade into his snout. Then she was hyena once more but with him rooting in her stomach, ripping free with her innards strung between the curved ivory blades of his tusks.

Effey was on him, Stepping to drive her spear into him and then vaulting over his shoulders, gashing his flank with her knife as he landed. He rounded on her, but she was already gone, and another of the pack lunged in to tear a strip off him, ripping through the tendons of his hindleg and crippling him.

Shyri watched and knew that none of the pack was watching her. They had someone even less fortunate to focus on. It was a good time to be the runt. She should be jostling for a place at the table, trying to get her teeth red to win Effey's approval.

No more. The thought of it bucked in her. Each time she bowed to Effey, she gave up more of the Hyena into the woman's keeping; each time her god became more Effey's god, defined however she wished.

And there was Effey, leisurely waiting to leap on the old Boar once he had been softened enough. More of the pack were driving the mother and the youth on towards the white walls, but Effey wanted her mouthful of flesh before returning to the chase.

She bunched to spring, eyes on the Boar as he faltered and sank to his knees, the trampled grass around him running with blood. Shyri left her treachery until the last possible moment, leaping out of the dark on hyena feet to Step just as Effey sprang, driving her blade into the woman, aiming to ram it up into her groin.

But Effey was quick – Shyri hadn't thought anything in her life right then would be that easy. The Hyena Malikah saw the movement and twitched aside, taking only a long shallow cut across her haunch. She was human when she landed, and for a moment she did not know what to make of Shyri, whether to kill her or applaud her for her boldness.

Then the cold part of her won out and she was crying out to her pack, calling them to heel because new game had presented itself. Her grin to Shyri was one of pure murder, but it sparked a jolt of connection too. The Hyena was suddenly in both of

180

them, and that was one too many right then. Before the night was out one of them would die.

Shyri matched her, grin for grin, and then turned tail and ran faster than she ever had before.

What happened to the rest of the Boar she never knew, nor did she care. Saving them was no part of her intent. Probably half the pack kept running them down, and for that service she was grateful for them. The other half were right on her heels, and none closer than Effey, whose breath she felt against her hide.

She dodged right, claws tearing at the dirt as she tried to gain distance. One of the pack was already there, trying to pen her in, but Shyri would not be penned. She threw herself right into the path of the flanking Hyena, Stepping for just as long as it took to put the bronze of her knife past the animal's eyes. The shock of it had the woman falling back from her on human feet, trying to defend herself from an attack that had never happened, while Shyri ran on.

She had that pale light at the edge of her eye, cutting a course across it but veering closer with each pounding pace. *It is like fire.* She was playing with something far too dangerous, which could reach out and consume her the moment she had its attention. What watch did the Plague set? Would the first she knew be a killing dart striking her down, or would it be the Terror . . .

But Effey was nipping at her again, heckling with glee whenever her teeth snapped on a tuft of Shyri's pelt. She had no fear in her, only the fierce spirit of the Hyena. Perhaps the Terror could not even touch her.

And now Shyri was leading her past the very footings of the white walls themselves. She saw, scuttling in the corner of her vision, spiders like the one they had slain, busy at their work. Yet there were no warriors, none of the Plague People themselves. The one time that anybody in the world might want to see one, they were all fast asleep in their beds. The cackling of hyenas beyond their walls meant nothing to them.

Then Effey's teeth closed on her, gashing at her haunches and failing to take hold by only a hair's breadth. Shyri yelped and tried for more speed, but the rest of the pack was outstripping her, closing off her path until it was them and the white wall and nowhere left save that narrowing path before her. She was running out of freedom, and when Effey caught her it would be no more runt, no more kicks and curses and menial duties. Nobody challenged the Malikah and lived to brag of it.

Her plan wasn't working. She could hear alien voices raised from within the compound, but none who had any time for her. She should have known that the Plague People were good for nobody, not even as executioners. She tried to break away, leaping for a gap and finding only bared teeth there that herded her back towards the walls. Effey was laughing as only a hyena can laugh.

I have made a bad job of this. But perhaps this was better. Let the Hyena see she was no whipped cur to be beaten and driven. *I fought the Hawk in the north; I fought Old Crocodile in the south. I will fight my sisters now.*

She made them think she had tripped and gone down, when she was just digging into the dirt to get purchase and turn about. Half the pack over-ran, speeding past and then kicking up dust as they tried to match her. She was already right under Effey's nose, though, the Malikah stumbling over Shyri as she tried to slow herself.

Shyri stepped and stabbed, in and out, not a mortal stroke but bloodying Effey's coat was reward enough. She tried to bolt, a hyena once more, but Effey snarled out her name and got an arm about her neck, ripping her back to her human form. They wrestled fiercely, and probably Effey could have cut her throat or carved out her kidneys, but she was determined to force Shyri's face into the dirt, to pin her to the ground and take out a proper revenge on her. Shyri was not cooperating, writhing and twisting in the other woman's grip. While she held her knife she tried to turn it about and get more of Effey's blood on it. After Effey slammed her hand into the ground to make her drop it, Shyri

182

snapped at her with human teeth, utterly unrepentant, utterly unwilling to give up. When at last Effey forced the side of her head to the earth, pinning Shyri's legs down with her own, she made do with curses. Every ill fate the Hyena ever visited on anyone was called down on Effey then, until the Malikah screamed at her and used both hands to grip her head and grind her face into the earth.

That left an arm suddenly unattended and Shyri found her knife somehow and tried to bury it in Effey's thigh.

Abruptly this was no longer a game that the Malikah enjoyed. With a sudden jerk she flipped Shyri onto her back, driving a knee into her victim's stomach to still the fight in her, if only for a breath.

She had her own knife out. The long death she wanted to inflict had been worn down into a quick one because Shyri would not be her prey and her patience had snapped at last.

Shyri stared past her, no eyes for the woman, none for the knife.

The Plague People did not care what two hyenas did, but human voices had brought them out. Shyri found herself repenting of her plan. A man hung in the air past Effey's shoulder, his shoulders glimmering in the darkness as his half-seen wings carried him over the walls.

Shyri was aware that the rest of the pack was fleeing. The Terror chased at their heels and must have caught the slowest of them. It washed past Effey and Shyri in an invisible tide, but for a moment the fire of the fight kept it off them, victor and victim both. Their eyes met.

The Hyena moved in them both, then, each to her own nature. Effey turned and leapt up at the newcomer. Shyri just stood and waited, feeling the Terror pile high over her like a mountain about to bury her.

Effey's voice got halfway through her warcry before it became a hyena's high whickering yelp. She was on four feet when she landed before the Plague warrior. The expression on his pale

183

face was revulsion, as though the very sight of a hyena, of any natural creature perhaps, was a horror to him. The rod in his hands snapped sharply and Effey – the beast that had been Effey – convulsed and died.

Shyri had no knife and she would not Step until the Terror made her take that shape for the last time, forever. She fought to stare defiance into the hollow face of the Plague Man. *I am Hyena; I will crack your bones!* But his bones were safe inside his skin and she had no way to get to them.

She did not see the wolf rush up behind the Plague warrior, but when it Stepped into the Champion of the north, vast enough to blot the stars, *that* she could not help but see. Maniye's great jaws closed on the Plague Man, rending his armour and his body with the sureness of iron. The Terror fled, leaving Shyri shaking with the realization that she was still herself and still alive.

There were more cries from within the Plague compound, and some at least sounded like pursuit. Shyri threw her arms about the reassuring hairy bulk of the Champion, released them from the wolf Maniye shrank down to, and then took to her own hyena paws to flee alongside her.

For a long time they fled wildly, the threat of wings always over-head, and Shyri was waiting for the Terror to catch up with her. She felt it nipping at her heels more than ever Effey had. She had sought to use the Plague People for her vengeance, and the thought made her sick to her soul. She deserved to have been overwhelmed by that fear. Who knows how many of the pack had been caught by it, or killed by the lethal darts of the Plague weapons?

But as she ran – with each loping step she took that did not rob her of her mind – she wondered about what Hyena thought. Because Hyena banned no weapons, nor any time for strife. Hyena was not a Riverlander, to build himself a tall chair and proclaim himself above the way of the world. Hyena knew everyone came to bones sooner or later. When the Aurochs had enslaved their mute brothers and brought the wrath of all the Plains down on them, Hyena had not stood back and said, *Enough spears are raised against them.* Hyena had taken his place at the carcass of that proud tribe and dragged off as much of it as he could to gnaw on. When the Horned Ones had raised their fortresses and built their Rat altars and killed one another, Hyena had not said, *We must save them from the vermin.* Hyena's people had gone to those places and faced down the Rat, one picker of ribs to another. When all the rest of the Plains had shrunk from it, Hyena had taken Rat's body in his jaws and shaken him until he gave up meat from his kills. And if the Rat, why not the Plague People? The world had many curses in it; Hyena survived them all.

Her mood lightened, and lightened more as they ran. It seemed to her that simply by living to see the dawn she had won Hyena's approval. Not won his blessing, but then Hyena blessed nobody – just like Maniye's Wolf god, as far as she could make out. Hyena laughed at everyone, but he smiled on those who survived.

In the morning, there were none of the Plague People to be seen above them or on their trail, and Shyri found herself grinning as fiercely as her god ever did. For a while Maniye just stared at her with a wolf's yellow eyes, but then she shook herself and Stepped, and a little of that Hyena grin crept onto her face as well.

'Why so happy?'

'You're alive,' Shyri said, the words surprising her even as she said them. 'I thought they had you. I told . . .' And then her words trailed off because a narrow green band was sliding from Maniye's human shoulders, looping halfway to the ground before it became a dark River girl with a covered head and rainbow scale tattoos. 'Her. I told her.'

'They had me,' Maniye confirmed. 'But I was freed.'

Shyri's grin faltered momentarily. 'I . . . I couldn't; not me, not into their camp . . .'

185

Maniye frowned at her. 'It's all right. You sent me Hesprec Essen Skese. Even the Plague People cannot stand against her.' She grinned wider at the Serpent's pained look. 'We live. We all live, all three of us.' And then a more sober look. 'What now, though? I fought with the Plains warriors, but the Terror struck them down. Where are my warband now? Did any live?'

'Tecumet's words are bringing together all the might of the river east of Atahlan,' Hesprec noted. 'The Plainsfolk who did not fight, or fought and lived, gather north of them. But when did Plains flow with River or River stand with Plains?'

'I met Asmander,' Shyri remarked. 'Asman, I mean. His mate couldn't stand him any more so she sent him to her brother.' For a moment Shyri's smile was braver than it needed to be. 'So, Many Tracks, how does the blood of Plague People taste to you now?' She let the question hang there, in her and Hesprec's expectant silences; saw Maniye understood what she meant. Shyri could not imagine what it was like, to be a prisoner within those white walls. Would anyone draw a knife against the Plague again, if they had been there? No shame in running, surely?

And Maniye did not leap to any grand declaration of eternal struggle with the enemy. She weighed the words and her own souls carefully. At last, her eyes flicked up to meet Shyri's.

'I know things of the Plague, now,' she said slowly. 'I have seen them live. I know their tribes and their habits, a little. If nothing else, I must speak what I know to someone wiser than me. For the rest . . . let me have time and distance, and the company of those with souls.'

Hesprec was thoughtful. 'There is one I would have you speak to. I have been a poor host to her, leaving her behind with Tecumet in my haste.' *My haste to find you* needed no saying. 'But she will interpret what you have seen better than any Serpent divination, I hope. Any knowledge of the Plague is a weapon.'

'So west along the river,' Maniye decided. 'Perhaps some of mine are with Tecumet as well.'

'West, and by boat if we can,' agreed Hesprec.

They made best time for the river, travelling by dark where they could, Hesprec like a loop of ribbon about Maniye's shoulders. When they came down towards the banks of the Tsotec they found no shortage of boats heading west, but it was not a sight they could take much joy in. The banks were jostling with warriors and Estuaryfolk of a dozen different tribes, all jumbled together. The water seethed with the backs of crocodiles, of turtles and toads; herons winged overhead. Every boat they saw was crammed, grim-faced men and women hanging from the rails until each vessel seemed on the point of foundering. Maniye, Hesprec and Shyri had no questions for them, no need to ask what it was they fled.

To the east, the floating ship of the Plague People was a dark shape coasting against the dawn's brightness. Beneath its lazy course were more boats, the stragglers of Tsokawan's warmuster. It was not the sunrise on the waters that blazed so brightly there. Where the shadow of the Plague Ship fell, boats burned and their crews turned to ash. The river itself was on fire.

* * *

Loud Thunder had wanted to take his fears to Mother, but doing so would mean airing them before Kailovela. And Mother would have no answers for him anyway, not because she didn't know but because she gave out her wisdom in her own time, and never on request.

So it was Thunder's problem to solve, just like everything seemed to be these days. Yellow Claw had gone dropping poison words into this ear or that, about the little monster who was Kailovela's own shadow these days, and how the thing's death would be a worthy gift to bring the gods of the Crown of the World south with them. The wise of the tribes had heard his venom, and each seen something there to recommend it.

So he had spoken long with Two Heads and Quiet When Loud and Empty Skin, the hollow Seal child who was often with

187

Kailovela and the little monster. Then he had declared that the Bear would offer a sacrifice, and let the word spread.

He had time to plan the place for his grand gesture. He found a rock that was hollowed out by water, a high lip on the side facing his audience, a sloping channel on the side towards himself. He found another rock, heavy enough that it took his two hands to lift, and a lesser man would barely have been able to roll it along the ground.

Meanwhile, the two Coyote had been busy.

That evening Thunder went to the open space he picked out, with the sunset at his back and a good number of warriors gathered to see what new foolishness he was taking up. Of course only Mother could really offer sacrifice to the Bear, and she would have no part of Thunder's ploy, no point even asking. She was there, though; perhaps Thunder's actions would be given vicarious power simply by her presence. It would have to be enough.

He waited until he saw the main voices in this mess were all present: Seven Mending, Aritchaka, Icefoot and a handful of other priests. And Yellow Claw, who should have been looking triumphant but was instead irritable and restless, as though he was missing something. He was not the only one.

Thunder let them wait there as he fussed with his dogs, scratching them under the jaw and telling them how good they were because he was still trying to get the words in the right order in his head. When he could delay no longer, he went over to the altar stone he had picked out. 'You want to shout to the gods, to make sure they know we're down here, then,' he started. Inauspicious words to begin a sacrifice and he saw the ripple of disquiet that went through them, but the Bear didn't care about formality and fancy phrasing, and neither did Thunder. He had a voice that carried to the furthest ear, which was all the gods could expect from him.

His eyes lit on Kailovela. The little monster was pressed close to her, like a near-grown child. Her taut features suggested she knew what demands had been placed on Thunder.

And Thunder would kill the empty creature in a heartbeat. He cared nothing for it; it was of his enemy, even if it had lifted no blade against him. He would throw it into the teeth of the Wolf, the maw of the Tiger, without hesitation – eagerly even. Except Kailovela valued it, as a pet, as a companion, as another pair of hands that had helped her when she was in need. And Thunder was about to defy every priest and maybe god, rather than take that from her.

'What do the gods hear?' he asked them all. 'Not just our voices, then? We've all been talking to the gods. I talk to the Bear. He doesn't listen to me, so it does no good, but I do it.'

The slightest murmur of laughter, despite everything. Everyone knew the Bear stories. Awake, Bear cared for nobody; asleep, he was so far from hearing that Coyote once removed his balls and replaced them with pine cones.

'So what will call to the gods and let them know what we're doing? Things that have value, things that are *us*. What do we give first, of those things?' Thunder scanned the crowd, terrified for a moment that Empty Skin wasn't even there. Then the Seal child was stepping forward, oblivious to the leery looks she got from the rest – everyone pitied Empty Skin; nobody liked her.

Thunder did not dare look down at his wide-planted feet. He felt movement at his ankles, but that part of the plan he must leave to more capable hands.

Empty Skin was holding something aloft – it was a fish as big as her hands, well worn, fashioned of whalebone and cut with scenes too delicate to make out. A toy, and who would make a fish as a toy save for the Seal? The easy sound of the crowd died to nothing staring at her: Empty Skin and the childhood the Plague People stole from her.

Wordlessly she held it out to Thunder, who placed it in the bowl of the altar and then, with great ceremony, heaved his big stone from the earth and up to his shoulder.

'Let the Seal know what has happened to his people,' he told them, no need to thunder now they were so quiet. He let a heartbeat go by, so everything was in readiness, and then lifted the stone above his head with a great cry, every eye on him. When he brought it down, the crash of rock on rock obliterated the sound of bone being crushed.

Empty Skin stood back, looking properly solemn about the whole business, and some of the others shuffled a bit, thinking it was done. The rest just watched. Enough of them had seen he had a heap of things piled beneath a cloak, half behind the altar rock.

What he had next was a bronze bowl, small enough to fit in the palm of one hand. It was fine work, the rim chased with beaten designs that suggested flames and smoke. 'So let the Tiger hear us,' Thunder called, holding it up and seeing Aritchaka and her people go still. How hard had they looked for this precious trinket, before finding it here in his grasp? Quiet When Loud reckoned from the smell that they kept oil in it, for their sacred smoky fires. 'Tiger, here is a thing of yours, dear to your heart,' Thunder thundered, and he placed it within the bowl of the altar and lifted up his hammer stone with a great cry. When he brought it down, he saw in their eyes the flinch as he hammered the thing flat.

There was a little goatskin bellows next, taken from Icefoot's own personal tools. The old Wolf priest actually stepped forward as though about to stop the sacrifice, but he bit down on his own protestations, though his eyes promised a reckoning. Then came a carved antler that one of the Deer wise women used for counting days, and then a Boar mask that was almost too big to go into the altar's bowl and disappear from sight while he held up his rock and roared, the muscles of his arms straining by now to heft its great weight.

By now every one of them was staring at him as though he was mad, but he was calling the gods to them, after all. It was a thing for madmen to do; these were mad times.

190

But he had saved the best to last, and anyone there who was counting must have realized that only the Eyrie had been spared his depredations. Yellow Claw knew, though. He knew what Thunder had taken, because he had been beating his underlings and cursing his women about its absence. Now Thunder kicked aside the cloak to expose the last prize that the Coyote had stolen away so stealthily.

The warriors of the Hawk went into battle with armour of bones, breastplates of ranked ribs that were about status as much as protection. When Yellow Claw and Loud Thunder had fought one another, Thunder had broken that armour, but Yellow Claw was Champion of the Eyrie. Of course he had a new set made, finer than the last. And it was beautiful indeed. The women of the Hawk had decorated it with beads and amber, painted it with wings and talons and the Hawk's staring eye. There was gold and copper and bronze worked in amongst the bones, turquoise and cat's eye and jet. So many hours, so many hands, to fashion such a thing.

'Hear us, Hawk! See where we are, so far from your roost!' Thunder cried, holding up the armour and enjoying himself just a little. 'Your sight is keen, but they tell me I must call you down, or else you would lose us in the vastness of the world.' He rolled the armour up and placed it in the hollow of the altar.

'Right, then,' he said, and went to lift up the rock, but then his dogs had finally got bored of sitting and wanted to investigate the bones. He had to shoo them away, and a ripple of nervous laughter went through everyone – not laughing at him, but laughing at Yellow Claw, who was tense as a bowstring and obviously about to leap in. It was not that he would lose his armour – his fingers hadn't made it, after all. It was that Loud Thunder was going to destroy it, right there in front of everyone. It would be shame, and Yellow Claw had already been shamed by Loud Thunder twice.

Then the dogs had been told off, and Thunder lifted the stone again. Yellow Claw twitched, but he could not say anything. Pride had him by one hand, shame the other and he was pulled tight between the two.

It was Seven Mending who spoke – the Owl priestess cared less about either emotion than her Champion. 'Enough,' she said.

'But, Hawk . . .' Loud Thunder kept the rock high, despite the burning in his arms.

'Enough. We cannot destroy the things that are of value to us, the things we *need*.' She had no expression and her eyes did not touch him, but he heard the concession in her voice. *You've made your point*, she meant.

'This is the gods' fight.' Five words and everyone was dead silent, dead still. Mother had spoken, and Thunder could only envy her instant command of them.

'Of course the gods are with us,' said she who ruled the Bear. 'Where else? The Plague People eat our world, wherever they go. You think they will not eat our gods? Of course they watch us. In the Godsland, they are running from the Plague as from a fire. They stand in our shadows even now.' She shook her head and gave Thunder a familiar look. *Why are you wasting everyone's time with this?* 'Go on then,' she told him, and he nudged Two Heads Talking where the Coyote priest crouched hidden behind the altar stone. He came up with the Tiger's bowl in his hands, and Quiet When Loud had the Deer antler. Each treasure, dropped into the altar's hollow, had been whisked out while all eyes had been on the raised rock, which Thunder now gratefully put down for his dogs to sniff disappointedly.

'Come get your things,' he said exhaustedly. 'Keep better hold of them.'

The priests themselves would not deign to, of course, but Eyriewomen came for the armour, a scrawny man of the Tiger for the bowl, and so on and so on until only Empty Skin was left. When she took the fish back she just looked at it curiously, then cast it aside. Whatever it had meant to her once had gone with the soul that had never come to her.

Thunder stayed there by the altar long after all the rest had gone save the Coyote, obscurely troubled. Quiet When Loud teased his dogs, then fed them scraps, while Two Heads Talking sat on the hollowed stone and looked up at him. 'You saw how they looked at you, of course,' he remarked.

Thunder made a vague noise deep in his throat.

'Bear takes from the tribes, but Coyote tricks Bear. You're making yourself into a story.'

'I don't want to.'

Two Heads sighed. 'You're asking them to travel half the world to fight the enemy of the gods. You'd better be a hero from the stories. Who'd follow a mere man, for that?'

18

Maniye's first sight of Galethea was almost too much. She was ushered into a tent in the midst of the sprawling River Nation camp and came face to face with human features without a soul behind them. Instantly the memories had come back: the reek of the trophy room, the cage, the children at their patient lessons. And the priest with his white eyes and grey face, who knew her and hated her as though it was *she* who had brought this horror to *him*.

She had Stepped to her tiger shape and yowled and cuffed at the creature, yet without wanting to touch her at all, then bolted outside. Hesprec had sat with her for a long span of heartbeats before she was ready to try again. Before she once again felt herself on solid ground, without her very identity constantly under attack from their Terror.

Their journey up the river had been in the company of Estuary warriors who had told of the fate of Tsokawan. The fortress was gone, the prince dead. Maniye thought of all the blood and ingenuity that had gone into saving Tecuman's life. Had he some destined role that would now go unfulfilled? She somehow felt that the Plague People erased destiny as they erased everything else.

Many people had told them that Asman was dead too. Shyri had taken the news with a tightened jaw and dry eyes. She had stopped her talk and her mockery and fallen into herself, clenching about the idea until Maniye felt that, had she touched the Laughing Girl, she would have been touching stone.

It was only when they were in sight of Tecumet's camp, with all its bright tents and bold flags, that Asman had found them – leaping in his Champion shape from the side of an overloaded boat, then coasting across the waters of the Tsotec on the leathery vanes of his winged form. He had landed before them, eyes wide and about to remark on the miraculous nature of their survival, and Shyri had attacked him. Not to kill, no knives or teeth, or he would have been a dead man, but kicking and punching and cursing his name every way the Plains knew how.

When she had done, the somewhat bruised Asman had looked down at her and said, 'On the River we just say we're glad to see our friends.'

'On the River you're all stupid,' Shyri had snapped, and Asman had agreed that, yes, probably that was so.

Now he had gone to tell Tecumet that her brother was dead and her eastern fortress lost, a story already running swift between the fires of the camp. Maniye had wanted to do many things. She wanted to go and find her friend Moon Eye, who was with Tecumet's Stone People Champion, Tchoche. She wanted to ask for any news of her warband that might come out of the chaos to the north. Most of all she wanted to sleep for two days and nights, but of all things that luxury would not be extended to her.

But Hesprec was politely insistent. She had explained what Galethea was, retold the tales of the Oldest Kingdom and the Pale Shadow People.

Galethea needed to hear what Maniye had seen. Hesprec had lived a long life collecting knowledge, and now she was faced with an enemy she could not understand. Perhaps the Pale Shadow could throw light on Maniye's experiences as a prisoner.

And so Maniye fought back her trembling. She found that part of her which feared, the last trace of that barb that had felt like a crippling wound in her. She called the Champion to her left side, the Tiger and the Wolf to her right, and told that fear: *I cannot indulge you. I am sorry.*

And she re-entered the tent, holding that part of herself tight in her hands to stop it running through her mind setting fires.

Galethea had a hollow face. It was pleasant enough, but she had exactly the same yawning hunger behind her that all the enemy did. And yet, as she sat there trying to be meek and unthreatening, she did something to herself. Maniye never saw her change, but heartbeat to heartbeat it was as though she painted herself, thicker and thicker layers over that pale face until she was beautiful and the hollowness was all but hidden.

It was Plague People magic, like their ephemeral wings, some way they drew upon the emptiness within. Such gifts! And yet Hesprec had said that the Pale Shadow would give it all up for a soul to stopper that hunger.

She sat with Galethea, listening to the woman ask questions in her accented speech, telling of all the madness she had seen. And she could see that so much of it meant nothing to the hollow woman. The flying ship with its fire, the killing rods and their invisible darts, even the different tribes of Plague People, all of it was either lost from the myths of the Pale Shadow, or else it had arisen after they fled their first home. And *that* was a strange thought: in the stories the Plague People were a force, forever waiting to devour the world, but a constant thing. Now it seemed that, in the long generations since they had lost their prey, they had been learning too.

Maniye studied Galethea as the woman spoke. Every so often the mask of humanity slipped, reminding her that she was sitting in a tent with a monster. And yet such a desperate monster, such an obliging one! *A monster that wants to be human.* The Plague People out there did not want to be human, Maniye decided.

Galethea agreed. 'They do not understand what it is. They do not understand there is any other way than their own. They look at you and see beasts.'

Maniye frowned at her.

196

'They were curious about you. They saw you Step but they do not know about souls, and what they mean. They could not understand you.'

Maniye thought about the two strange Plague People, the dark ones, and nodded cautiously.

'Tell me of the Terror,' Galethea prompted her, and so she did: how it felt in her, the way it affected others, the shield the Champion made that saved her.

'You were the first live human they ever saw,' Galethea identified. 'All the rest were corpses and animals driven mindless by the fear of them. And so in their minds they were fighting animals. And that is an easy thing for those without souls, who do not have . . . mute brothers?'

Maniye nodded. *So when the Plague People die, they're just . . . gone? No rebirth, no Godsland.* Looking into Galethea's deceptive eyes she thought she saw the truth buried deep there. *The Pale Shadow know. Another reason they are so greedy for souls of their own.*

'You must have baffled them,' the pale woman said in a small voice. 'They couldn't have known what you were. Perhaps it will make them think.'

Abruptly Maniye shook her head. 'Not the first human – the children, remember. What did they want with the children?'

Galethea opened her mouth and then shut it again. Maniye could almost see the thoughts moving behind her eyes. At last she said, 'I think they wanted to save them.'

'What?'

'We have children,' the Pale Shadow woman said. 'Do not think we don't have children of our own, and care for them. And so the Plague People came with their Terror, and they found deserted villages and maddened beasts, and children. Children who had no souls yet, and so children just like their children back in their home across the sea. What would they do?'

'Kill them, if they hate us so much.' But Maniye faltered in saying it. Except for the white-eyed priest, she had not felt hate from her captors. She would have welcomed hate; she would have understood it. Instead she had met with . . . not even incomprehension, but a failure to see there was anything to comprehend. The Plague People were obliterating her world without ever realizing what they crushed beneath their feet.

And the children they took would grow up without souls, and become more of the Plague People, and Galethea was saying that they would see this as some great kindness.

Abruptly she felt sick and could not stay in the tent any longer.

She woke next morning, fighting the blanket, waiting for the leaden weight of the Terror to descend on her. The sun against the cotton of the tent was light shining on her through pale shadows, and any moment the two dark Plague People would walk in and demand she Step for them. And it was worse now, because in some small way she understood. They wanted her to Step because they were trying to understand. They were trying to understand how it was she could take their shape, when she was just a beast to them.

But then a cool hand touched her, and became the dry scales of a serpent that wound herself about Maniye's arm. She froze, and for a long time just let Hesprec lay her little head upon the back of her hand, the slightest of weights, but no less comforting for that. She was no longer a prisoner. Her friend had come for her.

Later, when she was ready, she went to stand before the Kasra of the Sun River Nation, Tecumet in all her masked finery. Asman stood beside her, looking grim. Last night he would have given Tecumet the news of the twin wounds: her brother and her country. There were lines of small dark bruises across his face, and Maniye stared at them blankly before seeing them as the dents of teeth, where the Stepped Tecumet in her grief had taken her mate in her jaws. A testament to the Kasra's self-control, that she had gone so far and yet hauled herself from the brink.

Esumit, the Kasra's chief priestess, spoke for her, praising the Champion of the Crown of the World's victory over the Plague People, even as she praised Tecuman for defeating the enemy at Chumatla. No word was spoken about the sequel to that battle. The prince's victory was left to stand unchallenged. And so it should, Maniye knew. Travelling upriver, she had spoken to those who had fought there. She had heard version after version of that battle, each more lurid than the last, but the skill of the strategy and the courage of the fighters had shone through.

Beside the throne, fat Tchoche the Stone Man slouched, bedecked in the massive weight of his bronze armour. Maniye had fought the man before; Stepped, he was a monster, savage beyond the dreams of wolves and tigers. Her former follower Moon Eye sat at the man's feet, looking calmer than ever she had known. The Champions of the Stone Kingdoms knew a lot about putting a leash on rage.

'The Kasra asks what you will do now?' Esumit asked, and Maniye started.

Maniye could not remember how she was supposed to address Tecumet, or even who to speak to. 'I . . .' she said, feeling hollow as the enemy, not an idea inside her. *Help me*, she asked her souls.

The Champion rose within her. As so often, it knew what was right. 'I will go north to where the Plainsmen are. I hear there is a great gathering of them. I will tell them what I know of the Plague People. I will try to find my warband, if any yet lives of it. I will fight the enemy.'

Tecumet's mask nodded ponderously, and Esumit said, 'None would think any less of you if you thought your part in the war done, but the Daybreak Throne is not surprised. Your Champion soul will be proud of you.'

Maniye forced herself to nod back. She did not feel anything worthy of pride. She felt as though her Champion soul was a crutch, without which she would collapse.

'Will you travel alone, or would you go with my own emissaries to the Plains?' Esumit asked, for Tecumet. 'For I will march my own soldiers north soon enough, and I must prepare the path for them lest the Plainsfolk think we are their enemies still, and not their friends.'

'Will you send Asmand—Asman?' Maniye asked. Abruptly she wanted that very much. The company of another Champion would be very welcome indeed.

She saw Tecumet's beringed hands twist, her shoulders hunch within the heavy robe. Esumit was nodding sagely though. 'The Kasrani's presence will show our good faith. This is no time for mistrust between allies.'

Maniye confirmed that Asman's presence would be very welcome, and then shuffled aside so the next petitioner could stand before the Kasra, some clan chief come to boast of the spears he had brought. Released from the mask's august glower, Maniye backed away to the tent's entrance and then turned to leave.

She came face to face with a small man, half his face painted in stark black patterns, the other half plain. He was bare chested, his woollen tunic tied about his waist because it was too hot to wear in the southern heat, even with the breeze from the river.

She stared at him, heart hammering. He looked just as startled, regarding her with first one eye, then the other.

'Feeds on Dreams,' she named him.

'Many Tracks,' he returned. And here he was, the least reliable, the most troublesome of all her warband, but alive still. Here he was, with word from the north where some of her followers yet lived.

* * *

'I don't want to leave you here,' Asman said. Idly, he rubbed at the bruises left by Tecumet's teeth. He didn't begrudge her. Her reaction to the news of Tecuman's death had matched his own. She had Stepped on the instant, grief too much for a human frame to contain. When her jaws had closed on him, he had felt it the most perfect expression of their shared feelings.

200

'I don't want you to go.' They were both in Tecumet's tent, the regalia of the Kasra set aside for another day. She sat on her furs, wearing nothing but her shift, the cool air making the hairs prick up on her arms and neck. 'But I am facing the deed every Kasra before me has wished to do, and turned back from. I am leading all the River's spears into the Plains. If I arrive unheralded then the Plague People will find only the corpses of both sides.'

'There are others you could send,' he said, without conviction. 'The Serpent.'

'Oh, at least *one* of the Serpent will be with you,' Tecumet said, shaking her head. 'And too clever even for her fellows, that one. You have not spoken with the creature she brought from the south. Esumit does not know what to make of any of it. But the Plainsfolk never honoured Serpent's priests.'

'Nor will they honour me.'

'Oh, they will. A Champion and the Kasrani both,' Tecumet said bitterly. 'And coming to them with but a handful, barely a warband. Why else would I send you into their jaws unless I was sincere.' She spat. 'I feel like your father, to use you so. And yes, some other might serve, but you *will* serve. I must give my nation the best of chances.'

He sat beside her and she leant into him, huddling against him as he put his arms about her. The sounds of the camp were loud all around them, night notwithstanding, and yet that great murmur of humanity seemed tiny and fragile, somehow, against the greater backdrop of the empty dark.

Asman woke before dawn, hearing careful movement outside the flap of the tent. In an instant he had leapt from beside Tecumet, standing on the Champion's sickle-taloned feet within the stillness of the tent, imagining a hundred different enemies waiting outside in the grey light.

It was Tchoche's voice that sounded, though, a man simultaneously quiet enough to be deferential and loud enough to wake a sleeper. 'A messenger for the Kasrani, so.'

Regaining his human shape Asman ducked down to drag a robe about him, then stepped out into the chill.

Tchoche stood there with a handful of his Stone Men, Tecumet's bodyguard: stocky, ruddy warriors clad in heavy bronze. In their midst was an emaciated ash-skinned man wearing nothing but a loincloth, his body showing a life of poor meals and more than one whipping.

'Who's this?' Asman asked softly.

'Oloumec, so he says he is,' Tchoche replied, drawing Asman a little way from the tent. 'A slave, is also what he says, and bearer of a gift from his master, beyond those two things.'

Asman studied the man, guessing him for a Salt Eater, one of the island people who braved the sea north-east of the Estuary. Their land was little more than rocks amidst the spray and they lived off fish and madness, according to most. They had come in answer to Tecuman's muster, but this was none of their warriors.

'Who is your master?' he demanded.

'None, once you take my gift from me.' Oloumec's voice was harsh and cracked. 'I came all the way up the river a slave. I shall go home a free man.'

'Your gift is not given yet,' Asman pointed out, jabbing a finger at the leather bag Oloumec cradled in both hands. 'Who is your master?'

A smile that was at least three parts madness spread over the Salt Eater's face. 'He's here. I brought him.' He lifted up the bag, then flinched as one of the Stone Men snarled at him.

Asman's patience came to a ragged end. Lunging forwards he snatched the burden from the man and pulled open the thongs. One look inside was enough to confirm his suspicions. Salt; salt and a human head already wizened and dried.

'Someone doesn't know me very well, if this is what they send me,' he remarked, showing Tchoche.

'So it's your master's head you're bringing us?' Tecumet's Champion asked. 'Is this counted a good idea, among the Salt Eaters?'

'No,' Oloumec whispered. 'But among the Dragon, yes.'

Asman froze. 'You come from the Dragon Isles?'

'I was the slave of Gupmet,' Oloumec whispered, 'Gupmet who sat upon the Whalebone Seat and ruled the Black Teeth, greatest of all the tribes of the Dragon. I sat at his feet for many years and looked up to him. And then I carried him in a bag, and when I opened it up, he looked up to me.' He grinned, terrified, exhilarated. 'You'd know, *he* said. You'd know what the gift meant.' It was obvious that *he* was not the unlamented Gupmet.

Asman fought to still his racing heart. 'Is he coming? Will he fight?'

Oloumec's bony shoulders shrugged, slightly out of time with each other. 'It's what the Dragon do, isn't it? He spoke to my master's mate and won her over, and then he gave me my master's head, and he said you would know. Any questions, ask them of yourself.'

'It's a lot of teeth you're showing there,' Tchoche observed, 'for a man holding a head in a sack.'

But Asman let himself grin, because the Plague People were ending the world but at least Venat was on his way.

19

The dry warmth of the Plains was easier to bear Stepped than in human form, and easier at night than during the height of the day. It got hotter further south, so Loud Thunder was told by the Horse who were with them. He didn't want to think about that. Their tales of the River Tsotec and the Patient Ones who basked on its banks could remain mere stories as far as he was concerned.

They had left their own river, the Sand Pearl. Owls, Hawks and Ravens, and even the secretive messengers of the Bat had flown back and forth, scouting for where the Plainsfolk were. Not straight south, for certain. Not in any of the lands around Where the Fords Meet, or the lands west of that, or the lands west of that. There were signs of battle, bodies left for the hyena and the vulture, and there were abandoned villages.

At last one of the Crow caught sight of a great gathering of Plainsfolk and came back to correct their course.

'Are they mustering for a fight?' Thunder asked the man, suddenly worried that all this might be for nothing; that they would be too late.

'I did not see so many spears,' the Crow said, staring at the Bear from the painted half of his face. 'Many tired people. Too many. Everyone has fled the Plague.'

'Who can blame them?' But the thought gnawed at Thunder as they pressed on. He knew what contact with the Plague People could do. They were well named – not a disease of the body but of the spirit. They sickened the land wherever they set foot. They festered in the imagination. The Plains warriors had been fighting them for longer than anyone. What would be left of them?

He wanted to take counsel, but Two Heads and Quiet When Loud were asleep atop one of the travois the Horse were pulling, having been scouting about, or at least getting into unseen mischief, all day. He could not speak to Mother about it, because he feared that look of hers that was like being beaten with a stick for not knowing the answers. Who else, then? He was only impressed with his willpower, which let him at least exhaust the obvious alternatives before he went to seek out Kailovela.

He sought her in Mother's shadow, but found only Empty Skin and the little monster there, and Kailovela's cloak of feathers. Empty Skin held the baby, cradling the sleeping child with an eerie stillness that made Thunder think uncomfortably of death.

'She flies,' the Seal girl explained. 'I could see the wanting in her. I offered.' She looked down at the child in her arms, and Thunder reckoned that the little monster had more affection on its face than Empty Skin could muster.

'That was kind of you,' he rumbled.

Skin shrugged. 'You want her to be happy. I want her to be happy. Even *she* does.' A nod at the diminutive monster. 'It's strange, isn't it?'

Thunder shrugged, not thinking it was strange for *him*, at least. He knew exactly where his longings lay. But then Empty Skin snickered at him.

'You think it's your man-parts that want her,' she said. For a moment she was trying to leer, the expression horribly wrong on her normally bland face.

'What I think and what I want is none of yours,' Thunder snapped.

'Everyone wants her,' Empty Skin went on blithely. 'Good people want her to be happy. The rest want her to be theirs.

You're half and halfways. But it's strange, don't you think? She's not *that* pretty.'

Thunder looked up, trying to spot a hovering hawk against the stars. *A hawk flying by the moon.* But then it was a time for unnatural things. If the end of the world couldn't have a few good harbingers, what was the point of it?

Hawks were not night-fliers. In the Eyrie, the night was left to the Owl while the Hawk ruled all under the sun and the Crow picked at the boundaries.

But Kailovela hadn't had much of a chance to go and see the sun. Her flight to Thunder's cave had only come about after his great battle with her mate Yellow Claw. Even then, wings spread and bearing her unborn child away from the war host and the Bear's Mother, she had flown in his shadow. But at least she had flown.

She didn't know what to do with Thunder. He wasn't going away; nor was he pushing at her to become his – and how could she have refused the war leader of the Crown of the World? He just stood too close and looked too long and could not really help either of those things. She was run ragged waiting for his restraint to break. Thunder had taken it upon himself to be her protector against all the things of the world, but that left nobody to protect her against Loud Thunder.

When she flew, it didn't matter. With the cool night air coursing beneath her wings she could pretend there were no chains holding her to the ground. In all her life she had never been allowed freedom like this; in all the world perhaps no other Eyriewoman had such liberty. She could shed the weights life had hung her with, the expectations of the Eyrie, Thunder's wounded love and Claw's barbed love. Her child.

For whole breaths and heartbeats, here above the Plains, she could forget her child.

She was not the only woman carrying a baby towards the battle. More than a few of the warriors had their family along.

Some of those warriors were women. Even the Coyote, Quiet When Loud, had a child within her belly. Life went on, even at the end of the world.

She could not talk to any of them. She could not tell them what gnawed at her when she held her child to her breast or rocked him to sleep. They would see it as a vindication of all the Eyrie ways, that she who had slighted Hawk had been cursed like this. She could look upon her child's face and feel no instant wave of love binding the two of them together. In her mind she could tell herself, *this is mine*, but the other part of her, the deep physical part that let the mother wolf know her cubs, the hawk her chicks, it did not move within her.

He is no less my son, she told herself. Part of her wanted to believe that it was because she had never wanted the child – a burden forced on her by the warrior Yellow Claw had killed to possess her. And that dead warrior had himself killed the child his predecessor had planted in her, in the rough business of taking her from her previous mate. Small wonder that the result of their union had come into her arms without touching her. She could tell herself that she was saving her love for a child of her choosing.

Except she knew it was not true. No need to consult a priest, not that she would have dared. What she lacked did not recognize logic or reason. It was simply an absent part of her, a missing piece of hide from a robe or a tent, where only the cold came through.

I will fight for you, she told the child she had left in Empty Skin's arms, as she winged her way overhead. *You are mine and I will give you everything I can wrest from the world*. And yet she stood at the brink of a chasm, and she could not call forth that natural automatic love to bridge it. Her thoughts loved; her heart was cold.

And now she was chained again, her thoughts moving inescapably back to that vulnerable mote of life she had left behind.

207

In that moment she hated her son, because otherwise she could just fly away.

Even as the decision was clawing at her, a greater shadow sailed between her and the moon. For a frozen moment she thought it was the flying ship of the Plague People the warriors had spoken of, crept silently up to cast some blight down upon the war host. But no: something even less welcome had come to share the sky with her.

In his Champion's form, the great eagle, Yellow Claw's wingspan was five times her own. He filled the sky like weather, yet was nimble as a sparrow. He had been flying all his life, while she had only been chained to her human shape.

He swung low over her, as though buffeted by a breeze. She knew he was in total control of every feather, even when he made himself clumsy to menace her. His hooked talons flicked at her and she lost twenty feet of height, falling away from him before she recovered from his touch. He followed effortlessly, backing his wings for a moment until he almost stood still in the air before lazily recovering himself. She banked left and right but he was always there between her and the moonlight. Never a subtle man, was Yellow Claw. *You will always be in my shadow.*

Even though she had been about to descend, rebellion flared in her and she fought him – not claw to claw, but trying to find a way past the shade of his wings like a bird trapped in a tent and battering at the least hint of light. There was no out-flying the Champion of the Eyrie though, and now she felt the strain of it. Alone, she could have flown forever, but the mere presence of Yellow Claw seemed to sap her strength and her will until there was nothing for it but to circle down and down, seeking out the snaking line of the war host as it trekked its way across the empty Plains landscape.

For a moment, she seemed to see a shimmer in the earth they trod on, as though the whole strength of the Crown of the World walked a road that gleamed with rainbow scales. She stared, and the colours faded, until she was seeing nothing more than the first grey tints of dawn. Then she was down in a flurry of wings, feeling the great leaden weight of the ground recapture her. Overhead, Yellow Claw shrieked in mean triumph, his work done. She Stepped and became human again, not meeting the gazes of the Wolf warband passing her.

Two days later, an emissary came to Loud Thunder.

She had come down at dawn in an undignified battering of great black wings, narrowly avoiding Mother's shoulder – which roost would not have gone well for her. She had ended up clutching for the edge of the palanquin, a huge dark bird with a bald head and neck and a hooked beak. Until she Stepped, Thunder had not even known there was a Vulture tribe upon the Plains. Certainly the Eyriemen didn't seem pleased to be sharing the sky with more carrion-eaters.

Because the sun was already starting to bake the earth and the air, Thunder called a halt and the various parts of his host broke away and began to set up their separate camps. Today, Lone Mountain had challenged all comers to wrestle, and that would be a spectacle to keep this band of enemies from one another's throats for another sunrise.

Thunder went and sat before Mother, the two Coyote on his left hand and on his right the Tiger priestess Aritchaka, because she had been close by. 'What's this, then?' he demanded of the Vulture.

She was not what he would have looked for in an ambassador. Human, she seemed more hunched than ever the bird had been, and the robes she wore were tattered and multi-layered, as though she never replaced them, just threw new garments over the top of the old. Her name was Yaffel.

'What's this?' she asked, staring pop-eyed about her at the war host. 'What's this, you ask me? "What's this" is what they send me to find out. A hundred and five hundred spears come out of the north!'

Loud Thunder had to stop and think through that, before

answering. He came to the conclusion that he honestly hadn't thought how it would look to the Plainsfolk when a war host descended on them from the north.

'If we're here to fight, where does that leave you?' Aritchaka put in, unhelpfully.

'Dead.'Yaffel shrugged. 'No meat on my bones for you proud hunters. I'm ready to pass on under Vulture's wings anyway.'

'We're not here to fight,' Thunder said, and then, because that was palpably untrue, 'not here to fight *you*. Our enemies are everyone's enemies. We come to fight the Plague People.'

Yaffel made a hacking sound in her throat that might have been a laugh. 'Oh my, yes. Fight *them*, yes.'

'We fought them in the north. We won,' Thunder told her.

'Truth?' A little light came to Yaffel's eye with that. She looked from face to face, hunting out any deception, and then her gaze drifted to the spreading mass of the war host making its camp.

'We are coming to where the Plains people gather,' Aritchaka declared. 'Will we find warriors there?'

The Vulture ducked her head. 'Some, some,' she muttered, but she did not seem enthusiastic about it.

Nearing the Plains camp, Thunder realized his inner picture of it had been hopelessly inadequate. He had seen something like the rest stops of his warband, all the tribes neatly separated out and ready to move on or take up arms at a moment's notice. He had thought that this gathering of the Plains was *for* war, not simply heaped together *because* of it. This was no assembly that the Plainsfolk had ever sought or planned.

He could not count how many of them there were. He simply did not have words for the numbers involved. The advance of the Plague People had killed countless of the Plainsfolk – had obliterated entire tribes, even – but everyone not killed had fled. Some had fled south, some had fled further west or gone to find relatives in other tribes who might take them in – to flee again, if those relatives were in the path of the Plague. But far too many had come here.

The wind was at Thunder's back as he came close, but every time it wavered he caught the stench of too many people too close together. He smelled sickness,waste and sweat and spoiled food and . . . *people*, a great olfactory wall built up by those for whom everything else had been torn down. *How can they live like this?* was his instant thought, but the answer ran close on its heels, *Nobody who had any choice would live like this. Nobody wants to be here.*

There was some structure to the camp, he could see – some bigger tents, some cleared spaces. Those of the Eyrie who had flown over it said there were storehouses under fierce guard, constantly besieged by crowds of the hungry come to claim their meagre due. Thunder wondered how any human effort could feed so many, and now he came to the outskirts of the camp he could see that such efforts were failing. Plenty of those he saw here looked as though they had not eaten for days. He could count the ribs on them, no matter what shape they took. And there were more women than men, and the majority of those he saw were old or very young, or hearth-keepers whose hands had surely never held a spear.

'What now?' he asked aloud, feeling the great line of the war host pile up behind him.

Thankfully, Two Heads Talking was at his elbow. 'We should make our camp with some clear ground between us,' the Coyote suggested. 'They're looking at us as if we're here to steal what-ever the Plague left them. Then get the old bird woman to find some leader here, so they know why we've come.'

* * *

The Iron Wolves had put themselves outside one of the grain stores, lazing about in their Stepped shapes under the hot sun, growling at anyone they didn't know. They were still strange enough that most of the Plainsfolk gave them a wide berth,

211

despite their hunger. A couple of Lions and a Hyena had tried their bronze knives against the Wolves' iron skins, and the lesson had been well learned.

Kalameshli Takes Iron had already found a corner of the sprawling Plains camp to make his own. He had fenced it off with sticks, like a child's idea of a wall, and then he had ordered the Wolves to go find him good stones. Just because he was far from home and probably in no good odour with the Wolf didn't mean that proper religion just stopped.

They all thought he would pile up rocks in the vague shape of a dog-head and call it an altar of the Wolf, but he had been about something more important than that. Kalameshli had built a forge. It was not a good forge, and of course they had none of the twice-burned wolf-wood here in this dry land with too few trees. He did what he could with dried dung to stoke the flames, even so. He could not have drawn iron from the earth with it, nor tempered that iron into something strong enough to be used, but he could mend a few things, put his tools to use and pretend that the stinking air from the fire was the Wolf's breath. When he was beating his hammer on his little anvil, the others knew not to disturb him. And of all the people who should not disturb him, Feeds on Dreams headed the list. Kalameshli was no fool: the Crow's wings brought him news that nobody else could. But at all other times he was a babble of nonsense, and Kalameshli's rage at interruption ensured he would only ever see the man when word of real import was on the wind. Like now, apparently.

'They're here!' Feeds got out, even as Takes Iron rounded on him. The old priest's heart jumped. 'Maniye? Many Tracks is here?'

'No, no, no, *them*!' the Crow got out, withered a little under his glower, and visibly ordered his thoughts. 'Eyriemen, Wolves, Bears, everyone!' he managed. 'Hundreds from the north all come to fight the Plague, they say,' Feeds said with excitement.

'Who leads them?'

'Biggest Bear I ever saw,' Feeds reported dutifully.

212

Kalameshli wagered he knew who *that* must be, but the thought of that oaf *leading* anyone was . . .

'Well,' he said, half to himself, 'it's the end of the world, after all. Spear Catcher!'

'Hoi!' A moment later, a big wolf bounded into sight and Stepped to the old warrior in his iron-hair shirt.

'Find me someone else to waste their lives in front of this store,' Takes Iron told him. 'What about those Stone Men who came in yesterday – they looked well fed enough. Have them do some work for a change.' Seeing the unasked question on Spear Catcher's scarred face, he added, 'We have some old friends to meet.'

Feeds on Dreams stayed around the Iron Wolves until it was plain they had settled in with the other northerners for the duration, talking over what was going on in the crowded, stinking, desperate Plains camp. It was all very distressing, if you thought about it, but Feeds was extremely good at not thinking about anything save in hindsight. For him, the camp was a constant source of surprise and adventure.

Adventure needed someone to share it with, though. What point creeping through the sacred places of the Wild Dogs or stealing bead necklaces from the Hyena unless someone was there to see? And so Feeds took his friend, whistling softly for her and letting her trot at his heels as he headed back into the camp.

Sathewe was his friend, and she was a coyote. Once she had been Coyote, but then she had followed him one place too many, and Feeds on Dreams had found another helping of someone else's ruined life served up for him. He didn't mean it; he never meant it. But people always told him, 'Just think about what you're doing; just ask yourself if it's a good idea,' and somehow, in the moment, he never could. His mind was like a fly in a jar, all the motion in the world and no direction at all.

But Sathewe was still his friend, even though she couldn't talk

213

to him or laugh at him any more. She still knew him, and she knew the warband and stayed with them, rather than running off into the tall grass of the Plains. Perhaps, if they went north, she would go and find a pack to make mischief with, but here she stayed with people whose shapes she recognized. Most of all she stayed with him.

He talked to her, as they scurried through the winding back ways between tents and fires and bedrolls. There was a great mass of people here, of tribes he had never seen before. They had fascinating customs to watch, fascinating trinkets to play with. And they would chase him away when they found him, but he could fly and Sathewe had nimble paws.

Sometimes, surrounded by the wounded, the starving, the despairing, Feeds had to work very hard on not thinking about it all. Most of his mind cared nothing but for the next toy or diversion, the next wild idea for a game. Usually he could jeer down the little bit of him that understood the way others saw the world. He had to work hard at it here though.

It was not the hunger – just enough hard bread and dried fish was coming from the River, just enough weak beer and water from tribes to the west, that everyone's belly rumbled but only the weakest died. Feeds on Dreams had gone hungry himself – long nights with nothing but dreams indeed to fill his belly. The north was as hard as the Plains, just in a different way. Everyone starved sometimes. What threatened to break through to him was the sheer defeated misery. Everyone here had seen the Plague People or heard those who had. Everyone had lost their toys and tools; everyone had been driven from their homes; most had some friend or relative unaccounted for, or dead, or locked away in their Stepped form like Sathewe. But it was more even than that. Something was stalking the camp on sightless legs, not the Plague People but the shadow they cast. Nothing could live in that shadow. That was the truth Feeds worked so hard to ignore. Where that shadow was cast, there were no tribes or villages, no Stepping, no gods, no dancing or singing, no ritual, nothing of

214

all of the people of the world. There were only hollow human-seeming bodies without souls, building their webby little villages without any understanding. The Plainsfolk in the camp had seen their lives wiped away, like lines in the dust before a broom.

But Feeds' ability to ignore the world was truly vast, and boredom was a greater terror to him than the Plague People, and so he skipped off with Sathewe anyway to go and make trouble, following the little coyote as she sniffed and yipped her way through the broken lives of the Plainsfolk.

When she stopped, at first he thought she was just tired. After that he tried to invent a dozen other reasons she might abruptly have her tail between her legs and her head low, when there was no Kalameshli there actually telling them both off.

At last, though, he crouched down with her and tried to understand what she had seen or smelled or heard. Sathewe had never known fear for longer than it took to escape a threat. That had been why they were so well matched. When the Terror of the Plague People had caught her, she had not been able to escape fast enough, but even as a coyote she was bold and swift and careless. He often thought her soul was right behind her eyes, right at the back of her tongue – that any moment he would turn and see the skinny Coyote girl there, not the starved-looking animal. If anyone could find their way back from the Terror it would be Sathewe.

But now she was scared, and yet she fixed him with a look and he knew she was tracking something and wanted him to see it.

She led him to a tiny tent, just an awning held up by sticks and twine, like a child might build. It was tucked away at the back of a Boar tribe camp, hidden in the shadow of a lean-to where too many families crouched listlessly, talking in low voices.

There was little to see, though Sathewe growled at it, almost too soft to hear. Feeds saw some feathers and some bones – tiny ones. Something had been burned there, some minuscule offering. Officiating over it all, like the world's smallest priest, was a skull that would fit in the palm of his hand.

Feeds fought it, but the world seeped in anyway, sending a cold streak down his spine and twisting his bowels. He knew what this was. Not often it was seen, in the Crown of the World – especially not in the high reaches of the Eyrie that was his home – but everyone knew the stories. Everyone knew the one god who had no tribe, no people, but was always scratching about for the lost and the disaffected, to make them his own. And where better than here, to foster a nasty little cult of despair and picked bones? Someone had been invoking the Rat.

20

They made as swift time as they could. Galethea would have slowed them – she had no fleet shape to take on, nor would Maniye ever have consented to carry her. Tecumet had thought of this, as she thought of everything. Galethea rode, shrouded and cowled against the sun and against curious eyes. Those few Plains-dwellers who came close must have found them a strange sight: a lean woman without an inch of skin exposed to the sun, riding a Horse Society steed badly enough that the beast was constantly kept in place by a wolf and a hyena and the warning hiss of Asman's Swift Lizard Champion. Behind, a score of River Lord warriors kept up a punishing pace on foot, for the whole of the Sun River Nation could spare few mounts now the Horse Society had fallen.

The thought made Maniye shudder. What if the beast Galethea rode had been human once, had spoken and known and loved? Asman swore it was from the stables the Horse kept at Atahlan, but as far as Maniye was concerned there were no certainties any more. She had left a Horse youth at Where the Fords Meet, Alladai, who was lost and gone with the rest of his kin. For all she knew, some Plague warrior had a saddle on Alladai's back or had him drawing a load, no more than a beast of burden.

Hesprec kept her sane. Sometimes the little Serpent priest was a comforting pressure looped about Maniye's wolf ribs. At other times Maniye let her Champion out to prowl, and Hesprec rode on her shoulders like some tiny queen of the world. Hesprec said they needed Galethea. Maniye could not tell if she trusted the pale woman or if she was just keeping a close eye on her, but the two of them had walked a long enough road together that Maniye would follow her lead.

Feeds on Dreams flew over twice, Stepping to remark on how little ground they had covered, and how he'd told the warband she would be there already. Maniye reached inside herself each time, to see how she felt about rejoining them. They were her people; they had followed her as far south as she had ever dreamt the world went. But because she was their leader, they would expect her to lead them.

She flinched a little from the thought. She had failed them before, and the thought of being taken by the Plague Men, dragged back under their pall of fear, before their cold curiosity, was a dread to her. *But I am their Champion. I have no choice.*

Today she expected to see Feeds circling over them as though waiting for them to die, but he was absent. A worm of unease started turning in her, thinking that perhaps they were too slow, too late. Had the Plague come to the Plains camp already? Or had he just forgotten, as he was wont to do?

Towards day's end, though, she could make out a great shadow on the land that must be the camp. There was smoke there, but from cookfires, not from desolation. She almost fancied she could hear them, such a great gathering of humanity. Had it not been for the others she might have blithely assumed that such throngs were the normal business of the Plains – after all, she had heard of Atahlan and its many thousands, so why not here? Shyri was dumbstruck by it, though, shaken to her very core.

'Oh,' the Laughing Girl whispered. 'Not a good place, that. A dying place.'

'What's that?' Asman asked her.

'In the Hyena stories, in the hard times, he finds where the people of other tribes go. They gather together and they gnaw at each other, great chains of the hungry, until there's nothing left but carrion, and Hyena calls his people to . . .' She twitched and grimaced. 'Anyway, some of our stories. We have others. But *that* is a dying place.'

'That is an army,' Asman decided, but his voice lacked conviction.

'What about that?' Maniye Stepped to point at a great mound out to the east, its near side painted bright by the sunset. Her eyes tried to make it a rock, and then a hill, but at last the regular contours of it brought home that human hands had raised it, though not recently.

'Horn-Bearer fort,' Shyri said shortly. 'They're all over the Plains. From when they were many,' and then, an unnecessary addition, 'from when they were alive.'

'It looks strong,' Maniye said. 'Why aren't your people there, ready to defend it? Surely the Plague can't be far.' She heard her own voice catch a little, and hated the fear in it.

Shyri stared at her. 'Didn't help the Horn-Bearers. You don't know that story, truly?'

'How many north-stories do you know?' Hesprec pointed out.

They Stepped to make the most of the daylight. When Shyri shook out her blanket she stared off towards the great mound of the fort. 'My people tell their story the way it should be told, but there is a place for it. To tell it elsewhere calls to their ghosts, and nobody wants that. Say just that they were strong and that they feared. They went mad behind their walls. They sealed themselves away and never came out.'

Maniye digested that. 'And they're waiting in there, to come out and fight one last battle?'

Shyri cackled. 'Oh no, Many Tracks. We know the death that came to the Horn-Bearers. We of the Laughing Men know that most of all. We stole into the shadow of their forts after they were all dead. We know what tasted the meat of the Horn-Bearers.' She gave the words such a sepulchral edge that Maniye wanted to hear no more. In the dark, the great bulk of the fort seemed to loom larger and larger, until Maniye could not tell whether it was clouds that blotted the stars, or the haunted stones of the Horn-Bearers.

The next day they reached the outskirts of the camp that seemed to be growing and spreading even as they came to it. Ragged little bands of Plainsfolk were still arriving, carrying what they could, and few enough looked like complete families. Confronted with that great tangled snarl of humanity, Maniye and the others stopped, unwilling to just plunge in and be lost beneath its surface. It seemed impossible that they would ever find a familiar face in the midst of it all.

Then Feeds on Dreams was flying over them, low enough that Asman could have reached up and plucked a feather from his wings. He croaked out a welcome and then Stepped, dropping down into their midst.

'What's this?' Shyri demanded of him. 'This is going to fight the Plague?' as though it was his fault. She spoke loud enough to be heard by everyone around, and Maniye looked for an angry response in those nearest, but they just looked away. Everyone here looked so worn out and thin, as though, if you held them up to the sun, the light would shine through. The thought put her uneasily in mind of the hollowness of the enemy.

Feeds cocked his head at the Laughing Girl. 'Others fought,' he said simply. 'These lived.' His tone made no judgements, because Feeds' criteria for good and bad were different from sane people's, but the meaning came through anyway.

Asman needed to find some leadership within the great sea of people. Feeds claimed he could help. There was some council of chiefs or elders trying to accomplish something, he said. Shyri would dog Asman's footsteps, no doubt, and Hesprec would need to bring her pale guest to them and try to explain why the creature should not be killed out of hand. And Maniye . . .

She took a deep breath. 'Takes Iron and the warband,' she said to the Crow. 'Show me to them.'

She had expected to find just the bare bones of her people – the priest and whoever had survived of her band of followers – huddled miserably round a fire like an island of the north in the midst of all these Plainsfolk. They would look up at her, and she would read the demand in their eyes, that she somehow turn the world on its head and lead them to certain victory. Each step she took at Feeds' heels was slower, until he had to stop and wait, stop and wait, hopping from foot to foot impatiently.

Then there was a yip, and a stick-thin little creature bounded past the Crow and jumped up at Maniye. For a moment she could not understand who it was, because no coyote ever behaved so like a tame dog before. But it was Sathewe, who plainly knew her still. Maniye felt a deeper stab of pain, seeing her. *All my failures.* She had let the Coyote girl down, and then later she had let all her warband down, leading them into fear and death and gaining nothing.

But Sathewe yipped and danced; Maniye could see the girl so clearly in the eyes of the beast, her soul so bright there. She knelt down and put a hand on the coyote's head.

'Many Tracks . . . ?' Feeds on Dreams asked.

She was waiting for the Champion to just loom within her mind and magically dispel all her sour memories, her knowledge of her own fear and failings. She wanted to go before her warband cleansed of what had gone before, pure and worthy of them. Except the Champion slumbered at the back of her mind and she hesitated at the threshold. She had been given some small time when she need not be Many Tracks at all, just Maniye, as she used to be. Now that time was done.

She looked up, mouth open ready to deny them all. She would go. She would vanish into this huge maze of tents and camps and bodies.

Feeds seemed to cast a vast shadow, enough to block out the

sun. A moment later she reinterpreted what she was seeing, and leapt to her feet. Behind the Crow stood the biggest man she had ever seen, and a friend.

'Loud Thunder!' And abruptly all the dark clouds fell away from her, seeing him there: his slightly bewildered smile, the awkward way he had of standing that was a futile attempt to seem smaller. Even his dogs were at his heels as she remembered, staring suspiciously at Sathewe.

She ran to him and tried to throw her arms around him, but there was always too much of him for that.

'The Crow kept saying you were here,' he said, shaking his head. 'But you know how it is with him. He'll say anything.'

And there were more surprises in store for her. She followed Thunder's heavy tread to a camp much grander than she had been expecting. By then she understood that the Bear had brought a grand war host down from the Crown of the World, and it sat close by the Plainsfolk camp even now. There were plenty of visitors at her warband's fire, come to swap tales of the north. When Maniye walked in, a cheer went up that must have sparked a panic through all the neighbouring camps. She looked around her, seeing faces from what seemed like a lifetime ago. Each one of her band came to greet her, eager to re-swear their fealty to her. Where was all the blame she had been waiting for?

But here was one face who surely had some criticism for her. Kalameshli Takes Iron, standing back and waiting for the others to get it out of their system. No effusive welcomes from the Wolf's strictest priest. She looked into his leathery features, almost desperate for the condemnation she knew she deserved.

But she knew him too well now. Behind that harsh mask she saw the relief of a father whose daughter had come home.

It was too much, but she could not simply go and find somewhere quiet. All eyes were on her. She had to play the leader even if she wanted anything but.

'What welcome is this?' she announced to them. 'No salt, no meat? What sort of guest do you make me?' And they laughed at that, and Amelak scrambled to find her some token of hospitality so that things were done properly, and Maniye felt that the role of leader was like a cloak, shielding her from them, so that she could be with them and not be overwhelmed.

And there were others at the fire, too, Thunder's people. There was a pair of Coyote, and a limping old Wolf priest who had come to speak with Kalameshli, and there was one other.

Maniye felt the sight of him like a blow, like a spear going through her. He was a tall man, coppery like a Plains-dweller but with different features, angular and long-limbed. But he was handsome, still, and she remembered how kind he had been, when they first met up in the trading post on the Sand Pearl. He was Alladai of the Horse Society, and she had known him for dead the moment she had seen what the Plague had done to his home. And yet here he was.

Breathing was hard, abruptly, talking harder, but he seemed to understand that and just sat beside her and ate a little while she gathered herself.

He had been in the north, he said. When the Plague came to Where the Fords Meet, Alladai and an expedition of his fellows had been upriver. His family was gone, his hand-father and the rest, but he lived. He was glad to see her. He was here.

That was what finally let her move on and accept that the world would let her heal. She had no precise words for what she felt for Alladai, but all the colours in her world were brighter now she knew he lived, the fire warmer, the food had more savour.

For the first time in a long, long while she let herself relax and be safe.

She spent the next day hearing all their stories of what had happened since their parting, and then hearing Loud Thunder's own tales of how the Crown of the World had changed since she left it. When he told her how they had driven the Plague People from the Seal coast she dared to feel a stab of hope. Thunder talked dolefully about how that fight had gone – how many had died,

223

even though they had attacked by surprise out of a blizzard; how many of the Plague People had survived to fight another day.

'And yet here you are,' she pointed out. 'You brought all these spears to the Plains.'

'Because they must be stopped, and even though we are strong, we are not strong enough on our own,' Thunder said. 'You say the Riverlanders are sending soldiers, and there are Plains warriors who will bare a tooth still, and there are Stone Men come down from wherever they live. And it must be enough.'

Maniye nodded, but she was thinking of all she had seen of the enemy. *They will not care,* she thought. *Their killing darts will not care, and their flying fire-ship. And the fear will not stop, for all our numbers.*

'What if it is the end of the world?' she asked him.

Loud Thunder shrugged massively. 'I don't know. Are we supposed to do things differently if it is?'

Towards evening Hesprec sent to them. There would be a gathering of chiefs and the wise. Thunder and Maniye should both be there.

She felt like neither a chief nor one of the wise, but once she reached the heart of the camp and saw the assembly there, it didn't matter. It seemed that anyone who felt they had something to say had come, a great jumbled mass of priests and warriors, old women, young men, every tribe in the Plains rubbing shoulders uncomfortably, side by side.

Hesprec found them – no real art to spotting Loud Thunder in a crowd, after all. The Serpent priest led them over to where Shyri sat watching the proceedings with her Laughing Man sneer fully on show.

'What is this for?' Maniye asked.

'For making talk and nothing else,' Shyri told her.

'Words can heal, if you let them,' Hesprec said mildly. 'The Plains is bleeding. Here they try and staunch that wound. They need hope. Thunder, you can speak, tell them of your victory.'

He grunted, nodding reluctantly. 'If they will listen.'

'And Many Tracks . . . ?'

'I have only just found enough hope for me,' she said. 'I have none to spare for them.'

'That is not how hope works,' Hesprec pointed out.

'And will you tell them of Galethea? Do you see hope in her?' Maniye needled.

'I do.' Hesprec paused. 'But I don't know what I will make of her yet. So I will say nothing.'

'What is Galethea?' Thunder wanted to know.

'A long story, and a difficult one.' Hesprec shrugged. 'Later. Not here.'

Maniye tried to follow what was being said at the gathering. There were chiefs of the Plains tribes speaking, one after another, giving numbers of warriors they had which surely must have been exaggerations, trying to outdo one another. Then someone else would speak to say that some new village was gone, just gone, the Plague taken it. Perhaps some had fled and lived, perhaps not. And the boldness would go out of those chiefs with the warriors they might or might not have, and the mood of the crowd would waver again.

Then Asman got up to address them; Maniye hadn't even realized he was present at the council. The Champion was burning high within him – enough that everyone listened rather than talking over each other the way they had. For a moment she thought the River Lord youth would make some great sweeping speech and suddenly everyone in the Plains camp would have a knife in their hands ready to run off and throw themselves into the Terror of the Plague people. Asman was no great speaker, though. The greatness of his soul bottled itself up in the awkwardness of his words. 'We have fought them; we have won,' he said, but everyone there had heard about Tsokawan by then; the fortress's name was a susurration back and forth across the crowd. 'What else is there?' he demanded of them. 'The Sun River Nation is sending its soldiers, every one that can be spared.

The strength of the Tsotec and the Estuary both are coming to fight the Plague People with you!' And abruptly it was as though the Champion had his tongue and spoke through him, eloquence beyond anything he could normally boast. 'River spears coming to the Plains! No new story, I know. But you never saw so many spears as my Kasra is mustering right now. And for once we're not here to burn some village of yours, not here because you came and burned one of ours! Who would ever have thought the day would come when the north bank of the Tsotec was crossed in peace?'

And a little ripple of laughter eddied about them; Maniye saw heads lifted, saw the Plainsfolk re-evaluate Asman even as he mocked himself. 'I will not say the Plague People will drop dead to see so many spears! I will not say they are just a dream, and waking together will rid us of them. You've fought them; I've fought them; the northerners have fought them. We all know the cost. We know what they are, the horror of them.' And his voice had grown quieter and quieter, and so had his audience, to hear him. 'We know this; so we know they must be fought. Or there is nothing.'

Then one of the Plains Boar chiefs was standing, an old man who must have been huge with muscle when he was young, but had been hollowed out by age until only a cadaverous hulk was left. 'I believe we should go west,' the Boar said, fatigue in every word. 'The east is lost to them, but how far can they go? How much land can they use?'

A Lion stood, shouting down other voices to spit out, 'They don't *use* land! They just want to kill us all. And if you don't fight, then there isn't enough west you can travel, to save you from them!'

And even that's a lie we tell ourselves, Maniye thought, though she could never have said so to the crowd. *They don't even want to kill us, not like that.*

So many of the Plainsfolk clearly wanted the Boar chief to be right, no matter the evidence. They had fought the Plague People twice, three times, some of them. They had lost and lost, braved that withering fear and cast their lives and homes into it. They had so little left.

Hesprec was on her feet. Maniye had seen her quell a battle south of the River, but the Plainsfolk lacked that reverence for the Serpent, and none marked her. More and more voices rose in argument, as Asman stared about him in frustration. Impossible that anyone be heard now.

Except there was one. One thin old Plainsman, standing very still and wrapped in a blanket that had been brightly coloured once and was now just dust and loose threads. He stood so still that silence fell from him in waves, until when he raised his trembling voice, everyone heard him.

'There *is* a way,' he said, and all ears were ready for it. By Maniye's side, Hesprec had gone very still.

'There is one voice not heard from,' the starveling old man told them. 'One voice that you have all refused to hear. But there is a way.'

'No, no, no . . .' Hesprec whispered, and Stepped, vanishing amongst the bodies pressed around them, a fine thread of a serpent weaving between them. Maniye blinked, looking around in bafflement, surprising a predatory stare from Shyri as she looked at the old man. She could see Asman was blank too, but amongst the Plainsfolk she sensed a shared understanding, a name nobody spoke.

'The Plague People do not come to kill you,' the old man quavered. 'They do not come to raise their animals on your land, to take your treasure or make slaves of you.' A cracked titter of laughter escaped him, high and weirdly horrifying. 'They come to *undo* you. They come to replace you like you never were, and wipe you from the land. How will you fight that, River man? Will you stab it with a spear? Will you cut it with your stone-tooth sword? But there is a way, oh yes. There has *always* been a way. You tell your stories of Owl and Bat and Serpent, but you do not

227

say the other who stood against the Plague People, the *fourth* brother.'

'There is no fourth brother!' Asman snapped, and Maniye was of the same opinion, but the Plainsfolk had different stories perhaps.

'You cannot drive the Plague back by making war on it. List your great victories, and tell me what they have achieved. Some handful in the north, a stone tower fallen in the south? And all the while they grow strong and stronger. All the while more of them, for they come across the sea, and across the sea there are untold thousands of them, pressed closer together than you are now, like maggots in a wound.

'But there is one who will gnaw even hollow bones.' Again that weird, tittering laugh that seemed to come from no part of his throat or mouth. 'There is one who will visit such horror on the Plague People that they will flee to their boats and know our land is cursed for them, and never return. There is one who will devour their stores and starve them, who will bring plague to the Plague People and sicken them. There is one who will eat their dead and their living and leave nothing for them. There is one who will do all of this, if you give him the power.'

'*No!*' And Hesprec was abruptly right in front of the old man, shouting up at him. 'Not even in the face of the Plague. There is no place for you here.'

Serpent-swift, she lunged forward and ripped away the blanket from the old man's shoulders. Beneath, he was naked; beneath, he was skeletal, a body gone past the point of starvation. Maniye saw lithe grey shadows skitter across his hollowed flesh and flee out into the crowd, prompting panicked cries wherever they vanished. The old man's jaws gaped impossibly wide and a sleek, slick rat forced itself through them, so large that there was surely no room for tongue or teeth. For a moment it balanced there, staring down at the crowd in bristling contempt. Then Hesprec threw her hand towards it and Stepped, fingers becoming a snake's jaws that seized on the rodent and ripped it loose. A

228

widening circle formed, and Loud Thunder pushed his way to its edge with Maniye in his wake.

By the time they arrived, Hesprec was in her human form again, holding the dead rat by its tail. Beside her, the old man was not simply a corpse, but a body that should have been still and dead days before.

21

'There were never four brothers,' Hesprec said, after they had retreated to Asman's camp. There were already a surprising number of River Lords in amongst the Plainsfolk. Many had come with caravans of grain hauled from the stores at Atahlan, a gesture of friendship that said more than any number of spears. And still it was not enough for all those who had been forced to flee their homes, leaving their harvests and their stores behind them.

Now, the little knot of them huddled in the tent they had given over hurriedly for their Kasrani's use. Nobody had even asked the question, but Hesprec apparently felt the need to argue it.

'The lie is that when the Plague People drove us from The Place Where We Were,' she continued, 'the Rat and its people stayed behind to fight, and that is why the Rat has no tribe now, no human bodies for its souls.'

'I never heard this,' Asman said diplomatically, and if he had not, certainly Maniye and Loud Thunder hadn't. Only Shyri nodded, hearing a tale twice-told.

'You never heard it because it is a *lie*,' Hesprec said, her young face making her look sulky at having to speak the words, for all nobody was drawing them from her but herself. 'The Rat has no tribe because the Rat devours all. When we first came to this land, so the story goes, the Rat seized on the fear and suffering of the people, refugees as we all were in those days, and grew fat and had many followers. And even now, nobody from the desert south to the icy north builds a house without keeping the stocks out of the reach of vermin – yes, and the sleeping places too, if they have any sense. Or did you think the mounds of the Wolf and the stilts of the Horse were just to make them look grander?' Her face twisted, an old, old bitterness on such young features. 'No, the Rat came close to ending us before we began on these shores, and the Rat has never gone away – a god without worshippers, but a god who whispers in every ear come times of hardship and privation. A god that answers desperate prayers.'

'I . . .' Maniye almost thought twice, but pressed on. 'Years ago, when I was more of a child than I am now, I made an altar of rat bones. Because I was desperate, living under the hand of Stone River and Takes Iron. I was looking for something outside the tribe that could lend me strength.'

'Some strengths nobody needs,' Shyri murmured.

'I . . . felt that something answered, when I made that thing. So I smashed it and scattered the pieces.'

Hesprec gave a grunt of satisfaction. 'And found your own path out of your difficulties, as the Wolf teaches. You owe the Rat nothing. But there is always someone to open that door. The Rat comes to the starving and sends them to taste the flesh of their kin. The Rat promises a new world of power to those who slaughter the last of their cattle and spoil the last of their stores. But he has never been strong in the north – too cold even for him, up there. And along the River, well, there is nothing better for killing rats than a Serpent.'

'But we know him in the Plains,' Shyri put in.

'You do indeed.' Hesprec nodded grimly. 'And the Stone People remember him still.'

'We have seen their ruins,' Asman agreed, sharing a look with the Laughing Girl.

'Their Old Kingdom, which had silos overflowing with corn and roots, where the meanest labourer wore bronze at wrist and ankle and the kings wore gold,' Hesprec said, her intonation almost dreamy, one who has witnessed grandeur lifetimes ago. 'And they grew great, and could not imagine a limit to their power, and then seven dry years came together, and their wells parched, and their fields turned to dust, and in the deep, dark fastnesses of their stone halls strange priests appeared and whispered to them of a way they might preserve their majesty: the Rat Speakers. The Stone People did not make that mistake again. After they had fled their old cities and what swarmed there, they cast aside their enmities and opened their doors to the Serpent. But on the Plains it has been different.'

Shyri scowled. 'We always fought the Rat.'

'The Laughing Men did, yes. Because you frequent his places of bones and death. You met Rat's eyes too often over the carrion not to know his game. But the Plains – they do not fight all the time, like the River Lords claim. But when the Plainsfolk truly go to war, it is to lay waste to all – livestock, harvest and store. And so the Rat has always had a foothold and an ear to whisper in. More tribes have starved and died in the Plains than in all the other lands together, and the Rat has gnawed the bones of every one.' Hesprec took a deep breath. 'But since the Horn Bearers fell, I had not looked to hear another Rat Speaker stand before me and make demands, and I should have. Of course the Plague People are just another opportunity for the Rat.'

Maniye went back to her warband with much to think of. She sat with Spear Catcher and Takes Iron and warned them of this new threat, trusting they would pass it on to the rest. By then she was tired – not the healthy tired of a day well spent, but that leaching tiredness that crept through all the days since the Plague People took her, the memory of wounds and cages. Her body wanted to curl up and hunt dreams but her mind ran swift and forever like a mountain stream. With the camp growing quieter around her, she stood and stared up at the sky – crystal clear, speckled and banded with the stars. She could find most of the constellations she knew from childhood, save for those which

232

were northernmost in the sky. No doubt there were southern stars she did not know, which the Plains and the River people had new names for.

The thought brought back to her the sky above the Godsland, where the stars were in constant motion against the wall of the heavens trying to find a way in. *Are they the Plague People, those stars?* The thought seemed right, and yet not quite right.

I don't think we can win this war. Her distant ancestors had fled from the Plague People, back in the first days. Everyone knew those legends, yet the stories had nothing to say about floating ships or monstrous roaring metal boats, or rods that sent killing darts as swift as thought. *The Plague People have been busy, and we could not even fight them the first time.*

Abruptly she was trembling. Not fear for herself, not fear for her friends or her people even. Fear for all of it, all the ways of the Wolf and the Tiger, the Plainsfolk, the River Lords' over-complicated lives, all the stories and histories, how to propitiate gods, the memories of ancestors, the souls passing from body to body. Everything that made all the people *people*. She had spent her life hating and fighting and resenting, and yet there had always been that safety net: *if I die, I am reborn. If I die, life goes on, the cycle turns, and I will hear these stories again and walk these lands.* And if the Plague People could not be stopped there would be no stories and none who knew the ways of the land, not ever again. They would be gone and the Plague People would never know what was lost.

She held herself and shook, the thought like a knife in her and tears on her cheeks. Then someone was close behind her and she leapt away.

But it was just Alladai of the Horse, come to find her on a clear, chill night.

He spoke her name, both of her names. She forgot, when he was not there, how much she liked looking at him. He was so tall! She could rest her head against his chest, feel the strength there that had never been made to fight or kill anyone. *I will fight the*

233

Plague People, she thought. *I have to; who else will protect you, Alladai?*

She knew a few of her people marked her, when she took him to her bed. Sathewe lifted her coyote head and seemed to grin, and Amelak stirred where she slept, and probably woke enough to see what was up and smile a little to herself. And probably Takes Iron disapproved mightily, but that just showed that some parts of the world were still working the way they should.

She woke to the sound of an old woman wailing, the thin, high sound just going on and on, without any apparent need for breath. Beside her, Alladai was sitting up, very still. She heard the warband rousing, but beyond them, a greater furore, many voices asking questions of one another, and a growing turmoil of answers erupting in the midst of it all.

She Stepped, becoming the tiger that knew the night better than the wolf. The sight of her, flowing like embers and shadow through their midst, brought knives to the hand of more than one of her Wolves before they remembered.

Outside she knew she was seeing only the start of something. Most of the camp was still asleep, just waking enough to know something was wrong. But news was jumping from tent to tent like fire. Soon everything would blaze with it.

What has the Rat done? Hesprec's words of the evening before were loud in her mind. Surely only a half-eaten old man was the least of it. She prowled at the edge of her warband's little territory, wanting to rush out and hunt the word down, but knowing it would likely spread here while her back was turned.

Then a hyena's eyes gleamed at her out of the night, and a moment later Shyri was there, breathing heavily from weaving past so many confused people.

'What is it?' Maniye demanded of her, from tiger to woman even as the words formed in her mouth.

'They've been seen – near!' Shyri's eyes were wide, white all around them.

234

'The Rat?'

'The Plague People!'

Maniye's heart clenched and she stared at the Hyena. 'But how?' she got out, fighting to undo the knowledge, to change the world. And yet she knew how swift the Plague could spread. The wind had blown from the east and carried them in like seeds. And where they landed, they would sprout.

'We have to fight them,' she said, not because her heart meant it but because she knew it was right.

Shyri's expression was bleak. 'We who? You and your people? Three Boar here, two Lions there?'

'Loud Thunder and his people.'

'I think they're fighting already – or the Plague People attacked them first, maybe. Impossible to know what's real and what's shadow right now,' Shyri complained.

'Feeds! Where are you, Crow? I need you!' Maniye called, and then again until the dishevelled creature was before her, hopping anxiously and wearing no more than a blanket.

'Go to Thunder. Find out what's going on. Stay well clear of—'

'Yes–yes, I will,' he promised her. There was a lot of fear on the air tonight; even Feeds had caught a breath of it and was being serious. Moments later he was just black wings vanishing into the black sky.

Maniye turned to see Alladai behind her.

'You're safe,' she told him flatly.

'My people,' he said.

'No, just stay here, with us,' Maniye said. 'We'll find out what's going on.' His people were with Thunder's, of course.

She saw his soul kick in him, hauling him towards the rest of the herd. She saw him master it. When he nodded it was him forcing himself to trust her, and give his choices over to her. The faith of her warband had never shaken her so much as Alladai's trust. But then, worst come to worst, they could fight.

'Some nonsense is starting up over there.' Abruptly Kalameshli

235

was at her shoulder, shrugging his armour shirt on over bare skin. 'Get your iron on, child.'

She scowled at him, eight years old again just for a moment, and then she nodded. 'Bring it to me,' she said, craning to see what the closest shouting was. Her stature defeated her and she Stepped to the Champion, apologizing for using its greater height for such menial tasks. Reared onto her hind legs she would have dwarfed Loud Thunder's bear, as she looked past heads and tents to see some kind of half-ordered gathering there – a handful of Plainsfolk shouting orders to the rest, bringing them to their feet with weapons in hand.

At last. She Stepped back so Kalameshli could dress her, helping the iron links over her head, and then she pushed forward, the Champion once more, shouldering effortlessly through the roiling crowd until she could hear what was said and who was shouting. She knew one of them instantly – the Lioness Reshappa, who had fought alongside Grass Shadow and Maniye herself in that first, fateful battle. There were two others, a Boar and a Wild Dog, and they were going through camps striking people with sticks and calling on them to arm themselves.

Maniye pushed on until they saw her, and she could add the weight of her presence to their demands. Already there seemed quite a crowd of armed Plainsfolk here, and surely other bands were gathering elsewhere – not the warriors of any given tribe, just whoever was within earshot and could take up a spear.

'On, now!' Reshappa was shouting. 'On to defend your children! On for revenge for the dead we've lost! On for the blood of the enemy!'

But then a new voice spoke up, thin and piercing like a dagger-blade. 'You cannot kill what they are with spears!' it shrieked. 'You cannot kill it with tooth or claw! Bring war against the Plague as you would against your neighbour and you will die a thing that does not know its enemy, nor even its kin!' A haggard woman staggered through the crowd, arms thrown out, and the warriors fell back from her as though a single touch would damn

236

them. 'You cannot fight the Plague People with knives and arrows! You must fight them like you fight a fire.'

'Shut her up!' Reshappa bellowed, but though she raised her hand she would not strike the woman – another Rat Speaker, Maniye realized. The ragged robe the creature wore was rippling with a constant skittering motion. Maniye felt that laying a hand on her would transfer that burden of hidden vermin to her, and then perhaps the Rat words would be tumbling from her own jaws.

'You fight a fire with a greater fire!' the Rat Speaker screeched. 'You starve it. You burn all before it until it has nothing to sustain it. You fear the Rat, you brave warriors? Then you should let your enemy fear the Rat more. Clean hands will not wipe out the stain of the Plague People from our lands!' She shrieked out an appalling laugh, as shrill as if all the rodents about her had suddenly chorused it. 'Come to the Rat. Become his weapons against the Plague. Come feed the Rat to make him strong, to make him your Champion!'

Maniye was ready for the crowd to scoff, to throw stones or beat the woman out of their camp, but she saw plenty of fear in their eyes, and more than fear in some. Some of them had a kind of hunger to them. What had the world promised them that was better than this? What else was there, but the total extinction that Maniye herself had been contemplating? In that moment she felt the tug of it, the unspeakable appeal the Rat words held. *An end to worry. An end to loss.*

She was about to speak, to shout down the gaunt creature, but the Rat held her one heartbeat too long and someone else took her place. A shudder went through the Rat Speaker as though all those unseen rodents leapt all at once, and then the woman's grimy skin was ashen in the firelight. She tottered, mouth gaping but no more Rat words rushing forth, and then she fell. In her place, Stepping up from the shape of a viper on the ground, was Hesprec.

'For the gods' sake, make some *order*!' the Serpent woman demanded. 'I have been stilling the Rat's voice from fire to fire.'

'The Plague is here, River girl!' Reshappa shouted at her.

'Yes, yes it is!' Hesprec shot back. 'The Seven Tusks and the Torch Rock are out there trying to fight them, while you listen to the Rat here at your fires!' Her voice swelled to take in everyone nearby. 'The northerners are attacked even now. Ready your spears and bows! And have those who cannot fight leave their fires and go west, or would you have them here when the Plague arrives?'

Reshappa and her helpers went to the work with a will, trying to carve some semblance of order from a great mass of newly woken and terrified people. Hesprec shuddered and took a deep breath. Only now did Maniye see how tired she was.

'I have sunk my teeth into three Rat Speakers already,' she said.

'Messenger!' Asman bounded up. 'I've followed a trail of bodies, when I followed you.'

'This isn't the last,' Hesprec told him. 'Listen to me, Asman, Kasrani. Gather your people. You must keep my guest safe.'

For a moment Maniye couldn't understand who she meant, but then she remembered: *Galethea*.

'The hollow creature?' Asman demanded. 'Surely there are more—'

'No.' Hesprec's tone brooked no argument. 'Keep her safe. We have no more like her. I do not want to stand somewhere in ten days' time and say "If only we still had her." Go, keep her safe.'

'Where *is* safe? The whole camp's gone mad with fear. It's like a dam bursting out there!' That Asman would speak to a Serpent priest that way showed just how far he'd been pushed already.

'Take her to Loud Thunder and hope his shadow is big enough,' Hesprec told him. 'Go now, Champion.' When Shyri made to run after him, the Serpent priest caught at her arm. 'Not you. I need allies against the Rat, and Hyena are next best after Serpent.'

'I'm not yours, Snake,' Shyri snapped, but she stayed, eyes on Asman's disappearing back.

238

Maniye Stepped to stand tall and look around again. There were little islands of spears forming, scattered across the camp, but the great bulk of the people – all those who had fled the Plague and then fled it again – had no mind for fighting yet another doomed battle. She saw men and women snatching up whatever they could and fleeing, trying to push past others fleeing a different way. She saw children on shoulders and in arms, screaming with a fear they could not understand. Here an old man was knocked down, falling underfoot; here two women fought, Stepping into the shape of lions to snarl and cuff at each other.

She understood them. She wanted to rail and curse and decry them as cowards, but she felt the same fear within her. If she had not played host to a Champion's soul she would be running too. And the words of the Rat echoed in her head, surely spoken from a score of borrowed throats this night: you cannot fight the Plague as you would your neighbour. Not spears, not knives, not courage, not hope. None of these things would prevail against the Plague People.

'Many Tracks!' Feeds pushed up close enough that she almost stood on him, Kalameshli behind him. 'Many Tracks, Loud Thunder's people have fought. Some dead, some . . .' His hands clutched the air for a word which described what the Terror did. 'The Bear says he will go fight when the Plainsmen are ready.'

They will not be ready, Maniye thought. *Not this night.* She fell back down into her human shape, insignificant against all the confusion around her. 'The warband must go to him,' she decided. 'Bring all the Plains warriors they can. Spear Catcher?'

'Here.'

'Gather every spear, *every* spear you can find. Tell every warrior they must go to where Thunder is camped.' She looked around, feeling the fear rush in now she did not have the Champion's mass of flesh and thick hide to keep it out. 'No grand battle tonight, Spear Catcher. But there are far too many here who cannot fight and can barely run.'

'I understand.' And then Spear Catcher was off to round up the warband. She felt a sudden stab of worry for him, and it leapt to her thoughts of Alladai, and then everyone, everyone she knew.

She looked around for Hesprec – surely the Serpent would know what to do. After a moment she spotted her – the River girl was kneeling, hands to the ground; for a moment Maniye thought someone had struck her, but then she straightened up, a determined look on her face. *She has touched the Serpent's back,* Maniye thought. *She is hunting where the Rat has touched.*

Hesprec turned to her, about to give some order that would set all the world to rights and tie it all together with the wisdom of the Serpent, but before she could speak, someone slammed into her, knocking her off her feet. In the general panic, Maniye thought it must be mere accident, but then three or four ragged figures had leapt from the crowd onto her. One had a cord about the Serpent girl's throat even as the others wrestled with her limbs. Close by, another rake-thin figure rose up, hands lifted to the oblivious heavens. 'Hear me, and put down your spears and knives!'

Shyri had thrown herself onto the bundle of struggling figures around Hesprec and came away with one of them, hyena jaws closing on a thin arm with an audible crunch of bone. The others were already pulling their prize away, seeming to rush through the crowd with impossible speed, as though beneath them was nothing but a carpet of rodents bearing them in and out of the stamping feet. Kalameshli surprised Maniye by lunging past her, jaws snapping at their vanishing heels, and then the three of them were rushing, pushing, threatening and shouting their way through the press of humanity, hearing the crazed voices of the Rat Speakers rising on all sides.

And they were heading east, Maniye knew. When the camp suddenly began to thin out around them, she understood it. The fires were cold, the tents abandoned, possessions and the occasional corpse left in the wake of the fugitives; they were rushing

240

from the Plainsfolk *towards* the enemy, out into the night where the Plague People had come from.

And there was no sign of Hesprec or her captors then. They had spirited themselves away into the night, and even Maniye's wolf nose could not find their scent amidst such a morass of fear and desperation.

She turned away, her muzzle casting left and right, snarling in frustration. Shyri Stepped, though, knife in her hand and staring into the night.

'They will keep her alive until they can kill her properly,' she said flatly. 'The Rat doesn't often get a Serpent's bones to feast on, nor her soul.'

Maniye followed her gaze out into the dark, and remembered what she had seen out there, on her way in. Stepping, she asked, 'What does "properly" mean? A sacred place?'

Shyri met her gaze. 'Some place the Rat has touched, yes. Some place sealed away, where his reek is still strong. So, yes: the Horn-Bearer fortress will be closest for them.'

'But you said it was sealed . . .'

'Nothing is so sealed that the Rat cannot creep in.'

'Can we get in?' Kalameshli demanded.

Maniye stared at him. 'You?'

He scowled at her. 'The little Serpent and I have an understanding, priest to priest. And you stopped the Wolf eating her, so why should the Rat have the pleasure?'

'We can get in,' Shyri interrupted. 'I can get us in. The Hyena knows the Rat better than anyone.' She had more to say, and did not say it.

The Plague People were out there, on the ground, in the air, who knew? Perhaps the sealed fortress was already theirs, a trap even for the Rat that had claimed it. But Maniye needed Hesprec. She needed a world with Hesprec in it.

'Lead, please,' she said to Shyri, and the Laughing Girl was Stepped and running in the next heartbeat.

22

There was shouting all the way across the camp, and beyond it Loud Thunder could hear a great human rumble that was the panic of the Plains refugees, who had run this far and now were made to run again.

In the first moments of waking, knowing only that the sentries he had set had failed and the enemy were already here, he could understand none of it. He Stepped instinctively, bellowing out at the world to try and scare it into making sense. There were more frightening things abroad than a woken bear, though. He caught a faint whiff of the Terror and knew it was the Plague warriors.

He blundered between camps, man and bear and man again, until he found Mother. Of course the dutiful son must make sure that she was not in danger, and nobody would know it was Kailovela he was looking for.

They were all together: Mother, Empty Skin, the Hawk woman and her little monster. Some chiefs and messengers were already rushing up with news, babbled and contradictory. Thunder watched Icefoot and the Owl's Grey Herald and Seven Mending try to understand what was happening, each story coming in too late, while the unseen fight seemed to pluck at the edges of their camp like a swarm of flies.

Loud Thunder had just made up his mind to head east until he ran out of fires and see the enemy for himself, when two coyotes dashed past his ankles and then Stepped right in Mother's shadow. Two Heads Talking was gasping for breath, wheezing as he tried to recover. He pushed his mate forwards, Quiet When Loud sitting down heavily and shielding her belly.

'They've taken the Swift Backs,' Two Heads got out, loud enough to draw all ears.

'Taken how?' Loud Thunder demanded.

'Plague Men, come from the sky and killing. A dozen Swift Backs dead, and the rest taken by the Terror. The Plague Men hold their fire and strike out from it. I saw it with these eyes.'

'And escaped the fear?'

'Because I showed them a very fast pair of heels and sang Coyote songs in my head until I was clear of them,' Two Heads spat. 'I felt them scratching at the inside of my skull all the way.' He shivered. 'What will you do?'

Thunder rolled his shoulders. 'Fight. What else?' He made his voice sound as full and loud as he could, and hoped it didn't sound hollow with fear to anyone else. He should give orders now – this tribe and that, chosen to go into the fire with him. Who would be best? Whose lives did he value less today? But he was not that kind of leader – the good kind. Instead he must do everything himself. 'All of you, you warriors. Go get me a dozen, a score, whoever you can find. Bring spears and arrows and we will remind them of the Seal coast.'

Bold words from a big man. Will that substitute for courage? But they were on the move – Tigers, Wolves, Eyriemen, Boar, all rushing to get their friends because, if Loud Thunder said a thing, it meant they didn't have to think about it.

Thunder went to get his axe. His armour he abandoned, because the darts of the Plague People didn't seem to care about anything less than Wolf-iron, and precious little even about that. When he came from his tent, hefting the great weight of copper on its tree-branch haft, he found Kailovela standing there, fitful child in her arms and monster at her heels.

She stared at him blankly for a moment, as if surprised to find herself there. Thunder stared right back.

243

'You asked me for my blessing once,' she reminded him.

He nodded. That had been to guide him in the Godsland. The journey felt like a child's toddle compared to the war he had enmeshed himself in now.

'You have it.' She leant forward, hand warm on his bare arm, face deadly serious. Not the wishes of a lover but the benediction of a priest. 'Come back live and whole.'

The night was dark, and the sky shook with the cries and yells of all those who could not see a way out. But Loud Thunder felt as though he carried his own flame with him when he Stepped and lumbered off towards the Swift Back fire.

He had enough warriors at his back by the time he arrived there: the brave and the foolish and those few who knew what was going on and simply knew it had to be done. His great ally was the darkness; the Plague People warriors had no eyes for it. He had seen night or storm baffle them and spoil the reach of their killing rods. Even as he was crossing the abandoned group towards them, he saw another band who had the same idea. A dozen of the Tiger, all Stepped and racing through the dark that had always been theirs, were rushing the Swift Back fire. Loud Thunder saw them as no more than a sinuous suggestion of movement, while he saw the forms of the Plague People plain. There were a score of them caught clear in the firelight, the razor-edged hollowness of them outlined by the flames.

Even as he gathered himself to double his speed and back up the Tiger, something changed. One of the Plague People cast a stone towards the night sky; it flew there and lodged, and burned as though it was a false moon, shedding a cold white radiance across the camp. Thunder felt more than heard the stampede of panic behind him, anyone who had stayed anywhere near the Swift Back fire now bolting, and the Plague People's Terror ravening at their heels to drag them down. The Tiger were caught in plain sight, frozen like striped shadows under that hostile light, and the Plague Men loosed their killing darts instantly, cutting them down. Some ran, some tried to charge the fire, but they all died before a drop of Plague blood was shed. Loud Thunder fell back instantly, Stepping so that his human bulk might find some hiding place his bear shape was too large for. Above them all, the false moon was falling slowly, drifting a little with the wind and fading.

Thunder looked around. Some of his people had vanished away with this new development; others were with him, staring at him as though he had any answer for them. *We need more, to rush them.* And many would die when they made the attempt. He was struck with the understanding that these Plague warriors were acting differently – not oblivious to the world that they destroyed, these were hunters come to take human prey. Something had changed amongst them.

So we finally got them to notice us. Well done, us.

Thunder found a Deer hunter and a Hawk from amongst his followers. 'Go bring more,' he told them, because he was out of ideas that didn't involve terrible bloodshed. *We must drive them away. We can't just flee every time they come, or what kind of war host are we?* And yet he only had one success to his name, and it had come with surprise and favourable weather, and with all the advantages an attacker might devise or crave. Defence was an entirely different matter against an enemy as implacable as the Plague Men.

He felt their Terror, prowling around in that open space amongst the abandoned tents like something independent of the Plague People themselves.

More warriors were creeping in, one at a time, pairs or small bands. Soon there would not be hiding places enough. Thunder knew that the Plague People must grow tired of the Swift Backs fire soon enough, and then they would not lack for enemies to hunt. *So we attack and become the hunters.* But that ground between him and the foe was littered with dead Tigers, was strewn with more Wolves than he cared to think about, so many of his host just exterminated before anyone knew what was going on.

He Stepped, and it was the sign for all of them to ready themselves. *We are enough, or if we are not enough, we are all there are.*

He led from the front because that way he wouldn't have to see all those who wouldn't follow. He saw the Plague People in motion, and surely that ghastly light would leap up again to guide their aim. Thunder charged into their Terror like plunging into icy water, feeling it slow his limbs and sap his strength. His soul shied away from them, and he wished he could do the same.

Then there arose a sound that came to him through his feet and chest, not his ears. It was a keening, lonely cry, filled with centuries of bitterness and loss, and it left him cold and forlorn but the effect on the Plague Men was far greater. It struck them like a great wave, scattering them across the ground and up into the sky. It seemed to madden them; Thunder saw them clutch their heads and call out desperately to each other, their implacable order broken. The Terror broke too, in the echo of that unheard sound, and Thunder was abruptly at top speed, plunging forwards with a stampede of beasts at his heels.

The shivering sound came again, and now the stars were being swallowed by great web-veined wings as the Bat Society made their arrival known. Thunder saw the Plague warriors break, and for a moment they were utterly undone, prey for anyone who chose to cast a spear. Then they regained some semblance of themselves, pointing their rods at the wings above and spitting death randomly across the constellations. A moment later they fled, taking to their own wings and skimming across the ground, beyond Thunder's ability to make them out.

But how far will they go, and how many more are there? Thunder knew that this attack on his war host was only a part of the whole. This was no random blunder into their camp, but an assault backed by an intent the Plague People had previously lacked. *Now they know it's war.*

Kailovela wanted to fly, but her child weighed her down, and the night sky was full of terrifying sounds. The northern war host was still coming to order – some tribes had sent off their hunters without knowing what was going on. Others had already begun packing their tents determinedly, assuming the worst had happened. Kailovela could only stand in the shadow of Mother's sled, and hope that some stampeding tide of fear didn't come to tear her loose from it.

She had Empty Skin and the little monster with her, virtually hiding in her skirts. Mother herself stood atop the sled and stared out into the dark, occasionally barking out an order at any Bear unwise enough to be seen.

If my arms were empty, I would go away, she told herself. She was not sure if it was true. She did not love Loud Thunder, but his huge dog-like earnestness, his confusion, all the strength he was so careful about using, it was wearing her down. He would make a good friend if he was only content to stay at just that distance.

Abruptly new faces were pushing their way towards Mother, with a half-dozen of the Bear looming from the darkness to intercept them. Kailovela flinched back – *the Plague People!* But in truth that was her second fear. The first name that came to her mind was *Yellow Claw*. Her former mate had not forgotten her, of that she was sure.

The next heartbeat showed her they were neither Eyriemen nor the hollow creatures of the Plague. Mother's sharp voice hauled back her people, though she did not dismiss them. 'What do the Sons of the River want here?' she demanded.

Kailovela pressed close, seeing lean dark men and women wearing armour of ridged hide and padded cloth, wielding spears and swords edged with stone teeth. At their head was a youth – surely the youngest amongst them, and yet he had a presence to him she knew well from others: some Champion of the south.

The dark youth looked from Bear to Bear, in their great shadows yet fearing none of them. 'I seek Loud Thunder.'

Mother hunched forward. 'He is doing his duty. Probably. You

247

are the boy who came to the Stone Place and made peace with our gods. Asmander, the Serpent called you?'

'Asman now, Mother.' The Champion plainly re-evaluated who he was talking to. 'Mother, that same Serpent sends me to seek sanctuary here for a guest, a strange guest. May we have the hospitality of your fire?'

Mother shrugged hugely. There was no fire there by the sled, after all – the northerners found the Plains air stifling and precious little cool had come this night. 'If you must. Don't wander.' She sighed, shaking her head so that her long, tangled hair swayed like a grey curtain. 'My idiot son plays war leader, of course. I will go shout until everyone has stopped running about like mice. Stay here.'

She slumped off the sled and Stepped. The sullen, shapeless strength of her bear shape sent the southerners back a step as she shambled off into the dark.

Asman looked about, and gave a handful of brief words to his people that had them setting down their weapons but keeping up their watch – a neatly diplomatic balance. They did have someone in their midst – a slight shape, hooded and cloaked – but to Kailovela's eyes it seemed more prisoner than guest, and something more . . .

Empty Skin stepped out from behind her and skipped forwards, past the first of the southerners before anyone had seen her. Asman called her away, but in the next breath she was standing before that shrouded figure, reaching up to tug at the cloak. Kailovela heard her accusation: 'I know you!'

One of the southerners reached for her, arrested by the growling of one of Mother's people, who apparently felt possessive about the Seal girl. In that moment, Empty Skin had flicked back the stranger's hood and the moonlight fell on a face that matched it for paleness.

Kailovela froze, for she saw past the face into that emptiness – the same that gnawed within the little monster, and yet somehow

248

she had grown *used* to that. But here was one of the enemy, the very enemy themselves . . .

The Bears were reacting in shock – some Stepping to human forms with raised axes, others growling threats into the faces of the southern soldiers, who seemed none too happy themselves. Asman had his hands up, calling for calm, and then . . . and then . . .

The pale creature *did* something. Kailovela was watching her hollow face as it happened; she saw it as well as any pair of human eyes could see it.

It was a beautiful face. It had always been so, but the elegance of those white features had been destroyed by the hunger within. Now the beauty came to the fore, the emptiness masked and layered over until she really had to *look* for it, or she would pass it by. And the Bears' growls became uncertain and the loathing they all felt for the creature's emptiness ebbed. *Love me*, demanded the pale creature, and if they did not quite love her, still, it balanced out the hate a little.

Something moved within Kailovela, something resonating in empathy with whatever had been done.

In another moment, she would have said something. Any words would have been a mistake. Any kinship she claimed with this creature would have lessened her in the eyes of the world, and yet she felt it, just a sliver of it, as though some poisoned bolt had lodged in her at birth, and slowly festered into *this*.

Then Empty Skin had pushed forward, so heedless of the River spears that they did not know what to do with her. 'Is it you?' she asked, less certain now. 'You took me in . . .'

'I do not know you,' the pale woman said, trying to back away but constrained by her guards. Her voice was another shock: weirdly accented, and yet true words coming from that hollow mouth.

Then the little monster spoke, high and desperate, and the pale woman's eyes went wide as moons and she answered back in the same staccato language.

Kailovela felt a sudden access of jealousy, ridiculously. *She is mine. Only I can understand her.* But this pale creature knew all words, it seemed, one foot in two worlds. And on the back of that, a revelation that must have struck Empty Skin at exactly the same time. The Seal girl looked back at her, astounded. When their gazes met, Kailovela all but heard pieces closing together into a plan.

But then Thunder was back, bellowing orders. The Plague People were on the offensive. The Plainsfolk were already sallying forth to cover the exit of their wounded and helpless, and the Crown of the World would hear them. Those who would not fight must move. This land would be ceded to the Plague People by the morning, until a united front could be made to retake it.

Kailovela tried to speak – tried to force her voice high over the tumult at first, and then tried to bring that other force to bear, the way she had seen the pale woman do it. She had never had any mastery of it, though. It had always just acted through her, in spite of her, until she cursed it and cursed it without ever knowing that it was truly a thing apart from her, a magic in her blood that drew all eyes and hearts.

She could not do it. They would not listen to her. The Rivermen were moving off and yanking their guest-captive with them, leaving Empty Skin staring after them with hungry eyes. Kailovela shrank back against Mother's sled, drawing the little monster with her.

'You know, don't you,' she told it. A bare handful of words had passed between the creature and the pale woman, but there was an understanding there, a transfer of knowledge. *That we can use?* The hollow little thing stared at her, and Kailovela realized that it was as surprised as she was. Was the pale woman its kin, its ally or a familiar enemy? Plainly it had no idea.

As the camp began to disintegrate around them, all the warriors in the world rushing off into the night, Mother's heavy hand fell on Kailovela's shoulder.

'We will talk of this later,' the huge Bear woman rumbled. 'I know what is in your mind.'

'And?' Kailovela asked her.

'A fool's idea,' Mother told her flatly. 'But perhaps the wise have used up all of theirs.'

23

'The Horn-Bearers were proud,' Shyri told them softly, as the fortress loomed dark against the darkening sky. 'They were greater than other men – like your Bear, even – broader of shoulder, stronger of arm.' Her voice had a gentle rhythm to it, one recounting an oft-told story. 'The hide of their Stepped shapes was armour, and the armour they wore beneath was so thick and heavy that none other than their warriors could wear it. Across all the Plains, none dared oppose them.'

The fortress was of packed earth, its walls raised high and capped with a slanted roof. There had been projections once, Maniye saw, but they had broken, leaving irregular nubs that time had worn down. Perhaps there had been carving, too, but the hand of the years had smoothed it away. When they were hard up against the base of those walls, deep within their shadow, Maniye reached out and touched the surface, expecting to feel it crumble like dirt. Instead it felt like rough stone, abrasive to the fingers like sand could be, unyielding. At her back, Kalameshli growled quietly, still Stepped and plainly not liking the smell of the place.

'Who would not want to be strongest?' Shyri continued. 'Who would not want the earth to shake at their tread? To be proof against spear and arrow? Surely it is what all peoples want. And the wanting is good, sometimes. Sometimes it is better than the having. For in their strength and power the Horn-Bearers looked upon the world and asked, "We are supreme amongst men, and yet we are not gods, and the distance between us and the gods has not decreased, for all that we have climbed." And they looked into the great well of the night, and across the great space of the grassland, and began to wonder what still stood above them and around them, that they could not see, but that was greater than them.'

At last the old Wolf priest took up his human form, if only to snort derisively at the foreign story. 'All very well,' he grunted. 'How do we get in? You said they sealed themselves up.' There were no doors to be seen, nor windows in all that slab-like expanse, only little holes that Maniye could barely have put a hand into.

'Oh, seal the gates they did,' Shyri confirmed, breaking from her ritual cadence to grin at him. 'Old growler, know that the Laughing Men have ways even the Serpent cannot know, when it comes to the cracking of bones and the eating of dead flesh. When all was done for the Horn-Bearers, do you think we did not crack eggs like this, to suck the yolk inside?'

'So?' Maniye pressed, for all that seeing Kalameshli's nose tweaked was amusement in itself.

'We climb.' Shyri's grin that had excluded Takes Iron, let her in easily. 'I am a great climber amongst my people, but you are a tiger.'

'And I?' Kalameshli demanded peevishly.

I didn't ask you to come. The words hovered on Maniye's lips. She didn't know why he had, but that strange bond he had forged with Hesprec apparently extended this far, or else he wanted both the Plains and the River to acknowledge the superiority of the Wolf. Which superiority was not to be found in climbing walls, however.

Shyri did climb well, but Maniye in her tiger shape could flow up the walls like moonlight, wait at the top and then come back down to see what was taking the Laughing Girl so long. Kalameshli himself . . . well, wolves were no great scalers of walls, and nor were old Wolf men. He grunted and hissed and scrabbled a quarter of the way up before his pride finally gave way and he permitted them to help him. Even then he cursed them under his breath at every one of his own slips and mis-steps.

Then they were atop the wall, crouched in the gully between its top and the slant of the roof. Maniye had expected windows up here – places where defenders might have stood to fight off invaders who had climbed so high. She saw only shafts a fist wide that must give a fickle light onto the chambers below. Entry fit for serpents. *Or rats.*

Shyri was hunting, though, creeping along the gutter and testing the stone. As she moved, she continued to speak in a low voice, so soft Maniye had to stay on her heels to hear.

'As the years passed without challenge, the Horn-Bearers grew more and more fearful,' Shyri whispered. 'In their minds grew the shadow of some great evil that must come and consume them. And, as they were foremost of all the tribes of men, so would the shadow light on them first. And, as the eyes of all the other tribes were envious upon them, so might the strike come from any of those others.' To speak so, as they crept upon the enemy, might have seemed foolishness, but instead Maniye felt that the words were a kind of spell. By telling the fate of this place's masters, Shyri was weaving a shroud of dust and ages about them, to pass unnoticed by sentries who did not need ears or eyes to know their coming.

Now Shyri stopped, having found something to interest her. She drew a knife and tested it against the stone, its tip seeming to magically create a crack there that she traced until it outlined a square hatch.

'Oh, those Horn-Bearers,' Shyri murmured. 'They had the world, but all it won them was a fear that their treasure might be taken from them. And so they ceased to deal with other tribes, and spurned their traders and their priests. And the Laughing Men watched this, and drew closer, and waited, for we had the first hint of their long death in our nostrils.' She snickered, but even that was part of the telling. Then her knife blade bent alarmingly and she scowled, coming out of her reverie. 'Come make yourself useful, one of you. Bring your iron.'

It was Kalameshli who shouldered forwards, still smarting from his failures as a climber. He took his iron knife and investigated the crack around the portal carefully, listening to the sound the metal made.

'And they raised these walls, building great fortresses wherever they dwelt,' Shyri breathed, watching him work. 'And at first they placed great gates in their walls and spears about the gates to keep out all enemies, but as they sat in the silence, in the shadow of those walls, their fear did not lessen, but rather it grew in their minds, feeding on the silence and the shadow.'

'This has been barred from within,' Takes Iron growled.

'By the Horn-Bearers, or by whoever took Hesprec?' Maniye asked.

'If they took her some place other than this, we will never know where,' Shyri said in her normal voice. 'The Rat has her; this is a Rat place.'

'Well.' Kalameshli rolled his shoulders, which were still wiry with a smith-priest's strength. He took out the skin he rolled his tools, selected a bar of iron that narrowed to a flat edge at one end, and placed it in the crack precisely, feeling where the bar must be. 'We will not enter quietly,' he told them, 'but with all your gabbling, what chance was there of that?' In his other hand was one of his small hammers. Perhaps it was the very one that he had beaten out Hesprec's teeth with, the first time they met.

Maniye was anticipating a sound like thunder, like blasphemy in this quiet, dead place, but instead there was a single sharp beat, no more than two stones cracking at each other, and then Kalameshli was levering up the square stone. She could see the loops on its underside where a bar of wood had been slid, to hold it closed. The loops were stone, thumb-thick and ancient, but the wood was but a stick, torn from one of the Plains bushes, and it was fresh enough that the broken end was still white with dying wood.

She exchanged glances with the others, gathered around a square of darkness from which a cold, dead smell emanated. Not the reek of recent carrion, certainly, but something somehow worse. There was an edge of putrefaction, of excrement, of sour living bodies, but there was something that gathered all those scents to itself and smothered them, the patient odour of long-dead things and long-abandoned places.

Maniye dared to hang her head into that hole, looking about at a space crossed with the faint moonbeams let in by the holes in the roof. Tiger eyes showed her more: a narrow space, crusted with fragments of wood, desiccated cloth, the occasional bone.

'We'll need light,' she told them, when she was human again.

'Again, the Wolf provides,' Kalameshli said grandly, with a glower at Shyri. He swiftly had the makings of a torch, bundling cloth about an axe-handle he had brought and anointing it with a little precious oil – another of Wolf's secrets. Steel and flint soon had it burning at a steady pace, leaving all three of them staring at the hatchway without eagerness.

Shyri shrugged. 'Oh, those Horn-Bearers,' she murmured. 'The silence and the shadow began to eat them, and they raised great doors and set them at their gates, so that those who came visiting could not even see inside, and they threw earth over their windows so that they had no more eyes on the world, and they sought the guidance of their god, opening their minds to the darkness. But it was another god who spoke to them.' And then she was gone into the darkness, daring the others to follow her.

Kalameshli went next, and Maniye spared the moon a final glance before she descended. *In case I do not see you again.*

The jumping light of the torch revealed a low-ceilinged, cluttered space, but Shyri was already leading them away, finding a flight of steps that led downwards, and still reciting her litany. 'In the minds of the Horn-Bearers, the unknown enemy had grown and grown, until no spears could defeat it, and no walls could keep it out, and all their strength would be water against it.'

'Did they foresee the Plague People?' Maniye asked.

Broken from her story, Shyri glanced back at her, utterly without expression.

'I thought that was why you were telling the story, because it was about the Plague,' Maniye whispered to her.

Shyri shook her head convulsively. 'I tell it because it is the right story for this place. We tell the story of these ghosts and so we pass them.' Her eyes were wide, the torchlight dancing erratically in them, and abruptly Maniye saw just how frightened the Laughing Girl was. This was a place of terrible deeds that had been a part of her world forever. The story of the Horn-Bearers let her master it, place it within her shadow.

'Who knows what they saw?' Shyri added. 'Nobody can ask them now.' She continued, creeping down the stairs with Kalameshli's torch sending her shadow ahead of her. 'Those Horn-Bearers, they set guards at every window, even though the windows had been stopped; they put spears at every door, even though they had closed the doors and sealed them. They filled their cellars with dried meat, grain and honey, and all good things, and said, "Let the enemy come. They will not see us. They will pass on, and all will die but we." But the Rat came instead, who could creep into every little hole they had left in their walls. The Rat came, who could whisper into their minds even though they had closed them against the world. The Rat came, and dined well in their storehouses even as they stood guard against their own gates.'

And they came out of the stairwell and saw the bones.

This had been a gate indeed; from this side the outline was clear, though it had been sealed with the same hard stuff as the walls. And Shyri's tale was instantly gone from a fireside story to hard truth, because here were those guards, here were those spears.

Maniye could see that there was a passageway running around the outside of the fortress, curving away into darkness on either side beyond the reach of the torch. At their feet, it was

257

strewn with skeletons, enough for five men perhaps, though they had been jumbled together so that it was hard to be sure, interlaced with great plates of verdigrised bronze that had once been part of monumental suits of armour, as heavy as the mail worn by the Stone Man Champion she had once fought.

For a moment they were silent, even Shyri's words stilled on her lips. Then Kalameshli hissed and pointed. There were footprints in the dust – which living, human feet had made. Whoever it was had not entered the fortress at the same point, but had passed along this covered passageway and disturbed the bones a little.

'We follow,' agreed Maniye, and they set off again. Soon enough the trail led to more steps, delving further into the fortress through a door that would have let a horse and rider through.

'And who knows what the Rat whispered to the Horn-Bearers, as they trembled in the darkness?' Shyri said, her voice the merest breath in Maniye's ear. 'We know, for we came after and picked over their bones. Who knows what madness possessed them, after they sealed up all their doors and then discovered their empty storehouses where only the tracks of the Rat had passed?' And then her voice dried up entirely because the torchlight touched upon the bones of a monster. It lay before them at the foot of the stairs, long dead and yet still guarding this portal. It was as large as Maniye's Champion shape – too large surely to have ever moved from the room it had died in. Its bones were huge, not long but massive, made to bear colossal weights. Its skull, like that of a giant's horse, bore a long lance-like horn on its nose, and a short spike behind. Had it been alive and furious before them, it might have been the most terrifying thing Maniye had ever seen. But it was bones, bones and dust and withered slabs of hide that were too tough for even the Rat's sharp little teeth. Maniye could have stood within its ribs.

Only Takes Iron was untouched by the sad majesty of it. 'The tracks, look,' he told them, and they saw feet – more than one pair now – that had pattered past the great skeleton, heading down, forever down.

'And in the end, even their own fortress seemed too exposed, and they gave up their souls to the Rat, gave up their shapes and their god, and crept into the small, dark places to die.' And Maniye hoped that was the last of Shyri's tale because her own imagination was doing fine work in telling her what might be ahead, and needed no assistance from Laughing Men legends right then.

Then there was no more down, and they had come out into a low-ceilinged room that seemed to run off into the dark in every direction, supported by squat pillars cut with hard-angled geometric figures. The footprints ran everywhere here – mostly bare, large and small, as though a great many people had been scuttling back and forth in a chaotic host. *Like rats.*

Maniye Stepped to her wolf shape and sniffed the air. The prevailing scent of the fortress was stronger here, the over-whelming musk of old death laying a heavy hand on her, but she thought she caught the scent of something fresher. She started forwards, trying to turn that suggestion into a definite trail, but Shyri's hand caught in her pelt and pulled her back painfully. Maniye snarled, but then saw what the torchlight had touched: the edge of a shaft cut into the floor, round-sided, surely two men's lengths across.

Here in the chill, this was where the Horn-Bearers had stored their food, she guessed. As Kalameshli swept the light of the torch from left to right she saw more pits gaping blindly. Tugging the old priest's arm to bring the light closer, Maniye peered into the nearest one and recoiled.

Where had the Horn-Bearers gone? Down into the earth, down and down until only these pits remained to them. Bones large and small, she saw, but more small than large, and the torch-light lit mercilessly on the ragged edges, the dents and the cracks left by countless little gnawing teeth. And the rats had died down there too, their tiny bones piled in the gaps between the human remains, for the Rat cared nothing for the bodies it inhabited, of whatever kind.

Kalameshli spat disgustedly. In the echo of that sound and the minute spatter of his disdain Maniye heard more. Abruptly the buried darkness was not silent, but there came a pattering and a rustling, a hurry of small sleek bodies. And, almost lost within the susurrus, a choked-off human cry.

Maniye was moving even as her ears registered it. She raced ahead on tiger feet, Shyri loping as a hyena beside her and Kalameshli a step behind, the torch abandoned. She braced herself for the utter dark, but it never came. Even the Rat needed light to do dark deeds by. Ahead she saw the low glimmer of another fire and she made for it, letting its light warn her of the pits in the floor moments before her feet found them.

Then she discovered there was further down to go after all – a sudden slope that she half skidded down, claws digging at the stone to slow herself, and then a circular chamber, buried deep within the earth and thronging with shadows. Her paws struck a rough surface, lumpy and uneven, and for a moment the handful of small fires banked up there blinded her. She Stepped back to human, letting her weaker eyes overcome the glare, Shyri and Takes Iron catching her up.

The room was walled in bones. Bones were beneath her feet, but not scattered loose. Some madman's hand had fitted them one to another to make a grisly mosaic, set each in place so neatly that she could not have put a finger between them. Bones scaled the curved walls and the dome of the ceiling, so that skulls leered down surrounded by radiant sprays of fingerbones, marching spirals of ribs, the studs of vertebrae. *The Horn-Bearers' last work . . . ?*

But they were not alone in the chamber. Time enough later to admire the artwork.

She saw Hesprec instantly, held by a handful of scrawny, filthy creatures, a halter tight about her neck to keep her human. Standing beside her was a tall, gaunt Plainsman in an oversized

260

robe, a garment that had been fine once, studded with gems and gold, but was now threadbare and holed, some grave goods of the Horn-Bearers perhaps. The firelight played tricks; Maniye saw him standing stock still and yet that robe undulated and crept about him as though countless busy bodies were rushing about beneath it.

And he had at least a score of friends, she saw. Some held Hesprec, and others just crouched or crept about the chamber, the firelight wild in their eyes. They were cadaverous, streaked with dirt and excrement, their bodies covered with sores and welts, limbs like sticks, heads like skulls. They reminded Maniye of the Strangler cultists she had seen in the Estuary, and she knew the resemblance was more than skin-deep. People who had seen their world falling apart, who had no way to take their lives back and repair the damage: they despaired. These people had given over sovereignty of their minds and souls to a greater power because it relieved them of all burdens. The Stranglers, the Rat, these were known evils, better than the great collapse of the world that was going on outside.

All eyes were on them, not lost in some dark ritual or focused on their prisoner. Each gaunt face was turned to the newcomers, and the Rat Speaker's face was straining with an appalling smile.

'Always,' he said, 'there are those who follow the false trail of the Serpent.'

Maniye looked into the man's eyes and found something squatting there, leering back at her, but not the eyes' original owner. She had seen the hollowness of the Plague People; this was its opposite. The Speaker was stuffed with souls, hundreds of mean little rodent spirits crammed into his human shape until there was no room left for the man he had once been. Meeting his eyes was locking gazes with a god, albeit the most despised of all gods. The Rat Speaker was well named, no more than the Rat's mouthpiece.

'This will be a rare meal,' the Speaker announced to his followers. 'A Serpent of the River and curs of the north.' Maniye tried to gather herself to spring at him, but his words kept jarring her. In his voice she heard multitudes, tittering and rustling. 'But what's this?' He feigned exaggerated surprise. 'Are you a new guest at our fire, sweet one? Are these dogs your guest-gift?' His eyes were on Shyri. 'Oh, Laughing Child,' he sighed, 'this is the stuff of memories. You and I have stood here before.'

'We have not,' Shyri said shakily. 'I was in the stone ruins you left, above the Tsotec, but you were not there, only your memories.'

The Rat Speaker laughed, and it was worse than the smile. 'You mistake me, Laughing Child. Not this body, nor that you wear now, but I see Hyena in your shadow, and he and I are *old* friends. When we dragged down the last of the Horn-Bearers, all the peoples of the Plains made a great show of their despite, and yet some few crept in to share in our final feast. The Vulture was our guest then, and the Hyena too.' Again that laugh, and its echoes were the scuttling of countless feet within the stone around them. 'Do you think I would send Hyena away from my fire with an empty belly?'

Maniye glanced at Shyri, waiting for the heated denial, but the girl stood quite still, knife in her hand but no will to use it.

'Do you not tell of the time of corpses, when Hyena will pick over the bones of all the world? That is a Rat story, Laughing Child. That is the story we told you, long ago.' Abruptly he had swooped down and hauled Hesprec up, holding her by the halter so that she clutched at his arm to stop herself being strangled. Around them, the score of starvelings began a rapid patter on the stone floor with their hands and the sound swiftly took on a life of its own. Maniye remembered the Tiger being called forth by smoke and embers in the Shining Halls. Now she felt the Rat respond to its own summons, seething close within the dark beyond the fires, a tide of gnawing, ever-hungry teeth.

The Rat Speaker spread his arms wide, Hesprec still dangling from one hand. A flint knife was in the other. 'Laughing Child, know that the time of the stories is nigh. The Plains are already half strewn with bones. The enemy has come that no spear can fight, and only the carrion-eaters will live, who can survive on bones and the lost larders of extinct tribes. A brief but bounteous age, Laughing Child! And all we must do is rid the world of those who preach the poisonous creed of hope!'

Maniye felt the room was growing smaller and smaller, as though the walls seethed with an ever thicker layer of hairy bodies. She sought strength from the only well she had left; she let the Champion in and Stepped into that huge frame, brushing the stone of the domed ceiling with her back. And still the madness of the Rat stared undaunted at her from the Speaker's eyes.

'And there will be no more *Champions*,' he said, right into her snarl. 'No more old souls, no priests, no hope, no stories except those Rat tells Hyena over a picked carcass.'

Shyri stepped forwards, and Maniye read just a dull acceptance in her posture. She growled, deep in her throat, but the sound did not echo back from the stone, lost in the endless scuffling of rodent feet.

That ghastly smile stretched further, until the Speaker's face began to tear.

'No more Champions,' Shyri echoed, casting a moment's guilty look at Maniye, then stepping closer to the Speaker, virtually into his seething shadow.

Maniye lunged forward, but shied away at the last moment, backing off. The thought of taking that tainted flesh in her jaws, of feeling the bustling ripples of his robe within her mouth sickened her stomach, whatever shape she was in. She stared desperately at Hesprec.

The Serpent girl, still clinging gamely to the Speaker's wrist, chose that moment to conquer her own revulsion and sink her human teeth into the man's thumb.

There was enough living man left in the Rat Speaker that he barked with pain and smacked at her with the butt of the knife, and Shyri spat, 'There's one Champion I would keep,' and opened him up with her knife from navel to neck.

Instantly there was chaos. The Rat Speaker votaries leapt forward as though a single hand had hauled on them – knives and rocks and filthy teeth and nails. At the same time the wound that Shyri had carved was vomiting more than blood. A great flood of vermin was pouring out of the gash. Shyri stood before it for a moment, as though accepting the price for her treachery, but then a grey wolf had knocked her aside in its haste to get its teeth into one of the Rat cultists, and Maniye started back to herself, and ceased to be an observer. The Champion thundered forwards, spilling human bodies out of its way as easily as it crushed the fragile bones of the rats.

At first it was like fighting dead leaves. Everywhere she turned something crunched underfoot. The human servants of the Rat were so starved by their master that she barely felt the blows they aimed at her hide. She roared and cuffed, spilling them everywhere, knowing that the power of the enemy had been broken so very simply.

And yet they were not breaking, and there always seemed to be more of them. Coursing streams of matted little bodies were surging into the chamber from between the stones, from secret hidden ways. They surged like an unclean tide, seeking flesh to latch on to. Maniye had mad glances of a hyena shaking bodies in its teeth, their long tails flailing like whips; she saw Kalameshli's wolf pounce and snarl, and then he was a man again long enough to bloody his iron in the bowels of a human votary. A serpent ran its length through the chamber like lightning across the sky, now tiny, ambushing individual rats from behind their brethren, now huge, its scales warding off their dagger-like teeth.

Yet there were always more of them. Maniye's pelt crawled with little hand-like feet, and her back and belly became a constellation of pain as teeth began to gnaw and burrow. They were focusing their numbers on her, the greatest threat. Maniye began to panic. She Stepped to a wolf and tried to outrun them; she became a tiger and writhed and rolled, flinging the vermin off her only to have them swarm back with her next breath. She

264

snarled and cuffed, seeing a thousand little eyes throw back the firelight, backing away until the curved wall of the chamber was at her heels. She could not see the door; the Rat had closed the way somehow. She was buried deep within the earth and who would notice one more set of bones strewn in these dead halls?

A knife drove into her side and she turned on the wielder, crushing his brittle flesh in her jaws. A club broke across her back, sending a shock of pain through her. Her iron swallowed the teeth of the blow but the force still bruised her. She Stepped to the Champion again, but the slope of the ceiling cramped her, even as she scraped away a dozen little bodies against the stone. Some of the hands clinging to her were human, now, their weight dragging her down. Some of the teeth sunk into her were human too. She could no longer tell the difference.

Another cultist waved a burning brand at her face. Snarling, she closed her jaws on him, the moment's sear of the fire a cleaner pain by far than the teeth that were chewing at every inch of her, scrabbling to find the thinner skin where even her armoured hide could not keep them out.

And then the Rat Speaker rose up before her, his front a slick horror of gore and struggling rodents, and drove his knife at her neck. He made a broad sweep of it, the razor edge driven through her with mad strength. If she had been the Champion when he struck he would have flooded the room with her blood. Her souls knew better than she did, in that moment. She dropped down into the wolf-shape and the worst of the blow missed her, but still he knocked her onto her side. Instantly they were on her, more hands than she could count, forcing her down, grappling with the bucking, snarling beast until they had her by the throat and she was a kicking, shrieking girl instead, Rat bodies swarmed over her, burrowing at the hems of her mail, their filthy teeth worrying at her.

The Speaker raised his blade high. She could see he was dying; part of her whispered that he was already dead but such distinctions mattered nothing to the Rat. From the least of all gods to the greatest, feeding on the corpse of hope as the Plague People spread across the land. Perhaps Rat was right. Perhaps one day it would feast on Plague bones and drive them mad within their white-walled fortresses. Perhaps Rat would survive, the only remainder of all the ways and stories of the true people.

Looked at that way, she was playing her part by dying here.

The knife came down, but a lean grey wolf lunged past, jaws closing about the man's bloody throat. A hyena and a serpent were fighting the people holding her, trying to break her from their grasp. Beyond them all, the fires were dying. The darkness was descending on them, that had dwelled in this place for a hundred years. Maniye looked up and saw a great tide of vermin, high as mountains, high as the stars. It fell on them all and she lost hope and dropped into the dark.

24

Loud Thunder was waiting for her when she returned, with a face like his name. She had never really seen him angry – and he seemed like a man who perhaps could never work himself up to real rage, but he was close then. When Kailovela Stepped to drop down where Mother lounged in her sled, his face was all knotted up with the feelings he was trying to stopper.

'What have you *done*?' he demanded, flapping a hand at the open sky above that she had stooped from.

Kailovela took a long breath. 'I have seen where the Plague People are and what they're doing.'

'Why?' he barked out.

She faced up to him, knowing from bitter experience that the first step backwards from any angry man would never be the last. So she stood and told him. 'Because the Owl go only at night, and the warriors of the Hawk say many words but keep to their tents while the sun shines.' She scowled. 'It's been days now since they attacked our camp; since we fled them. And we have been blind. And I wanted to see.'

'Do you–?' Thunder started. 'What if–? They–!' The words crammed his mouth and refused to order themselves, and now his anger turned itself inwards on himself, because he was Loud Thunder and everything was his fault.

She thought of the Pale Shadow woman, the one the Southmen had brought who was somehow Plague and not-Plague all

267

at once. Without letting herself think or doubt, she put a hand to Thunder's bare arm, feeling the slab-like muscles there beneath their covering of fat and rough, hairy skin. He could snap her into pieces like kindling, but while her hand was on him he was powerless. *And could I have done this with Yellow Claw?* she wondered. She felt the power move in her. *The Plague People power. The power I shouldn't have.*

'You know the skies don't belong to the Eyrie any more,' he said harshly, but she could feel the anger drain from him, as though she had cut a hole in him with her touch.

'I saw them flying,' she told him. 'But they do not fly as high as a hawk, and a hawk's eyes can see from where the clouds sit.'

Thunder looked past her at Mother. 'Tell her,' he almost begged. 'Tell her she mustn't.'

Mother chuckled darkly. 'Oh, idiot child, when you set her free of all chains, what did you think? That she would roost on your hand and eat sweetmeats from your mouth?' Abruptly the huge woman pushed herself to her feet, the slow strength of the Bear moving in her, then fading again when she was standing, pretending to be just an old woman. 'Anyway, it's done now. She went; she came back. She saw things. Tonight the Owl and the Eyrie will come to my fire to tell me all that *they* saw. You, you with the long bird name, you'll come too.' She scowled at Kailovela for a moment as though she'd never seen the Eyriewoman before. 'Perhaps we need a proper name for you. "Kailovela" is like chewing sticks.'

'The Eyrie—' Kailovela started.

'They don't; with their women, they don't give names.' Mother's thick grey hair slapped about her face as she shook her head. 'So I shouldn't wait for them. I should do it.'

She Stepped, ending the conversation beyond any argument, and shuffled off, her swag-belly rumbling hungrily.

'Will you stand before the Eyrie and speak, then?' Thunder asked her. For a moment she thought he was taunting her as

Yellow Claw might have done, but his anger had washed away as it always would have done. There was only concern in him now.

Abruptly she felt sick that she had found that ability in herself and used it on anyone, let alone poor confused Loud Thunder. *It is wrong. It is a thing of the enemy. Why is it in me?*

'I'll speak,' she said. She would speak, but there were things she would *not* speak of. She had not just flown out to idly spy, after all. She had flown because she might have been needed to bear witness to a death.

'What is it, now?' he asked awkwardly, sensing the hurt but not knowing how to make it better. He stood very close, and yet he would not touch her. Perhaps he, too, was worried about breaking her.

I have found that I do not break so easily, since you freed me.

'I must go to my son,' she said, trying to make the words sound like a mother's. The thought only deepened the wound in her. *Is this why I don't feel for my boy like other mothers do? Because I am hollow somewhere inside?*

Thunder was mumbling a question about the child, who was with Quiet When Loud, the Coyote taking the opportunity to play mother before she must be one for real. Kailovela waved his words away. For a moment she was about to tell him the real reason she had flown out to watch the Plague People, but she bit back the words. Not while the anger was still cooling in him; not the best time to reveal one more little betrayal.

Later, Mother found a big rock out in the grassland and made herself a nest of furs there – or at least she had Loud Thunder build one, and then deigned to sit in it. Those who had some-thing to say could come to her there and speak, while Two Heads Talking and Quiet When Loud sat at her feet and murmured advice.

Mother had called for those who had flown over the Plains to the east, but plenty more had come to hear what the scouts had to say. A restless gathering of the wise and the wary and the

269

curious made a loose half-circle around Mother's rock, representatives from every tribe and warband.

They had lost many the night the Plague People attacked. The Swift Back hunters were almost all gone – some dead, but there were plenty of lost wolves at large on the Plains now. The Plague warriors had killed any other that the light of the Swift Back fire had touched, holding their weapons ready and taking any target that came. After the Bat had routed them from their post, they had joined their fellows in bedevilling the Plainsfolk. A great despair had swept the Plains refugees the moment word of the Plague People had come to them. What had started as an orderly retreat had turned swiftly into a panicked stampede as those who could not fight had fled with whatever they could carry, or just fled, empty-handed, Stepped, ridden by the Terror. Nobody knew how many had died, but the Plague People themselves had slain few of them. Fear and the heedless feet of the runners had done far worse.

Now here came an old hunter of the Many Mouths – not one of the scouts Mother wanted to hear, but he had sour news that must be told. His people cast down a score of wolf pelts before her rock. He and other Wolves had risked their souls to run east under the shadow of the Plague People, not to fight, but to hunt down their lost brethren of the Swift Backs. Each pelt was a former warrior lost to the Terror, soul now freed to be reborn in the north. No comment was made as the tally of those skins mounted. At least one hunting party had not returned.

Mother sat solemnly through this, though Thunder knew it was not what she was interested in. The Bear seldom had time for the griefs of others, but she had all the wisdom her people generally lacked.

There were others after, who wanted to speak – this Deer or this Tiger who had also braved the east – but abruptly Mother's patience wore through and she just looked straight over at the little knot of Eyriemen, her silent expectation drowning out everything else.

The Owl priestess, Seven Mending, spoke first, for those who had sailed the night skies. 'They have come to where the Plainsfolk were camped,' she said simply. 'Like they have with villages, they are making the place their own. The white walls are already up – they make a large circle. Their beasts are spinning their tents within it.'

'But what do they want, now?' an old Plains Boar demanded. *Haven't they taken enough?* was the echo behind the words, but Thunder shook his head. They were the Plague People. They were always hungry. There was no 'enough' in their world. Even as he thought it, Aritchaka of the Tiger was loudly saying just the same, full of scorn for a needless question, but the old Boar persisted.

'It is different now!' he told them, his harsh, cracking voice rising over the growing murmurs. 'Before, it was as if we were their dream that they never quite believed in. Now they send a warband to our fires.'

'It was the Rivermen!' someone else insisted. 'They fought them at Tsokawan and now they will come for every one of us!'

Thunder's heart sank, and he was braced when another voice called out, 'It was the Northmen!' for the same reasons, and it seemed the whole gathering would degenerate into finger-pointing. Then Mother stood, and that silenced everyone. She was not angry. Her expression was the usual one of sleepy boredom, but everyone's words made way for her voice when she said, 'Where is the Hawk woman?'

The Eyrie delegation exchanged glances, for certainly there were no women of the Hawk amongst them, but then Kailovela was stepping forward, her child fussing and whimpering at her breast. The assembled gaze of all the tribes was hard upon her, so many covetous eyes.

'You went by day over their places,' Mother pointed out. 'So, tell. What did you see?'

Kailovela swallowed but she kept her head high. 'This new

271

place the Plague People are building, it is not just some camp of theirs. There are not so many warriors there.'

'All Plague People are warriors,' one of the Lion called, and Thunder cut him off.

'They're not. When we came to their place in the north, some fought and some fled.' And apparently his voice was strong enough, too, to bring back the silence.

'There are many kinds of Plague People. The Champion Many Tracks said as much, when she escaped from them,' Kailovela told them all, and the name set another twinge of worry in Thunder's gut, because Maniye had not been seen since the attack either. 'This place of theirs is not a warband's camp, it is a prison.'

That stilled any errant muttering, set all ears waiting for her next words. Because the Owl could see by moonlight and tell what the Plague had built, but the Plague People themselves did not like the night much, and their business was done by day. Only Kailovela had seen them at it.

'It is a prison for children,' she told that horrified assembly. 'For the Terror cannot touch those yet to gain a soul. So they find our children, where they have killed us, and they bring them to their places.'

To convert them, to make them their own. A generation of Plains children who would forget their world and grow up soulless and hollow.

There were other reports after that. The flying ship had been seen again. Loose beasts of the Plague People – beetles and spiders as big as dogs – had been found far from their masters, gorging themselves on whatever came their way. It was Kailovela's words that stayed with them though.

He approached her afterwards, leery of scaring her away. His earlier anger still sat within him, making him feel sick of himself, and he knew his words now would carry the echo of it, no matter how he phrased them. 'You saw a lot, for one who flew so high.'

She gave him a guarded look. 'Hawk eyes.' When that didn't

send him away, she sighed. 'You cut my hair, Thunder. You *freed* me to fly. Must I just fly small circles about Mother's sled? Or did you think I would live forever in your cabin and keep your hearth?'

'I'm not trying to cage you. I just . . .'

'You worry.'

'Always I worry,' he agreed, rubbing at his head to make the words come.

'When the Plague warriors come, you'll go fight them again?'

'Of course.'

'And am I allowed to worry?' she asked. 'And if I do, does that mean I can tell you, "No fighting for you, Loud Thunder. My worry is more important"?'

He made a deep noise in his throat, unsatisfied but unable to muster an argument. And perhaps if she had been a sliver more sincere he would have left it at that, but there was something in her tone, a slight hollowness that suggested things hidden.

And then he had it, all of a sudden. For he had so seldom seen her alone since he called her to the war host, but here she was.

'Where is the little monster?' he asked her. 'Where is Empty Skin?'

* * *

Empty Skin had kept the circling speck that was Kailovela in sight all the way across the grasslands towards the white walls. It was good to know that, if this went wrong, someone would know what had happened to her.

She did not fear the Plague People the same way others did, because their greatest weapon was useless against her. She had stepped from child to adult within just such a set of white walls, after the Plague had come and destroyed the people she had been born to. The Seal had come to give her a soul and a shape to Step to, and the Plague People had barred their doors and kept him away, and now here she was: nothing more than Empty Skin.

273

Because she looked like a Seal, still – not the horrible pallor of the Plague People – and because she looked enough like a child, still, the others of Thunder's war host had not quite understood what she was. She was a grown woman without a soul. She was as hollow as the little monster currently by her side.

She was a Plague Woman. She had the mind of a Seal – she knew the stories and the ways, how to fish, how to mend a boat, how to read the sea and the weather. And yet it was as though all that childhood knowledge had become a lie, a fading dream. She would never be the woman she had aspired to.

None of the others understood just how much of a problem she represented. She was caught between two worlds; she needed to find her place. Having travelled so far with Thunder's host, she knew her place was not amongst any people from the Plains or the River or the Crown of the World. In her mind that only left one option.

When the Plague People had gathered in the Seal children, Empty Skin and her fellows had passed into the care of one of their womenfolk. And 'care' was the right word, for all none of the others would believe her. When Thunder's attack had come, that woman had even stood to defend her wards from their own people. Empty Skin had been in her care for a moon and more, hearing the sounds she made and trying to repeat them, trying to learn to be a Plague Person.

And then Thunder had taken her back, and she had tried to be a real person instead, but without a soul it was an impossible challenge. And yes, she could go begging the hearths for some other god to fill the gap within her, but she felt she would not be *her* if that happened, and there was so little of herself left to her. Yet she knew soon enough that everyone around her would realize she was an enemy dressed in the skin of one of their own. And so she had gone to Kailovela and explained what she needed. Kailovela had flown over the new village of the Plague People and told her what was there, and then Kailovela had granted her other wish, the big one, the one Empty Skin had been sure would be refused. Kailovela had given her the little monster.

Or she had freed the little monster, and it was returning to its people. Empty Skin couldn't know, because they only had gestures and grunts and so very few words between them. What did the hollow creature think was happening, and what hold did the Hawk woman truly have over it?

But she needed it. Without it, she was just one more lost child, and the Plague People would eventually imprison her with the rest, when they registered that she did not quite fit into the world they were spinning. But the little monster could talk to them and understand them. Empty Skin had even seen a couple of other diminutive creatures amongst the Plague People here, walking or flying through the air on unreal gossamer wings.

She had waited for the little monster to abandon her – to flee and put away the nightmare that its last few years must have been, trapped in a world of souls it could not understand, but it had crouched in her shadow and stared at the Plague camp and its walls with almost the same alarm a real person would have shown. Perhaps the creature had forgotten the Plague People dream while it had been amongst the Eyriemen.

For now, the creature was at her side, and they were within the white walls even as they were being raised. Empty Skin had watched, fascinated, as spiders larger than she was had woven them, all that patient industry at the direction of slender, pale men and women who might have been doing something as mundane as carding wool. She could look into their faces and see no sign that they knew they were destroying the world. From their perspective, no doubt, they were creating it, one strand at a time.

Empty Skin watched the children – far more here than there had been in the stolen Seal village where they had taken her. The Plague People were not sacrificing them to their gods, if they had gods. They were not torturing them or starving them. On the contrary, they sheltered them and they fed them, and if

275

what they fed them was the meat of their own kin, well, that distinction probably meant nothing to the Plague.

She walked among them. The warriors there – the hard-looking men in banded armour with the killing rods in their hands – they kept an eye on her, but she was not challenged. She was just one more child. Or perhaps they sensed she had crossed that boundary and already become one of them.

I will stay, Empty Skin told herself, but at the same time, *I must go, before they finish the walls.* And perhaps they would not let her go. Perhaps they would hold her here, to protect her against the last fragments of the world they were destroying.

She had brought the little monster as a talisman, and because she had envisaged feeling something definite in her heart, when she was amongst these, her true people. She had thought that the Plague-ness would hatch out of her like a butterfly, and she would know where she belonged at last. And then the little monster would go speak for her, and she would forget all the Seal stories and skills and just become one of the enemy. And it would not be good, but it would be something; it would be a place in the world, even if it was not the world she had been born into.

Here she was still, one foot on either side, though, and she looked to the little monster for help and surprised a new expression on the creature's face, one she could read as determination. All this time, she realized, the monster had been just as lost as she, unsure what its true destiny was. Now it had made a decision.

It laid a small hand on Empty Skin's arm, and then it was walking forward, out amongst these larger people who were just as hollow as it was. After two steps it was calling out to them, in those stuttering sounds that were its language. When they turned to stare, it was jabbing a little finger back at Empty Skin and all her choices had been taken from her.

25

Maniye stared up, and the stars of the Godsland stared down.

They were closer than she remembered, those stars. They moved busily about the sky with a terrible eagerness. Perhaps they sensed that the time was nigh when they would be let into this place with their devouring hunger.

She had been here before: to find a Champion's soul, to watch over the boy-Kasra Tecuman, to become sister to iron.

Only counting the visits did she realize that she had no idea why she was here now.

I was . . . but clutching at memories only scattered them. She must herd them carefully lest she lose them altogether and forget even her own names.

I am Maniye Many Tracks, the one I was born with, the other I earned.

Like floating embers from a fire, her memories ghosted about her. She had the sense that, when they were all within her again and she remembered everything, there would be a great deal of pain, but she would be no child of either Tiger or Wolf if she let that dissuade her.

She remembered the Plague People and their cages.

She remembered the Plainsfolk.

Hesprec.

The Rat.

There was no sudden awakening, no shock realization. She simply knew who she was and what had happened, now.

The Godsland stretched out around her. In a way she couldn't fathom, and yet which made perfect sense, she knew she was seeing the Plains and the Crown of the World both; that such distinctions did not make such a difference to the gods. And yet where were the gods? The hilltops, the great boulders, they were empty, and if she looked to the east (or was it east, here?) she saw that the dark of the night sky had already descended to touch the earth. The land there was . . . gone, taken beyond the reach of the gods because that was where the Plague People ruled, and they could not conceive of the gods of her people. In that bland lack of understanding, they unmade them, just as they unmade the minds of her people with their Terror.

And this was the land she had come to, after fighting the Rat for Hesprec.

'I thought I would be born again,' she told the seething sky, and someone nearby chuckled darkly. Her blood ran cold, because she knew that laugh too well; it had been the scourge of her childhood. But she was a child no longer, so she turned to face its maker.

Kalameshli Takes Iron sat on the hillside above her, as old and cantankerous as ever, wearing his robe of little bones and carrying his smith's tools, face painted in the careful patterns of the Wolf's priest.

'You think you're dead?' he mocked her. 'You're not dead. You should be so lucky. No simple life as a mute sister for you; you have to go back and mend it all.'

'Then why am I here?'

'I didn't say you were *well*, just not dead.' He shrugged, waving an arm at everything there was to see. 'This isn't real, anyway. This isn't the Godsland as the Wolf sees it.' That familiar expression, both sneer and scowl. 'Perhaps it's enough for Plains or River gods, but the Wolf wouldn't bother with this.'

'Then where is the Wolf?' she demanded.

278

'Comes when you call, does he?' Kalameshli levered himself up and rolled his shoulders; she heard his old joints crack. 'The Wolf in the sky follows the herds from summer to winter; the Wolf in the forests does the same. If all those other gods, Deer and Boar and the others, have fled these lands, you wouldn't expect Wolf to stay and starve, would you?'

His assurance in the superiority of his god, despite all he had seen, was almost comical. What it *was*, was familiar; the same faith that would have given Hesprec to the fire, but it didn't seem so terrible right now. At least he wasn't beating or threatening or cursing her.

The name echoed in her mind. 'Hesprec!'

Kalameshli sighed. 'Don't bring that Serpent nonsense here,' he told her, mildly for him.

'The Rats have Hesprec still. I'm fighting them—'

'That's all done,' he told her.

'Then . . . is she dead?'

'You place too much value in the little Snake.' Kalameshli spat, but without much rancour. 'But you know what? All that stone-wisdom, all that "the Serpent is within the earth", and yet the Wolf knows the secret of drawing iron from the blood rocks, hmm? Why doesn't Serpent know, if he's so wise? Don't forget where you came from, with all these travels and foreign friends of yours. The time will come when you need the Wolf.'

'Come at my call, will he?' she shot back. She was still waiting for that rise of anger from him, and yet he seemed weirdly placid, almost smiling as he cocked an eye at her.

'Are you not his Champion?'

'Not just his.'

'But his also. Child, you don't like me and you hated Akrit Stone River. Both your fathers, and neither one you would have chosen, eh? But we are not the Wolf. Even I am not the Wolf. Listen to the little Snake if you must, but don't forget the Wolf has wisdom too, and if you are strong, and if you walk

279

through wounds and cold and agony and pass out the other side, that is the Wolf in you that made you so.'

'Tell me what happened to Hesprec.' For the conversation was becoming less and less real to her.

Kalameshli fixed her with a sharp eye. 'Oh, she lives. You won, you and the Laughing Girl. Probably you should go back to her now, trailing after the Serpent like you always did. I should have cut the throat of that old white priest before he had the chance to turn you from your people.' And yet still without venom, and then he shook his head and chuckled. 'I tried to kill her, in that stone place on the river. And then she asked for my help. Me – and my jaws snapping for her scaly neck not ten heartbeats before! She asked me to help, in your name, as a friend of her friend. What do you think of that, eh?'

Maniye stared at him. 'And what did you do?' But she already knew the answer to that, of course, because the next time she had met Hesprec and Takes Iron, they were standing shoulder to shoulder, the world's most unlikely allies. 'I'm glad,' she told him. 'Hesprec was like a grandfather to me, when she was old, and a *he*. I'm glad she taught you to be a father.'

Kalameshli regarded her sternly, and she thought with relief that she had angered him at last, but then that smile slunk back, sniffing at the corners of his mouth. 'Perhaps she did teach me some things,' he allowed, and then took in a deep breath. 'Now, now, enough of this talk. Another thing the Serpent is about, too much talk all at the wrong time.'

Maniye opened her mouth to question him, but then the earth around them shook, and she saw cracks appear across the hills, raising great lines of dust. The ground heaved and groaned, and then something was pushing itself out into the night air of the Godsland. Not the Serpent, the god she would have wished to see born from the earth right then. Instead, another buried god was clawing its way into the open, fur matted with old blood, tangled with gnawed bones. It was the Rat, but it was far larger than the largest bear, or perhaps it was small but many, a rat made of countless vermin writhing over one another in constant turmoil.

'Go,' Kalameshli told her flatly, and she ran without question, pelting over the dry ground. Twenty steps and she turned to see him standing before the Rat still, an iron hatchet in one hand, a knife of the same metal in the other.

'Takes Iron!' she shouted, but he yelled, 'Go, idiot girl!' and she understood, fleeing the broken desolation of the Godsland for a land under a different shadow. When she looked over her shoulder she saw him as a tiny shape before the ever-growing bulk of the Rat, but he blazed with forge-fire, and when he opened his mouth the Wolf cried out of him, and she knew he would hold the way at her back, and let her return to the world.

She was right: there was pain. Every part of her ached, and she felt bindings about her, her limbs most of all. Beneath she could feel all the separate hot fevers from a hundred little bites.

She had been coming back to herself all this time while her mind soujorned in the gods' empty places. Now she hung just below the surface of the world, knowing she could put the revelations off no longer. Her eyes were gummed shut and she had to fight with the muscles beneath the lids, but at last she forced open a crack onto the world and looked out.

She saw the stars, and for a moment her eyes swam and they seemed to move, darting angrily about the barrier of night and looking for a way in. But then she made herself blink, the simple movement feeling like some colossal labour, and the stars fell back into their places, and the cold glare from the edge of her vision was not the lamps of the Plague People but just the moon.

She closed her eyes again, because listening hurt less, and doing both at once seemed a complexity she could not manage. There was a fire nearby – its warmth lost in the feverish heat that gripped her – and someone moving closer: soft footsteps, familiar.

'You breathe differently when you're awake, did you know?'

The words had that old dry humour but they were gentle and fond, the voice of a little Riverlands girl who had turned up from nowhere after an old Riverlands man had gone to the earth.

Maniye's intent was to open her eyes and leap up and exclaim over Hesprec's survival, but none of that happened; she managed a croak and a twitch at best. Moments later the cool edge of a bowl touched her lips and she was drinking as though she had crossed a desert.

Soon after that she was sitting up, feeling each part of her raise new complaints as she changed position. She had so many little wounds in her – shallow scratches and punctures where the teeth of the Rat had got past the Champion's thick hide and Maniye's iron coat. It was not the teeth that had laid her low, nor even loss of blood. The Rat's teeth were filthy from the middens and the graves where it fed. She could still feel the poison in her, the corruption it had driven into her with each tiny incision. But she was fighting it. She could feel her strength mustering like a warband ready to take back its home.

'Where . . . ?' She flicked her fingers at the fire, banked low and sheltered by rocks. Beyond, the grass ocean of the Plains waved silver in the moonlight.

'We went east,' Hesprec said. 'Probably it was a mistake, but when we were clear of the Horn-Bearer fortress, there were more Rat Speakers between us and the camp, and you were hard to carry between us. We were hurt, too. So we went east, because the Plague People have worse eyes, and were not looking for us.' She waved down Maniye's next question. 'Shyri is close. We have played hunter and hearth-keeper, she and I.' And then Hesprec waited, watching her face closely. 'Takes Iron is dead.'

'I know,' Maniye said simply.

Hesprec nodded. 'He taught the Rat to fear the Wolf before he went,' she said, exactly the words Kalameshli would have wanted to hear. 'We're clear of the fortress because of him, and him only. He died on four feet, believe me.'

'I know,' Maniye echoed. She reached inside herself to find

out how this made her feel, but there were so many pains there it was impossible to know. A father who had never seemed like one; a tormentor who thought it was for her own good. The man who had forced herself on her mother, when all Akrit's efforts had borne no fruit. Kalameshli had not lived a life of kindness, even by the Wolf's harsh standards. It was not Maniye's place to forgive him for the worst of it, but what he had done to her, she found she forgave. With Akrit dead and taken from the Crown of the World and the Wolf's Shadow, there had been another man in him, trying to reach the surface. She might have respected that man.

'So what's the plan?' she rasped out.

'The plan is that I wish not to have to rescue you and tend your wounds again, so you will have to be careful from now on, and not throw yourself away on small matters,' Hesprec told her, hiding behind the Riverlander way, formality and understatement.

'Like rescuing you,' Maniye pointed out.

'These things are known.' Hesprec smiled at her, but it was a terribly wan thing. 'But now you are awake, and if you can move, then we must walk. After the Plague attacked, everyone fled further into the Plains. What might be happening there now, I can't think. Perhaps the Rat rules on a mound of corpses. Perhaps everyone is fighting everyone else. I would not be surprised.'

'What about the Plague?' Maniye pressed.

'Well, bad news is like ants, they say; never going singly and everywhere you look,' Hesprec said dourly. 'Come, if you can.'

Maniye tried her human feet, but the challenge defeated her. As a wolf, though, she could limp along well enough, tracking round the fire to the edge of the rocks.

There was a great pale light out on the grasslands, beyond the stark shadow of the Horn-Bearer fort. It had not been just the moon, after all.

'They are still building it,' Hesprec told her. 'Many have come

283

from the east, warriors and the other sort, too. Our places fascinate them, I think.'

Maniye Stepped back, thoughtfully. 'I don't think they quite know they are our places,' she considered. 'We are beasts to them.' A dizzying thought took hold of her. 'Everywhere they go they find buildings and children and beasts. How puzzling it must be for them.'

'It was grown men and women they attacked four nights ago,' Hesprec pointed out.

'Four nights?' Maniye exclaimed.

'Four nights,' came a new voice, 'and you were quiet for all of them and did not call the Plague People down on us with shouting.' Shyri dropped down beside her, dumping down a couple of creatures like tailless squirrels. 'You look bad.'

'I feel worse,' Maniye said, honestly enough. 'But I can travel.'

'Good. Hunting is terrible here.' Shyri would not meet her eyes. 'Sorry.'

Maniye wondered what for. For the Hyena and its alliance of convenience with the Rat? For striking the blow that brought the fight that killed Kalameshli? But how would things have gone otherwise? None of it was the fault of either Shyri or her people's god. So instead she said, 'Sorry, are you? You told the Rat Speaker there was one Champion you would keep. Did you mean Asman or me? I don't know which you should be sorrier for.'

Shyri stared at her, aghast, and Maniye managed a weak chuckle that quickly threatened to get out of hand and tear something. The Hyena woman wavered between anger and hurt until the joke jumped over to her and she was the Laughing Girl again.

They set off before dawn, and would sleep out the hottest hours under whatever cover they could find and travel again when the sun was falling back towards the edge of the earth. It seemed a melancholy thing that each new day was born from the land the Plague People had already made their own, while each day died red over their fugitives and victims.

284

They made a wide detour to avoid the white walls of the Plague People camp, keeping within sight of it and seeing new figures arriving from the east, some on foot and some on the wing. Even Hesprec breathed a sigh of relief when its pale radiance was at their back, but they were still far from safe. They travelled on through a land abandoned, ceded already to the enemy.

The only human shapes they saw were skimming through the sky on shimmering wings, or penned behind the ever-growing white walls of the Plague People's new town. They also saw a handful atop the Horn-Bearer fortress, and perhaps their blank-faced curiosity would even root out the Rat from its dark places. The Plague People would ask their meaningless questions of that grand collection of bones and glean no answers they could understand.

Every so often Shyri would guide them to a village to pick over what remained there, taking food that had not spoiled, clothes, breaking up the pieces of lost lives for firewood. Often there were bodies, and many of them children who had been neither able to follow their transformed parents, nor gathered in by the Plague. Some had been killed and part-eaten by beasts, others starved. Some had fallen to knife or spear, and Maniye did not want to think about what had led to such a thing. There were adult corpses too – mostly the old but a few were warriors who had the marks of Plague People darts through their flesh. These the travellers avoided, because surely their ghosts would be clinging on within their ribs, waiting to blight the living who came near. Once they came across a village with dead fresh enough that vultures thronged the walls. The birds shuffled and shifted and fought, but they would not go down to feed because something worse was already in possession of the corpses. Maniye and the others watched a thing like a beetle, almost the size of a man, as it fumbled and chewed at the dead flesh, crushing and cutting with mouthparts like hammers and knives. Shyri was full of tales of similar sights. The Plague People were not good herdsmen; their monsters were getting loose into a land where nothing would threaten them.

And there was more. When they set a fire to watch out the night, hide it as they might, some beast would find them. A lion, perhaps, or a Plains dog, or even a wolf a long way from any place that wolves called home. They came and stared, those mute animals, and the firelight gleamed and danced in their eyes. Some part of them remembered, Maniye knew. It remembered other firesides, tales, family. She could look into those gleaming eyes and see a soul trapped within the beast, denied the freedom to take on its birth-shape. All she could do was wish them a rebirth, but the world of the spirit was unravelling, threads cut one by one as the Plague People spun their own world. In that world there were no souls and no rebirths.

The next village they came to was another trove of bones, the last testament to those who had not fled swiftly enough. Who had killed them, Maniye could not say. There were knives scattered across the ground and she had an image of them, men, women, children, hacking at each other, maddened with fear and desperate to flee in the only direction left to them. But perhaps that was just her imagination trying to digest all the rich food she had given it these last few days.

But the bones were all gnawed by hundreds of tiny teeth. Whether the Rat had brought death here, certainly it had followed soon after and taken what nourishment there was to be had. Every sack was chewed through, every pot upset and emptied, every shred of flesh stripped.

He said it is his age, now. And even rats starve, but perhaps that is his victory, to be the last on the hill of bones. Perhaps in the end it will just be Rat and Hyena at each other's throat. She stole a glance at Shyri and found the Laughing Girl looking back at her without expression.

They left that village as swiftly as they could, pushing on through a landscape that had begun to seem endless, just grassland to the end of the world, studded with the empty sockets of dead

286

villages, and not a single human being in sight from horizon to horizon. Maniye still needed much rest, slowing the other two down and knowing that any moment the Plague People might make a new push westwards and undo all their progress. And yet the enemy did not come, With her head swimming, and the fever still boiling her within her skin, Maniye padded on in wolf-shape, panting and shivering, and soon enough the world was swimming around her. The wind became voices of dead enemies and friends: Akrit, Kalameshli, Broken Axe. The tall grass rippled with the passage of tigers that were not there. After sunset, the stars came loose in the sky and wheeled about her. She felt the Godsland very near, just a sidestep away. At the same time she felt the heat of her wounds and knew that she could trust nothing of any of it, and must rely on Shyri and Hesprec to keep her walking straight.

What happened next was more like a dream than anything, or a nightmare.

They had camped in the shadow of a rock, choosing the west side so that it would shield them from the gaze of the Plague People, for all their new domain was not even a shadow to the east now. Shyri set a fire and they dropped down around it, more than ready to abandon the world to sleep.

Maniye thought she had dozed a little – it made what followed even more dream-like, draped with the confusion of a sudden waking. She came back to the world with the knowledge that Hesprec was standing right beside her, rod-straight and tense as a drawn bow. Hesprec said, 'We have a guest.'

'What guest?' Maniye fought not to just drop back into drowsing, pinching at her own arms.

'Something of theirs,' Hesprec murmured, and abruptly Maniye was wide awake, heart hammering away inside her. She Stepped, trusting to a tiger's eyes. Out there beyond the emberlight of their fire she saw a huge hunched shape scuttling on too many legs. Not the Plague People themselves but one of their creatures, and bigger than any she'd seen.

She took on the Champion's shape in case the thing skittered closer, but doing so caught its notice. It stopped, so still she almost lost it in the dark until the twitch of its antennae told her where it was. She growled then, deep and angry, hoping to drive the monster off. Instead, it pattered half a dozen steps closer.

Shyri was awake by then, knife in her hand, and the three of them just stared as the creature executed a curious little dance – a few steps closer, then one or two back, and then closer still – not attacking, not doing anything that they could make any sense of, but drifting slowly towards their fire nonetheless. Seen so clearly, it was awful in its clumsiness, legs flailing and dragging alternately, the curved shields of its wings half flaring out and then clacking back into place as though it didn't know what they were for.

Maniye found her human shape again, in case it was the Champion's bulk that was exercising such a fearsome fascination for the thing. The focus of those glittering, bulbous eyes never changed.

'It's you,' Shyri said. 'Why is it staring at you?'

Maniye shook her head, wanting to deny it, but that faceted regard was ignoring her companions utterly. Shyri could have gone up and driven her knife between the plates of the thing's hide, and it might have utterly ignored her. Soon its shell was dancing red with the last of the firelight and they had retreated to the far side of the camp.

'Is it diseased?' Shyri asked, wondering. Maniye shrugged, conceding the possibility. The Plague People's beasts had always seemed just that; yes, they were little soil-dwellers grown to monstrous size, but beasts still, with a beast's desires, or else on the leashes of their masters. This monster, this great-backed beetle thing, acted like something else altogether.

And yet we've seen this before. Maniye's insides lurched as she realized what it reminded her of. *Impossible . . .*

And then the creature had obviously gathered its courage, because it lunged forwards, almost running into the fire in its blundering advance, and then stopping, staring only at Maniye as though waiting for her to rebuke it.

She opened her mouth – to say she knew not what, for what possible words could there be? Even as she tried to speak, the thing changed. Without transition the great hulking insect had become a man. He was a fat man, dark and naked, sprawled before the fire. He clutched at the dry ground there and made noises, horrible word-like noises. He stared at his hands as though they were new to him, and then he looked at Maniye with his human eyes, and she knew him.

She had seen him day after day. He had come in with the woman, his constant companion, and he had tried to speak to her; he had tested and measured her. He had been curious. And hollow, for he was a Plague Man, but he was filled with something now. He was ridden by the soul of the beetle-thing he had become.

He goggled at her, eyes wide and white in a slack face; he beat his flabby fists against the ground and hooted desperately. Then he was the beetle once again, spinning in a circle on the spot, limbs mad with trapped meaning, and a moment later those many legs had carried him away into the night. They waited until the moon had passed its zenith, but not another sound or sight of the thing came to trouble their fire.

26

Speaking to the Pale Shadow woman was disconcerting for Kailovela, not for the burning emptiness within her, but for the predatory attention she paid to her visitor.

They were within a big tent set up by the Riverlanders; inside the cloth turned the daylight into near-dusk, for their prisoner-guest did not like the sun on her fishbelly-pale skin. Kailovela cradled her son, listening to him fuss and fidget, feeding him when he seemed to need it. In the gloom the pale woman stood out with ghost-like clarity.

The leader of the Rivermen sat close by. Kailovela was more familiar than most with that aura of strength a Champion's soul imparted, and this Asman had more of it than most, a man crammed with greatness so much that he sat in its shadow. He plainly did not relish being the Pale Shadow's keeper, and the continuing absence of the girl Serpent was obviously chewing at his mind. For now, he just sat and listened.

And Kailovela had come to gain just this from the white woman, but within a few words she was regretting her decision. The kinship between them horrified her, but for some reason Galethea of the Pale Shadow found it the most important thing in the world.

She was full of questions, all asked in that soft, strangely accented voice, occasionally pausing over a word as she translated the meaning from her own weird language. The thought of having two languages in one head was dizzying to Kailovela, as though languages were like a Champion's souls. Except this creature had no soul at all, and so perhaps that made room for all manner of knowledge and magics. Like the 'craft' she spoke of that allowed her to touch the minds of others, and make them love her, even a little.

'I have seen you do it,' Galethea said. 'It is a gift of our blood, the blood of the Families, and yet you have it. And you have a soul, a true human soul.' Her eyes gleamed with avarice. 'Where did you get it from?'

Kailovela started. 'My soul?'

'The craft, the way you touch them. Was it from your gods? Was it a gift?'

'It was just . . . born with me,' Kailovela said haltingly. 'It is no gift.'

Galethea chuckled, full of unwanted sisterly affection. 'Not to those around you, no, but to you? It makes you the centre of their world, does it not?'

'That is no gift either.'

The pale woman blinked, plainly unsure what she meant. 'It came on when you ceased to be a child? That is the way amongst us. And amongst you, it is when your soul comes, yes? Always we have wondered if, when the craft arose in us, it might open the door a little wider, so a soul could creep in?'

'I don't know what you mean. You have no gods. Souls come from the gods.'

'*But*,' Galethea interrupted urgently, 'what gods? The gods of your parents, but you can sever souls and invite new ones in, we know this. Among the Jaguar, back in our Kingdom, we have . . .' She faltered to silence abruptly, and so Kailovela's imagination had to supply the word *experimented*.

The pale woman pressed her lips together. 'We took mates from the Jaguar, when at last we began to feel the lack in ourselves. We thought it would be so simple, that our children at least would borrow the souls of their fathers. But they are as

291

empty as we. And our sons father only empty children on their Jaguar wives. But we never stopped believing that somehow we might find a god to favour us, to bridge the gap and bring us into your world. Because we like your world. Your world is so alive, and the world we left long ago is no longer ours.'

'The Plague People are trying to bring that world here,' Kailovela noted.

'We are not the Plague People. We fled them too, long ago. *Please.*' And Galethea reached out and touched her hand, where it rested on the baby's head. 'You have a foot in our world. A foot, half a foot, a toe. Please tell me how you did it. Tell me where the crossing is, so we may come to you.'

Dread and revulsion ripped through Kailovela and she pushed away, breaking that cool touch before something malign could leap from it to her child. The boy convulsed in her arms as she did so and began wailing, immediately and utterly inconsolable. She looked into Galethea's face then, expecting to see gleeful evil hidden in her eyes, but saw only utter misery. In that moment there was no craft, no magic, just a woman desperate for something she could not have.

Who knew what she might have said, in that candid moment, but her name was being called from outside, in Loud Thunder's booming tones. She stood awkwardly, eyes still on the beseeching figure. *We have stories of monsters who wear human faces and prey on the unwary. But what if they lived amongst us for so long that they forgot they were monsters? Can we trust them, these pale things?*

She ducked out into the bright day, into Loud Thunder's shadow. 'Mother wants you,' he told her awkwardly. 'And she wants the – the thing, the Pale Shadow thing.'

Kailovela frowned at him. 'What for?'

'Empty Skin and your monster, they're back.'

She should be happy they were still alive, given what they had been about, but the thought only brought Kailovela a shock of dismay. *Now I am punished,* she thought. Nobody had been pleased with her when they found out what treachery she had

292

aided. Only Loud Thunder's tacit support had staved off the repercussions. Now there would be a reckoning. Except . . .

'But why the Pale Shadow?'

A shrug. 'Your monster has something to say.'

There were plenty of angry people waiting to see what Empty Skin had to say for herself. The news of her recklessness had spread past the northerners' camp so that the Plainsfolk had come to scowl and finger their knives at her. Kailovela had the impression that the soulless girl had become somehow *to blame* in many minds. They thought she would stir up a new attack by the Plague People, as though their implacable enemy needed a prompt for anything it did. Those who knew of the little monster and understood what it was spoke of losing some great weapon against the enemy, for all that it had only ever been a tiny thing of no great use.

But they had gone, with Kailovela's own blessing, and now they had come back unscathed and full of words that nobody could understand.

Nobody except Galethea, but she had proved remarkably unwilling to act as translator. The sight of the little monster seemed far more abhorrent to her than it did to real people, until Kailovela guessed she was making it plain to everyone around her that the Pale Shadow and the Plague were utterly separate things. And there was a genuine fear there: she had not been lying when she said her people had fled the Plague, too.

It took Mother to bring the pale woman to heel. When Asman brought her into the presence of the greatest of the Bear, all the fight went out of her. She stood in Mother's shadow, face down-cast and shoulders slumped, and agreed that she would hear the little monster's words.

'And you will speak them *truly*,' Mother rumbled, and Kailovela imagined that 'craft', that hollow magic, reaching out to the Bear woman to try and alter her mind, and then scurrying back to hide behind its mistress's skirts. Galethea could move

293

Mother's mind no more than she could carry a mountain across the Plains.

So then it was down to the little monster talking excitedly in her rapid patter, broken by Galethea's occasional interjections, and everyone else sitting around and waiting. Empty Skin sat at the monster's side and faced down all the dark looks she was getting, unconcerned about anyone's opinion.

Kailovela watched and listened; she had lived with the little monster for years. She understood some of its words, but much more of the way it moved, its expressions and moods. A prisoner for most of that time, just as she had been, those moods had been in the main dejected. Now it was set on fire with purpose. She had never seen it so animated.

It looked at her often, as though seeking her approval. In some small way it was still the two of them against the world, just as it had been back in the Eyrie. She was the tether that had brought the little monster back. She was the one it was trying to save.

The thought made sense of what she was seeing. The little monster had a plan.

And then its words were done, and it was gesturing impatiently for Galethea to relay everything to the assembled crowd.

Their massed attention struck her like a blow, all that fear and suspicion and outright hate. Kailovela saw the exact moment that Galethea used her magic to blunt it, layering glamour over her hollowness until she could look like something other than her enemy. *This is how her people first came to our lands.*

'She has gone to the Plague People and told them of us,' Galethea announced, and if that 'us' rang false, then it was lost in the general uproar. Nobody liked the sound of what she was saying.

Then Mother shifted slightly, and the movement was sufficient to quiet people. 'Truly, pale one.'

Galethea flinched. 'It has told them of us,' she insisted. 'It says that in their minds we were a nothing, a dream people. She has made us a *real* people to them, even just a little.'

'So they will kill us as people,' one of the Wolves said, and for a moment Galethea was going to agree with him. Plainly whatever the little monster was suggesting was something she wanted no part of. Then she glanced guiltily at Mother and said, 'She says they will talk to us as people. Now they know we are people, she says they will send speakers. She says she argued long and hard to win this for us.'

'And then what?' someone demanded. 'Will they leave, when they have spoken to us?'

'It's enough if they will just agree to keep to the places where they are, and come no further!' shouted a Plainsman, and others began to argue, perhaps because those places had been their places not so long before. This time Mother had to cough twice before quiet was restored.

'She does not know what they will agree,' Galethea said, with a venomous look at the little monster. 'She does not know that they will agree anything. But she says they will talk, a few of them and a few of us. That is what she won from them, she says.'

'And why does it do any of these things?' The new voice sent a shock of fear through Kailovela, even now: Yellow Claw, of course. 'What does *it* want, out of this?'

The subject had obviously not come up. Galethea spoke to the little monster again, and it answered firmly, tiny fists clenched, staring at Yellow Claw and at anyone else who doubted it.

'It claims it wants to right a wrong,' Galethea said, trying to infuse the words with doubt. 'It has been our prisoner, it says. It could have just flown. But it knows us, as its people do not know us. It has seen the wrongs done to us. It will try, this once, to heal the wound. And then it will go back to its own places.'

The little monster's eyes were on Kailovela all through Galethea's words. *I do this for you, because you showed me kindness.* She needed no translator for that. The thought made her sick at herself. *It was not kindness. It was this craft, this magic I have. I was only ever your jailer.*

And of course everyone had an opinion that they needed to

express immediately, and very few of the voices Kailovela could hear sounded as though they were for the plan. Surely it was a trick of the Plague People. *As though they needed to use tricks.* Surely it was death for whoever went. *As though death wasn't already a guest at everyone's fire.* And there were far more who simply wanted no peace. They could not conceive of a world where they lived, and also the Plague People lived, the ensouled and the soulless in uneasy truce. *And yet what victories we have won are fleeting, and the Plague People only grow stronger.* There were a thousand real people for every Plague warrior, but the balance only shifted one way.

Galethea looked relieved, hearing the mood of the crowd, but then her eyes sought out Mother and found no condemnation there, only a sober thoughtfulness.

Two days later, a great host of spears was sighted to the south. A brief rash of panic swept all those who had fled this far, and were constantly on the point of fleeing further. It was not the Plague People. The soldiers of the River Lords had come.

Tecumet led them, carried at the fore, wearing the Kasra's fierce war mask and – Asman knew – armour beneath her fine robes. When the River forces arrived and struck their camp at a diplomatic distance from the rest, a delegation came to meet the leaders of the Plains and the Crown of the World's war hosts. Tecumet sat silent while the Serpent priestess told everyone how the River had come to fight the adversary of all humanity. Everyone already knew the truth. The Kasra's fortress at Tsokawan was ruins, her brother dead. Even the might of the Sun River Nation had not held back the Plague tide.

Asman went to her after all that formality was done, slipping almost apologetically into her tent to watch Esumit divest her of all the weighty regalia. Beneath it, Tecumet looked frailer than before, her eyes baggy and red with sleepless nights.

'All that work to muster the army, and half of me thinks the war is already lost. Half of me thinks that these men should put down their spears and return to their families for whatever time's left,' she admitted. 'And you have moved a long ways west since we set out. We have climbed here on a ladder of messengers, each with a different story of where your tent was pitched. Will you tell me there is some clever stratagem behind this.'

'It is . . .' But Asman had never been a man for comforting lies. 'Just what you'd think, Te.'

'Terrible things,' she supplied hollowly.

'Terrible things,' he echoed; their childhood game now turned into the end of the world.

Esumit had come and gone while they spoke, and now gave her Kasra a nod. Tecumet held her arms out abruptly. 'Hold me, Asa.'

He blinked in surprise but went to her, smooth skin against his own, her perfume and her sweat in his nostrils equally. 'What is it? More bad news?'

'For me? Probably. But never for you. Hold me now, because I know your loves and I want a moment where I don't have to share you.'

'Share me?' But someone else was shouldering into the tent, much to the helpless displeasure of the guards. Asman looked into that familiar lantern-jawed face, no different to the last time they'd met save for a new scar or two.

'He brought us a Dragon warband from all the way down the Tsotec. And probably raided every village on the way up,' Tecumet said, but Asman's heart leapt, because she was looking on the old pirate and there was none of the spite or loathing he would have expected. *It is enough that those I love do not hate one another.*

'You're chief of the Black Teeth now?' he asked the man.

Venat chuckled, then came over to punch him in the side for old times' sake – grunting with surprise when Asman hugged him fiercely, ending up with an arm over his shoulders, an arm over Tecumet's.

'When I left Whale Seat, I was chief,' he told them. 'By next

297

sunrise, probably not. They'll be cutting each other's throats all over the islands to see who's in charge, the stupid bastards. It got me the chance to raise a score of boats to come to the fight, though. If it's the end of the world, nobody's going to say that the Dragon didn't show.' He grinned, that vicious, ugly expression that warmed Asman's heart. 'So everyone over here's doing really badly then. Are they actually going to fight, some day, or just roll over and bare their throats?'

Asman had a quick answer prepared, but it died in his throat. He remembered that night of panic when the Plague People attacked. Overshadowing that, he remembered Tsokawan's fall, the tearing grief of Tecuman's death. *I loved three people more than life itself, loved them with my mind and heart, yearned for them, all three, with the burning passion of my body. One is dead, and the other two are here, where the blade will fall next. I fear no death of mine, but I fear the death that may come for them.*

'Or . . . what?' Venat asked, and Asman knew himself to have gone very still and solemn, holding them both. Tecumet looked into his face, seeking what had made him sad; as usual he buried it all deep, ready to shrug it off with a smile and a joke. But the sadness would remain, the fear of what even victory would cost, if to win by the spear was possible.

Unless there was another way.

'There is a plan.' His voice cracked over the words. It was not a good plan; in fact it was the worst plan, from the worst source, but it was a plan for something other than dying in a great fight, and suddenly he had more time for such a plan. 'The Iron Wolves and their allies, they have a prisoner, a little monster . . .'

Every fireside had its argument, it seemed. The tribes of the Wolf were at each other's throats about it, and the Tiger against the Eyrie, and every warband divided, but Kailovela thought the clear majority were against it, at least amongst Thunder's war host.

She had taken wing to listen to voices talking with Plains

accents, or the soft voices of the Riverlanders, and found no unity. The Plains, who had lost most, would be those paying the price of any compromise, and yet all the same, there were plenty amongst them who simply wished to lose no more – no more land, no more sons and daughters, no more tribes swallowed up. Just as there were those who had turned to the secret worship of Rat for salvation, so there were those who would clasp hands with the Plague People, if the Plague People would only stop their advance.

But it seemed to her, when sat at Mother's feet with the little monster squatting at her own, that far too few voices spoke for such a move.

Mother herself gave no sign of her opinions, but time was drawing back the bow, and all from the Crown of the World were aware of that absence of a pronouncement. The fact that she had not destroyed the little monster's plan with a few heavy words was more and more marked. *If she said yes to it,* Kailovela thought, *what would they do, all of them? Because the plan is nothing if they are all against it. You can't force people to make peace if they won't set down their spears.*

She went to sleep with that melancholy thought in her head, in the tent she shared with Empty Skin and the little monster, three freaks together. The moon was still high when she woke, though, hearing the distinctive sound outside that was Loud Thunder being stealthy.

Is it now that he has broken? She had been waiting for him to lose patience. He desired her, and who would waste a harsh word on him for taking what he wanted. And yet every chance given to Thunder, he had examined like a curious pebble and then gently put it down and walked on. And now she had found the ability to talk to him, and she had seen him lead in his humble-bumble way, and she had seen he was strong – not his arms or his bear shape, but deep in him. Hearing him outside, a shock went through her and she wondered whether she had come to want him after all. She was so unused to having it be her choice.

But no, he was here because Mother had sent him, muttering her name apologetically as though trying not to wake her even as he tried to wake her.

'Mother wants you. All of you. The River people have called a council.'

'Now?' she hissed, hearing Empty Skin groan and the little monster flourish its wings briefly as it woke.

'Now,' Thunder whispered – his whisper was a huge thing that seemed to cup the tent in the palm of its hand. 'Secret things are afoot.'

'Secret things,' she echoed. She looked over and met Empty Skin's gaze. Surely there was only one secret thing demanding Mother's attention, right then.

Perhaps she had expected a great moonlit gathering, but Mother sat on her rock and the small group around her seemed like conspirators. She saw the Coyote, Two Heads Talking, and Lone Mountain, who was Thunder's brother or cousin or some such thing, and who wanted to be war leader of the Bear. Icefoot of the Moon Eaters and Seven Mending of the Owl had brought wisdom, and there were a handful of old Plainsfolk too, mostly of the Boar tribe. Most of all there were the Riverlanders – their Champion and some of their warriors, and in their midst the Pale Shadow woman with her cloak pulled tight about her.

The River Champion, Asman, glanced over, but he was seeking the little monster. His eyes did not settle for a moment on Kailovela. 'Good. Bring it here,' he said, and she bristled a little at his tone. A moment later she did as he said, presenting the creature to the gathering there.

Asman knelt before it, staring into its face, or the hungry emptiness behind it. 'A trick,' he told it, though his words would mean nothing to the thing. 'You want us off our guard. You have begun to grow scared of us, is what they say? We are now so many – and with the spears of the River joining too! – that the

300

Plague People believe their killing rods and their Fear will not be enough. Hmm? So they send you with your offer to talk.'

He straightened up from that blank stare. 'Well, we've all heard the word about the camp. Nobody is off their guard. Nobody is tricked.' He grinned, teeth gleaming in the moonlight. 'But now Tecumet Kasra has heard the news. Tecumet Kasra thinks perhaps some small band might see if it is possible to exchange words with the Plague People. Small, so that if it is a trick, few are lost. And small because small is the number of those who believe it is worth the venture.'

Lone Mountain growled, deep in his chest; plainly he was not one of them. The slightest motion from Mother stayed him, though.

'What does the River propose?' she asked.

'Some few of ours, some few of yours,' Asman told her, bearing the weight of that gaze without flinching. 'Your little monster and its handlers; our Pale Shadow, to swallow one set of words and spit out another.'

There was an exclamation from the midst of the River warriors, and Galethea forced herself forwards. 'You *mustn't* do this!' she spat. 'There is no dealing with them.'

'They are your people,' Mother observed thoughtfully.

'Not my people! Not for many generations.' She trembled before Mother's solid regard. 'Please, if they see me, they will know we are there. They will come for all my people. Do not ask this of me.'

'We *ask* nothing,' Asman said shortly. 'We set it as the price of our aid. You came because your people wanted our help. Will you take that help from our bones and cold hearths?'

'I came with Hesprec,' Galethea told him, 'who would not ask me this!'

'And Hesprec is gone, not seen since the attack,' Asman told her harshly, as though it was her fault. 'And who will be next? And why should you not shoulder the risk, since the reward you seek is so great? There is nobody else.'

Kailovela could almost see the waves of glamour radiating from the Pale Shadow woman as she tried to twist Asman's mind about, but the Champion was like stone. At last, she herself stepped forward and touched Galethea's shoulder.

'I will be with you,' she told the hollow woman. She saw Loud Thunder start, because he hadn't seen her on this expedition, only Empty Skin, perhaps, to hold the little monster's leash. But she was needed. And perhaps the Plague People would see some kinship in her and stay their hands for her sake.

'I will be with you,' she repeated, and knew her own glamour was reaching out to touch Galethea. Surely it would slide from her like water off wax, for Kailovela's power was weak and this woman had lived and breathed it all her life. It caught, though, and she saw the white woman reluctantly let go of her tension. *She wants to believe me*, Kailovela knew. Here was one of the soulless, the enemy in all but name, and yet she was as lost and weak as any of them, and desperate enough to clutch at any comforting lie.

27

'It's still out there,' Maniye said. They were camped high up, nestled into a jumble of rocks and without a fire. She had hoped that the beetle creature would lose them, just blunder past in the dark. Her tiger eyes could find no trace of it, but her wolf nose told a different story. She had slept fitfully for a while, worn down by what should have been a modest pace, the poison of the Rat still sapping her body. Now she woke with that acrid, alien scent biting at her nostrils.

'We should kill it,' Shyri suggested. 'Crack its shell and see what hatches.'

'Probably.' But Hesprec's tone did not suggest total agreement.

'It's the Plague People and their monsters, all in one,' the Laughing Girl said, shaking her head. 'Is it the next way they'll come for us, the first of a whole war host of them, do you think?'

'There was only one,' Maniye noted.

'That we saw. So far.'

'It's following *me*.' The certainty had been building in her all day, as they tried to put distance between themselves and the unseen creature, and it stubbornly refused to let them.

'Why you? What's it to you, or you to it?' Shyri demanded.

'It knows me.'

'From the camp where they kept you,' Hesprec filled in, and she nodded.

303

'How can you tell? They're all just hollow things,' Shyri complained, in the manner of someone trying to convince herself.

'They have their hunters and their hearth-keepers, their priests,' Maniye said quietly. 'Only, not like us, not really, but I saw enough of them. This one I know. We would say, "One of the Wise", except the other Plague Men didn't seem to listen to it.'

'Just like one of the wise, then,' Hesprec put in drily, but Maniye shook off the humour, feeling through her memories to connect them to what she had seen.

'There were two of them. Like cousins to each other. They made me Step from shape to shape. They watched and watched.'

'Where is the other one, then?' Shyri eyed the moonlit grasslands suspiciously.

'Hesprec . . .' Maniye said, so softly they both leant in to hear her. 'When we fled them, there was . . . something had happened to catch their notice.'

'Yes,' the Serpent girl agreed, her mind already there.

'A terrible thing to them.' Maniye had left those memories alone, buried in the dark places of her mind: the story of 'When They Caught Me' that she had not wanted to uncover and look at. But now she forced herself. She and Hesprec had fled under cover of a great horror that had come even to the soulless Plague People. They had been gathered about a hideous, misshapen thing, a twitching, dying thing that had aspects of insect and human to it, running together like wax.

'I think it was trying,' Hesprec said unhappily. 'I think its companion succeeded. It is mad and does not know itself any more. But it knows you.'

'Does it think I can help it?' Maniye asked her.

'These things . . .' Hesprec shook her head. 'These things are *not* known.'

They saw nothing of it that night, no matter which of them kept watch, but somehow Maniye knew it was out there, tethered to her by whatever panic or revelation had gripped it, stumbling about in the grass on too many legs.

They made little progress the next day, as though the presence of the beetle-thing was gnawing at Maniye's strength. Her fever came back, and there was no shape she could take to escape it. Even the Champion felt like a prisoner of its own weighty flesh. Hesprec and Shyri tried their best to help her along, but she kept losing focus, the dry heat of the Plains desiccating her mind until she kept rediscovering herself stumbling through tall grass under an unfamiliar sky, as strange to her as the Godsland itself.

Is this how the beetle-thing feels? she wondered. She remembered the disjointed panic of its movements. Was that just how beetles were, or had it been dying even then, poisoned by the thinking mind that inhabited it, by the soul it had somehow swallowed.

She wanted to tell that to Hesprec, then, but there would be no need. Hesprec knew all that she knew, and kept her own counsel on it. Maniye had no revelations that would surprise the Serpent.

They rested up towards noon, finding a barrel-trunked tree standing alone amidst the grass and scavenging shade from it. The idea was to press on once the shadows lengthened, but Maniye could not. She felt that waves of sickness were pulsing towards her from the very earth, from the baking air. She shivered in her human skin, whined and gnawed at her wounds as a wolf. Shyri went to hunt but came back soon after; she had seen swift shadows passing across the earth and gone to ground, hiding from the eyes of the Plague People. There were many of them, she said – passing back and forth to some place ahead.

'Building some new den,' she suggested.

Hesprec nodded cautiously. 'First amongst Serpent's gifts is learning. Can you get close enough to see what they're about?'

Shyri's eyes widened at the thought but she nodded resolutely. That spared Maniye the rest of the day's march, leaving her to suffer in the tree's shade while Hesprec rationed out their water.

'Why is this come back to me?' she croaked, after waking for the fifth time.

'You walked too far, dipped too deep into your strength,' Hesprec suggested. 'We should have stayed still, even in the Plague's shadow.'

'We are still in that shadow,' Maniye said bitterly. She knew that their travel had taken them such a small way – she could have run that far in a day without tiring herself, if she was well and strong.

'We are under many shadows,' Hesprec responded.

When Shyri came back, it was with no story that made any sense. The Plague People had taken lanterns out to a great flat rock in the grasses. It had been the haunt of lions and lizards once; now they had marked it out as their place, as though some great Plague festival was due. Once sunset had been and gone, Maniye could even make out the glimmer of it, cold and still as the enemy's white-walled fortresses. And yet they had not brought their beasts to spin webs about the place and fence out the world. Instead they had just planted their lamps, marking out the spot and then abandoning it. Shyri said they were still nearby and overhead, but the rock itself they avoided. None of it made any sense. Maniye was still trying to formulate questions when Hesprec sat up with a hissing sound, then Stepped to a brown snake that lifted its head and tasted the air with its tongue.

Moments later she was a girl again, tugging at Maniye's arm. 'Go,' she said urgently. 'We go now.'

'The Plague?' Shyri's knife was in her hand, her eyes on the sky.

'Not the Plague. There are other shadows. Come on!'

They froze as a new voice broke in. 'What has no feet yet always runs?' it rasped, sounding as though it came from a man far closer to death than Maniye was. 'The Serpent never did stay to finish a fight, never! Why else would the world need a fourth brother, to have held back the Plague People? And yet where are our altars? Where our priests and sacrifices? Banned by the

Serpent that flees into a crack in the earth at the first tremble of the enemy.'

Hesprec was very still. 'There is no fourth brother,' she said, as much to herself as in reply.

Maniye's weakness was abruptly far, far worse. She felt panic start in her, that she would be unable to fight. The Champion caught it and stamped it out, and she Stepped into its great bulk, hoping that it would lend her the strength to move its ponderous limbs.

A cadaverous man was striding towards them through the grass, and for a moment she thought it was the same one, the same Rat Speaker they had faced in the Horn-Bearer fortress. This was some ancient who had once lived between the Lion's paws, though. He wore a cloak that hung about his bony frame and billowed like smoke, and his leathery skin was hideous, pock-marked and ragged with the traces of little teeth. About his feet the grass swayed and heaved with the passage of many bodies.

'Did you think I would not know, when you passed through my domain?' he asked. His voice was painful to hear, as tattered and scratched as he was.

'You have no domain,' Hesprec stated. 'You only hide in the Plague's shadow and eat their leavings.'

'I have all domains abandoned by other gods,' the Rat Speaker said, or the Rat said through him. 'The Plague has no gods nor souls. But it has bones and meat, even though it is empty. How's that for a riddle, Serpent Child?'

He strode closer, but Maniye saw how he stopped beyond the reach of Shyri's knife. The Rat valued its mouthpiece for as long as it wanted to hear its own voice. Her ears flicked, and she saw other spindly-limbed men and women creeping towards the tree, some limping on two legs, others crawling on all fours. Not many yet – a half-dozen maybe – but probably enough.

'You will run, O Serpent, as you always run,' the Rat Speaker sneered. 'As you fled your kingdom once, so you will flee back there again and live under the Pale Shadow, and tell your stories about how wise you are. And the rest of the world will rattle to our feet only, in the end.' His eyes flicked to Shyri. 'Oh, Laughing Child, what shame you bring to your god, to side against me now the world's end is come.'

Shyri's reply was to lunge forwards, leading with a knife that became the bronze-toothed jaws of a hyena. The Rat had misjudged how swift she was, and for a moment she had her teeth in the Speaker's hand, worrying off a couple of fingers, then snapping at the ground and coming up with a crushed grey body in her jaws. She fell back as the grass shivered with motion all around her, back to the clear ground about the tree. For a moment the Rat Speaker just stood there, staring at his mangled hand as though unsure what to do with it.

'The Champion and the Laughing Child will be our meat,' that wasted voice proclaimed. 'The Serpent we shall take, and torment and gnaw until she breaks and lets us in, and she shall be our Speaker to go to Atahlan. We shall make the Serpent eat its own tail.'

* * *

They all told each other they had chosen a meeting at midnight because the Plague People were more creatures of the sun than the moon, notwithstanding their recent night attack. The true people of the land had the noses of wolves, the glinting eyes of lions and tigers. The darkness was part of their world rather than the barren domain of the invader.

Kailovela thought to herself that it was a grand statement, but the truth of it was that they crept out under cover of darkness because most of those camped across the Plains there would have wanted to stop them. Yes, the Mother of the Bear had chosen this path, and the Kasra of the River, and some several chiefs and priests of the Plains, but even amongst the River Lords their ruler did not control the thoughts in their heads. How few would really countenance going to trade words with the

Plague People rather than blows. To most it would be foolishness at best, treachery at worst.

Loud Thunder led them, because he would not be left behind and because he could not accept that not every dire consequence was a weight for his shoulders. Asman, the southern Champion, walked at his elbow, speaking softly of old times they had shared. Kailovela caught the names 'Many Tracks' and 'Broken Axe', people she would never know; places she had never seen. Asman had brought a handful of River warriors, none of them looking keen on the business but all with bows as tall as they were. Thunder had a couple of Wolf hunters and Lone Mountain, his cousin. Mountain had also refused to be left behind, but Kailovela was worried about the set of his jaw. He had been the first to feel the sting of the Plague People. Their darts and their Terror had come close to killing him. Lone Mountain carried fear with him, now, like something lodged in an old wound. That was why he came, of course. What the Bear could not ignore, it would fight.

In the midst of these fighters came the talkers, Kailovela amongst them. They had the little monster, of course, and they had the reluctant Galethea, and Empty Skin. *And somehow we will turn the hearts of the Plague People, except surely they have none.* Mother had been plain, though: everyone knew that this first tentative contact would not end anything, or even change much. But it was something new, in a war that had been lost each day.

Would there be demands? Would there be any comprehension at all? Kailovela had a thought that even if the individual words could be translated from one world to another, the meaning would stop at the border. *How can we have anything to say to them?* Despite it all, some small part of her was curious, even through her fear.

And fear will kill us the moment it is off the leash. Or worse. Will my wings be enough to carry me away?

309

But by then they had already set out into the dark, flanked by wolves.

Kailovela wished that the two Coyote were with them. Two Heads Talking and Quiet When Loud had always seemed ready to dance past all the spears the world might throw at them. Except that Quiet had Kailovela's son in her arms right now, and besides, her own swelling belly had stripped her of freedom and fire; coming down to earth, becoming just as trapped as the rest of them. *And surely all my thoughts should be bent towards my son. Shouldn't he be all I think of, like a proper mother?* But she shook the accusation away. Right now her child was the last thing she could afford to think of; let her cover her guilt with that.

She was torn from her reverie by a shout from one of Asman's people, who had been watching the sky. For a moment their entire embassy was on the point of dissolution, everyone about to bolt into the grasses in every direction. Kailovela caught a glimpse of the swooping shapes, though, and knew them: not the ephemeral wings of the Plague People but the silent vanes of owls.

They stooped down before Loud Thunder and Stepped: two priests with grey faces, the white bar across their eyes standing out in the moonlight. The woman was Seven Mending, who had been a terror to Kailovela since she had left the Eyrie. The man was Grey Herald, who had gone to the dark places of the Plains to reawaken the Bat Society.

'So, you're going to do it after all, then,' Mending said, without preamble. Her blind-seeming eyes took them all in at once and disapproved.

'Mother's will,' Thunder mumbled, shrugging.

The Owls shared a moment of silent communion, and then Herald said, 'Someone will tell the others of your deaths. It may as well be us.'

'Raise no spear against the Plague Men unless they do it first,' Thunder warned them, and Mending laughed.

'If it comes to that, Son of the Bear, it will be too late to save any of you. The Terror will eat you whole.'

'And you?'

'Owl's first child fought the Plague when we came to these lands. We are proof against them.' Seven Mending stared past the Bear at Galethea. 'This is your great weapon, then, your tame monster? And you believe it will make peace with its words?'

Thunder had obviously run out of rhetoric for he just pushed past them with a mutter about needing to press on, and his entourage went forward under the shadow of the Owls.

Towards midnight they saw the glow, like a piece of the moon fallen to earth. There was where the Plague People had marked the meeting place, just as the little monster had claimed. Asman, Thunder and Seven Mending conferred briefly, and then one of the Wolves and Grey Herald were sent off to scout, to make sure there were no warriors waiting in the grass. Kailovela could only think about the speed the Plague People could fly. After all, Eyrie raiders would not need to be crouching within spear-cast to spring an ambush; why should the enemy?

And yet Wolf and Owl both returned, stating that there was a party of Plague People within sight of the rock but not hiding, and some of them at least not seeming to be warriors. Kailovela felt it, the last teetering moment when someone might say, 'This is a bad plan,' and lead them back the way they had come.

They went to the rock.

It was strewn with the cold lanterns of the Plague Men, which burned pale blue or greenish white, and put Kailovela in mind of ghosts and dead things, as if she needed much prompting. At the edge of the rock they paused, knowing that someone must ascend into that unwavering light to show the enemy they had arrived. And surely that first soul would not be instantly struck down, for what would that gain the Plague People? But the Plague People did not think like normal humans, and to stand unshielded before their gaze was a terrible thing.

She saw Thunder girding himself to do it, but in the end Lone Mountain went first, taking his fear in his hands and carrying it as he stepped from boulder to ledge until he was at the top, a huge man in a cloak of bright Riverlands cloth washed almost grey by the lamps.

He held out his empty hands and stood there and at first nothing happened. The breeze ran its hands whisperingly across the grass on every side and the enemy made no move, either in war or peace. Kailovela was close enough to see the slight tremble in Lone Mountain's arms.

She heard the sound too late, recognizing it only when the little monster tugged at her sleeve. The flurry of the grass around became the whicker of wings above, and with no more fanfare than that, the enemy were upon them.

She saw the warriors first, and part of her waited for the Terror to annihilate her, to make her no more than a bird, lost in a foreign land. They had their killing rods, and their eyes were on Lone Mountain, who would have made three of them even had they not been just hollow husks. There was a frozen moment when everyone was almost reaching for a weapon, almost running, almost losing themselves to fear.

But the warriors alighted on the far side of the rock and just stood there, and now there were more of them, not flying but pushing through the grass just like normal people. Some looked like the warriors, others were different – darker or stouter or more slender. One was a woman who might have been cousin to Galethea, though more pale even than she.

Lone Mountain backed off a few steps, to his edge of the rock. 'How was this supposed to work, then?'

'Come down,' Thunder told him. 'Unless you've learned how to make their words suddenly?'

Mountain scrabbled off the rock with more haste and less dignity than he had ascended.

The little monster stepped past Kailovela and her own wings flared into life, carrying her in a smooth arc past the bloom of the lamplight and off towards the Plague camp. Her high voice shrilled back to them in her chittering tongue, a clear invitation.

312

'Who goes up?' Obvious to all of them, what the creature was waiting for.

Galethea must, of course, but the silence stretched out. Kailovela saw that nobody quite trusted her on her own, yet nobody wanted to stand beside her in the harsh glare of the Plague People's attention. How long could anyone stave off the Terror, pinned by their gaze in such a way?

But someone must, and Kailovela even started to say 'I . . .' before another slight figure stepped around her.

'I have no soul to lose, no shape to be trapped in,' Empty Skin said matter-of-factly. 'So it shall be me. Come on, Pale Shadow. Let's go meet our people.'

She took Galethea's wrist and tugged, and then the two of them were ascending. That was their delegation then, an empty child and some bastard offshoot of the Plague People themselves.

She looked to the little monster, wondering if she would take her part in this, too. Perhaps she would stand there and talk on behalf of both parties, and then clasp her own wrist in agreement. But, bound to Kailovela as she was, the diminutive creature was not of the same world, and perhaps the Plague People did not trust her either. She had brought this meeting about, but now she kicked her little heels on the sidelines and looked often to the east, where her people reigned. She had been a prisoner of the Eyrie a long time, body and mind.

A heartbeat later the Plague ambassador dropped down to join them, and Kailovela's stomach clenched to see him. They were wrong, she realized; they were wrong to do this, but equally they were wrong to think that the Plague Men were things of daylight. This was a night creature, a shadow creature. It was their priest, the grey-faced man with the blank white eyes that the Owl's facepaint was only an echo of. He smiled, as a man of peace might, but it was only a mask stretched over the appalling hungry hollowness of him.

* * *

They had tried to fight, but mostly they had tried to run. The Rat Speaker himself seemed no great threat, but the grasslands around them were alive with movement, and ragged people would constantly leap at them, armed with no more than their grimy teeth and nails. Shyri tackled them for the most part, darting in to slash at necks and arms, or Stepping to crush legs and sever hamstrings in her jaws. Maniye just limped along as a wolf with Hesprec coiled loosely about her shoulders, an inconsequential and familiar weight. When any of the Rat's votaries came too close, the Serpent would strike out, driving her fangs deep for just long enough to leave behind a gift of poison and then recoiling back to her nest between Maniye's shoulder blades.

They made for the Plague People's rock at first, in the hope that the true enemy would bring out the Rat's cowardice. There were stooped human forms ahead of them, though, tattered cultists tightening their frayed net. Maniye and the others were driven away from the light, feeling as though they were caught up in a current sweeping them away from shore into the killing sea.

Then Maniye found a burst of speed from somewhere, tapping the last of her reserves to race out from under the Rat's shadow, clutching for precious distance with Shyri at her heels. She never had a sense that she had escaped. Every step told her that the shamblers and the scuttlers were drawing close from every quarter of the Plains. Yet when she found another rock and collapsed atop it, virtually dragging her hind legs and tail clear of the grass, she had some few breaths to regain her strength, some few moments for last words.

Hesprec's face was hard and angry. 'Always the Rat finds some bolt-hole, no matter how often we overturn his altars and burn his nests.'

Shyri sat down heavily. 'Yes, let's talk of past things. Not like we're in a hurry.'

Hesprec nodded to concede the point and turned her gaze to Maniye. 'There are fights knives can't win.'

314

'*Knife*,' Shyri corrected. 'Didn't see either of you stabbing anyone.'

'Just so. Maniye, I need you to come on a journey with me.'

Maniye frowned. 'What?'

'To a place you've been before, many times. Because we are not fighting those bodies out there. We are fighting the thing they have given themselves to, which lives elsewhere.'

'*Now?*' Maniye demanded. 'That journey now? What of your rituals, your places of power?'

Hesprec looked about them. 'Ah yes, those would be fine things, but I have only my two hands and the Serpent. But you have been in and out of that place since the Rat first sank his teeth into you. His filth is in your veins still, sapping your strength. Will it be enough to carry us to him? Unless we make the attempt we cannot know. Shyri.' She looked at the Laughing Girl. 'Can you keep your knife busy while we do this?'

'Hold them off, all of them, alone?'

'These things are known—'

'Yes, yes,' Shyri broke in. 'These things are known, nonsense nonsense River talk. Just get on with it.' She jumped to her feet and looked out at the figures drawing lines of motion through the grasses, all their sunken eyes on her. 'They found new friends,' she observed flatly.

Hesprec did have a knife, Maniye found. As gently as she could the Serpent took her arm and reopened one of the scabbed-over bite marks there before touching her tongue to the blood.

'Let us go find the Rat,' she said. 'You are quite the familiar of the gods, now. It was only a matter of time before you met this one face to face.'

28

When Mother had called Loud Thunder to bring the Crown of the World tribes under one banner and be their war chief, he had baulked at it. Lone Mountain would be better at it, he knew. Anyone would have been better at it.

And yet he had done what Mother said, mostly because not doing so would have been harder. But he had never wanted to be Warbringer, only Loud Thunder, living in his cabin on his own.

Now he felt that being a man of peace was harder. He had fought this enemy. He knew their hollow flesh ran with the same taste of blood as that of real men and beasts. He knew they could be killed by copper and bronze, stone and iron. He knew how to make war on them. He did not know how to stare at their warriors and stay his hand. He did not know how he was supposed to stand within the shadow of their Terror, knowing it could stoop on him at any moment and rob him of his mind. And yet this, too, Mother had asked of him. First make war; now stand idle while others tried to make peace.

Or that was what the Pale Shadow woman was supposed to be doing, but he had no guarantee of it. The only assurances came from her tone, for the creature's fear at facing her long-estranged kin was plain in every alien syllable. He could imagine that voice begging for its life, but not calculatedly betraying them. Her high, shaking tones rang out across the

316

sky from the rock, and Loud Thunder could understand nothing more than the anxiety behind them. Only that was truly human.

He knew what she was supposed to say. Mother had sat the creature down and schooled her. Galethea was playing emissary for every human in the world. She was asking the Plague People what they would take to go away or halt their killing. *Or just to kill us a little more slowly. Every breath becomes precious.* And what treasure might they demand, Loud Thunder wondered glumly. What could be traded for something as precious as life? Would they take a tithe of children each year? And if that was what they asked for, would the Plainsfolk pay the price? Would his own people, or the River Lords? Or perhaps the Wolf would cull the children of the Deer and Boar and send them downriver to Where the Fords Meet or what had once borne that name. Or the Rivermen would take the children of their subject peoples, or the Plains tribes would have a new reason to raid each other's villages.

Peace might destroy the world of the true people as certainly as war, but more slowly. For the Plague People's forbearance would surely not be bought with anything as mundane as pearls or amber.

Galethea's voice faltered again, and Thunder saw the little monster start forward from its stand between the two groups, obviously wanting to just step in and continue the words. One of the Plague warriors took her shoulder and held her back, though – not unkind, perhaps just seeking to protect her, but she seemed as much a prisoner in that moment as ever she had in Kailovela's tent.

Loud Thunder took a step nearer, trying to wring out every drop of meaning from Galethea's babble. As he did so, one of the Plague warriors did the same, like a crooked reflection. The creature was pale, clad in banded metal armour. Thunder had killed many like it, when he led his forces against the Plague nest on the Seal coast. He stared it in the eye, thinking, *How small you are, how empty*. Oh, perhaps a little taller than most Wolves, say, but everyone was smaller than a son of the Bear.

And yet the Plague warrior cradled that killing rod in the crook of his arm, directed at a slant towards the ground. He could point it at Loud Thunder more swiftly than Thunder could close the distance to him, yet there was a wildness in his eye, when he met the Bear's gaze. He looked on Thunder as though his enemy was not just a vast hulk of a man, but a ghost, a monster. His hands gripped the rod tightly – the moon showed Thunder how his knuckles were knotted with tension.

And all the while the talk went on, and Thunder and the Plague warrior stared at each other. Galethea's quavering tones rang out, and then, far softer, came the reply of the other.

And the other – the white-eyed priest – it wasn't speaking vitriol; there was no fire in its words. If Loud Thunder had heard that voice in the camp he would have thought it some uncle giving advice to a wayward nephew, some mild remonstrance from one of the Wise to one of the Foolish. Mother's own tones to Loud Thunder were harsher.

Except. Except that Thunder could hear Galethea's stammering responses, and knew she was not a woman won over or reassured. Her fear was being wound tighter and tighter, her words breathless with it as Empty Skin pushed closer and closer, little fists balled. That tone was a liar, Thunder knew. It was a boat painted to seem a friend, but it came carrying spears and knives. And when he looked into that grey face with its white eyes, he thought he saw a moment when the mask fell, and the creature's malevolence blazed brighter than the lamps.

He looked back at the Plague warrior and all the rest of them. Galethea's voice reached a new pitch. Was she demanding, now? No, she was pleading. For herself, for her tribe, for all the world's people? And the Plague priest just answered in his easy tones, but the tension was drawing about everyone there like a net. Thunder saw the Plague warrior's hands tighten further, his jaw clench as he regarded the Bear. *I have come closer*, Thunder realized. Each little shuffle of his, each idle movement had drawn him towards his enemy. *If I Stepped now, could I kill him before he killed me?*

He looked across at his own people. Lone Mountain was close to the rock now, his maul no longer butt to the ground like a staff, but slanted over his shoulder, ready to swing. The Wolves he had brought were Stepped, eyes throwing back the lamplight like white sparks. Thunder saw the readiness in every line of them. Seven Mending's hands were crooked like talons and Grey Herald had a hatchet in his hand, hidden mostly by his cloak but the bronze edge of it just peeked clear. The weapons were for when things went wrong, but they were for courage too. They were to hold on to when the Terror tore at them. Thunder could feel the air curdle with it, held back only by the fragile flame of their courage and hope. They stood right in the Terror's mouth now, its teeth on either side of them. The thought made him shiver and for a moment it was closing its jaws on him. *Hope*, he reminded himself. *Perhaps it will end here.* He felt it would end here for him, however it went.

And the Plains were not quiet, either. Distantly he thought he heard shouting, hidden in the echoes of Galethea's words. Somewhere across the grass someone else was fighting and dying. Surely that was a scream? He saw the Plague warrior twitch, hearing the same sound, perhaps suspecting treachery.

Now Galethea was almost shouting, her words washing over Thunder but hooking the attention of the Plague warrior across from him, drawing the creature's eyes. *They all understand, and we understand nothing*, vied in Thunder's mind with, *Now, now, kill him now!*

He fought back the impulse, hearing the fear in his own mind, which drove it. Even that little struggle brought him another inch, another inch towards his enemy.

Even Mother cannot bring some things about, he knew, with utter certainty. *This was never going to work.*

And then the scream came, tearing across the grasslands to

strike everyone there at once. It was so shrill and inhuman that Thunder thought at first it must be some Plains bird unfamiliar to him, but then it dissolved into a jabber of agonized, incomprehensible words. Plague words.

* * *

So Hesprec had sat down beside Maniye and now they were about some grand mystical business, which helped Shyri not at all. All she had was a knife and her teeth and her one body, and the Rat had who-knew-how-many Speakers and cultists, not to mention all those chittering little bodies.

My mistake was liking foreigners, she decided, balanced on the balls of her feet atop the rock as she watched the Rat's creatures rush her. Asman had made her his servant and never acknowledged that she would have been so much more to him if he had only let her. Maniye was like a sister, but sisters shouldn't get their sisters into this sort of trouble.

The Rat had no sense of strategy, or perhaps just didn't see the need yet. The first two to reach the rock were scrabbling up to her without waiting for their fellows, and she kicked one in the face and then cut the other: once, twice, her bronze gouging a shoulder, then hacking down to sever enough fingers to send the climber tumbling away. There was a third on the far side, making heavy going of the handholds, and Shyri had more than enough time to Step, bound over, and take the cultist's head in her mouth. No teeth were stronger than Hyena's; she clenched and felt the man's jaw pop from its socket, his skull crack where she sawed at it. Blood filled her mouth and made her want to haul the body away to feed, but she put Hyena's urges in her shadow and shook the limp body off into the grass. Let the rats feast, and let the feast delay them.

The rest had not hauled themselves from the grass and so she looked down at them, one side and then the other, heckling as only a hyena can until she locked eyes with the Rat Speaker.

'Oh, Laughing Child,' he told her. 'Your father and I, we are old friends. Will you not let us—' but she had been ready for that old song again. Stepping, she let fly with a good-sized stone that struck him in the teeth and turned his words to bloody mush. A ripple of outrage went through the other cultists as their priest reeled backwards, spitting out red strings of spittle and white fragments. He tried to speak again, whatever tedious threat or imprecation the Rat had for her, but the words were mumbled through torn lips and ragged gums. She saw the real anger then – the Rat blazing through his vacant eyes, because of all things it longed to listen to its own words.

'I don't know why anyone ever stopped to listen to you,' she taunted him, and saw the words strike a nerve; if people didn't let the Rat's words twist them, what was he? Vermin, just vermin.

Then they were coming in earnest, but clumsily, without discipline. They were half starved, these votaries; they were weak and diseased, driven by an energy their thin bodies could barely master. She cut at their faces, too fast for their hands to ward her off; she cut at their hands too swiftly for them to draw back. And there were not so many of them, but there seemed to be just enough to be too many for her to keep back.

And there was a swirling tide of grey-brown bodies roiling at the base of the rock, and she could easily imagine that tide rising to swamp her the moment the Rat put its mind to the task.

Then she had sliced up a Horse woman's face – some fugitive from Where the Fords Meet who had gone from bad to worse – thinking, *I am still fighting, and surely even Asman would have lost some blood by now*, and understood in that moment it had been too easy. She knew him even as she turned, seeing the gore-mouthed Rat Speaker standing behind her, his own knife out and poised over Maniye and Hesprec.

She had committed to that last slash, her balance tipped the wrong way for a sudden reversal. She Stepped even so, digging in with four feet to turn her faster, teeth bared. *But too slow! I can't—* and then the thunder came.

Not thunder. A sound from the sky that battered at them all just the same, but rhythmic, wordless, the night air being rent asunder by something impossible.

It fell on them from out of the night, wheeling like a mad thing, only the least thread of control left to it. It had its thorned legs outstretched in a doomed bid for balance. The thunder was its wings, three men's lengths across beneath the curved cases of its shell. Shyri had never thought the monstrous beetle-creature could *fly*.

Just barely, enough to come barrelling out of the night to crash blindly into the Rat Speaker. She saw the shears of its jaws close convulsively on one of his legs and sever the limb, bone and all. Its weight had smashed the rest of him against the rock and now it waved its grisly trophy like a standard as though rallying an army.

But the only army was the Rat's, and the loss of the Speaker did nothing to dispel them. Abruptly they were leaping up on all sides, and it was all Shyri could do to stand in the little space between Hesprec and Maniye and cut, cut, cut at every part of them that offered itself to her knife. At her back was the great domed bulk of the beetle, and right then she would take any ally she could. She only kept her skin whole because the Rat was far keener to kill *it* than *her*.

And she was thinking of the creature as something elemental, a monster from the stories. Was it not armoured on every side? Was it not armed with teeth like blades? She put her back to it and trusted in its indomitable nature while she got on with her own job of stamping on rats and carving slices from anything human-looking that tried to reach for her friends.

But the problem with the Plague People was that they deceived: they looked human but were not human; they looked like invulnerable monsters but . . .

She did not see what happened, but the behemoth behind her shrilled, some dreadful hissing noise no throat ever made. Some blunt part of it struck her across the shoulders and sent her to the ground, head ringing with the impact. There were Rat cultists clinging all over it, driving their knives through its shell, and she saw it rear like a horse, and then its wings flashed out, hurling thin bodies end over end on either side, broken shapes plunging into the tall grass.

And in the aftermath of that, the rock cleared of the Rat-followers for a handful of heartbeats, the beetle creature Stepped, becoming a naked man kneeling in a tangle of his own ravaged flesh and screaming in fear and pain.

Shyri half went to him, recoiling as his screech turned into a desperate babble of word-like sounds. She was willing him to Step back to his beetle shape, because everyone knew that if you died a human, then your soul . . . but what soul? Could such a hybrid thing have a soul?

He was not hollow. The emptiness in him had been filled, and now it was being emptied once again as his lifeblood left him.

Then she had no more time to speculate because the Rat had been driven away by the noise, but not far and not for more than a few heartbeats. She turned back to see its human votaries already surging back towards the rock, and around them the grass was thrashing madly with the passage of more bodies – not the scuttlings of the little rodents but something greater. She saw the whip of scaly tails and pictured rats the size of wolves slinking low-bellied towards her.

She readied her knife again, feeling bone-weary already, and hoped that Hesprec and Maniye were nearing the end of their journey, wherever that was. All the grasses were shivering with violent, low-slung movement. The human husks of the Rat gathered to swarm her, and a moment later the Plains erupted with jagged teeth.

* * *

Empty Skin saw it happen. The scream tore across the sky from somewhere to her right, far out across the grasslands. She heard the alien sounds in it and knew that one of the Plague People had

323

met a grisly end. She did not know the words but the meaning of it spoke to her: *Mother! Mother!* like any dying thing.

She was ready for the sudden chaos as warriors of both sides reacted. She almost heard the peace break as though it was a stick. But that was not what she *saw*. Her eyes were still fixed on the Plague priest.

His mild expression broke, a man who no longer needed his mask. He hissed something at Galethea and then one grey hand was coming up with a knife, a lean blade of shining iron. The Pale Shadow woman was already throwing herself back, but the razor edge still cut a path across her body, and the expression of the priest showed he was only sorry it had not gone deeper, for all the wound looked like it might be mortal.

But that was not what she saw, not the final truth of it, for the Plague priest stared at the blade of his dagger and then tore it viciously across his own arm, opening a long, ragged wound. He locked eyes with her as he did it, and his smile was pure spite.

Then he was backing away, kicking up from the rock and letting ephemeral wings carry him to the midst of his warriors. His bloody arm was up for them to see and she heard him calling them to arms with a cry that must have been *Treachery! Treachery!*

Then Empty Skin was scrabbling away, dropping back to where Galethea lay curled about her wound. She could hear the yells of both sides, words in two speeches competing against each other. The dying would start soon, and she could not be here for it. She got her shoulder under the arm of the pale woman and levered her to her feet, for all she screamed and thrashed. Of all the people in the world, with souls and without, only Galethea could say what had passed between her and the enemy. She must live; she must live long enough to spill those words out before someone who would understand them.

Kailovela came running to help her, flinching from each yell and roar. Empty Skin heard the howl of wolves and the bellow of bears and knew that everything had gone about as wrong as it possibly could. A pair of Plague warriors dropped down in front of her, landing in a shimmer of wings and then running somewhere. A glance around showed far too many of them – the enemy had kept forces nearby ready for just this moment. And yet they were not the only ones. Skin saw an Estuary warrior step from nowhere, bare skin shimmering and blurring as she rammed a knife into a Plague warrior's neck, and the keening of hawks was in the air above. Then a greater screech went up as one of the Bat Society overflew the rock. Empty Skin dropped to her knees, arms wrapped around herself to contain the shuddering vibration of it, and Galethea sagged in Kailovela's hands, eyes wide in horror as the sound swept through her. But the Plague warriors did not just fly away, but stayed on to make a fight of it, and now Skin was sure the Terror must be building around them, mounting to that point when it would begin locking away the souls of all those around them. All through the negotiations it had been waiting on like a bird of prey, kept at bay only by the hope of the true people that this talk might win them something. Now things had gone from talk to fight and in every mind a gate was opening, quicker or slower. Once the initial shock was over, they would find the Terror waiting to devour their souls.

Except me, for I have no soul to shackle, and nor does Galethea, for all she wants one. But Kailovela would be just a hawk then, and Skin had come to like her, so she forced herself up and dragged at both of them, the Eyriewoman and the Pale Shadow. A Plague warrior dropped down nearby, but whether he would have killed them or not she never knew, because a great owl was already stooping on him, claws fixing in his white face and beak ripping into his eyes. Even as he dropped, invisible darts were lancing into the bird, staggering it in the air. For a moment the priestess Seven Mending knelt there, vomiting out blood, pale eyes seeing nothing, but then the bird lay in her place, broken and bloodied.

Skin heard the voice of Kailovela's little monster, crying out in rage. She saw the creature held by Plague warriors, being hauled away from the rock and the fight. Its wings flickered erratically as it tried to escape their grip but they were intent on protecting it; it was one of their own, after all.

The Bat passed overhead again unleashing its silent scream on the enemy, and their busy darts followed it in the air, skipping and singing as they tried to tear its wings and bring it down. Then Loud Thunder was with them, his face bloody and his axe bloodier, virtually picking them all up to bundle them away. She thought that was it, but he stopped still in sight of the rock and in reach of the enemy, calling out a name. Skin looked about, seeing at last Lone Mountain, Thunder's cousin, as he charged down one of the Plague Men with a bear's sudden access to speed. Thunder called his name once again and for a moment he was human, his maul dark and stained, looking back with a dreadful wildness in his face. Then the air was alive with darts. Skin saw a Wolf go down, and a Riverman. Somewhere nearby Asman's Champion was screeching out a challenge, but there were more and more Plague Men coming, and they were incensed, fighting furiously and refusing to give ground even to the Bat. *Because they think themselves betrayed*, Skin knew, feeling sick. *All our work wasted.*

She saw the moment when Lone Mountain ceased to be Lone Mountain, the Terror ripping his human shape from him and leaving only the bear. The bear was fighting mad, though, and there was no such thing as *just* a bear. He tore into the enemies about him, bellowing and roaring. The Terror had robbed him of his humanity but it had taken away his fear of the enemy too. He was lost, but he was holding the way, drawing the enemy's rage.

They fell back, all of them. Lone Mountain was not the only one gone. There were men of the Plains and the River and the Crown of the World left there as sprawled figures or huddled mounds of fur and flesh. They lay amongst the torn corpses of the Plague Men they had fought.

★ ★ ★

The Godsland here was eaten away, as though Rat's hunger could not be sated on bones and grain alone, but had turned on the very earth itself. The grasses were patchy and dying as though the whole world was sick, and the rock whittled away to a crooked pillar of stone. Below, scattered across the earth as far as the eye could see, she saw bones. Some were human, most were animal. Some were huge enough to belong to gods. She remembered the buried chamber in the Horn-Bearer fortress with its intricate wall-coverings. This was just chaos, though. This was the desired end of the Rat, a world picked clean.

If she let herself drift, she could hear the clamour of a fight coming to her through her real ears. She was not firmly ensconced in the Godsland, straddling two worlds. Hesprec had done the best she could, but Maniye knew she had to block out any distraction or she would be lost back to the physical world. Part of her mind was constantly filling with images of Shyri falling, of the knives and teeth of the Rat's mortal agents poised before her eyes, caressing her throat. She bailed away at the thoughts like a lost boatman desperately trying to keep the sea from overwhelming his little barque.

When she had come over, there had been rats clinging to her, teeth latched into her wounds, and she had torn them away one by one, hurling the twitching little bodies out over the cracked earth.

She had never seen Hesprec in the Godland before; perhaps what she saw now was just the product of her imagination, but every movement of the River child seemed to trail a cascade of ghosts: men, women, old, young, dark and secret and painted with rainbow scales, receding back in some direction Maniye had no name for. She caught a sight of that lean old face she had rescued from the Jaws of the Wolf and felt a sudden stab of loss, for all he had not been taken from her, only changed.

Hesprec put her hands on her hips and called out, 'What a

poor host you are, O Rat! Here are the guests you have so longed to meet and yet your hearth is empty. Have you no salt or drink for your visitors?' Her tone was mocking and sharp but Maniye heard within it a tremble of fear.

There was nowhere for the Rat to come from, but it seemed to arise out of the earth itself, a great mounded form that grew and grew until it could stare at them on their pillar, eye to eye. It was almost shapeless in its gross bulk, its hide skewbald with patches of scabby hairless skin, with sores and maggoty boils. Maniye had seen days-dead corpses that looked more fit for life than the Rat. And yet she had no sense that it was in pain, that it suffered; the Rat revelled in the corruption and downfall of all things, even its own form.

Its eyes were pits of pure darkness; its filthy yellow teeth like slabs of bark peeling from dead trees.

'So the Serpent has finally come to see his brother.' The voice rose from its festering flesh like a chorus of whispers. 'Do you come to welcome me in, O Serpent? Do you finally admit that I was there when the Plague People were cast back and the sea rushed in?'

Hesprec stood very straight, looking into the face of the god. 'You were there, O Rat, but there is a reason you do not feature in the telling,' she said flatly. 'Serpent, Owl and Bat battled the Plague all night, awaiting the fire of the sun, but you lifted no spear against them. It was not *their* flesh you sharpened your teeth for. You are cut from the tale because you were there only for our bones should we fall. You could have taken your place with us and been our brother, but you chose to wager against us.' A curious authority had come into her voice, as though she was gathering some mantle about her, coil upon coil. The children of the Serpent had always enjoyed a close and strange relationship with their god.

Rat bared its dagger-teeth and the hateful voice hissed out, 'Then why come to me, O Serpent, if you only wish to dig up old corpses. You are in *my* place now. All the other gods are fled

328

and the Plague People have long ago forgotten their own. I am sole master of this land.'

'Not all other gods,' Hesprec said quietly, and then she looked to Maniye and only the girl herself stared out of her eyes. 'Bring your souls forward, Many Tracks, because we will need to fight.'

Even with the thought, Maniye felt the Champion close to her, padding massively across the ravaged land to stand beside the pillar. The Rat shrank back a little, seeming to diminish, until the Champion almost matched it, size for size.

'We can't fight a god, though, can we?' Maniye asked.

'This god we can fight,' Hesprec told her. 'This god we have fought all our lives, all of us, *this* god is starvation, deprivation, the loss of the self, the spiral of fallen tribes and kingdoms. The Rat is the enemy we always carry with us, just as the Plague is the enemy that we left behind. And now, with the world ending, the Rat has grown bolder, but bold for a rat is perhaps not so very bold.'

And indeed for a moment the Rat had seemed taken aback, cringing before the Champion's appearance, but now it bullied forward, growing greater again, bulking out in folds of greasy, patchy flesh. The Champion braced, and then thundered forward, lumbering like a bear, leaping like a cat, latching on like a wolf and shaking. Its claws ripped into the Rat's substance and tore it apart and it drove the squalling, squealing creature around the pillar, trying to gain purchase on its hide.

But the Rat was never still, and its bloated flesh seemed to flow and swirl about the Champion's attacks. Every gash and rent in its hide was gone the moment it was dealt, while its teeth left bloody puncture wounds in the Champion's body. Maniye felt each one: it was her soul that fought, after all. She stood on the pillar and yet she was simultaneously down there ripping and tearing, hunting for a throat that was just more bulbous flesh parting before her bite and then reforming after.

Something was happening around them, too: some terrible

deformation of the ground. Their pillar was now at the centre of a shallow bowl in the earth, and Maniye could feel everything around her sinking, the sides rising up to trap them. Time was running short, and she was losing to the Rat, carving into its substance without marking it for more than a heartbeat.

This is not how you fight a rat. But then there had never been a rat like this, not so vast and old and over-full of dead flesh. The thought caught in her mind like a fish-hook. *There never was a rat like this. This is the Rat as it wishes to be, but what is it really, but vermin that survives by hiding and creeping? This is not the truth of the Rat.*

With that thought, her other souls were with her. A wolf slunk to one side of the pillar, a tiger to the other. They were dwarfed by Champion and Rat both; they did not have that vast and ancient strength to them, but they were far better suited to the task of catching and killing rats.

She sent them forwards, committing every part of her, and they leapt upon the Rat's body. They were not seeking throats or eyes or other vulnerable parts, for the Rat had none of them. All the Rat had was its multitudes, and tiger and wolf tore into them, attacking not the great form but all the tiny bodies it was made of.

She was horribly aware of the land sinking and twisting around them, the sides of the pit so high she could see only a gash of sky above. The Rat was screaming out its rage in many voices as she worried away at its components, all the little bodies it was formed of. But there were hundreds, there were thousands. There had been too much death in this land, too much sustenance for this god of failed things. All she could do was hold it and occupy its wrath.

In her ear, Hesprec said, 'That is enough.'

Maniye could barely spare her any attention. 'What now?'

'Call back your souls. The fight is done.'

Looking at the high walls risen all around them, Maniye felt

330

a terrible despair. She felt her souls return to her, their physical forms fading, until there was nothing between them and the Rat.

'Kneel,' came that hissing choir of voices. 'Kneel and be my Speaker in the world, Serpent. Give me the blood of your friend and make yourself mine.'

Hesprec took a deep breath. 'O Rat,' she called to it, 'your brother is here to greet you.'

For a moment Maniye felt that she and the Rat were both staring at Hesprec with equal bafflement, but then the earthen walls around them rippled and she realized she had not seen them properly when they formed. She could look up now and see the curved fangs that cut into the sole remaining slice of sky; she could see the ribs lining the interior of the hole as it descended into the earth, a slope the Rat was even now scrabbling at, hampered by its quivering bulk. The earth had not sunk into a pit, but something had arisen out of the earth to surround them. They were within the closing jaws of the Serpent. She and Hesprec stood upon its forked tongue.

Below them, the Rat cried and clawed, but the walls around it, the throat of the Serpent, gave a great undulating heave and it vanished, swallowed into the depths of the earth.

Hesprec took her hand, not jubilant but only solemn, a priestess who has seen the greatest mysteries of her god played out.

'We have stayed too long here,' she said, 'and seen too much. Shyri will need us.'

Returning to the flesh was returning to weakness and pain, but Maniye remembered plucking the rats from her wounds and knew she would become stronger and that the pain would fade.

Around them were many bodies. Most were the starved followers of the Rat, but one was the still, dark form of the Plague Man whose captive she had been, who had been so curious about her Stepping from shape to shape. He had found his own

331

final shape now, contorted in death, and she could only stare at him and wonder.

And Shyri was there, but not among the dead. Instead, she sat atop the rock trading stories with an old friend.

'Venat?' Maniye demanded. 'How did you come here?'

The Dragon pirate grinned. 'Oh, the Great Kasrani was about a piece of foolishness, as usual, but not so foolish that he didn't want me and mine creeping about the place looking for surprises.' His smile slipped. 'It's all gone to ashes, from my best guess, but by then I'd heard Laughing Girl fighting, and come over to get stuck in.'

There were a handful of his people with him, big men with weapons of greenstone and shark teeth.

'They went to talk to the Plague People,' Shyri explained.

'Went about as well as you'd expect, I reckon,' Venat added. 'And we don't want to be here come dawn or we'll none of us see two feet again.' The note of caution from him brought home to Maniye just how bad things must have become.

Hesprec was kneeling beside the dead Plague Man, hands out and almost touching his torn-up flesh. 'He must have been so frightened at what was happening to him,' she murmured softly. 'And you were the only thing he knew that could make sense of it. I think he wanted you to help him.'

Maniye did not want to look at the creature – no, the *man*. A dead man, but a man nonetheless. 'I couldn't help him.'

'He didn't know that. What could he know? How strange it must have been for him.'

'To Step?'

'To have a soul.' Hesprec touched the dead flesh tentatively, and Maniye wondered if there was a ghost left there, unable to depart – and if it could flee that prison, where could it possibly go, to be reborn? Would it find one of the Plague People's pets, some hatchling monster to inhabit, or perhaps some tiny mote of an insect drifting on the wind?

Hesprec's face was devoid of expression when she stood up; that meant she was thinking very deeply indeed.

'Man of the Dragon, would you lead us to your Kasrani? You're right, this is not a healthy place to stay.'

29

Galethea had been brought before Mother as soon as the healers had finished with her. It had been strange, the healers said. She had screamed and thrashed just like a real person; her blood had been as red, her flesh as vulnerable. And yet the hollowness had been there always, beneath their fingers; the soullessness.

But she had been tenacious of life and clung on while they dressed and bandaged the gash the grey priest had made. She had lived, though her paleness was now an ashen, bluish colour. Then they had taken her on a stretcher up before Mother and the rest of the Wise, and she had stammered through her report: there would be no peace with the Plague People. They would trade no more words with the real people. All was war now. Kailovela had stood by and listened, and felt ice sink into her at the words. In her head the words, *It's the end of the world,* went round and round.

Mother had all but accused the Pale Shadow woman of bringing this about; everyone knew how reluctant she had been to play the peacemaker. Galethea had no strength left for her magic; her kinship with the enemy had been there for all to see. And yet she had wept and begged, desperate to be believed. She had done her best, but the enemy priest had no willingness to talk. He was poisoned from within by hatred for them all. In the end she had been believed.

Later, she had sat in Kailovela's tent, with Empty Skin and Hesprec the Serpent priestess, and told the full story.

'He said many things so the other Plague Men could hear,' she explained in her thin, exhausted voice. 'Peace words, as though he was there to treat with us. But in between those words he said other things with his craft, just for me. Because he needed to destroy us.'

'He hated us, you said,' Kailovela noted.

'That is not it. Or it is more than that.' Galethea's face twisted. 'I am trying to find your words for what he said. He said his family remembered, or his tribe, that is how you'd say it. He said the rest told each other you were animals who could trick them by taking man-shapes. He said that was best because then they would not feel guilt when they killed you, if all you were was animals. They do not have animals in their land, like you have here. Your wolves and bears and eagles are all monstrous to them. Killing you is easy, because they fear your claws and teeth.'

'But *his* tribe, his family,' Hesprec prompted.

'He said they remembered,' she repeated. 'He said they forget nothing, that all the lore of the Plague People is theirs. They are keepers of secrets, he said.' Her eyes fixed the Serpent girl. 'They know.'

'Know what?' Empty Skin asked, but it was clear Hesprec understood. She and Galethea stared at each other for a long time, and the Serpent spoke first.

'We have a legend; every tribe knows it, in one form or another. The legend of Where We Were, and how some of the people there made bargains with demons and became the Plague People. They spread throughout the land and devoured everything until the true people who were left had to flee. And, yes, the three brothers fought until the sun came and burned away the land, the sea rushed in, all of that. And I wonder about that last, and in truth I think perhaps the tale tellers made something grand out of something wretched. But we remember that the Plague People drove us out of our first home to these lands. And

335

the Plague People do not remember, because it is easier to forget the one you scar, than the one that scars you. The Plague People do not know us as those they once wronged, back in the lost days. As she says, we are just animals to them, who have learned a strange trick, monsters who deceive them with our human faces. Except for this grey priest's tribe.'

'But if they know . . .' Empty Skin started, because she was the youngest of them, and still innocent in some ways.

'Why would they let the killing happen?' Hesprec finished for her. Her eyes shifted briefly to Kailovela and saw the understanding there. 'What is easier for them to say to their kin? That these are beasts who have no right to life, no wisdom, no humanity; or that these are people, to whom your ancestors have done a great wrong, and you have done more great wrongs ever since you came to these shores? Which is easier? For who wants to think themselves a monster and a descendant of monsters? It is easier to think yourself just a killer of beasts.'

'But we can tell them . . .' Empty Skin insisted, voice petering out as she saw their expressions.

'How can we? They cannot hear our words nor will they let us get close enough to speak to them,' Kailovela told her. 'You said yourself, the grey priest went back to them with his own blood on his hands, crying betrayal.'

'But we're *human*!' Skin shouted at her. 'We're *people*! They can't not see that.' She bit back the words, and Kailovela guessed that she was thinking how the Plague People would accept *her*. How she had been made one of them when they chased off her soul.

'They will come and find my people,' Galethea said quietly. 'They will find some pretext to kill us too, because we know. Because we chose another way. And we will die without souls, and be lost.'

Empty Skin's mouth opened and closed as she fought for some magical argument that would prove them all wrong, and sought in vain. Kailovela could only think of poor Lone Mountain dead, severe Seven Mending dead, and so many others. And this was only the beginning of it. The Plague priest would be whipping up his followers into a frenzy of revenge against the monsters, and perhaps some of them would know those monsters were people, and perhaps they would not care. Easier to kill than change the way they viewed the world.

She looked to Hesprec to share her despair, but the Serpent priestess had a pensive look on her face, taken by some unexpected thought. When she did meet Kailovela's gaze, her face was full of secrets just like a Serpent priest's look should be, and not of despair at all.

Those who could, sent out scouts. Heron and Vulture, Owl and Hawk all took to the sky to go spy out what the Plague People were doing. Some did not return: the Terror had taken them, or perhaps the Plague warriors with their shimmering wings. Or perhaps they had fled, ashamed, but loving life more than courage. Kailovela could not blame them. She felt the sky calling to her as well. Sometimes her child seemed like the only anchor holding her to the ground. Now Kailovela wandered between the fires with her son clutched to her, and knew that, without that weight, she might just fly away and never be seen again.

She kept her distance from Loud Thunder, while everyone waited to see what the scouts would have to say. He was busy trying to be a war leader and she would put thoughts in his head he did not need there. She kept her distance from Yellow Claw, too, though she felt him stalking her. He did not go to scout but lorded it amongst the Eyriemen, or let his keen gaze follow his former mate from fire to fire. She felt it like an itching on the back of her neck.

Everyone now had some idea that things had changed. Most knew an attempt to treat with the Plague People had ended in ruin. And yet there was a sense of held breath, all across the camp. All those many hundreds who had been uprooted from their Plains villages, all those warriors come from the cold or the

337

River: they waited with a hope that Kailovela knew was wholly unwarranted.

She went to the Coyote, Two Heads Talking and Quiet When Loud, hoping they would have stories and wisdom to share, but he looked old and she looked frightened. The growing burden in her belly had become a curse to them: a child was of the future, and what future was there once the Plague People had done with them? Only a life like Empty Skin's, with no soul and no shape to Step to, and none of the stories and histories that made up their shared world.

She should go to Empty Skin, perhaps, who would at least understand her. She should go to Galethea and prise some truths out of the woman before it was too late, save that she was weak and slept, and anyway what truths could a hollow creature truly hold?

And so she returned at last to her own tent and there Loud Thunder was waiting for her.

She stopped awkwardly. He was sitting like a great lump beside her tent's entrance, looking like the most miserable man in the world. All his emotions were outsized, to match the rest of him.

'What is it?' she asked. The words came out more sharply than she had meant and he flinched. 'What do you want?'

His sorrowful gaze told the truth of that: *you*. But he shrugged massively. 'Just. Let me sit with you. Just for a while. I have lost my cousin and there is nobody I can share it with.'

'You have all the warriors in the Crown of the World to tell his stories to,' she pointed out.

'I don't want to tell his stories,' Thunder mumbled. 'I don't want to say how great he was, what a talker, what a hunter. I don't want to say all those things we say to stop us being sad. I don't know where his soul is. I don't know what's going to happen tomorrow. Tonight I want to be weak and be sad for Lone Mountain, and for all the rest I have to be strong. Please.'

She all but felt something break in her, some final barrier that had been keeping him out. The Eyriemen were braggarts, constantly flaunting their strength at each other. She had never before heard a man beg for the privilege of being weak.

'Come,' she said, pushing into her tent. Her child was sleeping by then and she settled him delicately, desperate not to set him squalling again. He had not wanted to leave Quiet When Loud's arms for hers. She couldn't blame him.

Thunder shouldered in, undignified on hands and knees. When he sat, he hunched forwards to keep his head clear of the hide stretched overhead. His eyes spoke mute gratitude to her.

With a sense that any choice now would be a mistake, she sat beside him and put her arms around him, easing the front of his robe open until she could feel the great rounded contours of his shoulders and chest. She laid her head on him, and tried to use what magic she had to salve the wounds he bore that the healers could not see or reach. Whether that did any good, she couldn't say, but he slept after a while, still sitting up, chin on his chest.

Before dawn next morning those scouts who would be returning were returned, and though the rest were still looked for, the word of their spying was swiftly all across the camp. At the Plague camp where Empty Skin had gone, the children had been taken away, and in their place came warriors. Plague Men marched in from the east, or flew, or rode in on mounts that might once have been men and women of the Horse. They came with their mail and their killing rods; they came with their skittering beasts. The walls of the camp were already a maze of webs strung higher than two men, but it was clear that they were not intending to sit there and defend.

They were not so many, compared to all the people of the world. When they went to war they would be outnumbered hundreds to one. And yet none doubted that they would bring the fight, and few doubted they could win. Their weapons and their wings, but most of all their Terror would carry the day.

But there was more and worse. The fleetest of the scouts had seen a shadow growing in the eastern sky; the Plague Ship was coming, ready to carpet the earth with fire. The Plague People would launch their attack from the shadow of their indomitable floating fortress.

Kailovela heard the voices at every fire, saying, 'But we are so many. We are all the strength of the world, all the spears there are, drawn together in one place. Surely they cannot defeat us.' But she listened past that cracked, desperate optimism to the others. She heard Plainsfolk who had lost their land a day at a time, and their warriors too, whenever they had turned to raise a spear. She heard Rivermen who had seen their great stronghold of Tsokawan fall in flames. She heard northerners talk about the horrors they had found on the Seal coast, and how many had been lost to drive away even a small band of the enemy.

That evening she stood and stared not at the sunset but at the darkness of the east, the realm light had already fled.

* * *

Alladai had made a little corner of the Horse Society within the Plains camp.

In his own tent he had made a den for Maniye, a nest of cushions and hides where she could lie and get well. She found him exasperating and was always on the point of leaving or telling him to go away, but he read her moods artfully, her frustration with how her wounds still dragged at her. He walked the line of her temper and never crossed it.

This evening he had more guests, old comrades. He had played host to them, long ago in the Crown of the World when Maniye had been running from her twin natures. Now, a fugitive himself, he could still find salt, milk and meat to perform the host's duties.

Loud Thunder had come, after a day of people running after him, all with the same bad news and demanding *What are you*

340

going to do about it? Asman was there, sitting close against Venat's dour bulk, and Shyri at his other hand, with more pointed distance between them.

Asman and Venat took the role that argued for a fight. The River Champion spoke of numbers, of a sudden strike, a surprise attack, keeping the momentum of a battle rolling against the Plague People so their Terror never had a chance to bite. He talked of the advantages they had, the different skills of the various tribes of people – who was fleet, who was strong, who flew, who walked unseen. He argued that they must attack the Plague People at their camp, burn their white walls and slaughter them all together, with Venat egging him on at every turn.

'This is a gift for us,' he insisted. 'They have brought all their strength and we can finish them.'

But sheer conviction would win neither battles nor arguments right then. 'They fly, Longmouth,' Shyri said tiredly. 'The moment they think they might lose they'll just go, and we can't stop them. They are not here with their families or children, to tie them to the land. They will just choose a different battle to fight.'

'And attacking their walls, that is no small matter,' Loud Thunder added.

'We can be the spearhead, Many Tracks and I, and all the other Champions. The Terror has no power to change us,' Asman pressed.

'There are maybe twenty Champions, if you gather all the Lions, all the Stone Men and the River tribes and the rest,' Thunder pointed out. 'And the Terror will sweep the rest away the moment they remember to be scared.'

'Some war leader you sound like,' Asman said desperately.

'I know, I know.' Thunder shrugged.

'And Many Tracks's not going to be fighting, not tomorrow, not soon,' Shyri pointed out.

Maniye saw that impact on Asman, just one more truth he

341

was trying to overlook. He tried a strained smile at Shyri. 'You're supposed to be agreeing with me, Laughing Girl. Surely Hyena is up for a fight.'

'Hyena can do what he likes,' Shyri said flatly. 'And if you think your grand fight is what he wants, then maybe you should think about that and what it means.'

Silence fell in the wake of that. Maniye could almost hear Asman taking down his carefully constructed hopes and stowing the pieces for some better day that wouldn't come.

'Some people have gone already.' Alladai broke the silence, ducking into the tent with a skin of mead he had somehow got hold of. 'One fire at a time, they're leaving.'

'Good for them,' Shyri said, but the Horse shrugged.

'Not many, though, not yet,' he explained. 'I think my people will leave with the dawn. We have lost too much already. But many are staying on, watching their war chiefs and their wise people, none of whom want to admit that the fight is lost.'

'It isn't lost,' said Asman, but his tone belied his words.

'We need to get people moving, at least those who can't fight,' Maniye said quietly. 'The Plague People strike fast. They can be here swiftly enough that we'll have no chance to get people away. We need to go to every fire and tell people: here is your choice – take up a spear or flee.'

A new voice broke in, 'No.'

They looked towards the tent flaps and saw a small figure there, just a slight dark girl with Serpent markings, but there was something dangerous and frightening on Hesprec's face.

'What do you mean, "No"?' Thunder asked her. 'They can't fight. If they stay here, they'll just make more bones.'

'They *can* fight.' Hesprec's voice shook; whatever idea had gripped her must be something audacious and desperate even for her. 'Not with spears, not with teeth, though we will need those fighters too. We will need people to play Three Brothers and hold the Plague at bay. But for the rest, there is something, something grand. Do not tell them to go.'

'What is it?' Maniye asked her. 'What will you do?'

'Something impossible,' the Serpent priestess said, and then shrugged. 'Again.'

30

Hesprec had sent word by every messenger she knew, Coyote, Owl and Bat going from fire to fire and speaking to the wise of every tribe. Her name, or that of the Serpent, carried enough weight that by the first shade of evening she had many of them gathered in an open space before the tent of Tecumet. Maniye looked from face to face, seeing fear and suspicion unhidden in many. The River honoured the Serpent, the Stone Men too, but the Plains had little reason to trust him, nor yet the Crown of the World.

Yet they had gathered, because they were desperate. All their wisdom had come to nothing, just as all the spears of the strong had broken against the Plague People.

Hesprec spent a while just watching her audience, as they muttered and shuffled. There were other Serpents there, that Tecumet had brought from the River, and there were priests of the many Estuary tribes. There were old Lionesses, gnarled Boar men, skinny-necked Vulture women with their hair shaved to a stubble. There were Wolves and Tigers, there was Grey Herald of the Owl, and a gathering of lean, silent Bats, and Two Heads Talking of the Coyote. She caught herself looking for old Takes Iron and her stomach lurched, remembering.

And there was Mother, wisest of all the Bear, looming at the back and keeping her own counsel, regarding Hesprec with a gaze heavy as stones. The little Serpent girl seemed too slender to bear it.

And yet when she drew herself up to her small height before them, she had the authority of ages. She had lived many lives, watched generations spring up and die down just like the Tsotec flooded and fell each year. She was old in a way no other tribe could imagine and she gathered all those years to her, right then. She stood before them with the Serpent at her back, one of the three brothers who had stood against the Plague People the first time.

'So we have come to it, then,' she told them. 'Most of you know we tried something other than fighting with the Plague Men, and it didn't work. But then the fighting hasn't worked either. Yes, we've bloodied them once or twice, but for every Plague warrior cut down, how many of ours? They gather all their strength at last. We have gathered ours. And so we go at it, spear on shield, do we? There are enough of us, far more than there are of them, that if we charge them with our fangs and our talons, we hope that they cannot kill *all* of us, their Terror cannot turn every mind amongst us. That is what we hope, is it? That is what is left for us?'

She plainly had more, but Mother's voice boomed from the back. 'The Snakes have many ways of speaking. Each word is a coil until they strangle others into agreeing with them. I am not here to be strangled, little Snake. So just tell us your other way.'

Hesprec held up her hands. 'Forgive me,' she said mildly. 'Old habits. But, yes, there is something. And it will not mean no spear gets bloodied when the Plague People come, because we will need our warriors to hold the eyes of the Plague People while we do what we must. Because if this war can be won, if our dream of the world can prevail over theirs, it comes down to us, because we are those who have spoken to the gods.'

She had begun walking back and forth before them, leading their suspicion left and right as it followed her.

'I have walked in the Godsland, just a few days ago. Who here

345

has seen it, since the Plague came?' Not many, but a few; Maniye could see the knowledge in their faces. She wondered what dire errands had driven them to it, and whether they had found what they were looking for in the ashes of what had been left.

'The Plague People are our enemy, and their very presence assaults us,' Hesprec told them. 'Even without meaning to, they destroy what we are, and now they very much intend to complete that job. But they are the enemy of our gods, more than us. Our gods have fled before them, because it is not just flesh and bone that the Plague People kill, it is all we are. They destroy our stories and our ways; they smooth away all the pictures we have drawn in the earth that tell us where we came from and who we are. And that is what the gods are made of. That is the death they bring to our gods and our souls.'

They were all silent by then, listening. It was no revelation to them, but perhaps nobody had stated the matter so bluntly before. Nobody wanted to believe that their gods were as fragile as they were.

'So we must fight, but we cannot fight alone. We must call back the gods who have fled, and have them fight the Plague People dream as our warriors attack their bodies. As our warriors lift their spears, the gods must be there, within and between them, giving them strength, fending off the Terror.'

It fell to one of the old Boar priests there to ask, 'How?'

'A hundred ways,' Hesprec told them. 'All the ways you have to catch their attention and call them from the far places they have gone to. Light your fires and play your music, dance your hunts, act out all the old stories; who am I to tell you how to speak to your gods?'

Maniye saw in her mind what that would look like: chaos, surely. And yet Hesprec spoke with such assurance, such passion.

'Above all, whatever you do must tell the gods, "We are here!"' she went on. 'You must remind the gods of who we are and who they are. You must tell the stories of your heroes

346

and how they bested each other. Tell of our fools and tricksters; tell of the great evils we have overcome. Tell the story of the three brothers, tell how Coyote stole back the sun, tell of First Eagle, how Serpent sought wisdom beneath the earth. Tell how Havesinder snatched his name from Old Crocodile's jaws, and how Leyri and Usri made the hills when they fought over who should be Chomaro's mate. Tell the deeds of your mothers and their fathers. Bring the gods close to the world until they are just the other side of the air, just beneath the skin of the earth. Because spears alone will not turn back the Plague People, not all the spears in the world.'

And she had them, Maniye saw, or enough of them. Some might yet steal away, seeking more life under the shadow of a rock somewhere south or west or north of here. But most would go back to their people, their war leaders and chiefs, and say what must be done.

Afterwards, she asked Hesprec, 'Why didn't you tell them what your plan really is?'

The Serpent shrugged. 'They wouldn't have liked it. And when did Serpent ever do anything the straightforward way?'

The next part of the plan had come from the Lion. An old priest named Oreto had come to Hesprec the day before, after he heard the Serpent had something secret hidden in its coils. He was thin as a switch, but he looked as though his wiry muscles were hard as stone. He came to them straight from some Lion ritual, coppery skin painted with reds and whites and a mane of dried grass about his face.

He invited them to his tent amongst the Lion fires, and they walked there beneath the suspicious glower of all those warriors, the heavy-muscled men, the strong, graceful women, all of them sharpening their spears for the battle to come.

'All my ancestors will curse me for this,' Oreto said, once they were inside and cut off from that fierce scrutiny. 'The Lion will take me in his jaws and tear me. This is a great secret of our people, and the Serpent has always been our enemy.'

Hesprec regarded him warily. 'Then why tell me? You're right, the Lion has never been a friend of the River or my people.'

He set out a bowl of water for them, and another of seeds, meagre hospitality for a lean season. 'I spoke with my wives last night, and my brothers,' by which Maniye had gathered he meant priests and priestesses of his people. 'We know it is the end of the world. Why keep secrets then? There will be a great battle soon, like none ever seen before. If we can add even one more cup of strength to the arms of the warriors there, then we must. So I volunteered to risk Lion's wrath, and lose our secret to the Serpent.'

Hesprec nodded, acknowledging the sacrifice.

'And for this one,' Oreto said, nodding at Maniye, to her surprise. 'We have heard of this one, the Champion of the Crown of the World. We have heard of the many gods who had the making of her. She is Lion's, as she is his sister, Tiger's. So some small part of her is of us, and she is your guardian and companion. So perhaps it is not so great a betrayal that we tell you this.'

'So tell,' Hesprec invited.

'We have Champions amongst the Lion,' Oreto said. 'More than many tribes, for we are strong. But, still, the Champion souls come to few. They cannot be everywhere and we *do* fight everywhere. All the Plains speaks in fear of the might of the Lion.'

Hesprec nodded diplomatically.

'But the Lion has long known how to share that strength, just a little,' Oreto explained. 'There is a ritual known to us, where our Champions give of themselves to make the whole pride greater. The fire of the Champion enters into each, some of that greatness of soul. One of my brothers came to this camp, just days ago, saying that he enacted this ritual before the Plague People came to destroy his village, and they held the Terror at bay just a little while, to let those who could not fight escape. Just a little, but it is something. And every tribe in the world has sent its Champions here.'

Hesprec's eyes had lit up, to hear that, and Maniye could almost hear her adjusting her plans.

Now, after her grand speech to the wise, Hesprec gathered all the Champions she could to stand before Oreto, who had a basin of red stone before him, and a copper knife heating in the ashes of his fire.

Maniye herself stepped forward first, because she knew she had given herself over to Hesprec's plan, and so she would follow wherever it led her. Asman was there too, and stout Tchoche who was Tecumet's bodyguard. There were other Rivermen – some so old they must surely have come from a peaceful retirement for this battle – and people from the Stone Kingdoms, and there were plenty of Lions, and a scattering from other Plains and Estuary tribes who had found a way to access those great souls from deep time. Even scowling Yellow Claw of the Eyrie had come, because he could not live with being left out of so great a gathering.

Oreto cut each of them and let a measure of their blood flow into his bowl. He anointed them with oil and ash, and each differently, his fingers finding the shape of the soul guesting within them. The blood he would mix with honey and beer, bone dust and the sap of certain plants gathered by the Lion on days sacred to them, until he had a great cauldron brimming with the thick brew. Then skins of the stuff would be dispatched to chief after chief, to pass amongst their warriors.

'And perhaps it is all nothing,' Hesprec confided to Maniye. 'But let the Lion brag of his strength, especially if, for once, he shares it. Let our warriors go to war knowing they are stronger, because that is all that matters when the enemy's greatest weapon is fear.'

'And maybe it will work,' Maniye said, because she liked the idea, and the Champion within her liked it too.

Hesprec shrugged. 'These things are known: drowning men

clutch at every straw. And also: it's late, and I have only one last loop of this plan to put in place. Morning will be best for it, and tonight you have other duties.'

Maniye frowned. 'What duties?'

Hesprec put a hand on her arm, stilling the world around her. 'Go to your friends, those you care about. Tomorrow we begin the ritual. Great things will be done, and probably done badly. And the Plague People will come, and bring their war and their floating ship to destroy us. Tomorrow will have no time for good-byes, so say them tonight, while you still can.'

Maniye sought out Alladai, just pushed straight past all his people with their needs and demands and threw her arms around him. He would not fight, tomorrow. His people would dance their Horse dances and speak long poems of travel and hardship and friends met at the end. She felt that, of all the people of the world, the Horse were almost a memory, the whole heart of their world eaten away by the Plague. And yet they had outposts in the north and in Atahlan and across the Plains, little seeds of the Horse Society that might yet grow, if the earth could be cleared for them.

She took him away from his responsibilities – they were the Horse, after all, a people used to counting and managing. They did not need Alladai this one night. He tried to ask her what she meant and what was the matter, but they were all questions he knew the answer to, and just did not want to face. At last he gave in and held her, unlacing her clothes with his deft care, letting a sliver of moonlight in to touch her body.

He was gentle; she was weak still, and shivered when he touched the scars the Rat had left, the scars of the hooks that had taught her the secret of iron, those given her by her father and by the man she had thought was her father, and all the other lines and blemishes that spoke of hurt and death.

'You will fight, tomorrow?' he asked. 'You are not strong enough.'

'Hesprec has other uses for me,' she told him, but would not be drawn. It was not her secret to share.

In another tent, Kailovela stood before Loud Thunder, looking into his broad, simple face and wondering if he would live. All his size and power would count for nothing against the killing darts of the Plague People. He would lead from the front, and he would be nothing but a greater target for their aim.

'I cannot give you what you want,' she told him. 'This thing you feel for me, it is too great, too all-consuming. I cannot feel that for anyone or anything. Not my own child, not my people.'

He nodded philosophically, but tonight she had sent word asking for him, rather than him coming to seek her, and so he waited, hoping there was more.

She put a hand on his arm, seeing him shiver a little at the contact. 'I wish I *could* lose myself in you, though. You are a good man. You are the only man I ever knew who took strength and power over others and did not twist them. You have all the tools to be a great monster amongst men and yet here you are, pining for your little cabin and your quiet. And so, what I feel for anyone, I feel for you. It is not enough; you deserve more from someone, but it is all I have to give.'

And, because he was who she said he was, he took that with a wide, incredulous grin.

She gave herself to him, thinking at first that she was like a sacrifice, that he might fight well the next day, but as his hands cupped her body, the act became more and more about her, needs she had always associated with pain and humiliation given a new life because she knew he would neither hurt nor cage her. And they were as quiet as they could be, and still the baby woke and cried, and had to be nursed back to sleep, and he was patient, and held her as she held her son.

This could be your life, said an insidious part of her, but she knew better than to trust it. Tomorrow, Loud Thunder would lead the war host of the Crown of the World to fight the Plague People who came by land.

And tomorrow, as she had told nobody, she would take wing and bring what magic she had against the enemy who came by air. One way or another there would be no long happy life for Loud Thunder of the Bear and Kailovela of the Eyrie.

The same night, once he had shed blood for Oreto, Asman went to Tecumet's side. He had seen plenty of tearful moments as he stalked through the camp. Warriors were with their mates for what could be their last night; parents and children knew that the coming fight would sunder families. The thought of the Plague People loomed large in every mind, the battle against the Terror already half lost.

Let my blood, all our blood, give them all courage. Even another ten heartbeats of fight might be enough to carry the day. In his mind he made the armed might of the true people a great tide sweeping away the Plague People, their beasts, their walls, their godless, soulless dream that they had brought to his world. He could almost believe it, even all mustered together, even with their sky ship and their fiery rain.

But then the images crept back, his memories: he saw Tecuman die; he saw the very Tsotec burn. The Terror could not destroy him, but he still knew fear.

He could only guess at the grim expression he was wearing when he sloped his way past the guards into the Kasra's tent. Tchoche had gone before him, and would have explained how the Lion ritual had gone and what Hesprec's grand plan was. Asman had heard the Serpent's words about the gods, but in his heart he knew it would come down to spears and swords and courage. *Let the gods strengthen men's arms and shore up their hearts, we will not see them walk the earth beside us. If they could do it, would they not have done so before?*

Tecumet was not one of the weeping women he had seen, already thinking of themselves as widowed, childless. There was a new expression on her face, though. The times had called on her to make many of a ruler's hard decisions, but now she had come to some final conclusion, and he could see it pained her. *Or perhaps this is her face beneath the mask, and I never knew.*

She sent Tchoche out and beckoned Asman near, looking him up and down as though he was new to her.

'Tchoche goes to his own people, to lend them his strength,' she said. 'The Stone Men, come down to the Plains to fight. Not something that has happened in two generations.'

'Now is a good time to do all those things we have put off,' Asman said. 'Tomorrow may be too late for them. Perhaps we should invade the Crown of the World or something.'

He scared up barely a ghost of a smile from her. She put a hand to his face, fingers digging slightly as though trying to find the real Asman beneath the calluses the world had put on him. 'I loved you as much as my brother did, you know that.'

'I know. I loved you as much as I did him.'

'But not with all your heart.'

He kissed her forehead. 'My heart is a pack of dogs straining after many quarries. It does not mean I do not love you.'

'I know. I knew before I made you Kasrani, but perhaps I fooled myself. But I cannot change that part of you and still keep the *you* I love. And tomorrow I may not even have that. And if not that, the day after I may be Kasra of nothing, and the River may not be the great Tsotec, but just a river with some Plague name no true human can say. But there is tonight.'

He moved to hold her, but she broke away. 'I believe you will live, Asman. I believe you will fight until the Plague People cannot threaten us. I believe you are the Champion of the Sun River Nation, a Champion amongst Champions. Hesprec Essen Skese will call close Old Crocodile and the Serpent and all the gods of the Estuary to stand at your back, and you *will* triumph. I believe it with all my life, with my soul. I wager everything on my belief that there will be another night for you and me, beyond this one.'

'I don't understand,' he confessed.

'I know your heart's loves,' she said. 'And there is one who goes to fight tomorrow who may yet die, for I have enough belief for you, and not for any other. I know you feel an ache for him, and that it does not lessen what is between us, son of Asman. And, though he would never admit a word of it, I know he keeps your name within him, as you keep his. And as I claim all your tomorrows, so I give you tonight.'

Asman blinked at her, and kept staring as she called her servants and had them load her with the mask and robe of state, so she could go amongst her people and have Esumit tell them they would be brave on the morrow.

Only after she had left did the tent flap part again to admit Venat, looking as baffled as he. Their eyes met, though. Asman saw some mocking comment occur to the man and get swallowed back down.

'Come,' he suggested. 'We'll drink.'

The Dragon rolled his shoulders. 'First sensible thing you've said for days.' He glanced back after the vanished Tecumet. 'I always reckoned she'd have my throat cut.'

'Because you don't know her. Perhaps I don't, either. But she knows my heart. And so she sent for you.'

Venat scowled at the sentiment, but Asman knew his moods, which were deep-carved, and which only painted on his skin.

'Tomorrow—' the Dragon started, but Asman hushed him.

'No more of tomorrow,' he said. 'Not when we have tonight.'

Elsewhere, but never too far away, Shyri drank and laughed with whoever she found, at whichever fire presented itself, and told herself she didn't care.

Elsewhere still, Hesprec went to where the sounds of grief masked by cheer were muted, where the wounded lay. Healers and the wise of a dozen tribes were still here, doing what they could for the sick and the injured and she passed amongst them

354

like a ghost. Her duty as a priest tugged at her with each cry for the Serpent's aid, but she plucked the hooks out the moment they latched on to her and went on her way. She was here for one casualty in particular.

The tent was quiet – so much so, Hesprec feared the woman had died. Galethea still breathed, though. Whether it was some innate hardiness of her kind or the half-hearted efforts of the healers, she could not say. Nobody had wanted to spend their time and medicines on the hollow creature, not when her glamours had dropped away. Hesprec had found some of the Milk Tear, who were the best healers the River had, and all but threatened them with the Serpent's coils. They had done what they could, and then left the woman to her own constitution, but it had been enough.

Hesprec slipped into the tent – no other of the wounded would share it – and heard Galethea's breathing change as she woke.

'Who—?' the Pale Shadow woman started weakly.

'I,' Hesprec told her. 'Only I, but with little time and much to ask. Where is your strength, Galethea? Did you leave it on the rock when the priest stabbed you, or do you have it still?'

'What do you want?' Galethea hissed at her. 'I went to the Plague People because of you and yours. I am stabbed because of you, and all for nothing.'

'Perhaps not for nothing. Your words, when you came back, taught me about the enemy. Other things I saw, while you were getting yourself cut open, taught me more. I have enough, now, for a plan. A plan that needs you.'

She heard Galethea turn over on her pallet, a laborious process carried out in stages. 'I have lost enough for your plans, all of them. And gained nothing, not for me or my people.' Then there was a sudden motion – Hesprec's eyes had adjusted just enough for her to see the woman sitting up, her pale skin luminous in the dark of the tent. 'And my people will suffer, once yours are no more. They will find us and kill us all.'

'So you have nothing to lose and much to gain, if I can turn back the Plague,' Hesprec pointed out mildly. 'But there is more than that. You came a long way, Galethea of the Pale Shadow, and it was for a purpose.'

The pale woman was very still. 'More tests, then? To prove myself worthy of your aid?'

'And if I said that it was more, that I had a grand experiment in mind?'

'I would not believe you. You have greater concerns than obliging me.'

Hesprec came closer and crouched down beside her. 'The Serpent has many coils, O Pale Shadow, but there is only one Serpent. Many things may be done, that are all to one purpose.'

'I don't believe you.' Stripped of her magic, Galethea's voice was a thin whine. 'I've seen the way your people look at me. I've felt their hands on me. They hate me. The rift between what they are and what I am is too great. I've been a fool every step of the journey. I should have stayed with my people and faded with them.'

'I will tell you what I have seen,' Hesprec said. 'And then you will change your mind and come with me tomorrow.'

Galethea's eyes were so wide that Hesprec could see them clearly in the gloom. 'Where?'

'Where your kind have never gone,' she told the Pale Shadow woman. 'To meet the gods.'

31

Some of the priests had begun their rites when the moon was up – those for whom the night was more sacred than the day. The Tiger and the Owl had been working to invoke their predatory deities, trying to replicate their northern mysteries in this unfamiliar land. But then the gods were all adrift now. Perhaps any land was home to them as long as someone lit the right fires and spoke the right words.

And Owl and Tiger both trained their priests to fight. When morning came they would form their warbands or join those of others. The night was their only chance to bring their gods near.

The dawn brought with it a bizarre air of celebration. Maniye heard voices raised in song, the sound of rattles and drums and shouting, as though the Plague was already beaten. Only after she had lain and listened for a while did she hear the crack of desperation in the voices, the fear that drove them. Only then did the purpose of all these sounds recur to her. She had been drifting in a sea of fond thoughts, still wrapped in the body-warmth Alladai had left behind him. Now she jumped up, wincing as her wounds snagged at her in a dozen places, insistent still that she not forget the god that dealt them to her, the one god she hoped nobody was invoking right now.

Alladai was outside, naked save for a loincloth and being painted by an old woman of his people. He was no warrior, after all. Horse would have run far, after so many of its children were

357

killed or driven out of their wits, but perhaps he could be lured back to lend his swiftness and endurance to the fight. Maniye could not throw her arms about Alladai without spoiling the old priestess's work, but she rested her head on the arm still clear of patterns, thoughts of strength and love passing between them silently, and then went to find Hesprec.

Others found her first, though, following her trail through the busy camp until she became aware of feet treading her own footsteps and turned to confront them. She thought they might be enemies, but that was her own guilt speaking that had recognized their tread. They were her own people, and only in seeing them did she realize she had been avoiding them.

Moon Eye was in the lead, the mad Wolf fighter she had left in the hands of Tecumet's Champion, Tchoche. He had been a man of mad rages, and Tchoche's people knew how to teach such a man control. Behind him were all the others who had gone with her to Tsokawan and fought alongside and against the River Lords at her command. Her warband had found her and they were ready for war, armoured in iron and bearing hatchets and spears.

'All the world is going to fight,' Moon Eye noted. 'Every hand that can hold a knife will raise it against the Plague People. And we are your warband.'

Maniye nodded soberly, looking from face to face. She felt as though she had not seen them for years, for lifetimes. They were all older than her, and yet they seemed young and earnest and fragile. They looked at her with such hope; if she was anybody's Champion, she was theirs.

A swift form weaved between their legs and jumped up at Maniye, and she knelt down to let Sathewe snuffle into her hand, the coyote's cold nose and rough tongue bringing a gift of more guilt. The Crow, Feeds on Dreams, stepped forward to bring the animal back, but Maniye scratched Sathewe's muzzle and ears because it was easier than telling the warband what they must hear.

358

But the silence stretched out until the words were drawn from her. 'I cannot lead you.' She should tell them she was too weak for the battle; it was probably true. And yet she knew it would not have kept her from the fight, not that alone, and her warband deserved only truth. 'Hesprec has a need for me.'

'The Serpent,' Moon Eye said doubtfully. He had spent a little time amongst the southerners and the Stone Men, both of whom held Snake in high esteem, but he was a Wolf at heart.

'If we are to defeat the Plague People, it will be by following the Serpent's back, no matter how crooked it is,' Maniye told him, straightening up.

'And yet we raise our spears.' Moon Eye nodded, understanding.

'All the Plague warriors in our world are coming,' Maniye said softly. 'And because our path is long and twisted, all the spears in the world must win us time to walk it.'

'I have seen my kin, the Moon Eaters, ready themselves for war, while Icefoot and his priests stoke the fires and shed blood into the Wolf's jaws,' Moon Eye said. 'I have seen the *soldiers* of the Sun River Nation,' he spoke the southern word carefully, 'with their stone-toothed swords, and all the people of their estuary, the Toad people and the Heron and the Capybara and the rest. Many spears there. I have seen the Eyrie with blades in their hands, and known they were not my enemies today. I have seen the Stone Men in armour that would crush slighter warriors. And the Plainsfolk! Lion and Boar, Horse and Dog! So many spears, Many Tracks. And all this to buy *time*?'

'You know the enemy,' Maniye said simply. 'You have felt their Terror. Tell me then how many shields can stave it off. You have seen them take wing like insects and rain death from the sky. How many spears must we fill the air with, to bring them down?' She knew that making them fear was exactly the wrong thing to do, but the words just cascaded from her lips.

It was Feeds on Dreams that saved the moment, bobbing up under Moon Eye's armpit, almost, to chirp, 'Yes, yes, so our place is with you, still. So these winged men can come to anywhere, at any time. So we are your warband, even I, and we will stand guard over you – yes, even over the Serpent. And you will know you are safe, for how could even the Plague People defeat such heroes?'

His grin was strained, and she thought, *One more dream for him to eat, and this time it's his own.*

'Of course,' she agreed, and she saw the pride in them, that their place would be at her side. The responsibility frightened her more than the Plague People. *What if this all comes to nothing?*

The answer was obvious. *Then none of it matters and you won't have long to feel the shame of it.*

They were her honour guard when she found Hesprec, who was sitting under an awning drawing lines in the dust. Galethea sat beside her looking like death. Nearby, the Eyriemen Stepped all together, Yellow Claw and his warriors thundering into the air, eclipsing the sun with their wings, circling higher and higher in the warming air. Sathewe yapped at them furiously as though it was some personal affront.

Maniye saw the Tiger leaving, too, in the company of the Lion of the Plains. For a moment Aritchaka, their priestess, stopped and met her gaze. They had been enemies and friends in turn, back in the north. Now Aritchaka fought alongside the Wolves she so despised. The end of the world made for strange allies.

'You want to go with them?' Hesprec was abruptly at her elbow.

'It would be simpler,' Maniye agreed. 'Why has this fallen to me, Hesprec?'

The Serpent stepped round to face her. 'People ask that question of priests. Most times I say it's the will of some god. But the gods are all in disarray now. I doubt any of them have the presence of mind to will this. Perhaps it is just chance that puts you here. Perhaps being born of Tiger and Wolf, both and neither all at once, has made you someone to whom odd destinies are drawn. And don't tell me you don't want them; who would? All

360

that matters is that your shoulders are strong enough to bear them.'

'I have the smallest shoulders of anyone here, save you,' Maniye pointed out.

Hesprec shrugged. 'Be glad the task is not mine, then. Galethea of the Pale Shadow!'

The pallid woman started, staring up at them. The skin about her eyes and mouth was bluish. Maniye half expected to be able to see through her flesh to the bones.

'I am here, Messenger,' she said, delivering the southern title flatly. Maniye had to lean in to hear her. Beyond Hesprec's little awning a hundred chants and instruments were clashing in appalling cacophony, each priest trying to drown out the next. The earth jumped without rhythm to the feet of many dancers. Sathewe huddled at Maniye's ankles, snarling at the noise with her tail between her legs.

'Sit with us, Champion,' Hesprec invited, dropping down beside Galethea. 'Sit and listen, for I will tell you of a land that must be as familiar to you as your northern home now. Few indeed have visited the land of the gods so many times as you.'

Maniye tried to let herself drift, but the resounding chaos all around kept tugging at her mind, never settling into a pattern, each shout or drumbeat treading on the toes of the last. Hesprec's hand was in hers, and she felt the connection there, the beginning of something, like a veil drawn aside just a sliver, yet not far enough that she could pass beyond. *It's her*, she realized. Hesprec's other hand was holding the Pale Shadow woman's. Maniye could feel the hollow creature like a weight she was trying to haul. *This can't work. This is no sacred ground. This is no Stone Place, made special to the gods over generations. And she has no soul. Galethea has nothing of the gods in her. She is like an empty jar. When the Godsland calls, nothing in her will hear it.*

'It cannot be,' she hissed. 'I will go alone. I will open the way somehow. Hesprec—'

'Patience, only patience.' The Serpent's words came to her

despite all the mounting noise. 'Patience, Many Tracks, for the gods are coming. Can you not hear them? There is Horse, his hooves like thunder.' Was there thunder? Impossible to tell in all the ruckus. 'There is Lion, striding proud, and Boar – can you not hear when he pauses to root at the earth?' Maniye's eyes were closed but she heard the grin in Hesprec's voice. 'I hear Old Crocodile drag his belly on the earth now. And here is Deer, his feet as fast and sharp as arrows.' Perhaps the awning snapped in the wind, perhaps some late Eyrie warrior put his shadow between them and the sun, but Hesprec said, 'There is Hawk, called from the high places because he is too proud to be left out. That thump was Toad, drawn from where he buried himself away, and even Dragon is here – how angry he is, to have to share the world with any other gods, but his people are going to shed blood today, and he would not miss it.'

Maniye did not want to open her eyes. She did not want to see all those thin, frightened priests and hearth-keepers stepping through their rituals, telling their stories, trying to tempt back their fled gods. She wanted the picture in her mind's eye that Hesprec was building, of the gods in their prime, in their strength, come to the aid of the people they tested and challenged and occasionally loved. The boom and rush of the rituals washed through her like a tide, like breathing, and her own breath caught when she realized it *was* a rhythm. If she let herself relax, if she stopped *listening* and only *heard*, there was a grand pulse that drew together every sound around her. The voice of Two Heads Talking and the stamping feet of the Deer, the dried grass rattles of the Lion, Mother's great bellow, the solemn formalities of Old Crocodile's priesthood, all of it blended into a single grand song that rode through the earth below her, and echoed far out across the sky. It was impossible – any moment surely it must break back down into all those clumsy human noises. And yet it pulsed and roared, ebbed and flowed, stronger and stronger until she was carried on it, until all that devotion had made this camp of fugitives the most sacred place in the world. She felt herself lifted, higher and higher, further and further from herself in that direction that she had no name for, and though there was a great weight on her arm where the clueless Pale Shadow creature clung, the current was strong enough to carry even her weight along with it.

* * *

Asman knew about armies and how slowly they moved, but apparently the Plague People didn't, for their force was coming across the Plains as fast as a man could run. There was a core that laboured along on the ground, but all around them were those Plague warriors who could fly. Handfuls of them would pitch up into the air and come down a hundred yards ahead, flushing out game from the grass and all too ready to do battle with anything that might bare a tooth at them. They killed what they scared into the open – animals of any stripe and nature, because they could not tell beast from man. All were their enemies.

Asman was with Venat and the fleetest of the Riverlanders, the first to throw themselves in the path of the enemy. It would be no easy job to inconvenience them, he knew: show a human face, and they would swarm from all sides. A charge of spearmen would be suicide, the darts would start what the Terror would end.

So Asman had left the regimented ranks of the Sun River Nation's army to be a final line between the great camp of refugees and the enemy, if a line even meant anything in this war, where the enemy could move about with such unnatural ease. Instead he had taken half fleet skirmishers and half archers with bows as tall as they were. A trio of other River Champions had come with him, deferring to him grudgingly because he was Kasrani.

They had planned to pick at the main body of the enemy but that was plainly not going to work. Instead he would have to hope that the Plague People would see his people as enough of a threat to slow for, rather than just butchering them all in passing.

'You've a better eye for this than me,' he told one of the other Champions, a lean woman who had brought a bow of her own. 'Have them loose as soon as a band comes in range.'

'Draw,' the woman said immediately, eyes flicking back and forth as she watched the Plague warriors cast themselves out across the grassland. A heartbeat later she spat, 'Loose,' and sent her own arrow on its way even as a flight of the enemy was descending. Asman would have thought they were out of range, but there was an archer's magic to the moment, the enemy dropping down as the arrows rose to meet them. A handful of the Plague People fell, either wounded or just knocked from the air by the impact, and the rest scattered.

'And loose,' the archer Champion said, quiet but confident, and for a moment they were harassing the enemy with arrows like rain and the Plague warriors were simply running around like mad insects. Then they came together and regained their senses, and they were up in the air again, swooping down to answer the arrows with the swift singing of their darts.

The plan had been for Asman's people to split off into groups to deny the enemy any one main target, but some of them just stood, staring horrified at the descending Plague People. Some of the archers stayed in place, aiming for one last strike against the fast-moving targets, while at the end of the line a whole clump of his skirmishers were rooted to the spot staring in horror at the advancing foe, so that the Plague warriors veered away to stoop on them. Asman Stepped and ran along the line, human for a breath at a time so he could shout orders. He was hoping to salvage the fighting but it collapsed before he ever got there. The darts struck down a dozen soldiers in a heartbeat, then a dozen more, and he saw the terrible moment when his people's nerve broke and the Terror struck them. Abruptly the grasslands were strewn with crocodiles and lizards, utterly out of their element and easy game for the enemy.

He saw one of the other Champions race in – an old man who had retired when Asman was just a child. He leapt into the air, his fighting shape still young, snagging a swooping Plague Man with his hooked claws and slamming the creature to earth. Moments later that fighting lizard was stumbling, blood written across the quills of his hide as the darts found him. Champions were proof against the Terror, but not against death. Death won every battle.

The archer Champion had kept pace with him, chivvying their people into falling back. Now she cried out, 'Smoke!'

Asman's head jerked up, looking towards the main body of the Plague advance. The haze in the air was not the dun of dust, but tinted blue and grey. Venat's people had been busy doing what the Dragon did best.

The grassland was not dry enough for a true inferno – it was not the season and the dew had been heavy. Still, Asman imagined the Dragon himself standing behind Venat's firestarters and breathing out, sending the wind rushing towards the core of the Plague People, and along with it a building wave of flame.

The Plague warriors above must have seen it, because they broke off their attack to swing back towards their own people.

But still: *Be safe*, he thought to Venat, and then he was shouting orders again, rallying the soldiers he still had, pulling them back.

He saw the Plague People break before the fire – a seeming chaos he knew contained a deeper order. A little flame would not drive them away.

But we have won some few heartbeats of time.

The archer Champion found him again in the retreat. 'Kasrani, go back to the spears. I will remind them of our arrows again.'

'Not yet,' Asman said, while considering his best move, until Venat and some of his people charged up, black heavyset lizards flailing through the grass and Stepping into brutish, sand-coloured men, laughing at the chaos they had wrought.

There were fewer Dragon warriors in his warband than there

had been, but Asman asked no questions: scattered, dead or lost to the Terror, it mattered little right now.

One of the archers called out, 'They're coming this way,' and Asman saw the sky to the east was busy with human-seeming forms.

'Go back, Kasrani,' the other Champion told him, and then she was running off at an angle with her archers, hoping to catch the enemy in the flank. Except the enemy had no flanks, an army that could swirl like mist and flow like water.

'Where's the rest?' Venat demanded. 'We're not *it*, are we?'

Asman tried to remember what the plan had been, mind momentarily blank. Given the choice he would be out there getting his claws bloody, not here giving orders. 'Tchoche,' he recalled. Tchoche and the Lion had a plan.

Reshappa of the Lion was dead behind the eyes, Tchoche had observed. Perhaps that made her the best person to lead the fight against the Plague People here. He could not imagine the Terror touching whatever lived inside her now. She had been fighting the enemy since Where the Fords Meet. The Plainsfolk told many stories about how Lion was lazy, how Lion loved a fight with the numbers in his favour. Since the Plague had come to the Plains, though, none had fought more than Lion's children. The stories about them were born from a resentment of their strength and domination of the land; they had the most to lose when a stronger enemy came.

Besides, Lions might be lazy, but Lionesses were proverbially fierce in all things save standing up to their mates, and Reshappa's mate was dead.

Even so, this was not the moment for a doomed charge into the killing teeth of the enemy. Reshappa had a far better way to cause the Plague People grief.

For a day and a night, her people had been hunting – not to kill, but to scare up a certain kind of game and make sure it was ready. They had not been alone, either. Once word of the plan spread, the best hunters of other people announced themselves proud to run with the Lion, and for once the Lion turned none of them away. There were some of the northmen, and the Plains Dogs, and even a handful of Hyena who seemed to realize that the best way to get their carrion was to contribute to the killing.

Reshappa and her people had gone north until they found a herd of aurochs, the huge horned beasts whose tribe was long lost in the Plains' bloody past. They had stalked about the edges of the herd, riling the beasts up with the scent of lion, forcing them across the grassland until they were between the Plague Men and the camp.

Tchoche and a hundred Stone Men had joined them after that. Half his force were White Face warriors, loaded down with thick bronze armour, carrying great shields that covered them from neck to toe; the other half were Snake Eaters, lithe men and women who moved like they were dancing and fought with javelins and short curved blades. The Stone Kingdoms were safer than anywhere, right now. Up in the mountains across the Tsotec's Back, who knew if the Plague People would ever come there? And yet the Serpent had called, who had once been their enemy but wormed his way into their friendship, and so here they were at the end of the world.

Now the scouts were running back – Lion and Dog and Snake Eater, two legs and four, shouting that the Plague Men were coming. Their warnings were unnecessary; the sky behind them was already whirling with flying men, advancing like a storm-front over the land.

Reshappa roared, and the sound was echoed back across the grassland. The aurochs had been cropping the grass, massed horns outwards against the predators they could still scent. Now the Lion hunters came at them, roaring and snarling, while behind them came more in human form, beating drums and clacking sticks together and waving bright torches. Tchoche imagined the herd stamping and bellowing, horns tossing in

367

defiance, but they were beasts, not men. There would come a moment when the noise and confusion was too much for them.

One of his people rapped on the side of his helm, and he craned past his shoulderguard to see a great curtain of dust thrown into the air as the aurochs began moving. The Lion and their helpers would be at their heels all the way, nipping and clawing, urging them on. In the rising dust, Tchoche seemed to see a shape, vastly muscled, head lowered as it charged over the backs of the animals. Perhaps Aurochs himself had heard the cries of the priests and come in memory of his vanished people. Perhaps this deed would bring them back to the world, who knew?

He had thought the Plains people would scatter and run before the charge, but only some of them could fly, and the rest dropped back to protect them. Tchoche's heart surged, because the aurochs were charging at full pelt now, an unstoppable force, and perhaps this was *it*. Perhaps the war would end here under the hooves of the bulls.

The dust was spreading across the Plains now, layering his view of the enemy with drifting veils, and he waited for the sound of that clash, feeling the earth jump beneath his feet at the massed charge of the aurochs.

The Plague People had formed lines, as though they could meet the aurochs as army met army in the south. Except nobody ever said the Plague Men just stood and fought with blade or spear, not when they had their killing rods.

And they were shooting, he saw. Two or three rows of them, shoulder to shoulder, shooting and shooting into that great unstoppable wave of meat and horn, *They are doomed!* Tchoche thought, and his heart surged, hearing the cheering of his people all around.

But the wave was cresting. His eyes couldn't understand what they were seeing at first – it was as though the aurochs were breaking against a barrier he couldn't see. As the jubilation of his fellows ebbed, he finally took hold of the sight and forced it to make sense. The Plague People were killing the aurochs with their darts. He had not believed that little slivers of metal could slay strong men the way he had been told, but now he saw the truth of all the stories. The charging herd met the massed wrath of the Plague People and died and died, huge beasts with thick hides pierced through and through until they dropped. Those behind were moving too fast in their panicked rout, stumbling over the bodies of those gone before, meeting the same fate even as they tried to regain their momentum. The Plague People just stood their ground, and Tchoche felt a worm of fear.

Then there was no more charging herd, just odd animals running off in all directions, and even these the Plague Men cut down, one after another. And then they were advancing again, coming across the grassland like the wind.

'What now?' one of the Snake Eaters asked, her eyes wide. Tchoche was momentarily without ideas, but then a lion was in their midst that Stepped into the shape of Reshappa.

'They barely slowed,' Tchoche observed.

'Then we will slow them,' Reshappa told him flatly. 'It will not be said that, at the end of the world, the Lion shied from the fight. Go back to your stone places, Stone Man.'

Tchoche took a deep breath. 'I will not.'

'All your bronze will not save you,' Reshappa told him. 'It will only slow you, old man.'

'It will not,' he said, and Stepped, first to the badger that was his people's totem, and then to his Champion form, the berserker wolverine that feared nothing and laughed at pain.

They flowed swift and low through the grass, and there was enough dust in the air that the Plague scouts did not see them until they were almost within striking distance. Then they did what they could, engaging the Plague People and trying to hook them down before they could fly, fighting a ragged running battle back and forth across the Plains and trusting to surprise and Champion's blood to stave off the Terror. For a few moments they were masters of the fight, and the Plague Men only reacting

369

to them. Tchoche let his angry spirit off its chain, feeling the fury take him in hand and throw him at the enemy like a stone.

He was the last one left, in the end. After his people had been killed, or the Terror had taken them, after Reshappa had been lanced with too many darts to fight on and all her hunters were dead or fled, still Tchoche remained, spitting and snarling and bleeding, surrounded by Plague Men regarding him with a horrified awe as they put shot after shot into him and he refused to die.

They would not come near his claws and teeth, but just circled and circled, shooting and shooting, and even a Champion's soul could not hold off the end forever. *Death wins all battles*, thought Tchoche, and the final bolt struck home in his skull and he died.

32

The rolling rhythm of the great ritual blurred in Maniye's head, receding but never quite going away. Hesprec's telling of the journey she was taking faded, becoming part of her mind at a level too deep to register.

She opened her eyes to the sight her ears had been telling her of: that waxing, waning sound, coursing towards her and then ebbing away, what else could it be but this?

She stared at the sea's great, black expanse, creased with the ridges of waves forever clawing at the shore. She had never seen the sea before, not like this, not properly, but it was embedded in her mind from the stories. Like a puddle, like a bowl of water, like a dark lake but bigger, bigger until there was no end to it and it could swallow the world and everything in it, *that* was the sea.

She wrenched her gaze from it to the barren shoreline, marked by a patchy line of driftwood and dead weed that the waves were creeping towards. Beyond, the land rose in jagged increments towards that unquiet sky she knew so well. *But why am I here? I was in the heart of the Plains, as far from the sea as I could be!* But in the mind of her people the sea meant the Plague People. The sea was to be feared because if you followed its roads long enough, you would find that ancient enemy. In the Godsland the sea was here because the land beyond this point had been lost.

The sea exhaled a chill that cut her to the bone, but that was not the breath she heard beside her. Galethea's voice gasped, 'What *is* this place?'

The Pale Shadow woman was with her. Her form was spectral and shifting; Maniye could see right through her to the blasted rocks beyond, to the hungry depths of the sea. She was there, though, or something of her was. The fact surprised her as much as it did Maniye.

'This is the Godsland,' Maniye told her.

'But how can I be here?' Galethea whispered.

'You knew this was Hesprec's plan.'

'But *how*?' the apparition demanded. 'Do I have a soul now? How else am I here?'

Maniye shook her head. 'You hollow people don't understand. There are souls and there are minds. If it were only my souls here, they would not remember me. My souls move from body to body, life to life. That part of *me* that knows the name Maniye Many Tracks, she is my mind. You can have a mind without a soul – look at Empty Skin. Look at you. Your mind is here but it has no soul to anchor it. A strong wind could blow you away.' She almost reached out to pass a hand through the ghostly figure, but the thought of what that might feel like stopped her.

'I don't want to blow away.' Even Galethea's voice sounded as though it came from far off. 'What can I do here?'

'You can stay close to me and hope my souls shield you,' Maniye told her.

'But where is Hesprec? I want Hesprec here. She knows what to do,' Galethea said petulantly.

'Can you not feel her at our backs?' Maniye asked. 'Can you not feel all of them, the priests, the dancers? Hesprec holds open the door that lets you stand here, that lets me stand here with you. So: it is up to us.'

'To do what? If this is the Godsland where are your gods?' Galethea asked her. 'What is any of this for, if they haven't come?'

'We are here to find the gods, yes.' And Maniye bit back the rest of it, because Hesprec had trusted the knowledge only to her, not to Galethea, not to Mother, not to any of the Wise.

'Then where are they?' The wind blowing off the sea caught Galethea's words and ripped them away from her, barely heard.

Maniye put the waves at her back, looking inland. There were mountains there, heights to scale. 'Come with me,' she ordered. A dozen paces up the slope she reached the first rocks and looked back. Galethea was still on the strand, the water touching her insubstantial heels.

'What is it?' Maniye asked her.

'I can't . . .' said the Pale Shadow woman's pale shadow. 'I'm hurt.'

'Your body is hurt, but that hurt does not come here, I know,' Maniye told her, but if what she had here was the woman's mind, it was a wispy, feeble thing without a soul behind it.

The only solution to the problem did not sit well with Maniye or any of her souls, but she knew the creature could ride a horse like a real human. Perhaps it would not be so bad.

She could not command, she could only ask, deep inside her. *I need you. I know you would rather be fighting. This is no fit task for a great soul such as yours but I need you.*

No words, but she felt the shifting of thoughts like ancient bones gone over to stone. It was acquiescence, and a heartbeat later the Champion's breath was on her neck and she stood in its shadow.

She climbed onto that broad back and held a hand out for Galethea, bracing herself. What touched her hand was not like a hand-clasp itself, but the memory of one, the after-impression once the hand is gone. Nonetheless she pulled and drew the spectre up behind her, feeling arms about her midriff no more substantial than thistledown.

'I'm scared,' Galethea whispered in her ear. 'I shouldn't be in this place. It's hungry. I could vanish into it and nobody would ever know.'

'All the world is hungry, and your kind are hungriest of all.

373

You've no right to complain.' Her incessant whining was setting Maniye's teeth on edge.

'They're not my kind,' Galethea sighed. 'Not any more.' She sounded fainter than before, and when Maniye craned back, there was almost nothing of her left. She had to shout the pale woman's name three times before the gossamer lines of her face sprang back like taut threads and she was present again.

'Remember why you are here,' Maniye snapped at her. 'You want souls for your people? Then you must work with us. You must help us defeat your cousins.'

'It's hard,' Galethea said. 'I'm hurt.'

'Just hold to me. Keep yourself real for me. You are the only one of your people ever to come here, Pale Shadow. This is the land all souls pass through, and here you are, laying eyes upon it. Let it be a lucky omen for your people and stay with me.'

Then she had bent down to touch her forehead to the hairy scalp of the Champion, communicating her desires, and the next moment the great beast lunged forwards and scaled the rocks without a pause, raking its way up with four sets of claws, and then running across the dry ground it discovered, heading against the slope all the time, seeking the highest ground. Ahead the mountains looked like broken teeth, shrouded in dust or cloud and circled by the angry gyrations of the stars.

The land around them was barren, but not featureless. The gods had been here. What they left behind was ruin. Maniye saw villages gone to fire or simply standing empty like skulls – the shadows of those places the Plague People had overtaken, perhaps the last monuments to where some small tribe and its god had made a final stand. There were bones, too, human interspersed with those of beasts large and small. In some places they formed a brittle carpet that the Champion picked its way over, the little ribs of rats and meerkats splintering beneath its pads. Elsewhere there were greater relics that dominated the scenery, the arching fingers, the boulder-sized skulls marking the fall of some ancient beast of deep time, or perhaps a god. Maniye didn't know any more. She didn't know what was real, what was her own mind dressing this dying place, what was built from Hesprec's patient words.

She had a dreadful sense of time flowing through her fingers like fine sand, the lives of Hesprec and the others before the advance of the Plague warriors that the war host could only delay? Or was it this place: was it the gods dying? She called out to them inside herself, for Tiger who dwelled in smoke and shadow, for Wolf who was fire and winter both. Was there a faint answer, her reluctant patrons howling back to her across the valleys? She could not say, but there was snow, then – and never in her life had she been so glad of it. Cold was her friend, a thing of her world sent by the Wolf to test his people. Her mood communicated itself to the Champion and it lunged ahead, loping swiftly across a ground patched with the first drifting scraps of white. Galethea's arms tightened – or perhaps became more real – and Maniye glanced back to see exhilaration on her waning face. The fierce coursing of the Champion beneath her, Maniye's own determination, *something* had crossed back into the world to haul her mind here, insubstantial as she still was, and commit her to this journey, to its reality.

And then the Champion was slowing. At first Maniye thought it was because the land ahead was broken, creased into canyons and ridges as though the mountains had twisted all the land around them on the way up.

It was not the land that had stopped the Champion, though. They were not alone. The starlight glinted silver in the eyes of something waiting for them in the darkness.

The Rat . . . Could Serpent not hold on to the creature just a little longer? Or was Serpent dying too, and the Rat the world's one true inheritor?

Or not the only one . . . and these bones are cracked and split, not gnawed by many teeth. 'Come forth,' Maniye demanded, truly not knowing what was ahead, knowing only that she must go forwards – and up, always up.

It stepped delicately out of its lair, claws rattling the bones of its feasting, a high-shouldered monster to put the Champion to shame, its back bristling with a ridge of hair and its massive jaws exhaling a carrion stench. Its flanks were dappled and spotted, and it snickered at them, a little sound of cruelty and mirth.

'Who is it still lives and breathes, here at the end of the world?' asked Hyena, in the voice of a woman who has seen much to laugh about.

'I am come to find the gods,' Maniye told her, because in the stories, questing heroes misled the gods as often as they told the truth.

'Your search is over,' Hyena pointed out. 'I am here.' She padded closer and the Champion growled a little and backed up. 'What other god did you expect to find at the world's sunset, little wolfling, little tiger cub? Do you not know my people's legends?'

'I do, for I have travelled with one of your daughters,' Maniye told those yellowed fangs. 'And yet I think they draw the wrong lesson from them.'

'Oho.' Hyena ducked her head until one eye was staring at Maniye's whole face, gleaming with captured starlight. 'Tell me how my people are wrong about me, little wolf-cat.'

'They say you will be the last god left on a pile of bones because you are last to the fight,' Maniye said, fists tight in the Champion's mane to keep her hands from shaking. 'But I think you are here because you are last to flee. All the other gods cannot abide the coming of the Plague People, but you know your children will stay until the last, for the dead meat and the easy kills. You are not the last to fight, you are the last to *run away*.'

Hyena was still for a long while, or at least half a dozen cavernous death-reeking breaths from those jaws seemed very long indeed. Then she cackled a little. 'You would make me a grand protector, would you?'

Maniye shrugged. Her words were spent now. She could only wait to see if they had been enough.

'There is some of me in you,' Hyena mused, eyeing the Champion. 'Is it enough to make you pass as mine? For this land is mine, now. Mine until they return to contest it, if they ever will.' She sniffed at Maniye, pushing at her gently. 'There is a little in your scent, perhaps. Perhaps it is my daughter, who ran with you once.'

'Shyri,' Maniye acknowledged.

'Such a wayward child,' the Hyena acknowledged. 'But mine, still, even when she does foolish things like make friends with foreigners and shed her blood for them. For the blood she has shed, for the hurts she has endured, for the joy you have given her, I let you pass, little wolf-cat. I give you safe passage to the end of the world. Much happiness may you have of it.'

* * *

Loud Thunder had his axe in hand, but nobody to use it on. He was the Warbringer, but the war was happening elsewhere. At his back were the fires of the camp, and the great song of the ritual rose up towards the sky – where he hoped some divine ears heard it. At his front . . .

The fight against the Plague had been going on all morning. The enemy had been far away across the Plains, too distant to see. Bands of the swifter warriors had set out at dawn, hoping to find the advancing warriors and slow them, even just a little. Thunder knew this, and he knew who had succeeded and who had failed. Somehow, word always got to him. Often it was by youths who had only just got their souls – Heron and Vulture boys and girls on clumsy wings. At other times it was the Horse, galloping up to him to deliver a breathless message before they Stepped and were off once more.

Thunder had tried to keep a picture in his head, of all the things they told him, but he kept losing his grip on them. Then Esumit the Serpent priestess had come to him, as though conjured by his mounting confusion. She had begun to draw maps in the dirt, showing who was where and how far the Plague Warriors had got, and she had made little pictures on the flat sheets the southerners made, which recorded the words each of the scouts delivered. It was as though she had become Loud Thunder's memory, freeing his mind up just when it would have choked to a halt with chewing over information.

The picture that she drew was not encouraging, though. War-bands were constantly striking against the Plague warriors, Stepped and unstepped, with spear, with arrow, with trickery. Each won a few heartbeats, no more. Many paid a savage price for it, for the Plague Men were killing anything that moved, now. They must understand that the whole world was against them, and if it had been Loud Thunder at their head he would have turned around and gone home. Their reaction was instead to kill it all, burn it all, tramp everything of this world beneath their feet, blot out the sky with their wings until there was nothing left that was not theirs. Thunder trembled at the thought of their belief in themselves, which eclipsed any other view of the world.

Asman was out there fighting. Perhaps the next messenger would swoop down and proclaim his death. Plenty of others Thunder could name were hazarding their lives against the darts and the Terror. And he was here, hearing of their courage and sending them to die.

Two Heads Talking was at his elbow then, shading his eyes. 'I see . . . smoke? Dust?' the Coyote said, voice shaking just a little.

Thunder squinted at the horizon. There was a storm there, the air dark as though a shadow came that the sun could not dispel.

'Not dust,' he said. 'Them.' He watched the cloud lift and then drop, thinking of starlings or schooling fish. The abrupt under-standing came to him that a whole double-handful of the Plague Men had just dropped down behind a force of the Boar and would be killing them, piercing them with their darts until the Terror took hold.

'The Tiger must act now,' he said. It was not meant as an

order but a young Heron girl within earshot took it as one and was off, spreading ungainly new-found wings and Stepping into the sky.

'More coming,' Two Heads Talking said through tight lips, and Loud Thunder saw that all their skirmishing, all their warbands, would not keep this enemy from their hearth.

It was only a handful that overflew the camp, and one of the Bat rose up shrieking to drive them away, but they would have *seen*. For a moment Thunder wondered what they could actually have understood of the sight. After all, surely the whole problem with the Plague People was that they were inimical to true humans. They did things differently and could not see any other way than theirs. But then Thunder thought of the Plague priest with his white eyes. *That* one would know. Galethea's testimony had been clear about that. In all the enemy, that one man knew exactly what the true people were and wanted them wiped from the world to cover sins remembered only in the stories of the true people, which told that the Plague had exterminated those who were unlike them in that place they once all called home.

'Who do we have left?' Again just an internal question that found his tongue, but Esumit was there with her little pictures telling him precisely who was still with the camp. They had River Lord spears, they had Plains Dog archers and the warband of the Many Mouths. Thunder sent word that they must stay close and be ready to fight.

In the moments when his attention had been off them, the army of the Plague People seemed to have covered half the ground towards the camp. Now there was a fierce skirmish as Boar and Tiger and some of the Estuary warbands tried to slow them again, striking from the long grass, loosing poison arrows, charging tusk-first into the metal rain of the darts. Thunder shuddered, stabbed by guilt because he knew that should be *his* charge.

Then Esumit gasped once and fell, writhing about a bloody tear across her breasts, and a score of Plague Men were dropping down on him. *They saw the camp,* Thunder's mind nagged at him even as he Stepped. *They saw the ritual, but they saw the war leader too.*

Two Heads Talking had fled instantly, because that was the wisdom of Coyote. Thunder had no such luxury, shackled as he was to leading. Pale, hollow men in armour were dropping down all around him, sending death at anything they could see, and he was the biggest target there. One came to earth incautiously close and Thunder bellowed and swatted the creature, feeling iron armour crumple, and bones and flesh too. They were all around him, and for a moment the Terror had him by the scruff of the neck, shaking him like a dog with a rat. As if summoned by the image, though, his real dogs were there – Yoff, Yaff and Husker came bounding to his aid, surely Two Heads had set them loose. Two leapt on a Plague Man at Thunder's back and bore him down, snarling and bloody-muzzled. Husker, the youngest and the biggest, just slammed into a Plague Man the way he would when greeting Loud Thunder – save that Thunder was twice the size of these empty monsters and the victim was thrown from his feet, weapon spinning from his hands.

Thunder lumbered forwards, feeling darts pluck at his hide, feeling one shot rip a shallow line of pain down his flank. He kept moving, the Terror always at his heels, scattering the enemy like handfuls of corn, getting his claws and teeth into any too slow to avoid him. He had heartbeats to live. He was too slow; they were too deadly.

Then there were Plains Dogs all around him, some band of them summoned by the fighting. They came Stepped and snarling and abruptly the Plague People had more to worry about than just a slow bear and a few dogs. The trap that was closing on Loud Thunder splintered into fierce close fighting, the Plague Men with their iron swords against the bronze axes and spears of the Plainsfolk. Thunder thought the enemy would fly then, but for hollow things they lacked no courage, standing their ground and killing with blade's edge, or with handfuls of fire conjured from nowhere.

Thunder took a blade in the side, the force of the thrust slowing to nothing in the bear's dense muscles. Brief flames washed over him and charred his pelt, and still the enemy skipped out of his reach, each one trying to get clear enough to kill him with their darts. Then half a dozen of the Plains Dogs were cut down in a single breath, and the Terror stooped on them all, ready to rip their minds from them.

Something else stooped too, putting them all within its great shadow. Yellow Claw blackened the sky as he fell on them, the vast-winged Eagle Champion of the Eyrie. His talons seized one Plague Man about the neck and almost wrenched his head away, and then he had Stepped to get his leaf-bladed knives into another, leaping up on the creature's shoulders to plunge them down past the edge of its armour. There were more Eyriemen wheeling overhead, and perhaps it was having their sky threatened that finally broke the Plague Warriors' nerve because they were fleeing, leaping up into the air and zig-zagging away, followed by arrows and stones.

Yellow Claw regarded Loud Thunder with distaste, as though he had not realized whose life he might save by indulging his bloodlust. Then he nodded once, full of a reminder of matters between them yet unresolved, and knocked half the Plains Dogs off their feet when his wings clapped down to lift him away.

Husker was dead and Yoff was scorched and limping, whimpering with pain beyond any healer's ability to help. Where Esumit had lain was a patch of bloody ground, but neither human nor snake body was to be seen. Plenty of the Plains Dogs had met their end too, and just to keep breath in Thunder's lump of a body. He felt sick of it all.

Two Heads Talking crept back then, a little shamefaced for all that he had been rallying help the while. He was about to say something, some comforting platitude perhaps, when the words died on his lips. Thunder followed his gaze – not only was the enemy on the ground dangerously close now, but they had brought their great weapon, of course they had. Sailing impossibly above them, already in advance of the skirmishing below, came the Plague Ship towards the camp.

'Well, we knew it would be like this,' Two Heads said, and his voice shook more than a little now.

All around them, every warrior who could Step to a pair of wings was taking to the air. The Hawk warriors of Yellow Claw were already aloft and now they were joined by Heron and Vulture and the lean, alien people of the Bat Society, and birds of a half-dozen small tribes from the Plains and the River. They had held back for this very moment. They were pitifully few compared to those who could fight on the ground, but to them fell the worst of all tasks. The floating monster of the enemy was coming, high beyond arrow-reach, growing to itself as it prepared to unleash scouring fire on all beneath it. All those who could take the fight skywards must do so.

And in the wake of that great tumult of wings came one more pair. After all the warriors had set off towards the approaching Plague Ship, one more hawk flurried overhead. Thunder felt his heart clench at the sight, knowing who it must be.

* * *

Maniye had travelled the Godsland more than once. Always before, the journey had been a symbolic thing, not distance but an attempt to find something within herself. This time was different. She was looking for something outside herself, outside the domain of the gods. And so she was lost.

She had taken the paths uphill, trusting that if she could just get high enough then the finer details of Hesprec's plan – such as how it could possibly be accomplished – would fall into place. The land around her seemed to crumple and twist even as she walked it. Canyon after canyon, ravine after ravine, sometimes riding the Champion's broad back, sometimes walking beside it as it negotiated narrow trails, hard rock to one side, empty air to the other. And always Galethea behind her like her own ghost arrived premature, her whispery voice coming and going with complaints of 'It hurts,' and demands to know what they were searching for.

'Where are your gods?' the Pale Shadow breathed, and Maniye wondered what she could possibly expect. Did she think she could stand before the Wolf or the Lion and beg souls for her people? The merest breath of a god would scatter her like spider-threads across a meadow.

Maniye had no answers for her, anyway. She could feel the gods' closeness – Hesprec's great ritual had done that much, at least – but they were out of sight, beyond the next rock, over the next ridge. And they would not go where Maniye needed to go. She would be on her own there.

Then at last the accusation came from behind her. 'You're lost, aren't you? You don't know.'

She turned, seeing Galethea glimmer and wane, ghostly arms clutched around herself as though trying to hold her filmy substance in. The pale woman's eyes were bitter. 'I'm dying. You've dragged me here where I don't belong, and for nothing. You don't know where to go. And my people . . .' Maniye braced herself for another recital of the Pale Shadow's fate, but then something changed in Galethea's face and she folded, sitting down and hunching over phantom pain. 'All our people,' she corrected herself, and the blame went from her face. 'Your people will die if we fail. We all will. So you have a plan. You must do. Even a desperate one. Please, tell me what can I do. I've come this far. I've come here, where I should never have been. Help me, Many Tracks.'

Maniye knelt by her, wondering if this access of humanity meant that there was some germ of soul in the creature after all. *Or was it always there, and I never noticed until now?* 'I need you to help me,' she said. 'Look above us, Pale Shadow.'

The angry darting stars of the Godsland – so far away no

matter how high they climbed – seemed to dance deep within Galethea's eyes.

'We need to reach them,' Maniye explained. 'There is a path to them, up this mountain,' *or so I hope, because all's lost if this cannot be done.* 'Do you not feel some call from them? Do you not hear a voice?' Hesprec had coached her, in this, but she found she had no belief in it. Hesprec could not have seen what an echo of a thing Galethea would be in the Godsland. Surely there was nothing to her that could hear any call at all.

And yet a spectral breeze seemed to stir the filaments of the pale woman's body, running through her just once and leaving the world changed behind it.

'I . . . hear,' she murmured. Her eyes brimmed with insubstantial tears. 'I hear something beautiful.'

Maniye had no doubt that if that call came to her own ears it would give her nightmares forever, but she and the Pale Shadow were very different things.

'Can you lead the way?' she asked, as gently as she could.

Galethea stood, briefly more real, filled with purpose. 'There is a sound, like the singing of wind-harps, like threads drawn taut.' She stared up at the mobile sky and Maniye wondered what she saw there – what she saw of the Godsland at all. Was it different, in her mind? Reversed so that the terrible was wonderful, the beautiful become a thing of fear?

'Take us to them,' she urged Galethea, and for a moment she thought it would be as easy as that. The Pale Shadow woman would play her part, lead her unerringly to where she needed to go, and then, and then . . . Except even Hesprec had not planned for 'and then' beyond the getting there. Maniye would have to take what spoor she found and hunt it any way she could.

But Galethea was not leading her anywhere. She wanted to, plainly. She started and stopped, started and stopped, sometimes thwarted by the rising rock walls, the brittle sharpness of jagged stones, other times by nothing Maniye could see. Now the song was in her, she was desperate to play her part, but the Godsland

384

hated her. It was not touched by her magic, or perhaps that magic had stayed behind with her body. She heard the song but had no way to reach it, and in frustration she tugged at her fair hair and tried to tear her face with her nails, save that neither had enough substance.

'It is there,' she spat out. 'Right there, but I can't . . .' She reached out fingers for the stars and they seemed to gather about her, as anxious for the union as she, but that was a mere trick of perspective. They were the stars, and as far away as ever.

At last the Pale Shadow woman collapsed back down, holding herself again, giving out a cracked, desperate cry. She was weeping, a real woman's bitter anger at being so powerless.

Kneeling beside Galethea, all the sounds in the world seemed to hush for a moment before resuming. She felt at her back the presence of Hesprec, and through her all the many rituals and stories, dances and songs of the priests and their votaries. Yet, for a moment, they had lessened and become further away.

'Galethea, please,' she said. 'We have no time.' She could picture the storm of the Plague army tearing through the camp, their Terror blotting out the sun like wings.

'I have no time,' the pale woman whispered. Her faint hands found Maniye's. 'I wanted so much. I came so far. It hurts, Many Tracks. It hurts more and more.'

There was a high giggle, from so close that Maniye could have reached out and touched the newcomer, grabbed her and shaken her. Instead she just stared. A girl had come to them, scarcely more than a child. She had sat to make a circle of the three of them and was staring at Galethea. Her lean Coyote features were unbearably familiar to Maniye, a face she had thought never to see again.

'How are you here?' she demanded. 'Sathewe?'

The Coyote girl looked at her blankly. 'What name is that? Is it mine?'

'Sathewe, I am Many Tracks. You know me.'

But she didn't, or not enough. A brief shadow passed behind

her eyes but then was gone, and back came the infuriating grin that had always meant trouble.

For a moment Maniye wondered if all whom the Terror had taken came to the Godsland like this, in their human shapes. But Sathewe-the-coyote lived still – was even now nestled in Maniye's lap back in the human world. And they had met no others, none of the multitudes the Plague People had destroyed by their very presence.

But Sathewe and fear had always had a strange relationship. The girl had always been strange, no common sense at all and up for whatever mad scheme Feeds on Dreams could conceive. When the trap closed on her tail yet again she would yelp, but she would never remember the pain. The Terror had taken her, but perhaps something of the girl she had been had clung on here in the Godsland, following her coyote body as it trotted at Maniye's heels.

'What's wrong with her?' Sathewe asked, passing a hand through Galethea's substance without hesitation.

'Many things,' Maniye said flatly. 'But she hears a song I cannot, and she needs to reach it.' In the back of her mind were all the stories people told – the ones the Wolf priests disapproved of, where Coyote's cunning and not Wolf's strength was lauded. Coyote was an uncertain ally, but often the only one in desperate times. Coyote was the great clever coward who went where no other god would dare.

She stared into the face of her lost friend and wondered whether she dealt with human or god.

'She cannot,' the Coyote girl said, with another laugh. 'I see the chains that bind her to her kin and the land beyond the seas. She makes her glamour from them, so she can paint her face and pretend to be real, but pretending is not being. You can never *be* if all you are is pretend.'

Galaethea gave a groan of frustration. 'This is meaningless,' she choked. 'What use are you?'

'At least I'm real,' Sathewe told her, stalking a little closer. 'At least I can look into the waters and see eyes reflected back at me, and not just hollow hunger.'

'I see eyes!' Galethea protested desperately.

'You see the eyes your craft paints onto your lids,' Sathewe sneered. 'How can you find your way with those?'

'And you can do better?' the Pale Shadow woman spat.

'I know *all* the ways of this mountain,' Sathewe boasted. 'I wager I could find your song. Just tell me if it's louder or quieter, each way you go?' She jumped to her feet, instantly impatient to be gone. 'We'll play a game. We'll call it *Can You Tear Off Your False Face?*'

'A game,' Galethea echoed faintly, but she forced herself to stand.

33

Even before she drew close, the Plague Ship seemed to grow until it could swallow the whole sky.

Kailovela had only heard stories of the monster before, and mostly from those who had seen it just as a shape in the sky. It hung impossible in the air without wings, they had said – and here it was, doing just that. It made a sound like a creature in pain, they had said, and they were right; not loud but penetrating, a constant complaint that seemed to reverberate from horizon to horizon. It vomited fire, they had said. That would come soon. It was drifting serenely towards the great camp, those many hundreds all desperately trying to call back the gods. She thought of how close-pressed they were, all those chanting, dancing bodies; all those sun-dry tents, the sick and injured, the children. *Her child*.

Ahead of her the great warband of the air seemed like a scatter of pebbles flung at the Plague Ship, Yellow Claw at their head. Already there were Plague warriors rising from below, and more issuing from the ship itself like angry bees. And perhaps the Eyriemen moved more swiftly and fiercely in the air, but how would killing those warriors stop the ship itself? No earthly thing was keeping it in the air, no wings moved it forwards. How could any of them halt or slow or turn aside such an unnatural beast.

They spoke of it as a beast, everyone who had a story of When The Plague Ship Came. Its pained voice was that of a living thing, and it moved. What else could it be but some great monster the Plague People had bound to their service?

Save that the thought did not sit well with her. She backed her wings, tilting sideways in the air and staring with a hawk's keen eyes at the prodigy before her, even as the others were diving in to fight.

The Eyriemen had few friends in the Crown of the World. They raided everywhere, secure in the knowledge that walls could not keep them out and they could come and go where they pleased. And yet they were not as many as most of the other tribes and so their depredations were in isolated places, against lambs and kids out at pasture, against children sometimes, whatever their talons could bear away. Most of the other tribes feared and despised them in equal measure. Many called them cowards for trusting to their wings rather than standing their ground to fight. And they were arrogant and kept apart from others. The Hawk were prideful and the Owl sinister, their only alliances those of convenience against common enemies. But this was their moment, their battle. Leading a ragged mob of Heron, Vulture and Shrike they surged towards the Plague Ship, armoured with the blood of Champions. Some broke off to fight the Plague warriors – some were already spinning away, pierced by their darts – while others soared against the immensity of the Plague Ship, keening their rage at it.

Kailovela saw seven or eight of the Bat Society, perhaps all that were left, throwing the shadow of their vaned wings across the bloated bulk of the ship, their screeching sending the Plague warriors into fits, knocking them from the sky or scattering them across the deck of the Plague Ship, twitching and foaming at the mouth.

The deck. The Plague Ship had a deck, where the Plague warriors stood to shoot. Kailovela had little knowledge of boats of any kind but a picture was coming to her of how the floating vessel was formed. There was an upper part, vast and bound like a full waterskin, and the Plague warriors were chasing their bird enemies across the face of it, determined to keep them from it. There was a lower part, smaller but inhabited by Plague warriors. They issued out onto its flat top from within, or they dropped out from openings in its belly. At its rear were great insubstantial discs that groaned and bellowed with the ship's voice – she saw one of the Heron dart through one and simply explode into a shower of blood and feathers.

The understanding came to her awkwardly, like an angular shape not meant to fit inside a human head. The ship was just a *ship*, not a monster. The front of that lower part was transparent, in front and below. She could see Plague Men within it, looking down. They would see the camp below them soon enough. They would know to drop their fire.

She had been keeping her distance, circling back over the camp as the ship groaned closer through the air. She could feel the Terror just touching her wingtips. How many of those wings out there now just belonged to birds, panicked and uncomprehending. How many were still warriors fighting the Plague?

Am I enough like them to be immune?

She watched a flight of Hawk warriors stoop down at the deck, Stepping just long enough to loose arrows before speeding off again, the air about them spattered with darts. She looked for Yellow Claw – surely his great wingspan would make him no more than a convenient target for their weapons? And yet he lived and fought still, now attacking the great bulbous bulk above with his knives, now swooping down to tear at a Plague Man with his talons.

I could watch like this until the fires come.

With that thought, she cast herself forwards, waiting for the dart that would kill her, for the Terror that would snuff out her mind. Or perhaps she was so filled with ordinary fear that the supernatural grasp of the Plague could find no purchase in her.

She beat her way through air filled with rage and death. On every side the warriors of the true people were dying, and killing too. The sky wheeled with Herons and Owls. Crooked men and women of the Vulture, black-clad with coppery heads shaved to the scalp, dropped down across the deck through a withering sleet of darts, but those that sprang up on human feet laid about them with knives and axes before taking wing again. Plague warriors in banded mail lifted their rods and sighted along them like arrows, trying to keep up with the manic, flapping throng around them.

Within the Plague Ship, their cousins calmly stared down through their clear walls and floor, untroubled by the chaos without. She understand that all the fight the Plague Men were giving was purely to allow those others within the ship a calm span in which to burn away the mass of their enemy.

Did they see the children below? Did they see the old women dancing, the antlers and the masks and the fires of devotion? Did they understand that those below were not warriors at all? She thought they lacked a hawk's eyes, to see so much. She thought they would not stay their hand even if they knew. The world was a mirror to them in which they only recognized their own face.

She flurried briefly against that clear wall, but it was hard and cold, like infinitely smooth stone. She slid off it without even scratching it with her claws. Briefly she thought of getting in through the holes the Plague warriors were issuing from, but that would be a death that would achieve nothing.

She would need help. Up here, riding the air above the end of the world, there was only one she could ask.

* * *

At first it seemed that Galethea heard that soundless song clearly. 'Yes!' she said, and 'Yes!', chasing one way and another as her image shimmered and waned and Sathewe watched her, head cocked to one side like a coyote. Maniye watched with mounting impatience as she seemed constantly on the brink of a revelation that never came. At her back she heard the great combined voice of the people falter, the unified rhythm of their invocation splintering as fear prowled between their fires. She felt *Hesprec's* fear.

391

Hesprec, who had been calm even old and alone in the Jaws of the Wolf. Maniye felt as though a great shadow was falling over everything she knew.

She felt a fierce knot of frustration with this pale woman, who had come so far, sent by all the gods and spirits for this one task. Or would the gods send a soulless thing like this? Perhaps Galethea was just the Plague with pleasing words on its lips that still ruined everything it touched.

Maniye could stand it no more. All that fear was standing at her shoulder, filling her with thoughts of death and burning and desolation afterwards. 'Come on!' she shouted at the spectre of Galethea. 'Why can't you find a way?'

The pale woman's look to her was desperate, teeth bared like the animal she would never be. 'I don't . . . the echoes . . .' Her voice seemed to come from miles away, borne on a dying breeze.

Maniye stormed over to her, wanting to rip that phantom substance apart, wanting to rage at the woman for her fallibility. 'Where is the power you're supposed to have?' she demanded. 'We don't have *time* for you to fail! Where is that Pale Shadow power even the Serpent fears?'

Galethea quailed before her. 'Just a ghost,' she whispered. 'A ghost in their minds that we steered them with, and it is not here. I cannot bring it here, before your gods.'

'Just a false face,' Sathewe chimed in, giggling like she always did when things went wrong. 'False eyes see nothing. No wonder you're so lost! Plague Woman has nothing but a big hole in her where her soul should be!'

'I'm not a Plague Woman!' Galethea hissed at her. Maniye had the sense of her trying to find her magic.

'Hollow body, empty mind. I can see through you, Plague Woman!' Sathewe leapt up and Maniye barely saw the blur as a stone whizzed past Galethea's ear. 'No place in the world, no right to be here, no soul for you, Plague Woman!'

'I'm not!' The Pale Shadow creature sounded like a child on the point of tears. 'We're not them! We don't want to be them!

392

We want to be *you*!' There was nothing good in her face, all those elegant lines crumpled by endless hunger and bitterness until she looked a hundred years old. 'We've lived a thousand years trying to be you! It's not *fair*!'

Maniye felt that horror at her back – all those who could not fight, but who had stayed to pray and dance, to beg and cajole and command their gods. 'We have no time,' she said, voice flat in her own ears, but Sathewe just capered and threw more stones.

'Hollow body, hollow mind! No soul for you, Plague Woman! Take your false face away, nothing-woman!' she cried again.

Galethea screeched, a sound that must have come from the vacant depths of her. Maniye saw her summon all her magic, all the craft of the Plague People. Her face shifted and writhed, layering beauty on beauty, glamour on glamour, paint over paint until what was left was hideous, features melted into one another, too many eyes staring out in taut rage. And Sathewe laughed and laughed.

'Hollow woman paints her face! On and on she paints her face!' the Coyote girl sang out. 'So much paint and so much weight! Drags her face down to the ground! Painted eyes see only dust!'

And this time Galethea went for her, a terrible blur of motion that had little of the woman to it. All the masks and guises seemed to spin and unravel in her wake, like fog, abandoned in her fury, her need to grind Sathewe between her hands, between her jaws. She went up the sheer rock like a spider, faster than Maniye would have believed possible, and her rage drew more substance to her so that she became a swarming grey shape, enough that she might have cast a shadow had there been a sun. The effect was horrible, profoundly inhuman, but Sathewe just squealed with mirth, always one step ahead.

Maniye realized with a start she was being left behind. The Champion had borne her this far but it was no climber. Instead an ember-furred shadow pressed against her side, and she crooked her fingers into the tiger's pelt and slung herself onto its back.

She had some catching up to do, by then, but her tiger soul could claw up the rock as well as any Pale Shadow. She saw them ahead of her: the little dancing speck that was Sathewe; the half-ghost that was Galethea, whose voice came to her on the wind, cursing the Coyote child. Higher and higher the Coyote skipped, riding a stream of taunting insults. Galethea skittered after her, more and more *here*, riding the tide of ritual to draw more of herself into the Godsland. Perhaps she had not believed, before, but she was so angry now that there was no room left for anything else. Her entire being was fixed on the mocking figure of the Coyote. Her nebulous shape seemed to boil with flailing legs and unblinking eyes.

Maniye lost them amidst the crags and the chasms – the whole landscape around her seemed broken, segmented, as though some great upheaval had riven it into splinters never to be made whole. The tiger leapt and scrabbled to keep up, and sometimes there was a wolf running alongside, a keener nose hunting out the scent of the two she followed.

She crested a rise, and there was Galethea standing very still. For a moment Maniye thought she had caught her quarry, that the Coyote's wrung body must be at her feet, but no, there was Sathewe sitting on a rock out of arm's reach, grinning from ear to ear.

'Galethea!' Maniye snapped. The woman didn't turn round, and so she slipped from the tiger's back and circled until she could see her face.

Her features were still recognizable, still that almost-human that passed for normal amongst the hollow people. Beneath translucent skin she seemed to seethe, and for a moment Maniye was afraid the Rat was here, somehow, come to spoil this last chance for victory. But whatever swarmed and ran within those hollow eyes was alien to this place as the Rat could never be.

'I remember you,' Sathewe said suddenly, but not to Maniye,

to Galethea herself. 'You hurt my hand. I was there with Takes Iron and Feeds on Dreams.' Then her eyes shifted. 'Many Tracks,' she said, sounding surprised at her own knowledge.

Galethea took in a harsh breath. 'I hear it.'

Maniye stared at her.

'I understand it now. It is like the story you tell, three brothers. But there is an older story you do not tell. Two sisters; we will call them two sisters. Two different paths, but they were sisters once, even so, who shared a world with vast powers. One sister looked on some of these powers and walked towards them, so she became like them and took their shapes and had children who took more shapes until the land was filled with a thousand tribes each casting a different shadow. And the other sister saw other powers, and took from them their aspects and their strengths, and instead of giving herself to them, she took these things into herself and made them her magics. And the sisters were not friends, and the world was not even, and so they parted in blood and have been parted ever since. Yet paths can be retraced.' The rage was leaching out of her, her grey substance shredding away like cobwebs. 'Oh, Many Tracks, I understand, I understand it all, but there is no time.'

'I know there is no time, so tell me,' Maniye snapped. 'Lead me!'

'There is nowhere to lead you. There is nowhere left to go,' Galethea breathed, and Maniye realized that the last rise she had crested was all the world there was. They were at the mountain's top, a barren plateau of cracked rock with only the stars beyond. They were close, those stars; close and fierce and hungry to touch the earth.

Galethea sagged to her knees as her borrowed strength ebbed away. 'I understand,' she said. 'I know why Hesprec sent me here. I know we are not betrayed.' She was weeping, silvery flecks like falling stars down her ghostly face. 'But it's too late. I have no time.' She was stripped of everything that had made her beautiful, all that guise and poise and craft, but what was left beneath was beautiful in another way, even as it faded.

'*We* have no time,' Maniye insisted, but the spectre shook her head.

'I,' she corrected, just a whisper. 'Too much, too much, and so little left of me. The grey priest's knife has cut my threads, Many Tracks.' She reached out to grip Maniye's arm and there was no sensation to the touch at all.

Galethea turned her face to the devouring stars and smiled. 'But they're beautiful, after all,' she said, and then, '*They have seen me!*' but with that, she was gone.

★ ★ ★

Kailovela found him sweeping across the deck of the Plague Ship. It seemed impossible that the broad sweep of his wings would fit through the tangle of beams and ropes that connected the two halves of the vessel, and yet there was none more born to the air than Yellow Claw. He turned and danced, pulling his wings in to thread needles through impossible gaps then throwing them wide to knock the Plague warriors from their feet or send them spinning away from him. Whenever they might have caught him, the shivering screams of the Bat were there to tear through Plague People minds like saws. Yellow Claw soared and tore through the fight like a man touched by the gods.

She flurried past him, keening, trying to hook his notice. The shadow of his wingspan dwarfed her. The first time he might have missed her. The second, she saw his round orange eye light on her and know her, and he turned away, tilting on a wingtip to seek a fight on the far side of the ship.

Desperately she flapped after him, screeching, catching him only because he stopped to fight. The air about them buzzed with darts – the Plague Men were defending their ship fiercely, and the deck was littered with the bedraggled, feathered mounds that were dead hawks and herons. Yellow Claw ignored them just as he ignored her, turning his back on her, then casting her to the deck with a single clap of his wings.

She Stepped. She had no option. She needed his help, for all it choked her.

'We need to break inside!' she cried at him, her words torn away by the wind. 'We need to get at the men inside. Yellow Claw, this fight means *nothing*!' She was waiting for the dart to find her human body and trap her ghost, to send her whirling from the ship until the ground caught her. 'Yellow Claw, curse you! We need to break through their walls!'

For a moment he was human, plunging his knives into a hollow body, eyes meeting hers. His face twisted with loathing – she saw the humiliation of losing her, the pain of the beating Loud Thunder had given him, all the frustrations that should only fall to lesser men, not the Champion of the Eyrie.

'Everyone will burn!' she screamed at him.

He spat. He was Yellow Claw. Let them burn.

She felt her fingers crook like claws, about to rush at him and tear at his face for sheer frustration. All her life men like this had held her prisoner, and even now she was at their mercy, even at this last fight.

A hand took her shoulder and hauled her back from her lunge without effort. She whirled, striking out, and her wrist was caught by another. She faced the fear-mask of the Owl Society: Grey Herald.

'Show me!' he shouted at her.

She Stepped, trusting him to follow, fighting the wind to reach the front of the Plague Ship again. She swooped a ring about those clear walls, hoping he would understand. In the end, when he just soared back and forth in bewilderment, she Stepped again and crouched at the front of the ship like a figurehead, poised over those industrious Plague People, beating her fists against their walls with all her strength like a child.

In that moment she felt the Terror rise up all around them. Enough darts had found a home in human bodies that the battle for the air had turned. Her body thrummed to the shriek of the Bats as they tried to turn the fear back on the enemy, but the whole sky sang to the Terror. In moments their warriors would be losing their minds, one by one, no more than birds fleeing the shadow of the Plague Ship.

Plague warriors were abruptly flurrying about them. *They know what we intend!* She clung to herself within the hawk's skull, seeing Grey Herald's owl driven away from her. Fire from their hands singed her feathers and she crashed down onto human knees right above the transparent wall, clutching at the smooth, cold stuff for purchase. A warrior dropped down right beside her and tried to bring his killing rod to bear, close enough that the barrel of it struck her above the eye. She raked at his face with her nails, but all she achieved was to drive him far enough that he could shoot her with ease.

Something stooped on him, wings enough to swallow the world. For a mad moment she thought Yellow Claw had changed his heart and put aside his pride, but these wings were no bird's, great vanes of leather that swept Plague Men aside with the force of them. Not one of the Bat, though, if any of them even still lived. For a moment the monster crouched here, some reptile thing with a long beak and a crested head, and then it was Asman of the River, hacking down with his stone-toothed sword to behead the Plague warrior, then Stepping again to his fighting shape. He ran precariously along the spine of the boat, leaping on another Plague Man and carving him up with brutal efficiency. In moments there were a half-dozen Heron fighting alongside him, the Estuary fliers drawn from across the sky to their Champion, and he led them up and down the deck in a storm of arrows and spears. He seemed frantic, and she knew he must have soldiers hard pressed on the ground, all his kin under the shadow of the Plague, but a call had gone out for anyone who could take to the air and he had answered.

Grey Herald Stepped down beside her, baring his teeth as he reversed the hatchet he carried and brought the back of it down hard against the clear wall. On the second blow she saw a maze of white lines spread from the point of impact. Then the third came down, with a great cry from the Owl priest, and the wall shattered into razor-edged shards of nothing.

What struck her was the surprise of the Plague Men inside. Their attention had been on their deadly work and, to them, the fight without was irrelevant, a problem for someone else. Now some of them cowered and others shouted, that staccato chittering of theirs that passed for language. Some drew out weapons.

Grey Herald landed in their midst, his skin drawn by a thousand little blades from the shattered wall. He yelled and put his axe into the skull of the nearest Plague Man, straight between the hollow creature's aghast eyes. Then darts were lancing him, two, three, a half-dozen, knocking him back against all their clutter and the broken shards.

Kailovela dropped down, Stepping halfway to spread her wings and slow herself, then landing on human feet: a young woman in a doe-hide robe and cloak of feathers, unarmed, her dark hair cut short so it might never shackle her again.

The utterly unexpected sight held them for half a heartbeat and she reached for the magic in her, that force that had blighted her life. For a moment, now of all times, it was absent, and she was just a savage woman before these implacable conquerors. She waited for the Terror to take her, or their darts. Despair emptied her and the magic rushed in like a tide to fill the void.

She touched their minds. She had never felt herself do this before, though she had been drawing people close to take and own and control her since she was grown. The Terror had stripped away all her masks. She had a moment of utter self-knowledge, as she watched how this thing within her went about its work.

They had minds, these Plague Men, even without souls. They had desires and longings. She felt the echo of them within herself, even as she tried to grip at them. They were warriors, these men. They had come to fight an enemy. Their purpose was like an arrow in flight – no small matter to pluck it from the air. And all the while the Plague Ship cruised on, towards the vast camp below that was to be fed to the fire.

She tried to make the magic control them and do her will, but it did not work like that, or how easy would her life have been? It spoke to them at a level below their waking minds, deep in the stomach and the liver where emotions were born. Their emotions were all of war and bravado, though – just as Yellow Claw's must be. She had no hold on them to turn them around.

And they had not killed her yet, nor had the Terror struck her, but the moment her magic parted ways with their minds, she would be dead. *What do they have that I can touch? They cannot just be blood and metal all through!* She dredged up all she knew about the enemy, and how pitiful that 'all' was! *If only I had Empty Skin here with me!*

The thought dropped into the centre of her like a rock thrown into a lake, and the ripples were understanding of the one thing the Plague People did know, the one thing of her world that they valued enough to repurpose.

Kailovela could feel the great strength of the ritual below her, all those minds, the fear, the desperation, the longing, the love. How many families crouched under the shadow of the Plague Ship? How many children? The Plague People had children, for they took in every stray of the real people to raise as their own. So Kailovela let her magic tell them of children. She filled their minds with thoughts of a mother's love, a father's pride, the burden of carrying a child to term, the pain of birth, the desperation of having such a dependent thing in so harsh a world. The gates were open then. She found herself channelling thoughts of lost homes left far behind, of loved ones gone too soon or too hard to their graves. A wellspring of feeling was funnelling through her and she could not stop it, but simply sped it on its way to the Plague Men before her, the world-burners in their invulnerable ship. And for everything she cast at them, she felt the echo: the homes they had left, the comrades and the kin they had lost to war or time, the sons they had watched grow, the daughters they hoped for. All the pathos in the world coursed back and forth through her, and she knew that these hollow men who had destroyed so much of her world without pity or regret were just men.

She channelled all of this, wielding this great emotional bludgeon, and she felt the wooden ground shift beneath her as the Plague Ship veered away. She felt them fighting her, fighting their own hands, holding back from unleashing their fire. Triumph leapt in her, but it was born of bitterness, because all these noble sentiments that she wielded against them were not hers. She reported them second-hand. She had no home she longed for. She had a child she felt only duty towards. She twisted their minds with all the finer feelings she had never known, and now she must face the truth: the lack was not in her kinship to the Plague, it was in herself.

She shuddered, and the belly of the Plague Ship unseamed itself, the fire vomiting forth towards the ground. But they were away, their shadow only clipping the camp below. She had saved everyone a burning death for now, and the end of the world was pushed one arm's length further away.

She opened her eyes and saw the grey man, the Plague priest, standing in the midst of the wreckage. He was staring at Grey Herald's painted face – that fear-mask that was just a mockery of his own grey face and white eyes. For a moment even he was on the point of some great revelation.

Then he reached out with his own magic and severed hers, ripping her from the minds of his kin without effort. He barked sharp sounds that must be an order to sail their ship over the camp again. The Plague warriors around him were blinking, dazed, but more and more their angry eyes were turning on Kailovela. No warrior wishes to be forced to face the pain of the world he contributes to.

The Plague priest drove forwards with his knife, as he had against Galethea, but he had forgotten he was dealing with one of the enemy, not just a shadow of his own kind. His thrust met empty air as she battered at the ceiling in a storm of feathers. She had never hunted as a hawk, but her talons were right here and so was he, and she dropped on him, latching on to that grey skin, tearing at those white eyes with her beak, feeling the bitterness of his gall on her tongue.

The fire from their hands seared her, the darts lanced her – at least one tore through the priest as well. As she dropped to the tilted floor, as her blood stained her robe and her own clutching hands and the Hawk stooped for her soul, she felt the lumbering slowness of the Plague Ship as it began to turn once more.

34

Hesprec held on to Maniye's hand as though she was drowning, gripping pale marks into the woman's skin, eyes closed, shoulders hunched against what was happening around her.

The vanguard of the Plague People had been holding back, she knew now. They had been waiting for the fire of their ship to do its work, so they could swoop in and finish off whoever remained. But then the ponderous shadow had begun to slip away in the air, nosing off to the south as though it had lost interest in what was going on.

Any relief was short lived. Moments after the sky had shrugged off that huge shadow, dozens of smaller ones were taking its place. The Plague warriors were scudding over the camp like bad weather, loosing bolts of fire and their swift darts.

Hesprec's plan had been *absurdly* ambitious. Even the long-lived Serpent had no memories of anything like it. So many priests, so many rituals; the tales, the chants, the drums and horns. Her fellows would have told her it could never work, and she would have believed them and not tried. That was why she had not shared her plans with anyone except Maniye.

But it had worked. The devotion of a score of different peoples had settled into the same rhythm and she had felt the gods turn back in their headlong flight. They had heard the music of their people and come to their aid one last time. Hesprec had felt them standing about the edge of the camp like tall shadows, now human, now in their true forms. Old Crocodile had been there, Wolf and Tiger, Bear and Boar and Plains Dog, Badger and Lion. All enemies, all of them, and yet they had been shoulder to shoulder passing their strength to their people, who passed it on to Hesprec. In that moment she had felt herself the fulcrum of the universe.

And she had passed it to Maniye and to the Pale Shadow creature, Galethea, because there was more to her plan than just this. But for a moment she had held the world in her hands and understood more about the nature of mankind and the gods than any priest before her.

Then the Plague had come, and her world had started to unravel. Hearth by hearth, song by song her great ritual was fraying. The Plague warriors dropped down, and the Terror stooped with them. She could feel the rituals ending like candles being snuffed, as the priests and votaries turned to flee or to fight. There were still warriors in the camp – more and more as Thunder's fighters had been forced back by the Plague advance – but they could not match the enemy for speed.

Her ears were full of the fighting and the dying and her eyes were shut tight as she held Maniye's hand and prayed that Serpent show the Champion her path. Galethea had already collapsed, lying on her side, curled about her reopened wound with the last few breaths of her life struggling to escape her.

Then the fighting was all around her and she could not close her eyes to it. The light let in a glimpse of banded armour, black and yellow, the flash of a blade. Hesprec held herself rigid, knowing that to even flinch would be to break her connection to Maniye and bring it all crashing down.

One of Maniye's warband was between her and the enemy in the next moment, a big dark wolf frothing at the mouth as it knocked the Plague warrior down. *Moon Eye.* The angry spirit was on him for sure, but it liked the taste of hollow flesh better than that of his friends, or else he had finally learned to leash it. It tore at the Plague Man's throat and then lifted its blood-stringed jaws to howl. Wolf bodies leapt and darted all around,

Stepping into iron-armoured men and women who threw spears or loosed arrows at the circling enemy above. And dying. She saw old Spear Catcher struck down, blood bright at his chest and lips and a look of bafflement on his face. She saw three darts find Moon Eye, and then the Terror come for him – it drove out the man he had been but the angry spirit in him fed on it and kept on fighting, sinking its teeth into any piece of Plague flesh it could reach.

Someone's knee impacted with the back of her head and she lurched forwards, clinging to Maniye. Someone was standing over them. Like a thorn in the corner of her eye, her peripheral vision caught the jut of a Plague warrior rod. She wanted to look at him. She wanted to meet his eyes and stare into the emptiness behind them, but she stared only at Maniye's face and filled her mind with the intricate workings of the ritual.

A thin bronze blade flashed, drawing a line across the Plague Man's throat, so that blood gouted hot across Hesprec's face. Moments later, Shyri dropped down beside her, eyes wild, gripping Maniye's shoulder as though trying to wrest some of the Champion's strength from her.

'Everyone's fighting,' she said, and to Hesprec's ears that sounded an utterly unnecessary thing to say. Then Shyri's meaning came to her: fighting was not *losing*. Fighting was not *dying*, even if it was not *winning*. All the warriors of the world were here to battle the Plague People, and by courage and numbers they were holding them at arm's length.

But not forever. The Terror was already claiming its victims, and that was the true plague of the Plague People, the thing that leapt from mind to mind like contagion. *We cannot last. Something must change.*

'Bring priests. Good ones.' She got the words out through gritted teeth.

'I reckon they're a bit busy right now,' Shyri pointed out.

'Do. It.'

The Laughing Girl hissed through her teeth but Stepped and

was off, and for a moment the space immediately about Hesprec was clear of living enemies.

The great ritual was disintegrating, eroded by the very closeness of the Plague People. *Because they don't understand it. Because they don't believe in it.* She felt the stifling presence of the enemy rolling over the camp, obliterating not just lives and minds but *ways. It will be as if we never were. All our histories back to the first of us, unwritten. And perhaps some Plague priest will find our bones and our tools a thousand years from now and make up stories about who we were.*

I'm sorry, she thought, the sentiment meant for all the people there had ever been, whom she was failing.

Then she had more company, even as the sky grew darker with the flurry of Plague warriors. Two Heads Talking and Quiet When Loud dropped down beside her, the latter still holding Kailovela's son, who was squalling fit to burst, little hands clawing at the shadows that flitted over him.

'I need—' Hesprec got out, but they knew, somehow. Coyote always was good at stealing the secrets of the other gods.

Others were coming now – those whose dance was done, whose song was cut short by the attack. Gnarl Hide of the Boar, Icefoot of the Wolf, Oreto of the Lion, Aritchaka of the Tiger with her knives steeped in blood. Crocodile, Snake Eater, and then a shadow that seemed as great as the Plague Ship itself as Mother came and sat beside them.

'I need—' Hesprec said again, feeling her heart strained to bursting by the effort of holding it all together.

Two Heads was explaining for her, though, not the long Coyote story but quick, concise words.

Hesprec closed her eyes.

* * *

Maniye stood before the stars. At her feet, Sathewe crouched, a thin Coyote girl or just a thin coyote, now one, now the other, but with head cocked waiting for her to do something.

406

When she had first come to the Godsland, the sky had frightened her with its busy malevolence. *Trying to find a way in*, she had thought, of all those swarming stars.

She had known nothing, back then. Now she stood on a mountaintop in the land of the gods, and the stars drew close to her, all of them. East and west, north and south, the sky was a featureless void of nothing, and all the stars were here, directly above her, clustered in a dreadful anticipation.

They're almost here.

When she inhaled, the air smelled of smoke and blood and fear. The wind in her ears sounded like screaming and battle. Her senses were constantly tugged at by the human world and what was going on there.

And yet she stood there, uselessly, unable to take the last step.

I wish Hesprec was here.

Even as the thought came, a small hand landed on her arm. Not Sathewe's: Hesprec. Maniye stared at her, not sure whether this was truly her friend or some phantom of the Godsland.

But then the Serpent girl smiled, that expression that called back to the old, old man Maniye had once known. 'You're here then. I knew you'd find the way.' She waved away Maniye's protests and glanced at Sathewe, who watched her warily.

'Three seems right,' she decided. 'Perhaps we're the three sisters, to follow after the three brothers.' She squinted at the sky and grimaced. 'There they are then.'

'I can't reach them,' Maniye told her. She had wanted a weapon, a cutting edge, when all those hungry stars had come to seethe overhead. In her hand was a hatchet of Wolf-iron and she knew it was Broken Axe's, somehow, an echo of his strength. Broken Axe, who had never given up. And now she was dishonouring his memory because she couldn't find a way.

Sathewe howled mournfully at the sky, and Maniye felt the sound through her whole being. The long, lonely call of wolf or dog or coyote that can travel the length and breadth of the Crown of the World. *I am here*, it said. *Even at the end of the world, I am here.* Maniye felt tears prick at the corners of her eyes.

Hesprec was still staring upwards. 'The gods of the Plague People,' she said, 'sealed in the cold sky for all of history. Surely we knew this, long ago, but we didn't want to, and so we forgot.'

'They're about to get their revenge for us sealing them there,' Maniye said bitterly.

'We didn't,' Hesprec said simply.

Maniye stared at her. 'But I thought—'

'Forgive an old Serpent. It's hard not to hold on to one last secret. Or else I'm wrong, and it doesn't matter.' Hesprec shrugged. 'Come on, then.'

'Come on what?'

Sathewe howled again, long and mournful, but defiant too. *I am here. No matter what you have done, I am still here.* Maniye felt the sentiment well up in her, the need of the wolf to answer that lonely call. *So am I. So am I.* With the thought, her soul was at her heels, sniffing the air and then lifting its head to cry out its own existence against the furious sky. *Here we are, all of us. So long as our voices sound, you have not destroyed us.*

The tiger was on her other side, ears flat and fangs bared. Maniye let her hand brush the fur of its scalp. At her back she felt the far greater shadow of the Champion.

'Maniye Many Tracks,' Hesprec said. 'Maniye Many Souls. Who'd have thought the angry girl I met in the pits of the Winter Runners would save the world? I think I did very well, saving you back then.'

'I remember it was me saving you,' Maniye told her. An idea was waking in her mind, the sort of thing that only worked in the old tales, but then they were in the Godsland, where things worked more like stories. 'And the world's not saved yet.'

'But the stories will say you saved it,' Hesprec pointed out. 'Or else there will be no stories, so what does it matter?'

Maniye nodded briefly, and then retreated a dozen paces back down the mountainside with her souls shadowing her. She looked up at that sky and gripped her hatchet. Then they began to run, all of them, the Champion in the lead.

* * *

Asman had done what he could up above, and as soon as the ship began to veer off course he had vaulted the rail and half flown, half dropped back to where the spear-line of the River Lords still held. What had undone the flying vessel he had no clue, but understanding this battle was something he had abandoned long before. He jumped back into the fray just as a wedge of Plague Men tried to push his soldiers aside – heavily armoured creatures that could not fly but still had the killing rods to strike men dead on sight. He gave the Champion its head then, leaping into their midst and trying his strength and claws against their mail, as his soldiers rattled arrows at them and drove at them with spear and sword. The Plague armour was proof against anything they had, but it had gaps. Asman tore at their eyes, their armpits, their groins. He kicked with the Champion's murderous strength at their knees and elbows, every part of them that could be made to break. Then they were trying to fall back, and the fighting spears of the River still held the strip of ground they had chosen to die on, but the skies overhead were overcast with a mass of the enemy who were not even stopping to kill them.

Asman broke away from his soldiers, seeing the camp behind him was suddenly alive with Plague warriors, their shadows mottling everything like patches of rot. Mobs of them were descending on anything that caught their eye, and Tecumet's tent was larger and grander than all the others. Of course it was, for she was the Kasra of the Sun River Nation, but that also made her the greatest target for the Plague.

The Champion gave him its speed and he leapt and raced between the hearths of the camp, springing over or dodging past the panicking crowds who were fleeing in every direction. Left and right he could see groups of priests and their followers still

409

propitiating their gods, calling on them for aid, but the ritual was being silenced one fire at a time as the Plague attack spread.

The Kasra's tent was on fire, he saw. There was a great skirmish about it as the Plague Men attacked, but others just glided over and spat flames from their hands, setting light to the silks and fine cloths. Tecumet would be in there. Asman pictured her in her formal robes and mask, because she would want to meet the end as befitted the ruler of the greatest nation in the world.

He let out a piercing screech to clear the way and picked up speed, aware that most of his followers were left far behind. A Plague warrior dropped down in his way, rod levelled to kill, and Asman leapt, hooking a sickle-claw in the collar of the creature's armour and ripping the metal off him, shearing straps and laying open the hollow man's chest to the ribs. He vaulted the folding body, using it as purchase for a final burst of speed that got him to the tent.

It was fiercely ablaze, and all around were Tecumet's servants and guard, trying to save what they could. He got to the flap and stared in, Stepping so that he could shield human eyes against the glare. For a moment all he saw was fire running along every outline of the tent's interior, but then he caught sight of her: the gold of her mask running bright with the flames, the great heavy robe alight as she stood straight-backed to meet her fate.

Asman bellowed and launched himself at the opening, but a heavy body crashed into his and slammed him to the floor. He glared up into Venat's scowl. 'Get off me!'

'No,' the old pirate spat.

Asman bucked under him, then got an elbow into the Dragon's jaw and writhed out from under him. Venat had his ankle even as he tried to charge for the flames, and furiously Asman Stepped and kicked him off. Even then, the pirate got between him and the fire. Asman screeched at him, threatening with tooth and claw.

'You're an *idiot*! You always were!' Venat shouted at him. 'Just as well your mate can do the thinking for you!'

410

Then the Dragon punched him. A hard fist cracked across the Champion's snout, more an affront than a serious attack, but it was enough to shock Asman back onto his human feet, and then Venat had hold of him, an arm about his neck to keep him that way, wrestling him away from the fire to where, to where . . .

To where Tecumet sat, masked by her servants, soot-stained and coughing, but the woman herself, not the Kasra's mask nor robes of state, but just Tecumet.

He threw his arms about her the moment Venat let him go, crying out, 'I thought you'd burned!'

She stood carefully into his embrace, staring upwards. 'We all may still,' she whispered.

He followed the line of her gaze. The Plague Ship was turning ponderously in the sky, coming around on a course that would bring it over the camp once more. Asman's mind flashed with images of the fall of Tsokawan, of Tecuman's fiery death. The Champion screamed within him, but here was another enemy it couldn't fight.

★ ★ ★

Thunder had gone to fight in the end. When the main force of the enemy were in plain sight of the camp, he could stand the burden of leadership no longer. And besides, the Plague People were making free with the sky. His ability to delay or corral them had been exhausted.

At the back of his mind was the tally of all those who he had sent to their deaths, that other burden of leadership. Better to lose himself in the fighting than consider it. The guilt would be waiting patiently for him if he lived.

He gathered up everyone who was close enough to hear his voice and led them out at a swift pace. Many were of his war host, the strength of the Crown of the World, though they had plenty of loose spears from other bands – Plainsfolk and Rivermen and Stone People. A great pack of the Plague warriors was within sight, waiting beyond the camp, and perhaps Thunder

411

and his forces could scatter them or occupy them. Perhaps a little more blood would give Hesprec the chance to act out the Serpent's plan.

It was the Serpent he found in his mind, as the greatest of the sons of the Bear charged out. Ever since Hesprec had guested with him over winter, he had been impressed with a god who actually helped people, rather than testing them like the Wolf or ignoring them like his own tribe's god. *If any power will bring us through this, it is the Serpent*, he knew, *so Serpent be with me now.*

He wanted to ask, *Make me your fist*, except what use would a snake have for fists? Could he be the god's fangs, its coils? The theology of it tied him up and made him forget his fear until he and his fellows were almost on the enemy. He had thought that their darts would start carving up his forces long before that, but the Plague People had something else on their mind. Their attention was on the sky, and he risked tilting his head for a glance upwards, seeing the great ship veering away. The expressions on the Plague Men's faces showed this was not part of their plan.

And then they realized they were under attack, and some started shooting, striking Thunder's people dead. A dart clipped his ear and another parted the hairs of his back, but most of the enemy were not standing to fight. They could have withered Thunder's charge away to nothing had they but tried, but they were taking wing, almost all of them, great handfuls of them just leaping up into the air. For a moment he thought they had broken – that some divine hand had sowed fear into them and the battle was won. Then he understood. With their flying ship foiled, they were going about the killing themselves. Scores of Plague warriors passed overhead, contemptuously dodging aside from the arrows and spears of Thunder's people. A kernel of them were left over, unable or unwilling to take to the sky, and these Thunder's force descended on, braving the darts and proof against the Terror for as long as they were winning. The luckless Plague Men were trampled down in short order, but Thunder played no part in it. His eyes followed the great swarm of the enemy as it surged above the camp.

'Back!' he cried. 'Back! Protect the priests!'

He thought he must be too late, that he would get back to only corpses, but the cloud of Plague warriors suddenly lost its menacing spiral and became just a scatter of individuals, crashing into each other or winging off wide beyond the camp's confines. Thunder didn't let his surprise slow him – and many of his people were already ahead, on fleeter paws. Had the Serpent reached up from the earth to attack the enemy? No – not the Serpent, but his brother.

There were few of the Bat Society left by then – many had died in clashes with the Plague before this final fight, and others were still bedevilling the Plague Ship. Some had held back, though, some half-dozen vast-winged shadows that plunged through the seething bustle of Plague Men with their soundless screams. Thunder had never understood their power, but perhaps of all the people, they had been the true killer of Plague Men back in the Land-That-Was. Something within the Plague warriors remembered them and their shrieking.

But half a dozen Bats against a hundred Plague warriors, how long could that fight sit in the balance? Everywhere the vanes of their wings darkened the sky, the Plague Men fled helplessly, some dropping their weapons, some falling to earth to be killed by the warriors below. And yet when they had passed, the enemy recovered their minds and their discipline, and Thunder knew that the darts would be sleeting like foul weather, wherever the Bats turned. He saw them falter and fall, one by one, each death buying another few heartbeats of life for those below.

Then they were too few, two left, then one, and Plague warriors were dropping down towards Hesprec's hearth. Thunder was powering between the tents then, shouldering aside anything that got in his way. He could see warriors there – that was Shyri, surely, and there were Wolves. He saw Aritchaka of the Tiger break from her devotions and hurl a spear into the groin of a

413

Plague warrior, doubling him up over it. Then she was leaping like dark flames, springing higher than a man to get her claws into another and drag him to earth. Beside her, Icefoot of the Moon Eaters died without a sound, a dart lancing the back of his skull.

Thunder burst out into the open, skidding to a halt before he ended up in a fire, then Stepping, coming to his feet with a stone in each hand. Yaff, his last surviving dog, caught up with him, barking at the sky as though to bring it down with sheer noise.

Hesprec still sat with Maniye, the motionless centre of the end of the world. The Plague Men seemed to know their true enemy, but a vast shadow stood over them and held them at bay.

Thunder knew Mother as harsh human words, but as a bear she had just been a great slow weight of ill temper, too sluggish to rouse herself to rage. Now he saw her angry, as he might have seen the Bear angry at the dawn of time, before he settled in to sleep. She seemed even larger than he was, rearing twelve feet and driving the Plague Men back by sheer bellowing fury. Her claws and teeth were bloody, and her pelt was already dotted with blood where their darts had found their mark, but the sight of her held them. She was like a goddess, like a mountain.

Thunder reached her side just as the next flurry of darts pierced her – her breast, her leg, her shoulder, and one drove a long ugly gouge across the top of her head. He felt the shudder through her, but she did not flinch, just made herself as big as she could and threatened them, all of them, the very notion of them.

He saw her skin ripple as a dart tore into her throat, another into her open mouth. He was human to touch her side, to let her know he had come to take her place when even her strength had gone. He could not catch her body when she fell. Instead, he Stepped and stood where she had stood, roaring defiance as his war host sent arrow after arrow at the swirling host above.

Something snagged painfully in the fur of his ankle and he thought they had shot him there, but it was a hand, a small hand, hauling on his pelt as though the owner was trying to haul herself up from out of the earth.

He risked a glance down.

Maniye's eyes were open. They were shining.

★ ★ ★

The Champion stood tall before her, braced with all four feet on the ground. Maniye leapt on its back, feeling all its solid strength that it lent to her in the physical world: her great soul that had saved her and made her what she was.

She became a tiger, and the tiger was also her soul, a gift from Joalpey her mother that had come close to getting her killed when she was just a child dwelling amongst the Winter Runners. The tiger planted its feet upon the Champion's back and readied itself.

And she became a wolf, which was her third soul, a gift from Kalameshli Takes Iron who had tormented her and whom she had hated and then accepted, but who had never hated her, for all that he had been a cruel man and done evil things. The wolf leapt to the tiger's back and the striped beast hissed at the indignity, but let it stand there.

And she became a girl, her first shape, the Maniye before the Many Tracks. She climbed the wolf's back and stood there with her hatchet in her hand, and the sky was right above her. The luminous gods of the Plague People were clustered just on the far side, within arm's reach.

They're about to get their revenge for us sealing them there, she had said, and Hesprec had replied, *We didn't*. No act of the true people kept these clustering, swarming things at arm's length, and so perhaps it was not the ruin of the true people that they had drawn close to accomplish.

Below, far below, Hesprec and Sathewe watched and held their breath.

She had her axe, and an axe was a weapon if you needed it to be, but only by extension. An axe was a tool for cutting, first and foremost.

So she drew back her hand, fixing the burning gods with her stare, and cut open the sky.

415

35

Mind still singing with what she'd done, Maniye opened her eyes.

They were fighting all around her. She saw warriors of twenty tribes with bows and spears, and above them the great swirl of the Plague army, reaching out across the sky to catch them all and crush them into nothing.

They were praying, too. She was jostled by priests on all sides, Boar, Plains Dog, Turtle, Coyote. They pressed at her because they were surrounded by the warriors trying to keep them safe. And some were dead, anyway, because the Plague darts cared nothing for a flimsy human body standing in the way.

She wanted to tell them, *You can stop now; it's done*, but she couldn't form the words. What she had seen, what she had done, normal human speech was insufficient to describe it. That was why such deeds became stories: to shrink them to a size that they could fit in the mind.

Hesprec was beside her, still holding her hand, eyes open as well. Their gazes met, and even though people were dying all around them Maniye saw the triumph there. Then Hesprec's gaze slid sideways, and Maniye followed it and cried out, lurching away until she reached the end of the tether that was Hesprec's arm.

There was a *thing* nestled beside her, cupped within the ring of priests. It lay on its bristling back, legs curved over in death,

416

yellow fangs half folded. Bulbous eyes stared out at her like stones. It was one of the Plague People's beasts, surely it was, and yet how had it come . . .

Belated realization struck her. It was not one of their beasts, nor quite one of them. It had a name, that curled husk, and its – her – name was Galethea.

The understanding turned the horror of the thing on its head, because Galethea was dead, but she had not died in a human shape. If Plague People could spawn ghosts, it would not be trapped in dead flesh. She had died Stepped. Her soul – the soul she had only now gained – would move on.

Maniye looked up at the circling host of the Plague warriors and watched.

At first there were only outliers, breaking away, clashing with their fellows, spiralling off in odd directions, but it was as though a disease spread through the mass of the Plague People, leaping from one to the other. She heard their voices calling out in a great murmur of confusion above.

She missed the first and the first several after that, but at last she was watching one of them when it happened. One moment there was a man, ephemeral wings ablur. He had dropped his killing rod and seemed to be fighting with his armour, or perhaps his skin, his bones. Then he Stepped. Where a human shape had been, now there was a wasp of human size, wings flashing errat- ically as it sought to free itself of the cloth and metal cocoon it had inherited. A moment later it was clear, and Maniye watched the creature arc over and over, struggling with its own shape, with unfamiliar limbs and senses. For a moment it was a man again, naked because the Plague Men had never trained to bring along their possessions. He was not flying any more and dropped ten feet before Stepping to the insect once again. He had been screaming, face gripped by an appalling horror at his own shape and form. The wasp crashed down nearby, flattening a tent, curl- ing over and over as though trying to sting itself. Then Loud

417

Thunder ran over and brought his axe down where the creature's body was narrowest, slicing it into two twitching sections.

Above them, the same drama was being repeated over and over. The Plague Men Stepped, Stepped back, Stepped again as the hollow spaces within them were filled with souls at last. They had no control over their shapes, their limbs. They fought each other or swung wildly back and forth across the sky. They crashed to earth or fled for the horizon or soared towards the sun as though it was a candle.

The warriors below needed no instruction. Every bow was tracking a madly buzzing body and those who had none picked up stones or hurled spears. It was no battle. The insect shapes the Plague Men stepped to were terrifying things of mandibles and stingers and hooked feet, but they were unfamiliar cages. They had no chance to learn how to control them before the warriors below picked them off. Only those who broke and fled at once escaped.

Overhead, the great bulk of the Plague Ship was drifting away, pushed westwards by the wind. Its hull was crawling with insects. Some deserted it and others just dropped off and plummeted, to break open on the ground.

A hand landed hard on Maniye's shoulder, its counterpart on Hesprec's. Shyri pushed in between them, demanding, 'What have *you* done?'

Maniye grinned. She felt utterly exhausted, as though her body had done in truth all the things her mind and souls had endured in the Godland. 'We opened the way to their gods.'

'You did what?' Shyri asked. 'But . . . that's a bad thing. Surely that's the worst thing?'

'Their gods were waiting for them, sealed away. Back in their home, who knows? They had a chance for gods and souls, and chose their magic, their wings and fire and glamour, instead. But this is a land of gods. Perhaps *we* only found *our* gods when we came here. And now it is a land of their gods, whether they want them or not,' Hesprec said. 'And their gods bring them souls, just

418

as ours do. Now they are not Plague People. Now they are just people. We can fight people. Every tribe has been fighting other people since time began.'

'But what about the rest?' Shyri demanded. 'All those at the Plague camp? What about when they can actually Step. Doesn't that make them worse?'

'I do not feel the Terror in the air any more,' Hesprec said. 'Perhaps it's just because we're winning here, but . . . that *difference* is gone, the gap is bridged. We can fight them if we need to fight them. And if we do not . . .'

'There will be few who won't want to fight them, given all they've done,' Maniye pointed out.

Hesprec shrugged. 'I have collected a hundred visions of the future, but that future is the past. I cannot say what will happen now. Which is a relief, believe it or not.' She sighed, and Maniye saw that, however tired she herself was, Hesprec was twice so.

'Old woman,' she asked the Riverlands girl, 'what will you do now?'

Hesprec chuckled. 'Oh, you think this is it, the world to rights again? Live as long as I have, Many Tracks, and you'd know there's always another problem.'

Just then a cold nose pushed its way into Maniye's palm and she looked down, thinking it was one of Thunder's dogs, perhaps. But the animal there was far smaller than any beast Loud Thunder would take in, just a starveling little coyote, head cocked on one side.

Maniye felt the clutch of that old guilt come back to her. 'I thought . . . She was there with us, right there. I thought she would come back to us.'

'She will be reborn in time,' Hesprec said. 'And I'm not sure it was Sathewe alone who was with us. I have a feeling one of the gods crept on his belly to where he was not supposed to be, to see we did the right thing.' She glared across the circle of priests in mock-censure and Two Heads Talking met her gaze evenly.

★

Later, there was time for mourning.

Some wanted to press on eastwards immediately – to catch the fugitive Plague warriors and shed their blood, to purge their camps and burn their white walls. The desire for more vengeance came shackled to a weight of loss, though. There was no hearth without empty places at the fire, no tribe that had not given of itself to win the victory.

And they were tired, all of them: those who fought, those who prayed, those who had fled their homes, those who had marched so many miles from the lands they knew. Hearts cooled, and by nightfall a great wake had been arrived at by piecemeal consensus, each people to its own customs.

Maniye went to the Wolves first, whose smith-priests had great fires banked up. Those who had died on four feet were celebrated, their souls fleeing north already to be reborn as cubs in the wild. Those who died in human shape were laid out where the priests could perform the proper rites over them, to free them for another life and be sure their ghosts would not sour within the decaying flesh. Grim work, but it was *their* grim work, their ways, their world. Maniye watched, and then she looked across the camp to other fires, heavy with smoke, where the patterns of light and shadow could be read as a great ember-striped form present to honour those of the Tiger who had died in his cause.

And is the Godsland crowded now, with all the Plague gods? Maniye wondered. *Or is it just larger, somehow?* She remembered her first view of it, her understanding of the great landscape of divinity, the gods and their kin-neighbours, radiating outwards in increments of likeness. Surely the gods of Spider and Locust and Scarab had some distant part of that land – as far removed in distance as their forms were from Wolf and Tiger and Crocodile, and yet all the same land. She would have to ask Hesprec.

Loud Thunder carried the torch to put his Mother to the flame. Not the woman who had borne him, but his Mother nonetheless,

420

the Mother of all the Bear, the greatest of them. Her vision had brought the Crown of the World together, for all that Thunder had been her tool. Her indomitable will had brought them all this way. But more than that, she had been the Bear's very soul in the world. She had made them great. Now the tribe would splinter into pieces, because to the Bear, the natural unit was one bear. It would be long years, generations perhaps, before anyone might cast a shadow as long as Mother had.

One cause for relief, though. No war meant no Warbringer. Thunder could shrug off the hated responsibility and return to his cabin. He could find new dogs to keep him company and serve the needs of none but himself, as he had always wanted.

It was cold, that cabin, even in summer. It was lonely, even with the dogs. All this while, ever since Mother called for him, he had pined for its solitude. Now he feared the hollow echo of it.

He had not seen Kailovela. Even the Coyote had not tracked her down, nor any word of her. She had gone to fight the Plague Ship and not returned. In his mind he made a decision: that she had played her part and then spread wing and gone her own way. She had ever loathed being tethered – far more than Thunder himself, for he had lived a life of his own decisions. She had been little more than a slave.

And so he pictured her, in his mind, sailing high over distant lands, and perhaps she found some place she could call home, or perhaps she just kept on flying, far above it all. In his mind, she never needed to land, to eat, to sleep. He saw her like that, and he ignored the cruel looks Yellow Claw gave him, so full of barely hidden knowledge. He ignored the child Quiet When Loud held and fed, an adopted sibling for the babe the Coyote woman carried.

She is free, he decided, and made himself believe it.

'It's all started again,' Maniye observed to Hesprec. They were at their own fire, at the camp's edge and looking over it. She had

421

expected the Serpent girl to be going from hearth to hearth, visiting all the world just as she had done before, and so much easier now the world had all come to one place. Except the world did not live with itself happily, as Maniye knew.

Instead, Hesprec had her own fire, and out of the darkness would come this woman or that man, mostly the Wise rather than the Strong. Few stayed long, but Hesprec would turn her calculating smile to any guest who presented themselves, playing host until they made their excuses. Early on there had been Estuary priests and Stone Men, paying formal respects from lands where the Serpent was known and honoured – if not loved, perhaps. Everyone knew Hesprec Essen Skese was the mind that had broken the back of the Plague Men, and Maniye Many Tracks was her hand. Respect aplenty, therefore, but not camaraderie. People looked on the pair of them as though they were story-figures, good to talk about, slightly awkward to share a fire with.

Right now, they were hosting Two Heads Talking and Quiet When Loud, who at least did not stand on ceremony. Two Heads had come with a jar of mead and a string of fish still warm from the fire, and they lounged about like the vagabonds they were, eating and trading news just as though the world was still the same.

There had been a fight already between the Tiger and the Many Mouths Wolves, which was the meat of the Coyote's news. The very night after the day when they had beaten the Plague Men, and vengeful memories were already finding generations-old grudges fresher in the mind.

There was a cackle from beyond the firelight, and then Shyri's spotted coat seemed to form out of the shadows, eyes flashing back the flames. When she Stepped, she was still laughing.

'Look at your faces,' she said. 'So solemn! This shows the world is going back to how it was.'

Hesprec's own smile was wan. 'Some of us might look for a world with more talk and fewer knives.'

422

'Can't cut your meat with talk,' Shyri pointed out, and helped herself to the fish.

'Why yes, of course you are welcome to our fire, as our guest,' Hesprec said pointedly.

'Hyena takes,' Shyri got out, around a mouthful.

'But you are welcome, nonetheless. You saved us in many ways the stories won't bother to recall, but I do. And I have a long memory.'

'Hyena tells his own stories, too,' Shyri said. 'And you can bet I'll be in *those*.'

'Is that what you'll do, when this is over?' Maniye pressed her. 'Back to your people?'

Shyri wouldn't meet her eyes. 'Probably. Or wherever I will.' Movement made her glance up and she rolled her eyes. 'Here they are, then, the Big Men the stories *will* talk about.'

Maniye saw Thunder's bulk first, but then, coming into sight around him like boats about a river bend, there were Asman and Venat too. She looked for Tecumet, but probably the Kasra of the Sun River Nation was not free to simply gad about between fires.

Hesprec's nod summoned them in, the circle expanding until everyone had a place. Thunder had more mead, sharp with the strange spices the Stone Men used. By unspoken agreement they let the jug pass about a couple of times before anyone spoke.

'Some of the Owl and the Bat are back with news,' Asman said at last. 'The Plague Men have abandoned their closest forts. They are trying to head east, those that can. There are a lot of their beasts loose across the Plains between here and the coast, and most of those beasts are men, some of the time.'

'They will die if they cannot come to terms with what they are,' Hesprec said.

'You make that sound like a bad thing,' Venat pointed out. 'Let them all die, and bury their ghosts in the sea.'

Hesprec shrugged, and the Dragon rolled his eyes. 'Here we go, the mystic secrets of Serpent. Give me any reason why we shouldn't want every Plague throat cut.'

'Galethea,' Maniye put in, when Hesprec was reluctant to speak. 'She was just such a creature, and without her we could not have found our way to victory.'

'And her people have souls, like real people, now,' Hesprec added. 'And that is more work for someone, because the Sun River Nation must have embassies south, for the first time, and that will be a fraying rope to walk, I'm sure.'

'And there was another one,' Maniye put in, then wished she hadn't when they all stared at her. 'There were two Plague People – a man and a woman – when I was caught. They were . . . curious about me, about my soul. They wanted to watch me Step. I think they wanted to find out how it was done. They found something. I saw one of them dead, when we escaped – she was halfway to Stepping, part insect, part human.' She shuddered at the memory. 'But the other, the man, he did it. He was like those out there, terrified and out of control, but he knew me. He followed me. He must have thought I could help. And he died fighting the Rat. And he was one of them, but he found his own way to their gods. Without him we'd never have known it could even be done.'

'Just one and he's dead,' Venat grunted. 'Doesn't mean we can't kill the rest.'

'It means they're more than just enemies,' Hesprec said slowly. 'And the Serpent has always tried to turn enemies into friends.'

She looked round the fire, and Maniye saw that there would be a lot of convincing before even these, her friends, would concede the point. *And how do I feel about this?* She found that she trusted Hesprec and the Serpent, in the end.

Then conversation moved on, more news, bragging of exploits, remembrance of the fallen, and at last Asman asked Shyri the same question as Maniye.

'There will be a place for you at Atahlan, if you wish,' he added, 'with honours and riches.'

Shyri looked at him uncertainly. 'You'd have some Laughing Girl creeping about your palaces, would you?'

Asman shrugged. 'I can even leave some trinkets out for you to make off with, if you felt Hyena demanded it.'

For a moment Shyri was very angry indeed, and then not at all, the emotion passing from her without leaving tracks. 'Oh, Longmouth, I would not be your pet. Not even for your Dragon friend, though I love to watch him needle you.' She stumbled over her next words twice, as though fighting parts of her that thought differently. 'I have already been invited to go to the Crown of the World by my friend Many Tracks, though. I would be a poor guest to deny my host.'

Maniye held her face still so no sign of the lie might be seen on it. She had not even decided to go back north herself. Only on hearing Shyri's words did she realize she would have to, at least for a little while. So much of her had been left behind there.

Asman nodded, a little sadly. 'Of course, of course,' he said.

Thunder cleared his throat, a heavy rumble like his namesake. 'We must go east first, though. We must see the end of it, what- ever the end is.'

★ ★ ★

Maniye had expected a month of fighting over every camp and village in the Plains, all the way to the sea. Her mind was full of the implacable Plague People, their deadly weapons, their utter heedlessness of anything that was not of *them*. And some part of her whispered what a lot of others were saying out loud. Surely gifting a people with gods would make them stronger, not destroy them.

Perhaps, left to come to terms with their new selves, the Plague People would have become stronger. Maniye hoped that Galethea's Pale Shadow People were better placed to greet their god and take joy in the souls they had long sought. To them, souls had been a lack they had felt in their hollow centre. The Plague People had known no gods or souls at all in their far land, having driven all such irrelevances out of their world countless generations ago when they had purged their home of Maniye's ancestors.

Everywhere the war host of the true people went, they found an enemy in horrible disarray. Often, the Plague camps were just abandoned, white walls already seeming tattered and threadbare in their absence, and perhaps a handful of Plainsfolk children left behind, bewildered and hungry. Sometimes the war host saw them leave, a sudden panicky evacuation the moment the warriors came into sight. Those early sights were comical and grotesque in equal measure, the Plague People fighting their own souls, crippling themselves as they struggled to stay in human form.

The countryside was crawling with their beasts by then, some just animals let loose in the general exodus, others maybe those Plague People who had lost control entirely. Great wasps blundered through the air, spiders and beetles skittered in meaningless patterns through the grasslands. The war host hunted them down where they could, but Maniye feared that would be a job for generations to come. Perhaps a job never complete – some of the monsters would no doubt breed and establish themselves, and be a terror to the future.

'Or a tribe,' Hesprec murmured, when she voiced those thoughts. At Maniye's startled look, the Serpent girl raised her eyebrows. 'The gods are here, their gods, but not just for them. What if some child sought them out, those gods, and begged a soul? What if some exiled pack of Wolves came south and, instead of begging the Plains Dog for patronage, sought out Spider or Locust? We have opened a bottle and lost the stopper, you and I. The world is saved, but it will never quite be the same.'

Without a strong force to oppose them, the war host began to break up. Keeping so many fed in ravaged countryside was next to impossible anyway, and many of the Plainsfolk with them simply stopped when they found their old homes and hunting grounds. Old enemies amongst the tribes began to remember who they despised – there were fights between Boar and Lion, between Dragon and Estuary tribes, and of course between Tiger and Wolf. Warbands were constantly packing their tents and heading home, openly or stealthily as their nature took them.

At last, in greatly diminished numbers, the liberators came to Where the Fords Meet, and there they found the Plague People ready to resist them.

Alladai was at Maniye's side to see his people's home again, unrecognizable as it was. This had been the heart of the Plague Dream in the lands of the true people, and they had built a bizarre maze of their web walls and left nothing standing of the Horse huts and palisades. At its centre, they had begun new structures, building with stone like the Rivermen did, and Maniye felt a weird shift of perspective as she understood that all their strange architecture had been merely transition, as though some completely different civilization would have hatched from that cocoon had they let it.

The Plague People were still in the midst of abandoning the place, trains of them heading east across the high passes towards the coast. There were not so many that the war host, even reduced, could not have destroyed them in open battle. They were ready to fight, though. They had been given enough time to learn a little about their souls. Maniye saw Plague warriors with their killing rods, and great heavy Wasps thundering through the sky or hanging upside down on the white walls. She saw them shift, one to another. Some even took their armour and weapons with them when they Stepped.

There were hurried councils between the surviving leaders. Some were all for attack, but more remembered the killing power of the Plague People weapons. Hesprec spoke most. While before, her words would have been shrugged off in anger, the sobering thought of another battle with the Plague warriors opened all ears.

Hesprec spoke of being human. The Plague People had never been human before. Probably they did not like it, certainly it did not absolve them, but they had become something more than the monster of stories. The hunger of their hollowness had been extinguished. Who knew what they might be, now?

Maniye heard Venat remark to Shyri that the Serpent just wanted the Plague's secrets for itself, which made as much sense as anything. What carried Hesprec's argument was the weariness of everyone there. They had been marching and fighting for a very long time, and nobody wanted to die in the cause of a war already won.

The war host stayed its hand and just watched as the remaining Plague People abandoned Where the Fords Meet. A great warband left then, judging that they would not be needed. Alladai himself gathered the remainder of his people, those who had been away when the Plague descended on his home.

'We will start to rebuild as best we can,' he told Maniye. 'I know you must see the end of this, but come back to me, when you have driven them into the sea at last.' He grinned. 'When I first met you, Hesprec – old man Hesprec – said you were a prophesied child he was fetching for the south. Was that a lie, then?'

'It was.' She remembered her bitter disappointment because, for a moment, she had believed it herself.

'It became true,' Alladai told her, and kissed her, and then it was time for the remaining warriors to move on.

They trailed the Plague Men all the way to the coast, watching them grow more and more used to their souls. The high passes were hard going, but they saw Plague People become beetles to haul loads, become spiders to weave rope, or flying insects to carry burdens. Maniye expected that to make them more fearsome, but instead the enemy just became more familiar now they were forced to live as real people lived, to solve problems as true humans had always solved them, with their souls and Stepped shapes.

And then, the sea.

*

Thunder remembered the sea from his own war host's assault on the Plague People up on the Seal coast. Of all the true people, only a handful dared to live with the great yawning abyss that was the ocean. The Seal, the Dragon, the strange, taciturn Lizard-people of the Salt Islands. All the rest had turned their back on the great water, driven by a deep and atavistic fear of the enemy that had forced them over it the first time. Now that enemy had come after them; now that enemy was going away, by that same road.

There was a last bid by the Lion and some of the Wolf tribes to fall upon the remnants and destroy them, but Hesprec again took the contrary voice. This time she said, 'There is a land out across the sea with a thousand thousand Plague People in it, without souls, without gods. These we see here are but a war-band sent across a sea that we ourselves cannot cross. Would you rather these survivors fled back to their people to tell them of the horrors that await them, should they send more? Or would you rather they come with more weapons and flying ships, at some other time of their choosing, to find out what happened to their fellows?'

The argument went back and forth, and Thunder felt that neither option was a guarantee of future peace, but then Hesprec never said everything that was on her mind, after all. What clinched it was the little monster.

Thunder had almost forgotten Kailovela's pet. It – she – had been taken by the Plague People after the failed peace talk, and he had assumed her dead or imprisoned, or just seamlessly become one of the enemy once again. Now she was here, springing from the jostling mob trying to get aboard the boat. She came to Thunder, and he saw her looking for another face, her former captor, her friend.

She read enough in his expression to understand Kailovela was not with them, and the sorrow he saw in her own was infinitely human, infinitely understandable. That was enough for him to add his voice to Hesprec's and carry the day.

Loud Thunder remembered the Plague People's metal beast. It had terrorized the Seal coast, and then he and his war host had watched it flee their spears, taking with it as many of the enemy as had been able to escape his attack up north. Now it was here, again the last sanctuary for the fleeing Plague Men. Except this time the sun shone on the thing and he saw it for what it was. A boat, that was all. A huge boat like a whole village, impossibly afloat even though it was armoured in metal plates like a Stone Man; a boat driven by the howls of tormented monsters within it. A boat, nonetheless.

The last of the fleeing Plague Men were just filing aboard under the sharp eyes of his war host. They carried only things of their making, nothing of the true people, who had come within a spear's throw, gathered within sight of the sea to see them go.

Maniye's Crow friend, Feeds on Dreams, had been out over the waves, watching the Plague People experiment using boats and their own wings. Go far enough from shore and there was a point when their gods finally let go of them and they were hollow again. The revelation was plainly a thing of delight to most of the Plague People, for once the news came back they redoubled their efforts to quit the land. Their souls horrified them and they wanted only to be empty once more. Thunder wondered if it was a revulsion at their changed state, or whether having a soul forced them to face up to all the things they had done.

And yet there were a few who felt differently, it seemed. A dozen only, but they had approached the war host with empty hands, and some of them Stepped into their six- or eight-legged forms, and then knelt or crouched, and waited. Hesprec had gone to them, and taken Empty Skin, the Seal girl, who could at least manage a few words of their speech.

These few wanted to stay, that much was plain. Whatever their lives had been like as Plague People, they had felt the absence within them that was now filled. They did not want to

430

lose their souls and return to what they had been. Thunder came down to look at them, Maniye and Asman by his side. They seemed a cross-section of the Plague People, some warriors, some of the solid dark people Maniye recalled as trying to study her; one was slender and fair as Galethea had been. One was a woman with grey skin and white eyes, like their priest, and this one Thunder wanted to kill out of hand, save that Hesprec stopped him.

'The Serpent will take them,' she said. 'Who knows what they may become in time?'

'You speak for the Serpent, do you?' Maniye asked her, and Asman made a doubtful noise. Tecumet had returned to Atahlan by then, and he was plainly not at all sure his Kasra would appreciate Plague People as guests within the Sun River Nation.

'I will talk my kinsfolk round,' Hesprec said. 'I always do. If these are willing to embrace their souls and live as we live, then perhaps the future can be a thing of hope and not just fear. I have had enough of fearing what is to come.'

'You cannot even speak to them,' Shyri pointed out.

'I will send to the Pale Shadow to come interpret for their kin,' Hesprec decided. 'And if they will not come then the Plague People will just have to learn to speak to me.'

Then there was just one farewell for Thunder to make. He sat down for it, to bring himself more to her eye level. 'Empty Skin,' he said.

The girl stared at him mulishly. 'I won't go back. Not to the sea, not to the Seal.'

Thunder shrugged ponderously. 'We have so many children back, now, left behind when the Plague Men fled. Some are too young for a soul, but there are others like you, whose time came and went. There are ways, the priests know. A soul can be invited again, or changed. Ask the Plains Dogs, who were Wolves once. You don't have to be this way.'

Empty Skin scowled at him so furiously he thought she would bite. '*This way* is me, Cave Dweller. Do you think that *this*,' and

431

she jabbed two fingers towards herself, 'is just the Seal child still? *This*, that walked amongst the Plague Men, that tried to save the world.'

'And helped save it,' he agreed. 'But what, then? You complain about having no place, but now you can have a place, you don't want one.'

'Can have a place if I become a different person. What if I want no gods, no souls. What if I want one of *their* souls.'

Thunder shuddered. There had always been something terrible about Empty Skin, and now he wondered if it was this moment, shining back through the months to when he first met her.

'They have wonders, you know,' the hollow girl said to him. 'I lived with them, a bit. I saw them. Their weapons are the least of it. What might their lands be like, where all such wonders are made? Don't tell me you never asked the question.' But she searched his big, honest face and had to nod resignedly. 'You never asked. And you never will again. But I asked. I want to know. So I will go on their boat with the little monster. I will be the first of the people to see the lands where Terror lives, and where men build flying boats and the houses are made of iron and gold.'

'And when they lose their souls and become monsters again, out over the sea?'

'Like me, you mean?'

'You're not—'

'Then why are they?' Empty Skin's face creased. 'Anyway, perhaps I will come back. Perhaps they will come back.'

Thunder felt a chill go through him at the thought. 'May they stay away for another thousand years.'

'But if they come back, don't you want them speaking our language, knowing our ways, *understanding* what we are?'

After she left, Loud Thunder watched the metal beast pull away from the shore, its innards roaring defiance at the land that had defeated its masters. There were ensouled Plague People

432

travelling as a makeshift embassy to Atahlan. There was a child of the true people venturing across the sea to the land they had been driven from at the dawn of time. The world had ended after all, and something new was being born.

Acknowledgements

The usual suspects: Simon Kavanagh, my agent, whose sterling work in all aspects of the trade keeps me busy; Annie, my wife, who provides the spine to my otherwise invertebrate existence; Bella Pagan and her confederates at Pan Macmillan, who have brought this series and this volume into the world, with a special thanks for Neil Lang, who has designed the best covers I've ever been blessed with.

Also, thanks to the voters and judges of the British Fantasy Society who chose *The Bear and the Serpent* as the winner of the 2017 Robert Holdstock Award for Best Fantasy Novel.

Read on for an extract from

Empire in Black and Gold

Book One in the
Shadows of the Apt series

One

After Stenwold picked up the telescope for the ninth time, Marius said, 'You will know first from the sound.'

The burly man stopped and peered down at him, telescope still half-poised. From their third-storey retreat the city walls were a mass of black and red, the defenders hurrying into place atop the ramparts and about the gates.

'How do you mean, the sound?'

Marius, sitting on the floor with his back to the wall, looked up at him. 'What you hear now is men braving themselves for a fight. When it starts, they will be quiet, just for a moment. They will brace themselves. Then it will be a different kind of noise.' It was a long speech for him.

Even from here Stenwold could hear a constant murmur from the gates. He lowered the telescope reluctantly. 'There'll be a great almighty noise when they come in, if all goes according to plan.'

Marius shrugged. 'Then listen for that.'

Below there was a quick patter of feet as someone ascended the stairs. Stenwold twitched but Marius remarked simply, 'Tisamon,' and went back to staring at nothing. In the room beneath them there were nine men and women dressed in the same chain hauberk and helm that Marius wore, and looking enough like him to be family. Stenwold knew their minds were meshed together, touching each other's and touching Marius too, thoughts passing freely back and forth between them. He could not imagine how it must be, for them.

Tisamon burst in, tall and pale, with thunder in his expression. Even as Stenwold opened his mouth he snapped out, 'No sign. She's not come.'

'Well there are always—' Stenwold started, but the tall man cut him off.

'I cannot think of any reason why she wouldn't come, except one,' Tisamon spat. Seldom, so very seldom, had Stenwold seen this man angry and, whenever he had been, there was always blood. Tisamon was Mantis-kinden, whose people had, when time was young, been the most deadly killers of the Lowlands. Even though their time of greatness had passed, they were still not to be toyed with. They were matchless, whether in single duel or a skirmish of swords, and Tisamon was a master, the deadliest fighter Stenwold had ever known.

'She has betrayed us,' Tisamon stated simply. Abruptly all expression was gone from his angular features but that was only because it had fled inwards.

'There are . . . reasons,' Stenwold said, wishing to defend his absent friend and yet not turn the duellist's anger against himself. The man's cold, hating eyes locked on to him even so. Tisamon had taken up no weapon, but his hands alone, and the spurs of naked bone that lanced outward from his forearms, were quite enough to take Stenwold apart, and with time to spare. 'Tisamon,' Stenwold said. 'You don't know . . .'

'Listen,' said Marius suddenly. And when Stenwold listened, in that very instant there was no more murmur audible from the gates.

And then it came, reaching them across the rooftops of Myna: the cry of a thousand throats. The assault had begun.

It was enough to shout down even Tisamon's wrath. Stenwold fumbled with the telescope, then stumbled to the window, nearly losing the instrument over the sill. When he had the glass back to his eye his hands were shaking so much that he could not keep it steady. The lens's view danced across the gatehouse and the wall, then finally settled. He saw the black and red armour of the army of Myna: men aiming crossbows or winching artillery around. He saw ballista and grapeshot-throwers wheel crazily through the arc of the telescope's eye, discharging their burdens. There was black and gold now amongst the black and red. The first wave of the Wasp divisions came upon them in a glittering mob: troops in light armour bearing the Empire's colours skimming over the tops of the walls, the air about their shoulders ashimmer with the dancing of nebulous wings. For a second Stenwold saw them as the insects they aped, but in reality they were armoured men, aloft in the air, with wings flickering from their backs and blades in their hands. They swooped on the earthbound defenders with lances and swords, loosing arrows and crossbow bolts and hurling spears. As the defenders turned their crossbows upwards towards them, Stenwold saw the bright crackle as golden fire flashed from the palms of the attackers' hands, the killing Art of the Wasp-kinden.

'Any moment now,' Stenwold whispered, as though the enemy, hundreds of yards away, might overhear him. From along the wall he heard a steady thump-thump-thump as Myna's huge rock-launchers hurled missile after missile into the ground troops advancing beyond the wall.

'They're at the gate.' Marius was still staring into space, but Stenwold knew that one of his men was positioned on a rooftop closer to the action, watching on his behalf.

'Then it must be now,' Stenwold said. '*Now.*' He tried to focus the jittery telescope on the gates, saw them flex inwards momentarily and heard the boom of the battering ram. 'Now,' he said again uselessly, for still nothing happened. All that time he had spent with the artificers of Myna, charging the earth in front of the gates with powder, and *nothing*.

'Perhaps they got it wrong,' Marius suggested. Again

the ram boomed against the metal-shod gates, and they groaned like a creature in pain before it.

'I was practically looking over their shoulders,' Stenwold said. 'It was ready to go. How could they have . . . Someone must have . . .'

'We are betrayed,' said Tisamon softly. 'By Atryssa, clearly. Who else knew the plan? Or do you think the people of Myna have sold their own to the slaver's block?'

'You . . . don't know . . .' But Stenwold felt conviction draining from him. Atryssa, so expected but so absent, and now this . . . .

'Spider-kind,' Tisamon spat, and then repeated, 'Spider-kind,' with even keener loathing. On the walls the vanguard of the Wasp army was already engaged in a hundred little skirmishes against the shields of the defenders. Tisamon bared his teeth in utter fury. 'I knew! I knew you could never trust the Spider-kinden. Why did we ever let her in? Why did— Why did we trust her?' He was white knuckled, shaking, eyes staring like a madman's. The spines flexed alarmingly in his forearms, seeking blood. Stenwold stared into his face but barely heard the words. Instead he heard what Tisamon had left unsaid, and knew not fear but a terrible pity. Spider-kinden, as Tisamon said. Spider-kinden, as subtle and devious as all that implied, and still Tisamon, with a thousand years of race-hatred between them, had let her into his life and opened the gates of his soul to her. It was not just that Atryssa had betrayed her friends and betrayed the people of Myna; it was that she had betrayed Tisamon, and he could not bear the hurt.

'It has been a long time,' Marius said quietly. 'A lot can happen that even a Spider cannot predict.'

Tisamon rounded on him, livid with anger, but just then with a great scream of tortured metal, a thundercrack of splintering wood, the gates gave way.

The ramming engine was first through, no telescope needed to see its great brass and steel bulk as it blundered over the wreckage it had created, belching smoke from its funnels. A ballista atop its hood hung half off its mountings, mangled by the defenders' artillery, but there were eyelets in its metal sides from which spat crossbow bolts and the crackling energy of the Wasps' Art. Swarming either side of it were their line infantry, spear-armed but shieldless. Clad in armour too heavy to fly in, they pushed the men stationed at the gate back through sheer force, whilst their airborne divisions were beginning to pass over the city. The guardians of Myna were a disciplined lot, shield locked with shield as they tried to keep the enemy out. There were too many of them, though; the assault came from before and above, and from either side. Eventually the defenders' line buckled and fell back.

'We have to leave now,' Stenwold said, 'or we'll never get out. Someone has to know what's happened here. The Lowlands have to be warned.'

'The Lowlands won't care,' said Marius, but he was up and poised, and Stenwold knew that, below them, his soldiers would be ready with shield and sword and crossbow. They went down the stairs in quick succession, knowing that, now their single trick had failed, nothing would keep the Wasps out of Myna. Their army had five men for every defender the city could muster.

What a band we are. The thought passed through Stenwold's mind as he took the stairs, bringing up the rear as always. First went Marius, tan-skinned and dark, with the universally compact build of his race: he had abandoned his people to come here, gone renegade so that he could fight against the enemy his city would not believe in. After him came Tisamon, still consumed with rage and yet still the most graceful man Stenwold had ever known. His leather arming jacket bore the green and gold colours, even

440

the ceremonial pin, of a Mantis Weaponsmaster. Stenwold had never seen him without it and knew he was clinging to his grudges and his honour like a drowning man.

And then myself: dark of skin and receding of hair; stout and bulky, loud of tread. Not my fault my folk are so heavy boned! Hardwearing leathers and a scorched apron, a workman's heavy gloves thrust through my belt, and goggles dangling about my neck. Not at first sight a man ever intended for war. And yet here I am with a crossbow banging against my legs.

Down in the room below, Marius's soldiers were already alert and on their feet, Some had their heavy square shields out, swords at the ready, others had slung them and taken up crossbows. Two carried the baggage: a heavy leather bag containing Stenwold's tools, and a long wooden case. Even as Stenwold got sight of the room they were unbarring the door, throwing it open. Immediately two of them pushed out, shields first. Stenwold realized that he had paused halfway down, dreading the moment when there would no longer be a roof above him to keep off enemy shot. Tisamon and most of the soldiers were gone. Marius, however, was waiting for him, an unspoken urgency hanging in his gaze.

'I'm coming,' Stenwold said, and hated the shaking of his voice. He clumped on down the stairs, fumbling for his crossbow.

'Leave it, and just move,' Marius ordered, and was out of the door. Following behind Stenwold, the final pair of soldiers moved in to guard the rear.

And then they were out into the open air. The sounds of the fighting at the gate were very close, closer than he could have thought, but this street had seen no blood – not yet. There were citizens of Myna out and about, though, waiting in a scatter of anxious faces. Men and women, and boys and girls still too young to be here at all, they were clutching knives and swords and staves, and waiting.

At his unheard direction, Marius's soldiers formed up: shields before and shields behind, with Stenwold, the baggage and the crossbows in the middle. Marius was at point, already setting a rapid pace down the narrow street. His troop's dark armour, its single purpose, moved people quickly out of the way without need for words or action.

'I can't run as fast as your lot,' Stenwold complained. He already felt out of step and was just waiting for the men behind to jostle or stumble over him. 'Where's Tisamon, anyway?'

'Around.' Marius did not look back or gesture, but then Stenwold caught a glimpse of the Mantis warrior passing through the crowd like an outrider, constantly pausing to look back towards the gate and then move on. He wore his armoured glove, with the blade jutting from between the fingers, flexing out like a sword blade one moment, folded back along his arm the next. It was an ancient tool of his kind and a laughable anachronism, save that Stenwold had witnessed what he could do with it.

'What about your man, at the gates?' Stenwold called, trying desperately to fall into step with those around him.

'Dead,' was the officer's curt reply.

'I'm sorry.'

'Be sorry when you know the full tally,' said Marius. 'We're not out of it yet.'

There was a ripple among the people of Myna, and not from the passage through them of this little squad of foreigners heading for the airfield. Stenwold realized what it must mean. All around now, they were brandishing their swords or workman's hammers or simple wooden clubs. It would not be quick or easy to capture this city, but the Wasps would have it in the end. Their dream of a black-and-gold world would accept no less.

Stenwold was Beetle-kinden and in the Lowlands his people were known for their industry, their artifice, even, as he liked to think, for their charity and kindly philosophy. The people of Myna were his distant cousins, being some offshoot of Beetle stock. He could spare them no charity now, however. He could spare no thought or time for anything but his own escape.

A brief shadow passed across him as the first of the Wasp vanguard soared overhead in a dart of black and gold, a shimmer of wings. Three more followed, and a dozen after that. They were heading in the same direction that Stenwold was moving.

'They're going to the airfield. They'll destroy the fliers!' he shouted in warning.

Instantly Marius and his men stepped up the pace and Stenwold wished he had not spoken. Now they were jogging along, effortlessly despite their armour, and he was running full tilt within a cage formed by their shields, feeling his gut lurch and his heart hammer. Behind him there were screams, and he made the mistake of looking back. Some of the Wasps, it seemed, were not heading for the airfield, but had stopped to rake across the assembled citizens with golden fire and javelins and crossbow bolts, circling and darting, and coming back to loose their missiles once again. This was no ordered attack, they were a frenzied mass of hatred, out solely for slaughter. Stenwold tripped even as he gaped, but the woman closest behind caught him by the arm and wrenched his bulk upright again, without breaking stride.

A moment later his rescuer herself was hit. There was a snap and crackle, and the stink of burned flesh and hot metal, and she sagged to one knee. Stenwold turned to help but nearly fell over the man reaching to drag her upright. The Wasp light airborne troops were all around them now, passing overhead, or diving at the citizens to

443

drive them off the streets. A crossbow bolt bounded past Stenwold like a living thing.

The injured woman was on her feet once more. She and the man beside her turned to face the new assault. Marius and the rest kept moving.

'Come on, Stenwold! Hurry!' the officer shouted.

'But—'

'Go,' said the injured woman, no pain or reproach in her voice. She and the man with her locked shields, waiting. Stenwold stumbled away from them, then turned and fled after Marius and the others.

Tisamon was beside him in an instant. He had a look on his face that Stenwold had never seen before, but he could read it as though the Mantis's thoughts were carved there. Tisamon wanted a fight. He had been betrayed. He had been broken. Now he wanted a fight that he could not win.

'Get a move on, fat-Beetle,' he hissed, grabbing one strap of Stenwold's apron and hauling him forward. 'You're getting out of here.'

'We are,' corrected Stenwold, too out of breath by now to say any more. He watched Tisamon snatch a Wasp spear from the air in his offhand and then the Mantis spun on his heel, launched it away into the sky behind them, and was immediately in step once again. Stenwold did not pause to look, but he had no doubt that behind them some Wasp soldier would now be dropping from the sky, pierced through by his own missile.

Myna was a tiered city and they hit a set of steps then, a steep, narrow twenty-foot ascent. Stenwold tried to slow down for it but Tisamon would not let him, grabbing his arm again and pulling him upwards, exerting every muscle in his lean frame.

'Keep moving,' the Mantis snapped at him through gritted teeth. 'Move your great big fat feet, you Beetle bastard!'

444

The sting of that insult got Stenwold to the top of the steps before he realized. There were more citizens up there, all trying to head in the wrong direction, directly towards the gates. Something in Tisamon's face or body language pushed them easily aside. Ahead, Stenwold could see Marius's squad taking the next set of steps at a run.

And Stenwold ran, too, as he had never run before. His toolstrip, and his sword and crossbow, all clattered and conspired to trip him up. His breath rasped as he dragged ever more of it into his lungs, yet he ran, because up beyond those steps lay the airfield. Then he would know if he could stop running or if it was already too late.

There were Wasp soldiers scattered across the airfield. At the far end, the great bloated bulk of an airship balloon was slowly settling into itself, gashed in a dozen places and deflating. Some half a dozen dead men and women were strewn like old toys between the flying machines, but a dozen more were putting up a final desperate defence, letting off their crossbow bolts at the circling Wasp soldiers from whatever shelter they could find. If the Wasps had been arrayed in military order they could have swept the place clean in a minute, but they were mad for blood, each one on his own.

Stenwold noticed one old man frantically stoking the boiler of a sleek orthopter that stood there like a tall ship, its slender wings folded together and pointing up towards the sky. A Wasp soldier passed close and caught him by the collar, hauling him ten feet away from the machine before touching down again and putting his sword through the old man once, twice, three times. A moment later a bolt caught the same soldier between the shoulder blades. He pitched forward, trying even as he fell to reach behind him and pull it out.

'That one!' wheezed Stenwold, stumbling towards the now deserted orthopter. It was stoked. It was ready to go. 'Come on!' he gasped.

In a moment Marius's men were around him, and then they were past him, deliberately moving away from the machine and making a brief wall of their shields with crossbows poised behind it, guarding the retreat as effectively as they could.

'Can you fly this?' Marius demanded. Stenwold merely nodded, because he had no more breath to speak, and no room left for doubt. The officer clapped him on the shoulder. 'Get it moving. We'll join you.' And then, as Stenwold hurried past him, 'Watch out for Tisamon. He does not want to leave this place.'

I know why. But Stenwold did not have the breath for it.

Tisamon was already at the orthopter, hand reaching for the hatch, then stopping. He looked back at Stenwold with an agonized expression. 'I— how . . .'

'The handle. Turn the handle.'

Hand on the lever, the Mantis shook his head, baring his teeth. One of Marius's men arrived just then, ducked neatly under his arm and hauled the hatch open, hurling Stenwold's toolbag inside. Stenwold reached the orthopter so fast that he bounced back off the scuffed wood of its hull. The soldier had already unslung his crossbow and was running to join his colleagues. Tisamon turned and went with him.

'Wait—' Stenwold got out, but the Mantis was already sprinting across the airfield with his blade drawn back ready for action. Even as Stenwold hauled himself up into the machine, the Mantis leapt and caught a passing Wasp by his black-and-gold boot, dragging the flailing man out of the sky and lashing the two-foot edge of his metal claw across the invader's throat. It would be a poor day for any Wasp who met with the Mantis just then.

Stenwold shouldered his way through the cramped interior of the flier towards the cockpit, there finding a single seat too small for him and unfamiliar controls. He

446

was an artificer, though, and had lived with machines all his life. A moment's observation told him which glass bar indicated the boiler pressure, which lever unleashed the wings. A Wasp soldier darted across the large and wide-open ports that were mainly what Stenwold had between him and the fighting outside. Then the wings clapped down and outwards with a roar of wood and canvas and the soldier was sent spinning by the concussion of air. Stenwold's feet found pedals in the narrow confines of the footwell. The boiler pressure was now closing on the optimal. He put his head back, peering through the open hatch for any sign of his comrades.

Half of Marius's men were already dead, he saw, and this jolted his heart. They fought beautifully: even he, though no warrior, could see that. Each man knew by heart the thoughts of his fellows, so they moved as one. They were so few, though, and the Wasps swarmed all over the field. Shield and crossbow were no defence against their numbers.

'Come on!' Stenwold bellowed. 'Let's go now!' He could not believe that they would hear him over the din of combat but one of them must have, and so they all did. They began to fall back, shields held high. Even as he watched, another was lanced in the side by a crossbow bolt, falling awkwardly before rising to one knee. The others continued to retreat, and Stenwold might have thought it heartless of them had he not been so sure that the fallen man would be exhorting them to go, to leave him there. Stenwold realized that he knew none of their names, had not even heard many of them speak.

Ant-kinden, he would never understand them or their communal world. Or how Marius had managed to leave that world and not look back.

The hatch went suddenly dark. A Wasp soldier forced his way in, the dance of his wings dying behind him. One open hand still crackled with the fire of his sting but he was now leading with his sword. Stenwold was lurching backwards even as the man's shoulders cleared the entrance, hurling the first thing that came to hand, which happened to be a mechanic's hammer. It thumped into the Wasp soldier's shoulder and knocked him half out of the hatch. Then Stenwold was upon him, grabbing for his sword arm with one hand, lunging with the other. He never got hold of the man's sword, but his right hand somehow managed to draw his own, and he rammed it up to its narrow guard in his adversary's armpit.

The Wasp spat at him and he recoiled in shock, then recoiled again as he saw the blood stringing across the man's lips. Then the dying soldier was falling out of the flier, the weight of him taking Stenwold's sword from his suddenly nerveless fingers.

He had just killed another human being. *There's a first time for everything.*

One of Marius's soldiers now reached the hatch and cast the wooden case inside. Marius himself and three of his men were still inching their way back, painfully slow.

'Tisamon!' Stenwold called out. 'Tisamon!'

He saw him then, the Weaponsmaster, moving in and out of the Wasps as they tried to corner him. But he stepped through the golden energy of their stings, their crossbow bolts that fractured on the hard earth of the airfield. He caught their spears easily and hurled them back. His blade, twisting and darting too swift to see, was never still for a second. It moved as naturally as his wrist and hand and arm could, and there were always the spines of his arms to cut and tear at anything the metal missed. Tisamon was going to die, but he would have more company on his journey than he knew what to do with.

'Tisamon!' Stenwold shouted and the Mantis-kinden broke off from the fight, danced across to him, casually cutting down a Wasp that tried to put a spear in him.

'Get Marius inside and go!' Tisamon commanded. 'Go! Just go!'

Stenwold's face twisted up in anger and fear. 'You bloody-handed bastard! If you stay here then you're taking me with you! I'm not going without you!'

Even as he moved to meet the next attacker Tisamon's face showed how utterly unfair he felt that threat was. Even so, he was returning to the orthopter in the very next instant.

'Marius, now!' Stenwold shrieked, and at last Marius and his two survivors broke into a run, shields temporarily slung on their backs. Stenwold ducked away from the hatch and even as he did so a lance of energy blasted a smoking hole in the rim. Hands shaking, he squeezed himself back into the pilot's seat, and began to pedal fast. He felt the entire frame of the flier creak as the wings moved, first up and then down, powered by the steam-boiler but guided by his feet.

Someone vaulted into the flier, and Stenwold flinched in fear, but it was only Tisamon, face grim. He set on the wooden case immediately and tugged at the buckles, his bladed glove now removed. A moment later a woman belonging to Marius's squad climbed in too and turned to help her commander aboard. By now Stenwold had the wings working smoothly and felt the orthopter lurch as though eager to be gone from here.

Marius was halfway in when he arched backwards without warning and began to fall away. The female soldier caught his belt and dragged him to safety, but Stenwold caught a glimpse of the leather vanes of the crossbow bolt buried deep in the commander's lower back beside the rim of his shield.

'Any more?' He could barely keep the machine on the ground.

'No!' the woman yelled to him, and he doubled his pace

and the orthopter sprang into the sky, spinning a couple of Wasps out of their way with the displaced air.

Stenwold risked a single glance behind him to see what was happening. Marius was lying on his side, his skin turned from tan to ashen-grey, his sole remaining soldier investigating the wound. Tisamon had opened his case and was stringing his greatbow. Another relic of the Bad Old Days, Stenwold knew, but he would not have swapped such a bow in Tisamon's hands for the latest repeating crossbow. The Mantis crouched at the still-open hatch and nocked an arrow. A moment later he loosed it and Stenwold saw, as he circled the airfield, another Wasp go whirling downwards, sword spinning off separately, out-reaching him as he fell.

'Away would be good!' Tisamon snapped, reaching into the case for another arrow.

'I have to gain height first,' Stenwold told him, knowing that the Mantis would not understand. He was pulling the orthopter into a ponderously slow upwards circle of the airfield as the steam-driven wings worked up and down. None of the other Mynan flying machines had got off the ground. He did not want to think about what might be happening in the city below them. He just pedalled and steered, watching a rising circle of Wasps below them, flying men with swords and spears milling in a furious swarm. Tisamon leant far out, securing his position with one knee and one elbow, and drew back the string.

High enough. Stenwold decided, and wrestled the orthopter out of its curve. But he had misjudged the angle and ended up sending it straight out over the teeming city. Below him a dozen Wasp soldiers passed by, oblivious, but Stenwold's attention was by now somewhere else.

'Hammer and tongs!' he swore. 'Will you look at that!'

It was ugly as sin and it hung in the air as elegantly as a hanged man, but nevertheless it stayed up and there had to be some craft in that feat. A heliopter in Wasp colours, a monstrous, uneven metal box with three spinning blades straining to keep it from crashing to the ground. There must have been hatches in its underbelly, he realized, because there was a stream of missiles falling constantly from it onto Myna. He thought they were rocks at first but, on seeing the explosions, decided they must be fire-pots or firepowder grenades.

Why am I still flying at it? He wrenched quickly at the simple wooden stick and the orthopter veered away, the Wasp heliopter sliding out of his frame of vision as he cast his newly acquired vehicle across the city and out over the walls. The orthopter was a simple piece of machinery, and the artificers back at his native city of Collegium, hundreds of miles away, would have called it 'prentice stuff'. It was all Stenwold needed, though, for it could outpace the Wasp light airborne, and in only minutes their pursuers were dropping back, turning for the city again, and Tisa-mon could lower his bow.

The Wasp heliopter, however – that was a crude and primitive piece. Any self-respecting artificer would have been rightly ashamed of it. And yet it flew, and only five years ago the Wasps had possessed nothing like it.

'Marius . . .' he began. He could crane over his shoulder, but even while letting the machine glide on its canvas wings he dared not take his attention from the controls. 'Marius, talk to me.'

'He is sorry,' said the woman, and after a moment's blank surprise Stenwold realized that Marius must now be too weak to speak, but strong enough to send his thoughts into her mind.

'We have to tell them what has happened here,' Sten-wold continued. 'Marius, we have to tell Sarn. We must warn your city.'

'He says we are considered renegades there,' the woman replied impassively. 'He says we can never go back.'

Beneath them the fields and small villages that were Myna's tributary settlements swept past. 'But Marius only left because he thought this was for your people's good,' Stenwold said stubbornly. 'He saw the threat even when they did not. You know this, and you have to tell them.'

'We can never go back there,' the woman said, and he realized she was speaking for herself this time. 'Once the bonds of loyalty are broken, we can never go back.'

'But Marius – Sarn isn't like the other Ant cities any more. There have been changes. There are even some of my own kin on the council there,' Stenwold insisted.

There was a lengthy silence from behind him, and he assumed that Marius must have died. He choked on a sob, but then the woman put a hand on his shoulder in a strong soldier's grip.

'He says you must do what you can,' she told him softly, and even her intonation resembled Marius's own. 'He says he regrets that things have ended this way, and he also regrets that the others, Atryssa and Nero, were not with us, but he does not regret following you from his city, and he does not regret dying in this company.'

Stenwold wiped a hand across his eyes and felt the first shaking of his shoulders. 'Tell him . . .' he managed, but then the woman's hand twitched on his shoulder, just once, just for a moment, and he knew that Marius was dead.

He let out a long, racked breath.

'We can tell nobody about this, because nobody will listen,' Tisamon said. 'We tried to warn your people at Helleron that the Wasps were coming, and what did they say? That nobody would invade Helleron. They claimed that the city was too useful. That Wasps needed to trade and deal in arms like everyone else. They look upon the Empire as just another Ant city-state.'

'And if we told your people?' asked Stenwold bitterly.

'Then they would simply not care. They have quarrels a thousand years old that they have yet to settle. They have no time for new ones.' And Stenwold heard, to his surprise, an equal bitterness in Tisamon's voice. The Mantis was hinging his metal claw forward and back, rolling his fingers about the crosspiece to lay the blade flat against his arm, then bringing it out to jut forward from his knuckles. It was not a threat, but just the man seeking reassurance in his old rituals.

'We saw their map,' Stenwold whispered. That one glimpse he had caught, of the Wasps' great map, had been a harsh education. A map of lands he had never seen, extending down to lands he knew all too well, the Lowlands of his home, and all sketched out with lines of advance and supply. A map of a projected conquest that stopped only with the Wasps' knowledge of their world.

'Nobody will care,' Tisamon repeated, and there was a rare wisdom in his voice. 'What is the Lowlands, anyway? A half-dozen feuding city-states, some hold-overs from the Days of Lore, when things were different, and perhaps a few men like yourself, trying to make sense of it all. The Wasps are a unity, we are a motley.' The gloom about him deepened, and Stenwold knew that his thoughts were turning inexorably towards Atryssa, towards the betrayal. Stenwold wished he could find some other way to explain her absence and their failure at the gates.

'What will you do,' he asked the Ant-kinden woman, 'if you cannot go home?'

'I will not be the first Ant renegade to go mercenary. If you now take us to Helleron I will sell my sword there,' she said. 'The market for us is good, and like to get better.'

'The same for me,' Tisamon confirmed.

'Tisamon—'

'No.' There was more finality in the Mantis's voice than Stenwold had ever heard from him. 'No return to Collegium for me, Stenwold. No debate and diplomacy. No society. No kind words, ever again. I followed you down that path once, and see where I am now.'

453

'But—'

'I will stay at Helleron and I will oppose the Wasps the only way I can.' With careful movements Tisamon replaced his greatbow in its case. 'You yourself have other means, Sten. You must go back to your college and your clever, machine-fingered people, and have them make ready. Of all of us, you were always the real hope of the future.'

Stenwold said nothing as, below them, the last of the straggling fields gave out, and a scrubby, dry landscape passed beneath them without so much as a whisper.